SACRIFICE ME

THE COMPLETE SEASON ONE

SARRA CANNON

Cover by Ravven

Get new release updates and exclusive content when you sign up for my
mailing list.

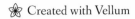 Created with Vellum

EPISODE ONE

THE DEMON

PROLOGUE

When you are about to die, they say your life flashes before your eyes. Life's last gift. A single moment of clarity so you can see all the things you did wrong.

Every bad decision.

Every mistake.

Every horrible word you said to someone when you really just wanted them to love you as much as you loved them.

It's easy to get lost in the regrets of our past, thinking that if we'd only chosen something different, we might have been able to save ourselves a hell of a lot of heartbreak.

Only, the thing is, we should really be giving ourselves more credit for just surviving the best way we know how. It's not like we made those bad decisions on purpose. Well, not most of the time, anyway.

At any given moment, we're all just doing the best we can to survive and make a place for ourselves in this shit-storm we call life.

Looking back, it's easy to forget just how broken we were when we made those bad decisions. And most importantly, it's easy to overlook the fact that if we were really able to go back in time and change things, sure, we might avoid some of the worst heartaches of our lives, but at the same time, we also might not be standing here, right now, with the one person we love most in all the world.

What if I'd never opened that invitation?

What if I'd thrown the whole thing in the trash and gone about my life?

What if I'd never stepped foot inside Venom?

These questions flash through my mind in those last moments, but then all I can think is that one small change— one *"better"* decision—and I might have missed him altogether.

So, you know what? If I had the chance to go back and do it all over again, I wouldn't change one painful, gut-wrenching, dangerous, terrifying moment of what I've been through over the past two weeks.

Even knowing it meant the death of me, I'd go through it all over again, just for him.

LITTLE BIRD

TWO WEEKS EARLIER

"Happy Birthday, sleepy head."

I pulled my pillow over my head, trying to ignore my roommate, Katy, but I should have known better. She was not one to give up easily when she set her mind to something.

"Get up," she called in that sing-song morning voice I hated and loved at the same time. "I made you breakfast and everything."

I peered out from under the pillow, one eye open. "Chocolate chip pancakes?"

She raised an eyebrow and tilted her head to the side. "Of course."

"With maple syrup?"

"I even made a Starbucks run this morning and got you a Caramel Macchiato," she said. "You're all set to go into a sugar coma before your first class of the day."

I rolled over and grabbed her hand, bringing it up to my lips in a quick kiss. "I don't deserve you," I said.

"You deserve so much better," she said. Her mouth twisted into a frown, and I knew she was thinking about my mother.

Katy had been my best friend for as long as I could remember, and I knew that look. She was feeling guilty because on her twenty-first birthday, a month earlier, her mother had shown up in a limousine to take her for tapas at Mercat.

My mother, on the other hand, was nowhere to be found. She disappeared on my eighteenth birthday, three years ago, without so much as a fuck-you.

"Don't give me your guilty face," I said. "I don't want pity pancakes."

She rolled her eyes. "These are not pity pancakes. They're friendship, happy twenty-first birthday pancakes and they were made with love," she said. She smacked my bare thigh. "Now get your ass out of bed before it gets cold."

I groaned and forced myself out from under the warm covers. Twenty-one. A major milestone in the lives of Americans everywhere, but I wasn't any more excited about this birthday than any of the twenty that had come before. Not that I could remember every single one, but you get the point.

I had already been drinking with a fake ID for the past two years, so the idea of going out to a bar didn't excite me. And the idea of being one year older was more terrifying than anything else. One year older meant one year closer to graduating and having to figure out what the hell I was going to do with my life.

But the smell of pancakes and coffee cheered me up.

Katy had set up our breakfast for two on the small bar that separated our tiny living room from our even tinier kitchen.

Beside my plate, there was also a long silver box with a dark red card on top.

"What's this?" I asked, eyeing her. We never exchanged gifts. Mostly because I could never afford it and she lived in constant guilt about being rich. "Katy, what did you do?"

She shook her head and sat down, taking a bite of pancake. "It wasn't me, I swear. Someone delivered them while I was out getting the coffee. They were waiting by the door when I got home," she said. "Have you been seeing someone new?"

This was such a ridiculous question that I didn't even justify it with an answer. She should have known better.

I was never seeing anyone new. Or old for that matter. I didn't believe in relationships, and no matter how many times Katy tried to set me up, nothing ever stuck.

I stared at the box as I took my first bites of birthday pancakes. I couldn't even think of one person who would have sent me flowers. I had no family. No close friends outside of Katy. I had never been in a serious relationship.

And nothing good could come of birthday flowers from a stranger.

"Aren't you going to open it?" she asked.

I eyed the silver box, a strange feeling fluttering in my stomach. "Eventually," I mumbled, mouth half full. "Maybe."

She grabbed the card off the top and waved it in my face. "Just see who it's from. Maybe you have a secret admirer."

I set my fork down and swallowed, hesitating. Part of me wanted to dump them, unopened, into the trash.

But my curiosity got the better of me. I lifted the silver lid off the box. Inside, nestled in black tissue paper, were the strangest, most beautiful black roses. I'd never seen anything like them, but they were exactly my taste. Rare and dark.

I bit my lip and shifted in my chair.

My hand trembled as I took the red envelope from Katy and tore it open. The paper was heavy. Expensive and smooth to the touch.

Inside, there was a short note written in large, swoopy black letters.

Happy Birthday, Little Bird
Don't you think it's time you learned to spread your wings?
VENOM, Hubbard Street, Chicago

MY STOMACH TWISTED at those two handwritten words near the top of the card.

Little Bird.

It was what my mother had always called me.

CATCH-22

I couldn't get my mind off those black roses. I walked around the whole day with the strangest feeling that someone was watching my every move.

I had become so paranoid that I nearly made some freshman piss his pants in the hallway of the student center. I thought he was following me. Apparently, he was just lost.

I didn't like the thought of someone sending me flowers and knowing my birthday and my mother's pet name for me. It had completely unnerved me, which I also hated because I figured that was probably the point of someone sending me black roses in the first place. By the time I met Katy for coffee after our last class of the day, I was a complete mess.

"I know you don't want to hear this, but what if the roses are from your mom?" Her forehead wrinkled as she said it, as if she half expected me to haul off and punch her in the face for even suggesting it.

The truth was, I had already considered that myself. Considered it and dismissed it. "She would never send me something so expensive," I said. I pulled the note out of my backpack where I had stuck it inside my Economics book. "Black roses can't be cheap, and did you feel this paper? No, someone spent some money on this. Definitely not my mother."

"What does this bottom part mean?" she asked. "What's Venom?"

"I'm not sure, but Hubbard is just south of here. I think this is close to the House of Blues," I said. "There are a lot of clubs and bars down there. Maybe Venom is a bar."

She started to speak, but I held my hand up, knowing what she was about to suggest.

"Not a chance," I said.

"But—"

"No." I slid the card back inside my book and pulled out a copy of today's newspaper. "I've actually been thinking maybe I'll stay in tonight. I don't really have the money to go out, anyway. I need to find a new job. Do you want to order pizza or something instead?"

I opened the paper and skimmed the help-wanted ads looking for something close to campus. I'd been working at a twenty-four-hour diner a couple of blocks north of our dorm for the past six months, but I'd had the privilege of being fired two days earlier.

It wasn't even my fault. One of my labs ran long and there was no way to sneak out without getting slammed with another absence. As much as I couldn't afford to lose my job, I definitely couldn't afford another absence in that class.

I was barely hanging onto my grades as it was. I had to maintain at least a B average to keep my financial aid and just one month into the first semester of my Senior year, I was already at risk of getting a C in two classes.

Of course, with my life, it was always a Catch-22. I was behind on my grades because I had to work nearly full-time to afford tuition and basics like, you know, food. But I was late for work because of class. Keeping things balanced was a nightmare and some days I felt more like a professional juggler than a college student. I resented people like Katy who didn't have to work at all. But I'd been making this work. Three long years of busting my ass to put myself through school all on my own. I wasn't about to watch it all go down the drain with less than a year left.

I needed to find another job.

"Pizza, are you kidding me?" she asked. "Seriously, what do you want to do? I told Jennifer and Ash I'd text them as soon as I knew where we were meeting up."

"I'm not going out," I said, burying my head deeper in the paper. Usually I was the first one up for a good time, but those roses had left me with a churning stomach. Besides, I was on the cusp of poverty.

Katy slammed her hand down on my newspaper and stared at me until I lifted my eyes to hers. "You can look for a job tomorrow," she said. When I reached for the paper, she pulled it farther out of my reach and stuffed it in her purse. "Please. Just for one night, let's go out and have some fun, okay? I need this."

I leaned back against my chair. "Well, as long as it's all about you," I said. "That really takes the pressure off."

She rolled her eyes and downed the rest of her coffee. "You know what I meant," she said. "We've all been looking forward to taking you out tonight. It's going to be fun, I promise. Just give me one night. Let's let go of the stress of jobs and school and guys and all that bullshit and just have fun, okay? You deserve it. You've been working so hard lately. It'll be good for you."

I sucked a deep breath in through my nose. I knew she was right. I really did need this. I was no fun when I was stressed and ever since the semester started, I'd been a big old ball of stress twenty-four-seven. Being without money and having no one to rely on sucked.

"I don't have any money," I said.

"It's your birthday. We'll take care of everything. All you need to bring is you. Besides, you'll get a job. You always do."

I could see the sympathy in her eyes, but I also knew she didn't truly understand what I was going through. She'd never had to work a day in her life, and if she ever needed money, all she had to do was call her mom. She had no idea how lucky she really was.

"Come out with us," she said, taking my hands in hers. "I'm begging you. We don't have to go to that Venom place if you don't want to. We'll go to Smart Bar or something. I promise, we'll make it a night you'll never forget."

I finally gave in and agreed to go out, not knowing at the time just how much that night would live up to her promise.

LYING TO MYSELF

Four hours later, I had managed to squeeze myself into my tightest pair of jeans and a plain white tank top. I couldn't afford fancy clothes, so instead I went with tight and sexy.

I was relatively tall at five feet eight, but I still loved to wear super high heels. The higher the better. I'd managed to snag a pair of used white Christian Louboutin knock-offs at a thrift shop downtown a few weeks ago and I proudly pulled them on tonight, instantly growing three inches taller. The black rose lace overlay on the shoes gave me chills. It was almost as if I could feel fate tapping on my shoulder.

"Wow, you look hot," Katy said when I walked out. She had already started drinking and her face was flushed.

I twirled, my long black hair flying up around my face. "Better than my diner uniform, eh?"

She rolled her eyes. "Anything is better than that hideous thing," she said. "Plus, no hat. Win, win."

"You ready to go?" I asked.

She wore a skimpy black dress that showed off her curves. Unlike me, she was petite at five-foot-four.

"Yes. I just need to grab my ID."

"Okay, me too," I said. I walked back in my room to grab my license and the last of my cash, just in case. As I pulled them out of my top drawer, a tattered picture fluttered to the floor and my heart sank.

I should have just left it where it was, but what can I say? Sometimes I can be a real glutton for punishment.

I squatted down to pick up the folded picture. It was worn thin from folding and unfolding and being carried in pockets and wallets for years, but the smiles on our faces were still visible despite the creases.

This was one of the only pictures I had of my mom and me. I had a clearer, less messed up version on my computer, but in a rare not-drunk-or-messed-up moment, my mom had been sweet enough to actually have this one printed out for me. As much as I wanted to hate her for all she'd done to me, looking at this picture of us together still brought a smile to my face.

And tears to my eyes.

God, I missed her so much.

Three years ago today she had vanished from my life without a word. No note or text. No phone call. Nothing. She just packed up all her stuff and took off, as if she'd been counting the days until my eighteenth birthday so she could abandon me without taking any grief for it from child services.

She'd broken my heart more times than I could count, but none of it compared to the brutal beating my heart took when she left.

At first, I'd told myself she was coming back. She'd just

gone on a bender somewhere, too drunk to come home or too high to remember her own address. It wouldn't be the first time she'd done something like that, right?

But after a month had gone by, the truth had started to sink in. I tried calling the police, but they weren't interested in tracking down a woman like my mother. She was a grown woman, free to come and go as she pleased. There was no sign of a struggle or hints of foul play, so what could they do?

They told me they'd look into it, but that was the last I ever heard from them.

It was as if she'd simply disappeared into thin air.

Some birthday present.

"You coming?" Katy yelled from the other room.

I took a deep breath and stuffed my sorrow back down in my gut where it belonged.

She isn't worth my tears.

It was a lie I'd told myself a thousand times, but sometimes lying to myself was the only thing that allowed me to keep putting one foot in front of the other.

"Yep, be there in a second," I said.

I refolded the picture and stuffed it back into the drawer, then headed out to celebrate.

Tear-free.

TRUE FRIENDS

"Here's to twenty-one effing years," Katy shouted. She lifted two shots off the top of the bar and handed one to me, then raised her hand high into the air with a whoop.

I bit back a smile as she downed the shot like a pro.

Jennifer and Ashley were more tentative, almost sipping their shots, then both scrunching up their noses at the taste.

"What is this?" Ashley asked, coughing.

"Franki's choice," Katy said with a laugh. "Don't look at me."

"Scotch," I said, raising my full shot glass up in a slight salute before throwing it back and downing it in a single gulp. It burned all the way down my throat.

"It's disgusting," Jennifer said, setting her empty glass down on the table.

I winked at her. "Don't be such a wimp."

"Want another?" Katy asked.

I bit my lip. I was tempted.

Hell, who was I kidding? I wanted it like a dying man in the desert wants water. The growing warmth in my stomach and the loosening of the tension in my shoulders felt amazing. I'd been wound so freaking tight lately. Katy was right. I really had needed this.

But at the same time, I didn't usually let myself drink too much. I'd seen where that could lead, and I knew from watching my mother's addiction grow out of control over the years that I needed to be careful.

But it was my twenty-first birthday and I wasn't in the mood to be responsible.

"Let's do it," I said.

"Hell yeah." Katy leaned over the top of the bar, looking for the bartender who had served us a few minutes ago.

After a delicious dinner at my favorite sushi place, we'd ended up at a pub near campus. Being a Wednesday night, the place was practically dead.

Normally, that might not have been such a bad thing. The more I had to drink, though, the more I wanted Katy to deliver on her promise to make this a night to remember. The alcohol made me feel wild and different and loose.

I wanted more.

"This place is lame," I said, ignoring the fact that my words were slightly slurred. "Let's do something wild."

"Oh, yeah, that's my girl," Katy said, landing a wet kiss on my forehead. "I was starting to think you'd disappeared on me."

"Like what?" Jennifer asked.

Her less-than-enthused tone wasn't lost on me, nor was the fact that Ashley had glanced at the time on her cell phone four times in the past five minutes.

That was the down side of constantly keeping everyone at arm's length. You ended up with very few true friends.

"I don't know," I said. "Let's go dancing."

"Yes," Katy squealed. "Let's go to Smart Bar."

Ashley shook her head. "No way. Alex is working there now. I'm not taking the risk of running into him right now."

"Poop," Katy said, frowning. "Not even for Franki's birthday? Besides, you look amazing tonight. It would be the perfect night to run into him. Make him see what he's missing."

"No," Ashley said. She grabbed my hand and squeezed. "Sorry, Franki. I can't do it. The girl he cheated with works there too. If I had to see them together right now, I would just die."

I squeezed her hand back. "I get it," I said. "It's fine. There's got to be another place we could go dancing, right? There are tons of clubs on that side of town."

"We'd have to take a cab to get anywhere good," Jennifer said. "And it's already getting late. I have to be up pretty early."

"Party poopers," Katy said, standing and putting a knee in her chair. "Let's shake things up. We're failing on our best friend's twenty-first!"

I shook my head. "It's okay, really," I said. I caught the disappointment in my own voice and cursed myself for letting it slip through. "I have to be up early, too."

I wondered if it was too late to grab a six pack and head to the one place I knew I shouldn't go tonight. The place I'd spent every birthday since the one three years ago when she disappeared.

"Don't even think about it," Katy said, as if reading my mind.

"What?"

"You know what," she said through clenched teeth. "Your mother has messed up enough of your birthdays. I'm not going to let you go back to that old house and think about sad things. We're going to have fun tonight if it kills us. Come on, ladies, we're going out."

She downed the rest of her drink and went to pay the tab.

I had a nearly-full glass of Jack and coke but took a deep breath and drained it in ten seconds flat.

Jennifer and Ashley shared a look.

Annoyance bubbled to the surface. Why were good friends so hard to find? I mean, it's not like I expected them to stay out all night with me, but it was my birthday and it was only eleven. Was it really so much to ask that they hang out a couple more hours?

Apparently, it was.

As we made our way to the door, Jennifer put her hand on my arm. "I'm sorry, sweetie, but I think we're just going to head home," she said.

Ashley threw her arms around my neck, a fake smile plastered on her lips. "Love you so much, girl. Happy birthday."

"Thanks," I said, amazed at how easily some people tossed around the word love. "I'm glad you guys came out."

"Screw this," Katy said. "You guys suck. It's not even midnight."

I pressed my lips together, not wanting to smile too hard. I could always count on Katy to say what needed to be said.

Still, if they didn't want to be here, I wasn't about to beg them to stay.

"I know," Ashley said, wrinkling her nose. "But it's the middle of the week and—"

"Blah, blah, blah," Katy said, rolling her eyes. "You suck."

"Maybe we can do something this weekend." Jennifer hugged me.

"Sounds good," I said, even though I knew I wouldn't be able to get out again over the weekend. I needed to focus on finding a new job and saving money.

"Good night," the girls said as they waved and took off down the sidewalk in the direction of their apartment.

Katy threaded her arm in mine and sighed. "Assholes," she said. "I'm sorry."

"It's okay," I said. "Maybe we should call it a night, too. We could rent a movie or something and grab a bottle of wine."

"No way." Katy shook her head and pulled out her cell phone.

"Who are you calling?" I asked.

"I'm calling a cab," she said. "There's no way I'm letting this night end before midnight. We're going to go find some fun. We're going to find this place you were invited to. Venom."

THE ALLEY

I protested, but Katy's mind was set on taking me to this new club.

The truth is, I was curious. Who had sent the roses? No one else I knew called me Little Bird, but there was no way my mother had bought those expensive roses for me. Well, not unless she'd magically gotten her shit together in the past three years. And if that was the case, there was no way I was missing out on seeing that.

But what if they truly weren't from my mother? What if there was someone else who knew about her? About me? What if they were from someone else in my family?

The note had been on my mind from the moment I first opened it, and even if I protested, there was no denying that I wanted to see what was going down at this club and why I had been invited there.

Our cab picked us up within minutes, but when we asked him to take us to a club called Venom on Hubbard, he stared at us like we were high.

"You don't know it?" I asked.

He shook his head. "There's no club by that name."

"Well, a bar, then. Or a restaurant."

"No," he said. "I would know this. There is no place in this city by the name."

Katy showed him the card and he just shrugged.

"Then just take us to West Hubbard," Katy said with a loud sigh. She turned to me. "We'll find it."

I let my head fall back against the seat of the cab. I really didn't want to spend all night on some wild goose chase. If a cabbie had no clue where this place was, it was either brand new or it didn't exist. This was definitely not turning out to be the birthday of the century, but I guess anything was better than drinking beer in my mom's old house, thinking about old times, and where the hell everything seemed to go off the rails for me.

Ten minutes later, he dropped us off at the Paris Club.

Katy asked a few people standing out front if they'd heard of Venom, but we got the same blank stares we'd gotten from the cab driver.

"Maybe we should just pick a place and get a few drinks," I said. I was curious about the note and who it came from, but there was also a part of me that was scared of finding out anything beyond what I already knew.

"Dammit, if you say that one more time, I'm going to kick you in the tits," she said. "We're going to find this place. Come on."

She looked both ways down the street, then just randomly picked one and started walking down, her eyes sweeping back and forth, looking for the name on a sign.

Half an hour went by and Katy was near tears. She raised

her arms, then let them slap back down against her legs. "I've totally failed you," she said. "This is the lamest birthday ever."

I shook my head and looped my arm in hers. "I've been with you, so it can't be lame," I said. "Really, it's fine. This whole thing was probably someone's idea of a bad joke. Let's just pick a place where we can drink and forget all about Venom and the black roses."

She sighed. "Okay, you win. Pick any bar you want. I have no idea which ones are good down here, so just follow your gut instinct."

I closed my eyes and twirled around, my world turning like I was on some wicked merry-go-round.

Follow my gut instinct? I usually tried to do exactly the opposite. I always figured my instincts were screwed up after such a crappy childhood.

I'd never known my father. Or any of my family, for that matter. We were one-hundred-percent loners, my mother and me. She refused to answer any of my questions about where I'd come from. Or where she'd come from. I guess I'd always known she had run away from something. She was always running.

Late on rent? We'd just pack up and move to a new city before they could kick us out or take her to court.

Meet a guy who actually seems nice and treats you well? She'd almost give in, then would dump him so fast, it would make your head turn. I had no idea why she was so scared of getting close to anyone, but it happened without fail. The second she thought a friend got too close or a man seemed too interested, she would wake me up in the middle of the night and tell me to pack my shit.

Running is just what she did.

The one thing I never thought she'd run from was me.

No, I didn't trust my instincts.

But tonight, something was different. Maybe it was the full moon. Or maybe it was the drinks still sloshing around in my stomach. As I twirled on the sidewalk with my eyes closed, something tugged at me deep down.

I stopped, listening to that whisper of instinct or pull.

"This way," I said, grabbing Katy's hand and walking toward the quieter end of the street.

She giggled, tripping over her own feet. "You're going the wrong way. The bars are all the other way," she said.

"Shhh," I told her. "I'm following my gut, like you told me."

I paused in front of the open door of a bar toward the end of the street, letting that feeling deep inside guide me.

This was the last place on this side of the street, so I expected to feel the urge to go inside, but no, there was something else. I couldn't explain it.

I should have ignored it. I should have turned back toward the lights and looked for a more normal place with actual people coming in and out.

But I was feeling wild.

"Wait," I said, pulling Katy back from the bouncer she was already handing her ID to. "Not here."

"This is the last place down this way," she said.

"I don't think so," I said. "Follow me."

The bouncer raised an eyebrow and threw a glance toward the alley, which is exactly where I was feeling pulled toward. It was completely empty and very dark, but I stepped into the alley between two tall buildings.

Katy gripped my arm. "Okay, so I know I told you to follow

your instincts, but I didn't expect your instincts to lead us to a dumpster."

I shook my head, feeling breathless. "I think there's something down here."

"It's creepy down here," she said, the excitement from earlier fading from her voice.

"Yes, it is," I whispered.

I kept my eye out for a door or something, but this place was just dark and dead. What the heck was I doing?

Being stupid, that's what.

We were way out of our element just being off-campus and here I was dragging us into a back alley where girls like us probably got murdered on a regular basis.

But I pressed on, the tug in my core growing stronger. Undeniable.

"Let's turn around, Franki," she said. "I don't like this."

I frowned. There had to be something down here. I could feel it.

A few more steps, though, and I was ready to turn back.

"I'm sorry," I said. "I don't know..."

Someone stepped out of a door in the middle of the alley.

For a moment, the entire alley lit up with an eerie electric green light, but when the door slammed closed, everything went black all over again.

"Wait," I said. "There."

Katy mouth twisted. "You sure? It looks sketch."

"Let's check it out."

"I'm only doing this because it's your birthday," she said, taking a deep breath. "But if we get murdered, I'm coming back from the dead, so I can murder you myself."

I knew it was crazy, but I knew I had to go to this place. "Deal."

When we got down to the door, I was surprised to see that it was just an unmarked door. No club name. No bouncer. Nothing.

"I think maybe this is the back door or something," Katy said. "Let's go around and try to find the front."

I reached forward and placed my hand on the rusted metal handle. Static shock surged through me and I pulled my hand away.

Katy shrieked, and I laughed.

"Just a little shock," I said. "Don't be such a baby."

She put her hand on her chest and took a deep breath. "You scared the crap out of me."

I reached for the door again, knowing with all my heart that everything that had happened since the moment I woke up this morning had been leading me here, to this door. As if my future had been waiting for me right here in this dark alley.

I wrapped my hand around my future and pulled, opening up a whole new world.

A world I had no idea how hard my mother had worked to keep from me for so long.

NO. FREAKING. WAY

The door opened up to a long, narrow corridor. The black walls made it seem like the inside of a very dark box, the only light came from two long plastic tubes running along the ceiling. They were filled with some kind of glowing green liquid. Not quite like neon. More like a lava lamp with a ton of bubbles. I'd never seen anything like it.

I stepped forward and could hear Katy gasp behind me.

"What is this place?"

"I have no idea," I said.

A feeling deep in my belly told me I belonged here, though, which I realized was a ridiculous thought. How could I belong somewhere I'd never been?

A heavy black door closed off whatever was in the next room and as I stepped closer, the door opened and a young girl who didn't look much older than us stepped out.

I moved aside so she could pass, but she just stopped and stared at us.

Her hair was bleached very white-blonde and cut in a

short pixie cut. She was a little taller than me and had these gorgeous sky-blue eyes. To say she was stunning would be the understatement of a lifetime.

"Good evening, ladies," she said. She had an Australian accent. "Don't think I've seen the likes of you around here before. Is there something I can help you with?"

I paused and looked at Katy. She was usually so much better at bullshitting her way into places, but I could tell from the look on her face she was way out of her comfort zone.

I turned back to the girl and smiled. "I have no idea, to be honest," I said, choosing truth over bullshit. "It's my birthday and we were out looking for a place, and I don't know. Does it sound stupid to say I was drawn to this place?"

She raised an eyebrow and studied me closely. "Not stupid, no. Strange, more like."

Katy gripped my arm, her fingernails digging into my flesh. I sucked in a breath and turned to tell her to let up, but her eyes were crazy wide. "Look at her shirt," she whispered in my ear.

I glanced at the blonde girl's shirt and swallowed. It said VENOM in bright green letters across her chest.

No. Freaking. Way.

"Is that the name of this place?" I asked.

She cocked her head to the side. "Who told you to come here?"

I bit my lip. "No one," I said. "Not exactly."

She shook her head, all traces of her smile gone from her pretty pink lips. "Don't bullshit me. How did you find out about this place and what's your purpose here?"

Shit. The one time I choose not to bullshit someone, I get accused of it anyway.

Katy tugged on my arm. "Maybe we should just go."

"I'm not bullshitting you," I told the girl at the door, shrugging off Katy's hand. I didn't want to leave now. Not after searching for it for half the night. I needed to know what was inside, and why I had somehow known it was here.

"I got an invitation," I said. "But we've been searching for this club for the past half hour with no luck. No one even seems to know this place is here."

"So, how did you find it?"

"I don't know," I said. "I just felt drawn to this alley. Like I belonged here. I know how weird that sounds, but—"

"I've heard much weirder," the girl said, a smile tugging at the corner of her mouth. "You said it's your birthday today?"

"Yes," I said. "Twenty-one today."

She pressed her lips together and looked at Katy, then back at me as if trying to decide what in the world to do with us.

"Okay, then tonight's your lucky night," she said. "But we have some rules here at Venom and you'd better follow them as if your pretty little lives depended on it. You got that?"

We nodded.

"Number one, don't go off into any dark corners or back rooms with someone you don't know. Number two, don't leave here with any strange men. If either of you ladies is looking for a one-night-stand, this is not the place for you."

I studied her, my eyes narrowing. "These are the club's rules?" I asked. What kind of club has a rule against one-night-stands?

She returned my stare, her face dead serious. "Not exactly. These are my rules for letting you in, okay? If anything were to happen to either of you, I'd never forgive myself."

The concern in her voice sent chills up my spine. Since

when does a bouncer at a club give a crap about what happens to random girls who come in? And since when is it so incredibly dangerous to go into a dark corner with someone?

What kind of place is this?

The door girl pulled a small pen from the pocket of her jeans and reached for my hand. She turned my hand over and placed the pen against the inside of my wrist, then pushed. Instead of an actual pen, it was some kind of stamp. In the green glow of the hallway, the stamp also glowed green, like it was under a black-light. The stamp was a picture of a coiled snake.

She stamped Katy, then put the pen away.

"My name is Selena," she said. "If you need anything, you can come find me. I'll be here the rest of the night."

I nodded. "Thanks," I said. I glanced toward the heavy black door with a matching carving of a snake in the wood. "What kind of a club is this, anyway?"

She smiled, placing her hand on the metal handle. "The kind of club people don't find by accident."

RED DRAGON

Thumping bass greeted us as the door opened. We had to walk down another long black hallway to get to the main room of the club, and Katy grabbed my arm.

"What have you gotten us into?" she whispered, clinging to me. "What if this is some kind of sex club?"

I smiled at the thought. "Well, if we walk in and everyone's having sex, we either join in or turn around and walk right back out."

She smacked my arm. "You are so disgusting."

I bit back a laugh. If this was a sex club, at least we'd end up with one hell of a story to tell about this night.

But as we walked down that hallway, I knew this club had much deeper secrets than that. Much more dangerous secrets. Whatever this place was, it was going to be a real adventure. I knew it from the knot of fear in my core.

It scared and excited me at the same time.

I pressed forward, giving Katy's hand a reassuring squeeze.

Like the front entrance, this hallway had long tubes of colored liquid that bubbled and swam along as we walked, giving off an eerie glow.

The closer we got, the louder the music and voices became. I'd never been to a club that made you walk through a tunnel to get to the main room, but our small journey added to the mystery of the place.

Walking through that final archway and into the main room was like walking into a brand-new world. My senses were assaulted with beauty and mystery and noise.

The room opened into a large two-level dance floor filled with beautiful, elegant bodies. On the upper level, a balcony wrapped around the dance floor with tables that overlooked the spectacle below. People sat drinking, talking and laughing in the shadows.

Large booths lined in plush velvet wrapped around the entire bottom floor of the room.

Dancers with perfect bodies danced in cages lifted just off the ground.

A long bar to our left took up the entire wall on that side of the room. It was unlike any bar-top I'd ever seen, in life or in the movies. Instead of wood, the bar was made of thick clear glass, bright colors rushing back and forth in waves inside long tubes that ran the length of the bar.

It was the lighting of the place that amazed me and made me have to physically close my own jaw. It was magical and mysterious. Dark and shadowed, yet filled with so much color and light. A neon jungle of glass tubes.

I studied the tubes, trying to figure out exactly how they were lit, but it seemed that the liquid itself was alive with light. How could that be? It had to be some beautiful illusion.

"Wow," I said, taking it all in. "This place is incredible."

Neither of us had moved from the archway.

Servers with clear glass trays passed in front of us wearing skimpy outfits adorned with jewels. One girl with long black hair and a killer body came out of a back room and stopped.

She stared at me for just a moment too long, then shook her head as if realizing she'd been staring. She smiled, meeting my eyes for a brief moment before disappearing into the crowd, presumably to deliver her drinks to a table.

"I've never seen anything like this," Katy shouted in my ear.

Techno music blasted throughout the room and I suddenly felt the urge to dance.

"Come on," I said, pulling her toward the dance floor.

She hesitated and threw a glance toward the bar. "I want another drink. My buzz has totally worn off after all that walking."

I nodded. "Okay, let's grab something and then dance."

"Deal," she said, leading me toward the bar.

The long counter was crowded with people, but we managed to squeeze ourselves into a small opening somewhere near the end. As we waited for a bartender to take our order, I studied the other people crowded around the bar.

Every single one of them was gorgeous. And I'm not just talking about I've-had-too-much-to-drink-so-everyone-is-beautiful kind of gorgeous. I'm talking about perfect skin, gorgeous glittering eyes, and banging bodies.

Never in my entire life had I seen so many good-looking people packed into one room like this.

I shifted my weight on my hand-me-down heels and pulled my tank top down on my hips. I might have felt like I belonged here when we first walked up, but I was quickly realizing how much I did not match up to the money and style of the people in this room.

My face flushed, and I suddenly felt as if someone was watching me. I glanced around the dance floor, then turned my eyes toward the bar. I was assaulted by the darkest, blackest eyes staring back at me. My stomach flipped, and my heart skipped a beat. Or twelve.

If the people in this club were gorgeous, the guy attached to that set of mysteriously beautiful eyes was a god. I forced my mouth closed, realizing my lips had parted and I was beginning to breathe heavily just looking at him.

His eyes were locked on mine. He wasn't smiling or nodding or trying to approach me. He was just staring, his body frozen and tense as if the sight of me had put him into some kind of angry trance. Around me, the thundering music muted and there was only him.

I could not force my eyes away no matter how hard I tried.

He stared at me as if he could see straight into the core of who I was. As if he knew something about me I had yet to discover for myself. I felt the pressure of his gaze like hand on my heart.

I heard Katy say my name, but I couldn't drag my eyes away from the guy behind the bar.

But then he seemed to wake up. His eyebrows wrinkled in the middle and he shook his head, then turned away, as if we hadn't just shared some incredibly strange moment.

"Earth to Franki," Katy said, shaking my shoulder.

I took a deep breath and slowly came back down to reality. "I'm sorry," I said. "What did you say?"

She whistled, her eyes wide. "Where the hell did you go just now?"

"Nowhere," I said, forcing a smile. I didn't dare look back toward the hot bartender. I was already way out of my comfort zone here. The last thing I needed was to get lost inside his eyes again.

"I asked what you want to drink," Katy said. "I can't do another shot of scotch. I swear, I'll puke."

I laughed. "I'm game for whatever."

A female bartender came over to take our order and looked at me with expectant eyes. The bar was extremely busy, even for a Wednesday night, and I'm sure the last thing she wanted to do was stand there and wait for us to make up our minds.

I leaned forward over the counter. "We've been drinking Scotch all night, but we want to mix it up. What kind of vodka do you have?"

The corner of her lip twitched. "Is this your first time here?"

As if she didn't already know the answer. The two of us stuck out like two sore thumbs in here.

I didn't answer. I just leaned against the bar and raised an eyebrow.

Her face broke out into a smile. "Hold on," she said.

She reached down low behind the bar and pulled up a clear glass bottle with no label or markings of any kind.

She poured two full shots and set them down on the counter in front of us. "What is this?"

"We call it the Red Dragon," she said. There was a mischievous gleam in her eyes. "Trust me. You'll love it."

I studied her. Was she fucking with me? This drink was totally clear and was probably either a shot of straight vodka or nothing but water. Why did everyone here act like they had some big secret they were keeping from us?

"This place is weird," I muttered, eyeing Katy as I snatched the shot glass off the counter and downed it in a single gulp.

I don't know what I expected, but nothing could have prepared me for the sweet, cinnamon flavor that slithered its way down my throat. It was warm but didn't burn the way vodka or other alcohol usually did.

I set the glass down on the bar and felt the world around me shift. I closed my eyes, then opened them wide, drawing in a long, heated breath. I could swear a haze began to form around my vision. My entire body relaxed. I reached for the bar to steady myself, wishing I hadn't worn such high heels.

"Holy shit," Katy said, leaning against my shoulder. "What the hell was that?"

I couldn't answer her at first. I could still feel the warmth of it sliding all the way down into the pit of my stomach. Heat traveled through my veins and branched out, making its way to the very tips of my fingers and toes. I let my own hand move down my arm, loving the way my skin felt. It was as if every nerve in my body had been set on fire. It was as if my every inhibition had been cast into exile.

I wanted to dance.

I shook my head, not sure if I was drunk or what. "I have no idea, but whatever it was, it was amazing," I said. "Do you feel that?"

I turned to look at Katy and saw that instead of sensual and uninhibited, she looked like she was about to yack all over me. Her face literally had turned gray and her lips were pressed tight, like she was doing everything in her power to hold it in.

"Oh, god, are you okay?" I grabbed her arms to steady her.

She shook her head, her mouth closed tight. There was raw panic in her eyes.

I turned to the bartender. She was helping some people just down from us, but I caught her eye and mouthed the word, "Bathrooms?"

She jerked her head toward the entrance and I looked up to see a set of doors near where we'd first come in.

I grabbed Katy's hand and led her in the direction of those doors, praying we'd find a toilet before her stomach released whatever she'd just put inside.

We barely made it inside the women's restroom when she made a guttural noise that sounded more like a strangled cat than a human. I aimed her toward the closest trash can and winced as she threw up. I gathered her shoulder-length hair up into a pony-tail and held it back from her face.

The shot had not agreed with her, to say the least. Which only made me feel guilty for how I was feeling.

I was alive. Every sense was heightened and every tiny breath of air that brushed against my skin felt like a caress.

I didn't tell her how amazing I felt, though, because I could tell she was miserable. I just held her hair back from her face and rubbed her shoulder, waiting for it to pass. When she steadied and leaned back against the tile wall, I reached for a wad of paper towels and ran them under the water.

"Are you okay?" I asked, handing her one towel to wipe her mouth and running the other gently across her sweaty forehead.

"Fabulous," she said, her voice strained and rough.

"Is it over?"

She closed her eyes and breathed in through her nose. Long deep breaths.

I waited, doing my best to comfort her. At the same time, though, hearing the thumping of the bass outside made me wish more than ever I could be out on that dance floor.

"I'm okay," she said. "I think it's passing. Man, that was disgusting. How are you not ill from that taste?"

I frowned. "You thought it tasted bad?"

She looked up at me like I had lost my damned mind. "There is no way you thought that tasted good, right? I mean, it was like someone wrapped a knife with rancid meat and shoved it down my throat."

I shook my head. Did we have the same drink? I mean, I'd watched the bartender pour our shots from the same bottle. How could we have possibly had such different experiences?

"It tasted like cinnamon," I said.

Her face twisted, and she brushed her hair off her shoulders. "Cinnamon? No. Just... no."

I shook my head. It didn't make sense. Either we had extremely different taste buds or something had gone terribly wrong with her shot.

I didn't want to push it and tell her how delicious and buzzed I felt from it, but at the same time, I wanted the chance to describe it. I wanted her to feel it too.

And as bad of a friend as it made me seem, I wanted to beg her not to ask me to take her home.

I desperately wanted to stay. There was something different about this place, and I wanted to figure it out.

"I think that bartender was trying to drug us or something," Katy said. "Did you see that smile on her face? Like she was playing with us. I think we should get the hell out of here."

My shoulders fell. "I don't want to go home," I said. "I think this place is kind of cool."

"Cool? It's freaking me out," she said. "There's not a single fat or ugly person in this whole place. And that drink was not normal. There's something more than weird going on in this club. I think it's dangerous here. We need to go, Franki. I know it's your birthday and all, but I don't feel right about this place."

I sighed. What could I do? I couldn't abandon my friend and tell her to find her own way home.

I was trying to find the cab driver's number in her phone when the door to the bathroom opened and the bartender who'd served us walked in. She was carrying a small bottle in one hand. Water, maybe.

She approached us with a sympathetic look on her face. "I'm sorry," she said, looking at Katy. "I didn't know you weren't... Well, I didn't realize. I wouldn't have given you that shot if I'd known."

"Known what?" I asked.

She turned to look at me, confusion wrinkling the skin around her eyes. "I didn't know you weren't both the kind of girls who belonged here."

Her words were gloriously vague. I wanted to ask her what kind of girls did belong here, but she didn't give me the chance.

"Here," she said, pushing the clear bottle into Katy's hand. "Drink this. I swear it'll make you feel right again."

Katy held the bottle at arm's length. "I don't think I should take anything from you, no offense."

The bartender's face softened. "I know. I completely suck for doing that to you," she said. "We don't get many normals in here, and I was getting such a strong vibe there by the bar. I didn't read you right and I messed up. I'm genuinely sorry, and I don't blame you for not trusting me."

"Normals?" I asked, but neither one of them even acknowledged my question.

"Do you think you could call us a cab or something? I just want to get home and get to bed," Katy said, shoving the bottle back toward the girl.

She wouldn't take it back. She closed her hands around Katy's and pushed it back toward her. "I promise you, all you have to do is drink this and you will feel completely, one-hundred-percent better. Just take a sip. You'll see."

"It's not water?"

She shook her head. "It's more like an antidote for a very nasty shot. Please."

Katy stared down at the drink in her hand for a long moment, then unscrewed the cap and took a single sip. She waited, and I held my breath.

She took another sip, then let her head rest against the tile wall.

I waited, completely, acutely aware of the weirdness of this entire situation. Who had an antidote for a shot? Or even a hangover? And why had she come in here after us?

Katy's eyes opened, and she let out a long sigh of relief.

"Better?" the bartender asked.

"Much," she said. "Wow. My head was pounding, and my stomach was all twisted up, and now I feel fine. What is this stuff?"

The girl's entire body relaxed. "I'm so glad," she said, avoiding the question. "I would have felt awful if you went home sick. I swear I just didn't realize."

I took a step back and crossed my arms across my chest.

"Okay, so what's with the cryptic messages and the weird drinks and everything? What is this place?"

I loved the way the shot had made me feel, but I didn't like the way this girl was implying that my friend was '*normal*' and I wasn't. That had not been totally lost on me, and I wanted to know what the heck she meant by it.

The bartender shook her head, her long blonde curls caressing her shoulders. "You really have no idea where you are, do you?" she asked.

It was a question with too obvious an answer. We obviously had no clue where we really were.

"How did you end up here, then? I mean, it's not like we're on the main strip with a big sign out front. Most people don't find us on accident."

Her tongue tripped over the word people and it sent a shiver up my spine. Plus, her words were eerily similar to the ones Selena had used out front.

"Franki here got an invitation to come to this place, but no one seemed to know where it was," Katy said. "You know, you really shouldn't put your main entrance down a dark alleyway. That can't be good for business."

"So, how did you find us if no one told you where it was?"

Katy pointed at me. "Psychic wonder over here had a feeling about it. She just knew it was here. Don't ask me how."

The bartender turned her focus on me, looking me up and down. For the first time since she'd come in here, I noticed how icy blue her eyes were. I shifted uncomfortably, not sure if I should thank her for helping Katy or punch her in the face for serving us something weird to begin with.

"What?" I asked, annoyed. The booze—or whatever it was —flowing through my veins was taking away both inhibitions and good sense. I opened my arms and stepped forward. "Why does everyone here keep staring at me like that? Just what do you think you see?"

Her eyes widened, and a startled smile broke out on her face. "I see—"

Someone pounded hard on the bathroom door. "Azure? Get your ass out here. We've got customers."

The bartender shrugged, her thoughts cut off. "Sorry, that's my cue to go," she said, turning toward the door. "Stay and hang out a little bit if you want. Drinks are on the house. No funny stuff, I promise."

I was supremely annoyed. None of my questions were being answered and the strange warmth flowing through me only seemed to heat up, the angrier I got.

"Wait," I said, taking a step in her direction. "What was in that shot, anyway?"

She opened the door and stood half-in, half-out, the noise of the club almost deafening after the silence of the bathroom. "I really have to go," she said. Her icy blue eyes met mine. "You guys should stay, if you want. Just be careful not to leave with anyone you don't know. Selena will call you a cab and make sure you get home safely when you're ready to go, okay? Promise me."

I nodded as she turned on her heel and left the room. The bathroom door closed, leaving us in muted silence again.

This was definitely turning out to be the strangest night of my life.

And it had only just begun.

TRUST ME

Katy and I walked out of the bathroom and back into the neon glow of the main club.

"If you want to go home, I completely understand," I shouted over the music.

She turned to me, her green eyes bright. "I feel great," she said. "And I realize how completely insane that sounds after you were just holding my hair back, so I could throw up in the trashcan, but whatever she gave me really helped."

She looked down, as if realizing she was still holding the bottle of clear liquid.

"I wonder what's in it?" I asked. "And what was in that shot to begin with?"

She shook her head and shrugged. "Hell if I know," she said. "But the way I see it, we're here, there's music, there are a ton of hot guys on the dance floor, and there are still fifteen minutes left of your birthday. Let's just have a good time and forget about the rest of it."

She reached for my hand and I placed it in hers, smiling.

"Sounds good to me."

"Just no more funky shots." Katy laughed and together we worked our way through the crowd and onto the dance floor.

The buzz from the shot was still flowing strong in my system, somehow amplified by my anger earlier in the bathroom. And now that we were out here on the crowded dance floor with the strange lights and pounding music, my entire body began to hum with energy.

I looked around, at first feeling a little bit self-conscious around all these beautiful people. But then I started to lose myself to the music.

I closed my eyes, letting go of everything else but the vibrations running up through the floor and into my bones. My lips parted, and the lights and energy seemed to flow straight into my mouth and through my soul. My blood pulsed with the rhythm of this place.

I had always considered myself a pretty good dancer, but tonight, I was electric. It was as if someone had plugged me directly in to one of the speakers and turned me on.

My body moved in ways I never knew were possible. Smooth and fluid. Sexy and sensual and confident.

The taste of the cinnamon-flavored shot lingered on my tongue, warm and slightly sweet.

I pulled my long black hair up, letting the air blow across the back of my neck. Every one of my senses was amplified.

That's when I felt him watching me.

A darkness washed over me, dread pooling in my stomach. The sticky sweetness of the drink went sour in my mouth, making me long for water and fresh air.

His gaze passed like a shadow across my skin, pulling me

into the dark places where no one would see me. No one but him.

I let my hair drop heavily down my back and opened my eyes. I didn't stop dancing or try to draw attention to myself, but I no longer felt free. Sadness and fear pushed through me and I shivered.

Who is he?

I knew it was a man, even if I couldn't tell you how I knew. I just felt the maleness of him. The territorial claim of his eyes on my body. I didn't like it.

I didn't like it at all.

I turned and scanned the crowd behind me, concentrating on the shadowy places beyond the dance floor. He was up there somewhere, sitting down. Watching me from the darkness. Whatever I'd done to get his attention, I wished I could take it back.

Was this the same person who had sent the invitation?

I swallowed, my throat thick with syrup. Someone had invited me here, but who? Katy was right. It had been a mistake to come.

In my bones, I knew this wasn't just some secret admirer or old friend trying to reconnect. This definitely wasn't my mother. There was something much darker at play here.

And much more dangerous.

Strong hands encircled my waist, fingers slipping into the belt loops on my jeans and pulling me back. I gasped. My body tensed, and I tried to pull away. To turn around and see his face.

But his strength was too much for me.

He leaned forward, his warm breath against my ear.

"Don't struggle," he said. His voice was rough and deep. "Just play along. Trust me."

It was the way he said the word trust that calmed me.

This was not the man from the darkness. This was someone trying to protect me.

Only, I couldn't shake the question of what, exactly, I might need protection from.

I turned my head, but still couldn't see his face.

"Keep dancing," he said.

Our bodies moved together, his hands firm on my hips as he pressed his solid, muscular body against mine.

I moved my hands to his and when our skin touched, an electric shock went through me for the second time that night. It was like a static shock times ten. I gripped his wrists and pulled his fingers from their hold on my jeans.

"I need to see your face," I said, turning my head slightly so that my cheek was practically touching his.

He gave way, letting me turn around, but never taking his hands from me.

In the pulsing lights, I recognized the deep black of his eyes and the wild black hair.

The bartender who had been staring at me earlier.

I stepped back in surprise, but his arms reclaimed me, pulling me closer, as if we were lovers reuniting after being apart for far too long. My heart pounded so hard against my ribs, I was sure he would be able to feel it beating against his chest.

"What's happening?" I asked, barely able to hear my own voice over the music. "Someone is watching me."

"Now they're watching us," he said, a hint of a smile on his lips that disappeared so fast I wondered if it was ever really there.

I let my hands wander up his arms, gripping the muscular biceps that bulged against the sleeves of his black t-shirt. He was taller than me by several inches and I had to look up to meet his eyes, pools of black liquid with veins of silver running through them. I disappeared into them for a moment. My knees went weak, and I fell against him, blinking to force my gaze away.

I was not the swooning type, so I refused to believe I had just swooned over this dark-eyed stranger. Maybe my blood-sugar was low. There had to be a logical explanation.

"You okay?" he asked, steadying me.

"I'm fine," I said through clenched teeth. "Or at least, I think I am. Something is definitely not normal about this place."

His smile played another disappearing act. "You're just now figuring that out?"

I wasn't sure if I wanted to punch him or pull him closer.

"Care to explain?"

He raised an eyebrow and shook his head, amused.

Punch. I definitely wanted to punch him.

But that was impossible considering the fact that our bodies were pressed tighter than I'd been with any man in months. And like it or not, mine was definitely responding to him. If I thought my skin was on fire earlier, it was burning up now. I thought I might turn to ash at any moment.

"If you didn't know what kind of place this was, why did you come here?" he asked.

I narrowed my eyes at him. Why did everyone keep asking

us that? "It's a public place, right? People come here all the time? Why not me?"

He cocked his head slightly, studying me. "Not many people wander in here on accident," he said. "It's not that kind of club."

"So I've heard," I mumbled. "What no one seems to want to share with me is exactly what kind of club it is."

The music changed, and his hands shifted on my hips. The tip of his thumb brushed against the bare skin at my waist and I tensed, flames rising up through my core. I gasped for breath.

He raised his eyebrow again. He was getting a kick out of my reactions, and I hated him for it. I hated that one tiny touch of his skin against mine could tilt my entire world on its axis.

Maybe it was the alcohol still working its way through my system. That had to be it. Men just didn't affect me like this. At least none who had ever touched me before.

"You're not going to answer me, are you?" I asked, my voice unsteady. I straightened my shoulders and tried to put a little space between us, so I could think straight.

"Not until you answer my question first."

He was toying with me. Why come over here to protect me from some unseen stranger if he just wanted to play with me?

I didn't like to play games.

"I was invited by someone," I said.

Darkness crossed his features. That wasn't the answer he'd been expecting.

"Who?"

I shook my head. "I have no idea." I shrugged, trying to pretend I wasn't completely distracted by the way his body moved against mine.

"Someone you don't know invited you to a strange club

and you came?" he asked, his voice raw with anger. His muscles tensed against my hands. "Expecting what? Some kind of affair? A fun time?"

I pushed against him, but he only held me tighter.

"Who the hell are you to judge me? I don't even know you."

"You don't know the person who invited you either," he said.

"Why are you getting mad at me for that?" I raised my voice over the music a few heads turned toward us. "You don't own me. You don't even know me. If I want to come to a club to meet up with a guy, that's none of your business."

The muscles in his jaw tensed and he took a deep breath. "Lower your voice," he said.

"Or what?" I challenged him. I had been on my own for most of my life. I didn't do well with people spouting orders at me. I certainly didn't need this asshole telling me what I could or could not do on my own damned birthday.

He pulled me closer, bringing his mouth close to my ear again. "Or you're going to end up getting into a lot more trouble than you bargained for when you walked through that door tonight. Trust me."

There went that word again. Trust. Not a word to be taken lightly in my experience, and I wasn't about to let this guy threaten me.

I moved my hand up his arm and shoulder, then around to the back of his neck. I threaded my fingers through his long dark hair and tugged slightly, pulling him toward me.

"In my world, people have to earn my trust, so don't throw that word around like it means nothing," I said. "Just because you're stronger than me doesn't mean you have the right to push me around, you got that? So, if you have something to say, you'd better start talking."

I loosened my grip on his hair and he pulled his head back, his eyes wide and the first solid smile on his lips.

At first, he didn't say a word. He just stared at me, as if in shock. Then, after a long moment where I thought my heart might beat completely out of my chest, he pulled away from me and held out his hand.

I stared at it, not knowing whether to take it or turn and walk away.

"You want to talk?" he asked. "Come on, then. Let's talk."

Was he really offering me answers? Or was this just another part of whatever game he was playing with me? There was only one way to find out.

I took a couple of deep breaths, then placed my hand in his.

IN THE SHADOWS

K aty grabbed my arm as I passed by her. "Who is that?" she asked, her face turned away from him, so he couldn't see or hear.

"One of the bartenders," I said. It was the best answer I had at the moment.

"He's hot," she whispered.

"I'll be right back," I said, biting my lip. Yes, he was hot, but he was also mysterious and way out of my league.

"Don't you dare leave me here by myself," she said with a nervous laugh.

"I won't," I said. She should have known better.

She squeezed my arm and went back to dancing with the guy beside her. I hadn't noticed him before and wondered if he had appeared on the dance floor at the same time the bartender had.

"She'll be fine," the bartender said. He was still holding onto my hand. "That guy's a friend of mine. I told him to keep an eye on her."

I opened my mouth to protest, but he tugged on my hand, pulling me through the crowd. People seemed to part for him with ease, letting us pass. A few of the people smiled, but many of them lowered their gaze as he moved by, stepping back to give him plenty of space.

Who was this guy? I certainly couldn't just call him the bartender all night. Especially not after he'd had his hands all over me.

I followed him to the edge of the dance floor, past the bar and into the shadows at the back of the room. He finally stopped in a dark corner. Hadn't the girl out front made me promise not to go into any shadowy places with a stranger?

A shiver traveled down my spine and moved into my stomach, making me feel jittery and unsettled. The alcohol in my system wouldn't let me think clearly. All I could concentrate on was how I felt. And how his hands felt on me.

He finally released my hand, but the warmth of his skin lingered on mine. I stuffed my hands into the pockets of my jeans and leaned against the wall, hoping I looked casual instead of completely and utterly affected by his presence.

"Let me see it," he said. He had this way of giving orders that made me both angry and aroused.

"See what?"

"The invitation."

"Oh," I said. So not what I thought he meant. I reached deeper into my pocket and found the folded piece of red paper.

Before he'd even touched it or read a word of it, his face turned almost pale. I held it out to him, but he hesitated, just staring at the paper as if it were made of thorns.

He drew in a loud breath, then reached out for the red

invitation. He unfolded it and stared at it for a second. I knew he was reading the words I'd seen this morning when it had arrived with the mysterious black roses.

Happy Birthday, Little Bird

The address to the club was typed in neat letters at the bottom of the paper.

The bartender crumpled the invitation in his fist, squeezing it down into a small ball. His lips were pressed tight, and his shoulders were tensed.

"Where did you get this?"

"Hold on just a second," I said. "You haven't even told me who you are or why you care. I'm not going to tell you everything if you aren't going to talk to me first. You said you'd explain what was going on."

He stuffed my invitation into his back pocket, then ran a tense hand through his hair. "What do you want to know?"

"Your name would be good for starters," I said.

"Rend." His eyes followed someone walking past us, then moved back to my face. Every time his eyes met mine, it sent a warm rush of desire through my body. "Now will you tell me where you got this invitation?"

Rend. An unusual name for a very unusual man.

"What's going on in this place?" I asked, determined to get some answers while I still had the upper hand. "Why did you say people don't typically come here on accident? And what was up with that Red Dragon stuff your friend gave us when we first got here? Why did it make me feel good and make my friend feel like crap?"

He raised an eyebrow again. That seemed to be his signature look. "Anything else? You sure you don't want to ask me a few more questions?"

I didn't humor him with a response. I just stared at him until he started talking. I didn't owe him anything, so if he wanted me to talk, he'd better start answering my questions, too.

"You don't give up, do you?" he asked. "Look. None of those are easy questions to answer. You've walked into something here you couldn't possibly understand, and I'm trying to protect you. You have to believe that."

"I don't have to believe anything," I said. "This whole night has been incredibly strange and not at all what I expected."

"What you expected? So, you did have some idea who might have sent this?"

"No," I said. "I don't know. Not really. I thought there was some small possibility it might have come from my mother, but then, why would she send me black roses? None of this makes any sense."

His eyes flashed almost silver in the darkness, which was impossible right? Had I imagined it?

"Black roses?" He ran a hand across his face. "Did you touch them?"

I shrugged. What kind of question was that? "Of course. I put them in a vase with some water."

His shoulders relaxed.

This conversation was getting stranger with every word. He'd seemed worried about the roses. I'll admit, black roses are a weird choice, but they were strangely beautiful. Exotic.

"Listen, if you ever get another box of black roses, just throw them in the trash. Don't even touch them with your bare hands, okay? Promise me."

"I don't understand you," I said, anger growing in my voice. I was sick of people telling me to promise them things when they refused to explain why. "You come out of nowhere and tell me you know someone is watching me. You touch me like you have some kind of claim on me. I can't wrap my head around it. What do you think I owe you? What is going on? Stop talking in circles and just come out with it. I'm not some stupid little girl who doesn't know how to take care of herself. I've been through shit, okay? I can handle it. Just tell me what you think you know about that invitation and the roses. Tell me who was watching me out there."

Anger flashed in his eyes again and he gripped both my arms and lifted me off the ground. He moved me into the corner and pushed my back against the wall.

"An attitude like that will get you killed in a place like this," he said, almost growling. His face was so close to mine, I could feel his breath against my cheek. "I've only seen red paper of that quality one time before in my life, and I'm telling you, if the same man who sent that to me also sent this invitation to you this morning, you ought to run as far away from this place as you can."

He lowered me until my heels touched the ground. Tears stung the corners of my eyes, and I was not the type of girl who cried. Ever. But his outburst had scared me.

He released his grip on my arms, and I resisted the urge to rub the spots where his hands had been.

"I'm sorry." He ran his hand through his hair and closed his eyes, taking a moment before he spoke again. "I know you didn't know what you were getting into by coming here. It's not your fault, but I really wish you had just thrown that paper away and never walked into this place."

I wanted to be strong and tell him to leave me alone, but I was frozen to the spot, unable to talk back or argue with him. I had no idea why he was so angry or why he wanted to keep me safe, but I understood now that he honestly believed I was in some kind of danger.

I thought about my mother and how it was exactly three years to the day since she had disappeared from my life. I'd convinced myself that she left of her own will. She'd never been a real mother to me, anyway. I couldn't remember a single day of my childhood when she wasn't high or drunk or completely disconnected from life. All she'd ever wanted to do was escape, and the day I turned eighteen and could legally take care of myself, that's exactly what she had done.

Escaped.

She'd left me alone without even bothering with goodbye.

That was the real reason why those words on the invitation haunted me. Those two words were the real reason I had come.

Little Bird.

Standing there with Rend, I finally admitted to myself that in some strange way, I had hoped I would find her here. In some secret, hidden part of my heart, I had hoped those roses were from her and that she would be here, waiting with open arms and ready to apologize for all those years of heartache.

I should have known better. This whole thing was stupid.

"I shouldn't have come," I said. I cursed the teary sound of my voice. I was stronger than that, even if this guy didn't know me well enough to understand what I'd been through. What I'd overcome to get this far.

"No," he said. "You shouldn't have. You should go. Get out and forget you ever came here."

I breathed through the threat of tears, reaching deep down

to find the strength I knew I had. I refused to let a single tear hit my cheek.

I looked up into his eyes, no longer feeling weak-kneed. What I felt instead was a mix of anger and regret and disappointment.

Disappointment that the first man who had actually made me feel something was mixed up in something dangerous and untouchable. It wasn't fair. Why couldn't I have met someone like him under different circumstances?

But my mother had always told me I had a personality meant for trouble and that I was no good. Maybe that's why I was so attracted to him. The scent of danger rolled off him like cologne. On one hand, I wished I'd never met him. On the other, I wished I didn't have to walk away and never see him again.

"Want to get out of my way so I can leave? Or are you planning to hold me prisoner back here in the shadows?" My voice was strong again despite the queasiness in my stomach.

His eyes widened, and that secret smile tugged at his lips as he moved to the side.

I held his gaze for a second longer, then walked back toward the crowd on the dance floor.

BLOOD-THIRSTY

I needed to find Katy and get the hell out of this place.

The dance floor had only become more crowded in the past few minutes. The later it got, the more people poured into the club, even on a Wednesday night.

I found her dancing with the same blond-haired guy as before, and I could tell by the way their bodies were pressed close together that she wasn't going to be happy about me dragging her away from him. Still, if he was a good friend of Rend's, I was doing her a favor. Hopefully they hadn't thought to exchange numbers. If we were lucky, we would both be able to walk away and forget this night ever happened.

I had to wade through the sea of people to get to her. They didn't part for me now that Rend wasn't leading the way. When I'd almost reached her, a strange sensation pricked at my heart. I stopped cold and looked around.

This was different from earlier when I had felt someone watching me. This was more like a familiar presence. It reached inside my chest and squeezed my heart until it stopped beating.

I looked up just in time to see her long black braid and the shadowed profile of her face.

My mother.

I couldn't breathe. She was really here. After all this time. It was like seeing a ghost.

All of the heat in my body dissipated, and I shivered, clutching my arms close to my chest.

She was with three men I didn't recognize. They were dressed in long black cloaks even though it was still late summer and warm out.

All I caught was that flash of her before she opened a door and disappeared through it. The men followed her, then closed the door behind them.

I couldn't move at first. I couldn't think. Part of me wanted to grab Katy and run away, like Rend had told me to. My mother never cared about me, so why did I even want to see her? It had taken me a long time to get over the heartbreak of her disappearance. Did I really want to relive that?

But another part of me—a stronger part—knew I couldn't walk away.

I had to follow her. Even if just to get the chance to tell her how much I hated her. How much she had broken me.

I pushed my way through the throng and sprinted for the door.

With both hands, I pushed it open and felt the humid night air wash over me. It led into another back alley. I stepped out and the door slammed shut behind me, the music now muffled and distant.

There were no lights out here and I struggled to see in the darkness. I thought I saw a pair of red eyes turn toward me, then giant black wings rose up into the sky. I fell back in surprise, shielding my face with my hand, and when I looked up again, the bird was flying off overhead. It looked to be a normal size, and I wondered if my eyes had been playing tricks on me.

I caught my breath, then looked again for my mother.

But she wasn't out there.

Instead, the three men who had followed her were standing side-by-side, their eyes locked on me. Hungry smiles marred their faces.

"Well, well, what have we here?" the tallest one said. He moved one step closer to me.

I reached back and tugged on the door handle to get back inside, but it was locked.

"A juicy little treat," another one said. There was laughter in his tone. "Perhaps the night is not lost after all."

The third one, a man with broad shoulders and pale skin, moved toward me so fast, his body was a blur of shadows.

I gasped as he ran a jagged fingernail across my cheek. He closed his eyes and leaned forward to smell my hair. I pulled away, but his hand darted out to grab me. He held on so tightly, I whimpered in pain. That was going to leave a bruise.

"Do you smell that?" he asked. "It's been a long time since I tasted one so powerful and pure."

The tall one rubbed his hands together and took a few more steps toward me.

Bile rose into the back of my throat, tasting faintly of cinnamon and scotch.

What did he mean by taste?

I didn't want to stay here and find out, but there were three of them and only one of me. It didn't look good, but I wasn't going down without a fight.

"I don't know what you guys think you're doing, but you'd better get your freaking hands off me."

I lifted my knee and stomped the heel of my shoe down on the guy's foot as hard as I could. He loosened his grip for a split second, and I wrenched my arm away.

I darted around him and ran toward the lights of the main street, but before I could get more than a few steps, the tall one was in front of me. It was as if he'd just materialized out of thin air.

He made a clicking noise with his tongue. "Bad little witch," he said. "Don't make this any harder than it has to be, or we'll make this a very unpleasant experience for you."

"As if you ever had any intention of making it pleasant," I muttered, clenching my jaw and backing away.

He smiled, and my stomach turned.

Two large fangs protruded from his mouth.

I shook my head and stared at those fangs, unable to believe what I was seeing.

Vampires weren't real, yet I could swear that's exactly what I saw standing in front of me. I screamed and turned to run the other way, but it was no use. The three of them had me surrounded now.

And all three of them had fangs.

Suddenly the word taste took on a whole new meaning.

"We're going to be the strongest demons in this world after this meal," the pale one said.

He opened his mouth and reached for me. In my panic, I must have summoned up some kind of superhuman strength because I kicked him in the chest so hard, he nearly flew back several feet until his back hit the brick wall behind him.

Shock registered on his face, followed by an insane fury that literally turned his eyes red with hatred.

A hand gripped my shoulder, and I threw my elbow back with all my might, hitting the tall one in the gut. He let go of me and doubled over with a grunt.

I spun around toward the smaller one, my body buzzing with adrenaline.

He blocked my way toward the main street, but I knew I needed to get past him fast before his two friends recovered and came back for vengeance.

I ran toward him, a strange energy gathering in my fist. I reared back and punched him in the face as hard as I could. A horrible crack echoed in the alley and blood splattered through the air. I didn't even take the time to wonder how the hell I'd been strong enough to do that. I just ran, kicking off my heels as I went.

But it wasn't enough. Again, the biggest of the three materialized in front of me, this time not bothering to smile or make some snide remark about how tasty I smelled.

Instead, he grabbed the front of my white shirt and twisted, lifting me off the ground so that my bare feet dangled in the air.

I screamed again, terror pumping through my veins. I kicked and scratched, but soon his buddies joined him, holding my arms.

There were no smiles. Just blood-thirsty vengeance.

"You're going to pay for that, witch."

The pale one pulled me to him, his fangs shining white as he opened his mouth wide toward my neck.

I closed my eyes.

STRONGER THAN SHE LOOKS

"**P**ut her down."

The vampire's fangs brushed against the bare skin of my neck. I felt the pressure of his bite against my flesh, but he froze at the sound of the voice behind me.

My eyes snapped open as he pulled away. He did not, however, put me down.

I turned my head but couldn't see the newcomer. I recognized his voice, though. That rough, deep bass sounded different without the thumping of the music to cover it, but I knew it was Rend.

I wanted to tell him to go back inside. That these guys were too strong. Too dangerous. Too completely unbelievable to be real.

But considering the fact that his presence had just saved my life for the moment, I kept my damned mouth shut.

"I said put her down. Don't make me ask a third time, or you'll wish you'd never set eyes on this girl." He chuckled.

"From the looks of it she already put up a good fight on her own."

I couldn't see the other two, but my eyes had adjusted enough to the darkness to see the pale, broad-shouldered vampire in front of me. He looked pissed, to say the least.

I expected him to tell Rend to get lost, but instead, like some miracle, he opened his fist. I fell to the pavement like some ragdoll. Both of my hands went down on instinct to protect my fall, and I ended up scraping the hell out of both palms and my elbow as I hit. I felt the blood trickle against my skin.

Rend cursed, and all four men in the alley reached for me.

Luckily, Rend got to me first. Even though he was the farthest away, he somehow got to my side and lifted me into his arms. He backed toward the door to the club.

"Don't you dare lay one finger on her," he said.

The smallest of the three vampires dropped to his knees and licked the pavement where my blood had spilled. The tall one kicked him aside so hard he went flying into a dumpster.

"You took it all, you asshole," he yelled.

The two of them began to fight until the pale man lifted his fist. "Shut up, both of you."

Everyone grew still. The only sounds were the distant thumping of music and the occasional car passing on the main street at the end of the alley.

Rend set me down gently, then brought his arm out in front of me, shielding me from the other three.

"She one of your girls?" the guy asked. He brought one hand to his side where I'd elbowed him, and I wondered if I'd really managed to hurt him. "I've never seen her here before."

"Yes, she's mine," he said.

I opened my mouth to protest, but a side-glance from Rend shut me up real quick.

"She's not wearing one of your shirts. She doesn't have the mark," the tall one protested. "How were we supposed to know?"

That's when I realized that these guys weren't just listening to Rend. They were afraid of him.

"We didn't mean any harm," the broad-shouldered vampire said. "We were outside the club. We didn't break any rules here."

The three of them waited, barely moving a muscle. What exactly were they scared he was going to do to them? I mean, I could tell he was built, but what were muscles against mythical beings of the night?

Unless Rend wasn't exactly human himself.

"I'll give the three of you a pass this one time," Rend said. "But only because she's new and isn't in uniform. I haven't had a chance to mark her yet."

The three vampires visibly relaxed.

The tall one wiped dark blood from his nose. "She was being a real pain in the ass anyway," he said, snarling. "I think she broke my nose."

Rend glanced back at me, shaking his head, and laughing. "She's stronger than she looks."

"Tell me about it," the small one said, clutching his side.

"We didn't mean any disrespect."

"You may have been outside of my club, but you should know better than to feed less than three feet away from my back door," Rend said. "The ones who come here have a right to feel safe whether they're coming or going. You know that.

Like I said, I'll let you live. This time. Don't let me see any of you around here for a while."

"But—"

The tall one started to argue, but his friends cut him off. They all bowed, said their thanks, then right before my eyes, each of them turned from solid men into dark, swirling shadows.

I reached up to hold onto Rend's still outstretched arms, my eyes not leaving the spot where the shadows gathered and then flew away into the night.

"What the hell were those things?" I asked, breathless. I wasn't even sure I wanted to know.

Rend pulled his arm away from me, then walked over to retrieve my shoes.

He glared at me as he handed them over.

"Remember when I told you this place was dangerous, and you needed to go home? What happened to that?"

I shrugged. "I thought I saw someone I knew."

He walked past me and pulled open the door.

"Hey, that door was locked a minute ago," I said.

"This door is never locked to me," he said. He stood there, waiting for me to go in.

I straightened my shoulders and took a deep breath to calm my fractured nerves.

Demons. Vampires. Whatever they were, he wasn't joking when he told me I shouldn't have come here.

But I still had a lot of questions. Especially about the woman who had led me out here in the first place. Where had she disappeared to? Was it even really my mother or was it just some trick to lure me out here?

I was afraid that asking those questions would lead me down a path I wasn't ready to walk.

"Come on," he said. "Let's get you inside."

I couldn't argue with that. I walked past him and back into the neon glow of Venom.

I wanted to do what I should have done half an hour ago. Grab Katy and get the hell out of there.

But when I started toward the dance floor, Rend called out to me. "Hey, Franki."

"What?" I said, turning back to him. I didn't remember ever telling him my name.

He motioned for me to follow him, then leaned over the top of the bar and grabbed a black t-shirt. He threw it at me, and I nearly dropped my shoes to catch it.

I held it out to get a better look at the shirt. The word VENOM was written in bright green across the chest. On the back was the word STAFF.

I swallowed. "What's this for?"

He raised an eyebrow.

"You're one of mine, now," he said, a smile playing at his lips. "You start tomorrow."

EPISODE TWO

THE DREAM

A BLACK CROW

Large black wings rise up against the shadows. I stagger backwards, tripping over something soft on the ground.

I look down to see a ratty old teddy bear. Something from my childhood that tugs at the edge of my memory. I pick up the small tattered thing and bring it up to my chest, hugging it close. It smells like home. My old home.

I hear the fluttering of wings and look up, but I'm no longer in the dark alleyway. Instead, I'm in a long, narrow hallway that stretches out as far as my eyes can see. Doors line both sides. A light above flickers on and off.

I clutch the bear to my chest and walk forward. I'm not sure what I'm searching for, but I think it must be this way. I follow the sound of the crow's caw.

On each side of me, the doors are marked with different symbols. A horse. A serpent. A flower. A butterfly.

I keep to the center of the hall, not daring to reach out and touch any of the doors. I half expect one of them to open and reveal some chamber of horrors on the other side. I can't shake the feeling that someone is watching me. Following me.

But when I turn to look, there's no one there. I am alone.

Alone except for the crow.

I keep moving forward, my steps tentative, like a little girl. I feel small and frightened.

The sound of flapping wings echoes around me, but I can't see the bird. She's here somewhere. If I could just find her, I'd be safe.

I'd be home.

The overhead light finally flickers one last time and then dies, dousing the hallway in darkness. I stop, unsure what to do without someone to guide me or tell me where to go.

But then I see it. Just up ahead, one of the doors is glowing.

I force my feet to move, feeling that if I could just reach that door safely, I would find the answers I've been looking for.

The hall is long and dark, but when I finally reach the glowing door, I gasp. The symbol carved into the wood is the outline of a black crow.

With a trembling hand, I reach for it.

THE DREAM

The buzzing of my alarm ripped me from the dream. Sweat poured down the back of my neck, and my heart pounded against my ribs.

Holy crap. Last night had really done a number on my head. It had taken me forever to get to sleep in the first place, and I must have spent the rest of the night lost in the same dream, walking down that endless hallway over and over again.

I pushed my hair off my face and sat up. The black t-shirt Rend gave me was lying on top of my desk. I just stared at it, as if looking at it long enough might make it disappear. How could he expect me to go back to that awful place?

I'd almost died last night. If he hadn't shown up at just that moment, I would probably be sprawled out in a dumpster, drained of every single drop of blood.

The image of that guy licking up a few drops of my spilled blood from the ground invaded my mind, and I squeezed my eyes shut, begging it to go away.

This couldn't be real. Vampires didn't really exist, right?

They were myths or make-believe, not something you actually encountered in a dark alley. Maybe I'd just gotten hold of some really bad drugs last night and went on some kind of weird trip. Maybe I'd get to the club and realize it was all just one, long nightmare.

But I knew in my gut that it was no dream.

I thought about crawling back under the covers and ignoring the rest of the day. What would Rend do if I didn't show up to work? It wasn't like he knew where I lived.

I hope.

Still, he struck me as the kind of guy who would know how to find people. And I most definitely did not want him to have to come looking for me.

Random bartender or not, those guys last night had been scared of him. Terrified. So, what did that make him?

More than just a bartender, that's for sure.

And if he expected me to work for him at Venom, I didn't have much of a choice but to show up.

I forced myself out of bed and climbed into the shower, turning the water up as hot as it would go. I washed off the stench of sweat and cigarette smoke and let the hot water wash the crusted blood from my palms and my elbow. A large black and blue bruise had formed on my arm where the tall guy had grabbed me.

I knew I was lucky to have gotten out of there without more damage done. What would happen if I had to work there now? Night after night?

I couldn't do it. I'd have to go in today and tell Rend that I'd work off whatever debt I owed him and then I was out of there, gone forever just like he'd wanted in the first place. I would find a way to wipe the whole experience from my mind and move on.

When my skin had turned bright pink from the heat of the water, I turned it off and got dressed, pulling on a clean pair of jeans and the black Venom Staff t-shirt.

The only consolation as I grabbed my keys and headed out the door was that he'd asked me to come in at ten in the morning instead of ten at night. I didn't think I could face that place again after dark.

THE BOSS

T he outside of the club looked very different in the light of day. Less dark and dangerous and more like any other rundown building on this side of town.

I parked in a nearby lot and headed toward the alley entrance, wondering again why they didn't have a more normal entrance facing the main street. I also realized I had no idea where that back door must have taken me last night. If this was the back alley, where the hell was that?

I shook my head. Maybe there were just some things I was going to have to let go of about this place. I took a deep breath and steeled my nerves for whatever may come. There was no doubt I owed this guy Rend for saving my life. I just hoped I didn't have to run into anymore demons or vampires while I was there.

I'd be good with never having to see fangs again in my life, thank you very much.

Inside the first hallway, the green liquid still glowed as

brightly as it had the night before. Were they open all day? Or did they just leave these lights on all the time?

The tunnel-like entrance beyond was still lit up, too, but this time there was no bouncer waiting to check my ID. I went straight through to the club and looked around for Rend. He hadn't told me exactly what to do when I got here or where to go, so I had assumed he'd just be waiting for me.

I checked my watch. It was three minutes after ten and there was no one else in sight.

The lights were all on at this time of morning and the place looked far less exotic. I walked over toward the bar, then flipped around as one of the doors on the other side of the room opened.

I hoped to see Rend, but instead, the other bartender from last night appeared. Azure. She was dressed almost the same as she had been the night before. We could have been twins except that her hair was blonde and curly and mine was black and straight as a board.

She smiled when she saw me. "Franki, right?"

She held her hand out and I shook it.

"Yes," I said. "I guess Rend told you I'd be coming in today."

She nodded and motioned toward the bar. "I have to tell you, I was really surprised when he told me you'd be working here."

"Me too," I mumbled. I followed her to the bar and took a seat on one of the stools while she went back behind the counter and started unloading a box of new glasses onto the bar-top.

"Just out of curiosity, what made you want to work here?" she asked. "I mean, no offense or anything, but I've never seen you around and you and your friend seemed pretty freaked out by the place. We don't get a lot of newcomers around here."

"That's kind of what Rend was telling me last night," I said. "Why is that exactly?"

Other than the whole demon vampire thing.

She shrugged. "It's the kind of place that caters to a certain... clientele. Most of the regulars have been coming here for years."

"Okay, but why don't new people stop in all the time? I get that this place isn't exactly on the main strip or anything, but if you guys put a sign out front, I'm sure you'd get a lot more business."

"More business isn't something we're looking for," she said. "And to be honest, I'm not sure the boss would want me to explain it even if I could. At least, not until you understand more about what it is we do here."

Great. More cryptic answers.

"Okay, so how do I find out what it is you do here?"

I had obviously already figured out this wasn't a typical bar or nightclub, but I still didn't understand what it was that made it so different. Surely everyone who was here last night wasn't some kind of demon, right?

"I think it's safer if I just wait and let the boss man tell you when he thinks you're ready," she said with a laugh. "In the meantime, he asked me show you around the place and get you started on some of the basic morning tasks."

I slid off my stool and followed her back toward the other side of the room. "So, when will I get to meet him?" I asked.

"Who?"

"This mysterious boss man," I said. "Rend didn't say anything about him."

She stopped, a huge grin spreading across her face. "You are so adorably clueless," she said. "You really don't know?"

"Know what?" My cheeks flushed.

Azure laughed and opened a black metal door just off the dance-floor.

"Rend is the boss."

DON'T GET USED TO IT

I felt like an idiot.

"Oh, god, I thought he was just a bartender," I said. "No offense. I mean, I have nothing against bartenders, it's just that, crap. I had no idea he owned the place."

"It's his baby," she said. She led me down a narrow hallway painted in all black, then opened a door and motioned for me to go inside.

The storage room was huge. Metal racks lined the walls from floor to ceiling, stacked with boxes.

"I'm not surprised he didn't mention it," she said. "He's a real hands-on kind of boss, always working behind the bar and making sure things are running smoothly. Still, did you really think a guy behind the bar could just hire you on the spot and demand that you show up the next morning?"

I shrugged, feeling stupid. "After the night I had last night, I didn't even think to question it."

She frowned. "Did something happen? I mean, besides your friend getting sick? I saw Rend go out on the floor to dance with you and at first, I figured maybe he knew you from somewhere else."

She climbed up on a step-ladder and pulled down a box, handing it to me before grabbing another and climbing down.

I didn't know where to start. Was I supposed to keep what happened in the alley a secret? I wasn't about to tell her about my mom, but I didn't really want to tell her I'd almost been eaten by vampires, either. "I'd never met him until last night," I said, deciding to leave it at that and let her push for more if she wanted to.

She made a face. "You guys got pretty cozy with each other there for a while," she said. "I've never seen Rend do that with a customer before. Don't get used to it."

Was that a hint of jealousy in her tone?

"I'm sure it won't happen again," I said. "I think he's pretty pissed at me."

"Pissed enough to hire you?" she said, laughing again. "Set that down over here and open it up. I want to show you something."

I brought the box over to the middle of the room and pulled the tape off the top. She set hers beside mine and opened hers, too. Inside both boxes were plastic shot glasses in various neon colors. Stacks of them were wrapped in brown tissue paper. Each glass had the Venom logo on it. A serpent with its fangs outstretched. I shuddered at the image, wondering if snake fangs had anything to do with human fangs.

"This, obviously, is one of the main storage rooms," she said. I was grateful to be talking about the job and out of the line of fire for a minute. "We keep all our merchandise-type items in here. Shot glasses, t-shirts, novelty type stuff. On this other side, are the paper products, like napkins and toilet paper. Your first job is to unwrap all the glasses in these two boxes and bring them up to the bar area for me. Sound good?"

"Sounds easy enough," I said.

"Great." She slapped her hands against her legs and looked around. "So, I'll just leave you to it for now. I'm going back up front to work on washing the other new glassware. Come back out when you're done, and I'll finish showing you around."

I nodded and sat down on the floor next to the boxes.

"Oh." She turned around as she reached the door. "By the way, welcome to Venom."

"Thanks," I said as she disappeared into the hallway, leaving me alone with the boxes.

THE REAL QUESTION

I n an hour, I had all the glasses unwrapped and stacked
on the edge of the bar. So far, it wasn't a bad job, but I
wished I had thought to bring some headphones with me
so I could listen to music on my phone. Anything to distract
me from thoughts of what happened last night.

Azure showed me around the rest of the club, but there
wasn't that much to see. At least not that she was willing to
show, anyway. She took me on a tour of the main sections of
the club like the dance-floor, the exits, the second-floor
balcony. She showed me where the bathrooms were, even
though she knew I'd already been inside them last night. She
took me to a second storage room where all the glassware for
behind the bar was kept, and finally, she showed me to another
room on that same hallway where the employees took breaks
during their shifts. There was a coffee pot and snacks on the
counter, some well-worn couches, and a TV, but other than
that, nothing else to see. Just your basic break room.

"That's everything," Azure said, ignoring the fact that

she'd walked me past at least half a dozen doors that she didn't open. "When you start your shift, you'll come here to the break room and clock in on this computer. I don't think your name is listed officially yet, though."

"I haven't filled out any paperwork," I said.

She shook her head. "We're all kind of off the books here at Venom, so to speak."

I studied her to see if she was just messing with me. "What do you mean? Like, no taxes?"

"I mean, no official documentation that you work here. No taxes, no W-2's, no paychecks."

"So, how do you get paid?"

She smiled. "Rend pays us once a week."

"In cash?"

"In cash and other things," she said.

I wanted to beat my head against the wall and tell her to stop messing around with me. So far, this place was full of secrets. It was driving me mad.

"What kinds of other things?" I figured she wasn't going to tell me, but I needed to ask because I didn't want to end up working here and getting paid in plastic neon shot-glasses.

"Most of us who work here have our own special needs that only Rend can meet," she said. When she saw the disgusted look on my face, she laughed and touched my arm. A static shock went off between us. I jumped, but she didn't seem surprised. "I'm not talking about anything gross, so get your mind out of the gutter. I just mean he has some particular talents that are in high demand in our world."

I was relieved she wasn't talking about sex. The idea of Rend touching me again wasn't exactly offensive, but I did not want to be a part of some sex-demon freak show. Still, the way she'd said '*our world*' made my heart beat a little faster. As if stepping into this nightclub meant stepping into another dimension. One where reality ceased to exist and creatures from the world of nightmares came out to play.

Or feed.

Rend had used that word last night in the alley, and it still haunted me.

"I'm sure he'll go over all that stuff with you when he gets a chance," she said.

"Is he here?" I asked. I hated that I sounded eager when I'd meant to sound completely uninterested. Had she noticed?

"He's completely off-limits. You realize that right?"

Oh, yeah, she noticed.

"He's my boss, I get it. I just have a lot of questions after last night."

She stared at me, and I tried to act cool. I had a feeling she could see right through me. I hated that almost as much as I hated the fact that I kept thinking about the way his thumb had brushed against my skin.

"I've seen that look before," she said. "Trust me, every girl who comes through those doors wants a piece of him. And every girl ends up leaving sorely disappointed."

"I'm not trying to get a piece of anything," I said, snapping at her more sharply than I'd intended. She was annoying the crap out of me. So what if every girl wanted him. I wasn't like every other girl.

Besides, she was the one who had said she'd never seen him dance that way with anyone before.

And, as much as I hated to admit it, no one had ever made me feel the way he had last night. Some nagging part of me wanted to know if he had felt it too, or if he'd just truly been trying to keep me safe.

A bolt of fear shot through me.

In the excitement and horror of the back-alley drama, I had completely forgotten about the fact that someone else had been watching me from the shadows. Someone who had sent me black roses and invited me to Venom in the first place.

Whoever they were, they knew about my mother. I could feel it in my bones. If nothing else came from the fact that I had to work in this place, I wanted to at least get to the bottom of that red invitation.

Rend had recognized the paper. He'd said the man who used that type of paper was dangerous. But what he didn't say was why someone like that would be interested in a nobody like me.

"Azure?"

She was making a pot of coffee and turned when I called her name.

"I know you said you can't tell me everything about what happens here at the club, but I do have one question," I said. "What was in that drink last night? The Red Dragon?"

A small smile played on her lips. "You liked it, huh? Want more of it?"

"It's not that," I said. "I mean, yes, I loved it. But I'm more interested in finding out what it was and why it made Katy sick when it made me feel so great."

She bit her bottom lip and avoided my gaze as she poured some coffee into a thick paper cup.

"In the bathroom last night, you gave her something to make her feel better," I said, not letting it go. "You told her you didn't know she was a normal. What did you mean by that?"

She poured an obscene amount of cream and sugar into her cup and stirred it around before taking a sip. "Look, I get that you're curious. I would be too. But I don't know that it's my place to talk to you about—"

"Dammit," I shouted, slamming my hand down on the counter. "I'm tired of everyone giving me the run around. What's with all the secrets? I'm here, aren't I? I'm wearing the t-shirt, right? If I'm going to work here and possibly risk my life to come to this place every night, I have a right to know what the hell is going on."

"You're right." Rend's voice startled me.

I turned and sucked in a deep breath. Damn, he was even more gorgeous in the light. I didn't know that was even possible.

Even though there was a good twenty feet or so between us, my body reacted as if his hands were on me. My skin burned for the feel of his warm fingertips on my skin.

And that reaction was immediately followed by anger at the fact that I wanted him so badly. I had dated my fair share of guys and none of them had left me feeling so helpless and needy. I felt out of control around him. Like I wanted to know where I stood with him and if there was any way he was feeling even a fraction of what I was feeling right now.

I hated that he had this power over me. No one had ever had power over me. Not even my own mother.

Especially not my mother.

Yet here he was. The one person in the world who might have answers about where she was or what kind of mess she'd managed to get herself into, and all I could think about was if I would ever again feel the burning heat of his skin against mine.

"Morning, boss," Azure said, looking from him to me and

back again. "Seems your new employee has a lot of questions, so, I guess I'll just leave you guys to it."

Rend nodded, but never once took his eyes off me.

Azure passed by him, then threw one last bitter glance back toward me before she walked out the door.

"Do you want a cup of coffee?" he asked.

"I'd rather have some straight answers about what's going on and what I'm really doing here," I said.

He gave a slight smile, amusement dancing in his dark black eyes. I wanted to get closer to see if there was still that hint of silver in them, or if I had dreamed it up. "It wasn't an either-or kind of question, you know."

I relaxed my shoulders and walked over to pour myself a cup. "I'm sorry," I said. "I don't do well with secrets and vague hints at things. I like honesty."

"Even when the truth is hard to hear?" He crossed over to stand beside me and grabbed a cup for himself.

"Especially when the truth is hard to hear."

Our arms nearly touched, and I had to work to control my heartbeat. Dammit, this guy was really getting to me.

"You keep surprising me," he said. "I've been around for a very long time, and believe me when I say that not many people can surprise me anymore."

I laughed. "You can't be that much older than I am. You're what? Twenty-seven? Twenty-eight?"

He gave me a sideways glance and a somewhat frustrated groan.

"What now?" I asked.

He laughed. "Come on. Let's go to my office where we can talk."

I finished pouring some creamer into my coffee and

followed him down the hallway toward a set of black double-doors at the very end.

Azure hadn't brought me back here to this end of the hallway.

I expected to walk straight into his office when he opened the door, but instead there was a large open seating area with a door on the left, a door on the right, and a wide staircase straight ahead that led up to a second floor.

Rend headed for the door on the right, opened it, and motioned for me to go on in.

His office was not at all what I'd expected, either. I had pictured a small room that looked like the manager's offices in other bars or restaurants where I'd waitressed. Usually there would be the standard metal desk cluttered with bills and note-books and binders. Maybe a few pictures of family members. A filing cabinet or two. Harsh fluorescent lighting.

But this was nothing at all like that.

Rend's office was a work of art. To begin with, it was huge. Instead of bright overhead lights, there was a warm amber glow coming from a series of round orbs hanging like pendants from the ceiling. A dark leather couch was pushed against the wall on one side of the room with a gorgeous Persian rug and a deep mahogany coffee table in front of it.

His desk was an equally gorgeous color of deep mahogany brown, intricately carved. A real antique that looked like it probably cost a fortune. Instead of stacks of papers and binders, his desk was clean and organized. A sleek, flat-screen computer monitor was angled off to one side. My eyes were drawn to a beautiful green stone sitting on the edge of the desk. It almost looked as if it were glowing from within. I wanted to touch it but wondered if it would be rude.

Behind the desk was a wall of floor-to-ceiling bookcases lined with leather-bound books. Some of the titles weren't even in English.

And he thought I was full of surprises. He didn't seem like the literary type.

The entire room was decorated to perfection. It was warm and comfortable, yet somehow strong. It matched him perfectly, even down to the strange painting of a dark and stormy sea with high cliffs as black as obsidian.

He followed my gaze toward the painting. "Do you like it?"

"It's beautiful," I said. "Haunting and sad in a way. Violent. Like a scene from a dream."

When he didn't say anything else, I tore my eyes away from the painting to find him still staring at me. Would I ever be able to look into his eyes and not feel breathless?

He looked away first this time. "Have a seat," he said. "Make yourself comfortable."

"Thanks."

I sat in a large comfortable leather chair across from his desk as he took his place behind it.

"What kind of stone is this?" I asked, again wishing I could touch it, but feeling that, like him, it was off-limits. "Is it an emerald?"

The question was ridiculous. An emerald that big would cost a fortune.

"No," he said. "It's actually something I made in my lab."

I looked up, questioning.

"We'll get to that," he said. "Eventually. But first, you had some more pressing questions you wanted answered?"

I took a sip of my coffee. It was strange. Now that I had

him here, I couldn't think of exactly what I wanted to ask him most. All of my questions were jumbled up inside my brain like a ball of rubber bands.

"Why am I working here?" I asked. "It's obviously not something you wanted when you told me to get lost and never come back."

He cleared his throat and leaned back in his chair. "That was before you got attacked in an alley and needed rescuing. What in the world possessed you to go out that back door, anyway?"

"I thought I was asking the questions," I said. His was not one I was prepared to answer just yet.

"Fair enough," he said. "For now."

"You told those men I was one of your girls," I said.

"To protect you," he said. "If you work here long enough, you'll begin to see that this club is a sort of middle ground. A safe zone for people from all sides of the game to gather and have a good time. It's a place where people from different sides can come to talk things out without fear of a war breaking out around them."

War? Jesus.

"Why is it that everything you say just leads to more questions?" I asked, shaking my head.

He laughed for the second time since we'd met, and the sound sent a shot of warmth through my middle.

"I know you're hungry for answers. I can't blame you," he said. "But I need you to understand that I couldn't possibly explain everything to you all at once. It would probably leave you comatose and drooling on the floor if I did that to you."

"That's a pretty image," I mumbled into my coffee cup.

"If I had my way, I'd turn back time and convince you to

think twice before ever walking through the doors to my club," he said. "The world you've stumbled upon here isn't like the world you're used to. There are people, things—dark things— here that can't be easily explained. It's very dangerous, especially for a girl like you."

His tongue stumbled a bit over the word girl.

"And what kind of girl am I?" I asked.

He leaned forward and placed his hands together on the desk, looking me right in the eyes.

"That's the real question here, isn't it?"

THE POSSIBILITY OF MAGIC

I gripped the edge of the chair.

"Your whole life, you've been different, right?" he began, but didn't wait for an answer. "Strange things happen around you when you get angry or sad. Any time you have a strong enough emotion to really move you, you feel something deep inside you shift. You feel like you're on the verge of something both exciting and terrifying at the same time."

I listened without taking a breath. I was afraid that if I breathed or moved or reacted in any way, I might break into pieces. He was talking about my darkest secrets, rattling them off as if they were common.

"It manifests in different ways for different people," he said. "For some, it's objects that fly across the room. For others, it's a thunder storm that can't be explained. Or maybe it's an extreme heat that gathers at your fingertips."

He paused and even though I tried to hold it back, a memory flashed through my mind.

"Tell me," he said, his voice low and oddly comforting.

I gripped the chair harder, resisting.

I had never told anyone these things. Not even my closest, most trusted friends.

"Franki?" he said after a moment had passed in silence.

I shook my head and looked away, feeling those damned tears welling up in my eyes again. I hated that he could bring this out in me. I had worked so hard for so long to control every emotion, and here he was, breaking me down as if I were made of paper.

He stood and moved around the desk. Panic tightened my chest, and I wished I could just disappear into nothingness.

Rend knelt down on the floor beside my chair and placed his hand on top of mine. My entire body tensed, and with that one touch, a raging river coursed through me, threatening to crash over every single wall I'd built up to keep others out.

I yanked my hand away and stood, walking over toward the painting of the dark cliffs and the violent sea.

"I know it isn't an easy thing to talk about," he said. "Not when you've spent a lifetime with no one to confide in about it. But, you have to believe me when I say that it gets easier once you realize you're not alone."

I refused to look at him even though I could feel that he was moving closer.

"There are so many others who are like you," he said. "Thousands of women and girls who have abilities that can't be explained without opening your mind to the possibility of magic."

I flinched at the word. Magic was a kid's game. Cheap tricks and illusions meant to awe and entertain crowds. It wasn't real.

He was standing behind me now, so close I could feel his warmth radiating against my back. I didn't know if I wanted to lean into him or move away. All I could do was stand there, staring at that painting.

"A good friend of mine painted that," he said. "Years ago. More than a century ago by now."

I glanced over my shoulder so I could see his face. "How is that possible? How could you have a friend that old?"

"That's what I'm trying to tell you, Franki. Not everything in this world is what you thought it was," he said. He lifted his hand to my arm, running his fingertips across the dark bruise. "People like those men in the alleyway last night? I know it sounds impossible to you now, but some people can live for a lot longer than a normal human lifespan. Some people—some beings—are immortal, while others are human but capable of great power. Once you open your mind to that truth, a whole new world will open up right before your eyes."

My body trembled at his touch. At his words. I wanted to dismiss them and tell him he was crazy. But I couldn't. I knew he was telling me the truth. I had denied it for so long, but there was a reason I had worked so hard to control my emotions.

I'd pushed the truth of it so far back into my mind that I refused to discuss it or even allow the thought to enter my consciousness most of the time. But I couldn't ignore it any longer.

"That's why Katy got sick when she drank that Dragon stuff last night, right? Why she threw up and I felt so alive?" I asked, turning slowly toward him, my heart beating so fast I thought it might escape from my chest and fly away with little hummingbird wings. "She's not like me."

He shook his head. "No, she's not."

I brought my eyes to his, afraid of the way it would make me feel, but needing to be able to look at him when he said it.

"What am I?" I asked in a whisper, my voice quivering.

He met my stare and brought his hand to my cheek.

"You're a witch."

THE MAGIC WITHIN

For a moment, I thought he might kiss me.

His face was so close to mine, and oh god, I wanted him to. My mind and body were on the edge, emotion flowing so strongly inside of me that I needed some kind of outlet. I needed something to balance me out before I lost control.

He must have felt my need, because he pulled his hand away as if I'd burned him. He stepped back, every muscle tense.

"I know it's a lot to take in," he said, his tone matching my desire. He was just as on edge as I was. "You need to know the truth, though. Understanding the threat is the only way I can protect you."

"From people like those three guys last night?"

"Them," he said pacing the floor in front of the couch, "and much worse."

I took deep breaths, trying to still the wave of emotions crashing over me.

"Worse?"

"There is evil all around us," he said. "Back home, living your normal life, you probably weren't using your powers at all, I'm guessing?"

I shook my head, rattled by the use of the word powers.

"If someone extremely sensitive to our kind got close to you, they would recognize you for what you are, but most people would never know," he said. "The second you walked through the door to this club, though, you introduced yourself to a whole world of those who would kill to take you for their own."

"Why?" I asked, my hands curled into tight fists at my side. "If there are thousands out there like me, then why would anyone care about one more?"

He let his head fall back slightly, as if I'd asked him an impossible question.

"On this side of the curtain, there is a constant war for each and every witch or demon that walks this earth," he said. "Lesser witches than you have started battles that saw a hundred dead in a single afternoon."

He came close to me again and my need to touch him flared like hot coals pressed against my skin.

"And Franki, whether you realize it or not, you are..." His words broke off and he stared deep into my eyes, as if searching there for the right words. "I can't explain it. I've never felt energy quite like yours before. Powerful, but something beyond that. It's as if darkness and light have always been fighting over your soul."

His words cut me to my core. I knew their truth in the deepest, most secret part of myself.

Fear and anger and years of holding back the truth from

anyone who tried to get too close all came to a head in that moment. I fought it as hard as I could, but I felt it slipping through the cracks like sand through an hourglass. I pressed my hands tightly against my chest and squeezed my eyes shut as if maybe I could keep it inside, but it was no use.

Control slipped just out of reach, and I felt the magic within me ooze through the cracks in my resolve.

I cried out as a gust of wind blew my hair across my face. My arms thrust out, palms open as the air moved faster around us, circling the room like a tornado. It roared in my ears, drowning out the sounds of my despair.

Glass flew up and shattered into tiny pieces that whipped around, cutting the skin on my face and arms. Furniture shifted and toppled over.

Despair poured from me like tears from a grieving widow, raw and painful and full of regret.

Rend's arms wrapped around me, shielding me from the glass and debris. He pulled me down toward the floor and covered me with his body as the wind storm destroyed his office.

"Franki," he said, his voice distant but commanding. He placed a hand on my cheek and pressed his face close to mine. "It's okay, Franki. It's going to be okay. I'm going to help you. You're not alone anymore."

His words slowly calmed the storm raging inside me. The winds died down as he held me tight against his strong body.

I put my arms around him, clinging to him for dear life as my heartbeat slowed and the storm passed. I gasped for air at first, then concentrated on the slow, rhythmic rise and fall of his chest against mine.

"Just breathe," he said as he stroked my hair.

Despite his soft tone and caressing touch, his entire body was tense and hard, as if he was struggling to hold on to his control, the same way I had struggled.

After a few minutes, I pulled back but didn't let go.

"I think I ruined your office." My breath hitched in my chest.

I was scared to look, so I kept my eyes on his, still matching him breath for breath.

A sad smile wrinkled his eyes. "I don't care about my office," he said. "I just want to know that you're all right."

His face was inches from mine. I had never wanted to kiss someone so badly in my entire life. But at the same time, I felt completely exposed and afraid. No one was ever supposed to see me like this. I had worked so hard to conceal and control it.

This power of mine had terrified and pushed away the only person I had ever loved, and when she left me three years ago, I promised myself I would never let it happen again. I would never lose myself to anger like that again.

And I would never let anyone close enough to see it, just in case.

Now I had let a stranger bring me to the breaking point. I wanted to hate him for it as much as I hated myself.

I reached up and took his hands in mine, then slowly pulled them down, away from my face. It was too intimate. Too revealing.

Trust was too damned hard.

"I should go," I said. I tried to stand, but my knees gave out, and I fell back to the ground with a whimper.

Rend stared down at his hands, now smeared with red blood.

His fingers trembled, then curled into strong fists. He

stood, turning away from me and wiping his hands on his jeans.

"You need to rest," he said. The tenderness that had been in his voice earlier was replaced by a stiffness that punctuated every word. "Something so powerful can take days of recovery until you're feeling normal again."

"I should get home," I said.

"No," he said. He practically growled it. I shrank down, away from him. What had caused this sudden shift in him? Was he angry about the office? "I'll take you home later, but first you need to rest for a while."

He picked me up into his arms like I weighed nothing. I tried to protest, but all the strength and fight had been sucked from my body.

He lowered me onto the soft leather couch and pulled a blanket across me. I looked up into his eyes, begging for some return of that softness he'd shown earlier, but he stood quickly and backed away, putting distance between us.

"Franki, there's something else—"

A frantic knock on the door interrupted him.

"What is it?" He reached for the back of the leather chair that still stood upright in the chaos of his office, gripping it so hard his knuckles turned white.

"Is everything okay in there?" A man's voice.

"We're fine."

"We heard—"

"I said everything was fine." His voice was rough and commanding, leaving no room for argument. "Wait for me in the bar. I'll be out in a minute."

"Okay, sorry, boss."

Rend glared at the door, his jaw rigid and hard-lined. He

released his grip on the chair and when he turned back to me, I knew whatever moment of closeness we had shared had passed. Whatever he had decided to say to me was bottled back up inside.

He said he wanted to protect me, but there was something bothering him. Like, he wished he didn't have to protect me.

I wanted to tell him I didn't need him and that he could just leave me alone, but the thought of those men coming after me in the dark, fangs flashing, had me settling back under the covers like a good girl.

"I'll be back in a few hours," he said. "I have some things to take care of first, but I'll be back to check on you when I can. I'm expecting you to really rest. If I come back and find that you've cleaned up one piece of this office, you'll have to answer to me, you understand?"

I swallowed down my normal smart-ass-response instinct and nodded instead. I was so exhausted, rest wasn't going to be a problem. There would be plenty of time to be a smart-ass later.

Rend turned off the lights as he left, leaving me alone in the darkness.

DANGEROUS OR NOT

Whe I woke up, I was back in my own bed in the
dorm apartment I shared with Katy. The room
was nearly pitch black. What time was it?

I sat up, my mind fuzzy, like I had slept for five days. My
mouth tasted of ash and cinnamon. Not a pleasant
combination.

I grabbed my cell phone from the side table and hit the
power button to bring up the time. Fourteen after eleven. I
checked the date just in case, relieved to see that I hadn't
somehow missed a day.

But how had I gotten home?

I climbed out of bed and padded into the small living area
Katy and I shared. We were seniors and after three years in
crappy small rooms on campus, we had practically won the
lottery with our small dorm apartment in the middle of
campus this year. It had two small bedrooms, a bathroom, and
a separate living and kitchen area. Katy had her laptop set up
on the kitchen table and was checking email.

"Thank God, you're awake," she said, barely looking up from the screen. "I was starting to think you'd sleep the rest of the night away. What happened to you? You were gone when I got up this morning."

"Were you here when I got home?" I asked.

She shook her head. "No, I was at the library studying this afternoon. Why?"

I yanked on the door to the fridge and stood there for a second trying to decide what my best option was for washing this taste out of mouth. I grabbed a Pepsi and downed half of it in a couple of seconds.

I was also stalling. How much should I tell her? I didn't want to get a lecture from her, but I guess she needed to know that I had a new job. I knew she wouldn't like it, though. Especially not after how spooked I'd been when we left the other night.

"Franki?"

I leaned against the bar that separated the living room and kitchen. "I don't know how I got home," I said simply.

That got her attention.

She turned in her chair, her eyes fixed on me. "What do you mean? Where were you?"

Apparently, she hadn't noticed my t-shirt yet. I stood and pointed to the front. Her eyes grew wide.

"You went back there? Why?"

I turned around and pointed to the back of the shirt. "I sort of work there now."

"Holy what?" she said, popping up from her chair and coming to stand across from me. "I knew you needed a new job, but I thought you were totally creeped out by that place?

You yanked me off the dance-floor so fast last night, I got whiplash."

I took another drink of my soda. "I don't know. I guess it's not so bad," I said. "That guy? The hot bartender? Turns out he owns the place. He offered me a job and I really couldn't afford to turn it down."

I always believed honesty was the best policy, but when it came to vampires and indoor tornadoes and magical powers, I decided Katy was better off not knowing the whole truth. So how was I supposed to explain my new job?

"You're acting strange," she said. "Last night, you were acting like you never wanted to step foot in that place again."

I shrugged, trying to play it casual. "I had given the bartender my number and he called this morning and told me they had an opening if I wanted it," I said. "He said I could make some killer tips."

I cringed at my own words. Killer. Yes, I was now working at a place where people had tried to kill me. And probably would again.

Rend said he could protect me, but for how long? And what if one of the vampires from the club figured out where I lived? It wasn't like I could expect him to keep me safe when I was home or walking around campus.

Still, what choice did I have? He assured me that those guys didn't mess with his girls, and now, apparently, I was one of his girls. Whatever that meant.

"Are you sure it's worth it?" she asked. "That club was weird, to say the least. And wait a second, if you were there today, why don't you remember how you got home? Did something happen?"

"I passed out," I said, running a hand along my head. A sharp pain was forming just behind my left eye.

Katy propped her elbows against the bar. "Franki, this is insane," she said. "You kind of look like hell, to be honest. Are you sick?"

"I don't know," I said, which was the truth. Rend had said using that much magic without practice could be draining, but damn. I wasn't expecting that to mean hours of feeling like crap. "I think I just pushed myself too hard after being out drinking late last night."

"Do you think that guy brought you home?" she asked, a curious smile on her face. "The bartender or owner or whatever he is?"

"His name is Rend," I said. "And I don't know. Maybe, but how did he know where I live?"

"Did you fill out paperwork and stuff to work there? He probably just read it on there."

"Oh, yeah," I said absently. I didn't want to tell her what Azure had said. We technically weren't on the books. Paid in cash every night. It seemed sketchy.

Besides, the dorm apartment wasn't even my real address. My driver's license still had my Mom's old address on it and my mailing address here on campus was a P.O. Box. So how the hell did he figure out where I lived?

It spooked me, for sure. What was I getting myself into with this new job?

"When do you go back?" she asked. "Do you have a schedule or anything? I'm going to be sad if you're working late nights again, like you did when you worked at Shade last year. That sucked. We never saw each other except in class, and we don't even have any classes together this semester."

"We didn't get a chance to go over my hours or anything," I said. "But they don't even open until, like, eight every night. I can't imagine he hired me to work during the day. Besides, I've got class every day except Fridays this semester."

She groaned. "I still don't know how you managed that one," she said. "I'm so jealous I could die."

I laughed. Yeah, I had gotten super lucky with my course schedule this semester. I had a three-day weekend every single week, and it was awesome. Of course, now I was probably going to be working late on weekends. The club didn't close until three in the morning, so that could mean I wouldn't be home until nearly four. Ugh, that was going to suck.

Unless the money really was good. I could certainly use it. Rend and Azure had both failed to mention money at all.

I had a small scholarship, but most of my expenses were being paid out of money I'd earned over the past few years, working sometimes two jobs to make ends meet. I had no idea what I was going to do when I graduated in May.

I'd need some starter money, though, regardless of what I decided to do. A down payment on a new apartment and new work clothes, and stuff like that wouldn't be cheap.

I envied girls like Katy who had their parents to fall back on when they needed it. Her entire college education was paid for. They even gave her money for food and clothes and books and anything else she needed. She only worked part-time so she could have money to go out on the weekends. I don't even think she realized just how lucky she was to have that kind of support.

I'd been working since I was fourteen, babysitting and picking up neighborhood jobs just to put food on the table.

As much as the truth of what Rend had told me earlier

scared the mess out of me, there was a part of me that was relieved to know I wasn't the only one out there with these kinds of powers. I had spent so much of my life thinking I was a freak, worried about how to hide it so that no one ever found out.

What would it be like to just be myself around people? What would it be like to meet an entire world of people who were like me?

Dangerous or not, it was exciting.

And if I could make some good money in the process, I was all in. At least until graduation. I could make anything work for the next eight or nine months.

"Well, you know I'll support you no matter what you want to do," she said. "I just hope you don't disappear on me."

"I have to work," I said. "There's no getting around it. But you know I'm always going to make time for you."

Katy smiled and before she even opened her mouth, I knew what she was thinking. We hadn't been friends for the past three years without me learning how to read her boy-crazy smiles.

"Hey, maybe I can come hang out with you at the club. That guy I was dancing with, Marco? He was gorgeous. I wouldn't mind seeing him again."

I rolled my eyes and downed the last of the Pepsi. "I doubt I'll be able to hang out much while I'm at work," I said. I didn't want to hurt her feelings, but I really didn't want her coming back up to that club. Not if it was really as dangerous as Rend said.

"I don't want to get you in trouble or anything, but maybe once you get settled, I can get some of the other girls together and come out there sometimes on the weekends."

"We'll see," I said.

She pouted, and I could tell I'd hurt her feelings. She wouldn't understand why I wanted to keep her away if I couldn't tell her the truth about the place. This was exactly why I hated not just being honest. Lies and half-truths complicated everything.

But, there was no way I could tell her the truth this time. Not without admitting what I was.

And that was something I just wasn't ready to do. Not when I still didn't completely understand it myself.

"Let's watch a movie," I said. "I need to veg out for a while. Your choice."

Her face lit up. "Deal. You start the popcorn and I'll pick the movie. Meet you on the couch."

A VERY NASTY END

By Saturday morning I felt much better, but a twinge of headache still lingered behind my eye.

I had no idea when they were expecting me back to work at Venom, but I had voluntarily taken Friday off to sleep and lounge around the apartment. I considered it a birthday present to myself.

Besides, I didn't have Rend's phone number and when I tried to look it up, I couldn't find a general number for the club either. In fact, I couldn't find a single mention of the club on the internet anywhere.

Weird, right? Most clubs had a website, but even if they didn't, there should at least be some reviews and mentions of it somewhere. I couldn't find as much as a mention of it on twitter. Not a whisper. It was as if the place didn't even exist.

I considered just going about my normal life and waiting for Rend to call or come by and insist I show up for work. If he'd wanted me there, he should have left a note or something when he brought me home.

If he brought me home.

But I knew he wasn't going to let me off the hook altogether. He'd said my life was in danger, and after everything I'd seen, I kind of believed him. Plus, I really did need a new job, so after hours of telling myself I wasn't going to go in, I got dressed and decided to head downtown anyway.

It had absolutely nothing to do with wanting to see Rend again. Nothing.

Or so I told myself.

I was glad to see my car was parked in its spot outside in the dorm parking lot. Of course, that just made me wonder again exactly how I got home the other day. I certainly didn't drive myself, but whoever had brought me back knew exactly where I normally parked.

I shuddered.

I didn't like the idea of someone knowing so much about me when I was still so much in the dark about them.

I took the 'L' to the club instead of taking my car. This time, though, instead of the club being deserted, the bouncer was already sitting in her spot in the tunnel.

I started to reach for my ID, but she waved me off.

"Franki, right? Rend told me you might be coming in today," she said.

"Hey," I said. "Selena, right? I wasn't sure if I was supposed to come in or not."

"Good memory," she said, her Australian accent thick and beautiful. "It's good that you're here. It's going to be a busy night, so we can use all the help we can get."

"Is Rend here?" My voice made this little crack when I said his name, and I scrunched my nose. Dammit. I definitely did not want anyone to know that I was attracted to the guy, but it was going to be obvious if I didn't get my shit together.

"Not yet," she said, an eyebrow raised and a knowing smile on her face. "He'll be in later, though. Azure's here. She'll tell you what you need to do. She's kind of in charge around here when Rend's not available."

"Thanks," I said, cursing the blush that warmed my cheeks and neck. I was glad that she, at least, had not bothered to tell me just how off-limits Rend was for a girl like me.

The lights inside were on full blast like they had been yesterday, but this time there were at least ten other people rushing around to get things set up. I wondered if it was always like this on a Saturday or if there was something special going on tonight.

Azure stood at the end of the bar talking to the guy who had been dancing with Katy the other night. Marco. I made my way over to them and they both got very quiet, very quickly. A dead giveaway that they'd been talking about me. Great.

"Hey," I said, forcing a smile.

"Well, if it isn't sleeping beauty," Azure said. "We missed you the rest of the afternoon Thursday."

"Yeah, sorry about that," I said. What had Rend told them? Had she seen him carry me out of here? "I wasn't feeling well."

"Uh-huh," she said, exchanging a look with Marco. "I'm glad you're here tonight. We could really use a few extra hands."

"That's what Selena said. Is something going on tonight? Or is this just normal for a Saturday?" I turned to Marco and held out my hand. "You're Marco, right? I'm Franki, by the way."

"Nice to meet you, carino." He took my hand and kissed the top of my knuckles. He had a thick Spanish accent.

"We have a few special guests coming in tonight," Azure said, but didn't elaborate.

I had a feeling special guests in this type of place meant something, considering almost everyone here was special. I was dying to ask Azure about her own powers and to find out if all the staff here was some kind of witch or demon, but now wasn't the time.

"What do you need me to do? I have some experience bartending and waiting tables." I assumed I'd be back behind the bar with her or serving out on the floor. Of course, thinking about that shot she'd served me on my birthday, I doubted I would know the recipes for the drinks here. Still, I was a fast learner and a hard worker, so I knew I'd figure it out.

She turned her head sideways and studied me with a strange smile on her face that made my stomach tighten. "I have something else in mind for you tonight."

Marco stiffened and leaned in toward her. "Azure, be careful. You heard what Rend said. He's going to be—"

"Rend put me in charge," she said, cutting him off. "Follow me."

Marco ran a shaky hand through his hair but stood aside to let her pass. I followed Azure back toward a set of long black curtains near the bar. She hadn't shown this part of the club to me the other day, and I had no idea what she had in mind for me. The way Marco acted, though, I got the feeling it wasn't going to be something fun.

She pulled the curtain aside and walked into a small, dark room with a plush, burgundy velvet couch and shiny black tables. A crystal chandelier hung in the middle of the room, throwing bits of light around the room.

It was slightly more elegant and intimate back here than the rest of the club. "What's this room?"

"This is where Rend likes to bring some of his more important clientele. Especially when they have some private business to discuss."

I swallowed nervously. So, why the heck did she want me back here? I didn't like the idea of being hidden away in a place where no one could really see what was happening. It may have been decorated nicely, but it felt just as ominous as the back alley.

"Don't worry, you won't be in here," she said, putting her hand on my shoulder. "The dressing rooms are back this way."

"Dressing rooms?"

"Yeah, we need to get you in something more appropriate," she said. She didn't bother explaining herself, which I was starting to understand was a theme of hers.

She led me back through another doorway that opened into a large dressing room adorned with mirrors, racks of clothes, and tables where makeup and hairspray and brushes and things were set out. There were already five other girls inside getting ready, and all I had to do was take one look at what they were wearing to want to turn around and head back out again.

"Do you need me to help them get ready?" I asked, which was my little way of saying I couldn't even imagine that she wanted me to actually put on one of these costumes.

The girls in the room were dressed in tight spandex outfits that looked straight out of Vegas or something. Thigh high boots, thick makeup, low-cut necklines. Nothing too revealing, but none of them completely clothed either.

Azure put her hand on my shoulder like she owned me. "We had one of our dancers call out sick tonight, and we really need someone to fill her spot," she said. "I think you'd be perfect."

I didn't even tell her what I thought of her idea. I simply turned around and walked out the door.

She caught up with me in the middle of the posh sitting room.

"Franki, sweetie, wait up," she said. She grabbed my wrist a little tighter than she should have.

I wrenched out of her grasp. "First of all, don't call me sweetie. That's so tacky. Especially when you know I'm upset," I said. "Second of all, I agreed to work here thinking I would be running errands, cleaning up or serving alcohol or whatever. I did not sign up to be a stripper."

She smiled a sickly-sweet smile, giving me such a clear view of exactly what kind of person she was. "These girls are not strippers." She lowered her voice and leaned in closer to me. "You'd better not let them hear you call them that either. They are dancers, that's all. It's very hands-off, trust me."

"I don't trust you as far as I can throw you," I said, returning her smile so she could understand what kind of person I am.

Her smile disappeared, and her eyes widened. "Rend told me you need this job." She put her hands on her hips to show me just how serious she was about telling me what to do. "I don't think you want to upset him by walking out that door. You have no idea what he's capable of when he's upset."

This chick had no idea what I was capable of, either.

"I don't answer to Rend, and I certainly don't answer to you," I said. "Now, if you want to give me a job I'm comfortable with—one that doesn't involve getting half naked in front of a crowd of strangers—I'm one-hundred-percent on board. But if you tell me to walk back in that room and play dress up, you can both go to hell."

She didn't say anything for a long moment. She just pressed her lips into a tight line, her nostrils slightly flared as she stared me down.

I turned again to go, ready to walk out and leave this place in the dust, but my entire body stopped working. My feet froze in place. I literally could not move a muscle. I could breathe, but not so much as blink my eyes or swallow.

Fear rolled through my veins as I struggled against whatever magic was holding me. No matter how hard I tried to move my arms or speak out, I was completely helpless.

Azure walked around me slowly, taking her sweet time to make her way into my line of vision. Her smile was back, but this time it was ringed with a sort of joyful mischief.

"I realize you're new," she said. "Not only to Venom, but to our whole world."

She lifted both hands to dramatically indicate the world around her. In my mind, I imagined what it would be like to grab her by those arms and body-slam her.

"For that reason, and that reason alone, I'm going to take it easy on you instead of turning this whole thing into some kind of living nightmare," she said, as if being unable to move my entire body wasn't nightmare enough. "You are here because you need protection. I get that. As long as you work here, none of the big bad boogeymen will bother you. But it's extremely important you understand that the second you walk out that door and leave us behind, you become free game for all those unknown evils that got a whiff of your scent the other night. And trust me when I say they will come looking for you. Until Rend gives you his mark, you're still fair game."

Saliva gathered in the back of my throat as hatred grew in my chest.

"Unless you want to come to a very nasty end by tomorrow morning, you should stay here and accept the gracious protection that Rend has offered you, despite his better judgment," she threatened. "As it turns out, the job we have open tonight is as a dancer, so that's what you will be doing, do I make that clear?"

Of course, she knew I couldn't answer her. If I could have, the answer might have come in the form of a punch straight to her throat.

She laughed. "So much anger in those pretty blue eyes," she said. "You really need to try to get that under control before you damage this room like you did Rend's office yesterday. He would not be happy about a mess in here with his friends coming into town."

She walked over and pulled back the black curtain leading into the bar.

"The other girls will help you find something to wear."

With that, she disappeared into the next room, releasing me from whatever hold she'd placed on me.

I doubled over, coughing and rubbing my eyes. A slight breeze flew across my back, blowing the hair off the back of my neck. I closed my eyes and forced several deep breaths. She was right about one thing. I needed to calm down. I could not let myself lose control again.

Not because Rend might get upset, but because I needed all of my energy and wits about me if I was going to survive this night.

WORTH SAVING

I sat down on the expensive velvet couch and took a
minute to think this through.

Yes, okay, I wanted to leave. No doubt about it. But
that witch Azure had a point, whether I liked it or not.

Rend had basically said the same thing to me about those
guys in the alley, not to mention all the others of their type
who frequented this club. For whatever reason, showing up
here the other night put my life in danger. I needed Rend's
protection now, as much as I hated that. If I walked away, I'd
be on my own.

I was, admittedly, shocked at how well I held my own with
those three out back that night, but in the end, they had me.
And what if they came with more than three, next time? I
could be putting Katy's life in danger, too, and that thought
was really what sealed my fate.

I had no choice. I needed this job in more ways than one.

As much as I hated the idea of having to dance around in
front of an entire club full of people, I'd worked at question-

able establishments before, and I could do this if I had to. Hell, I'd once willingly worked at a bar that made the bartenders wear hot-pants and sports bras. At least here she'd said there was a strict no touching policy. That would be a step up from that other place.

I stood up, resolved to make the most of this. I had been kicked when I was down before, and I always had the same philosophy when it happened. Pick myself up and find a way to walk back out there with my head held high, like I was the one in control.

And that was exactly what I was going to do now.

I straightened my shoulders and took a deep breath, then walked back into the dressing room with a confident smile on my face.

"Hey," I said, strutting in and walking straight to the rack of clothing. "I'm Franki."

"Hey, Franki," several of the girls called out. One girl with short brown hair and a banging body stood and came over to introduce herself.

"I'm Lyla. That's Cherish there with the green shirt, Misty in blue, Peri, and our resident redhead is Shay," she said. "You must be the new girl Rend was telling us about."

"That's me," I said. "Azure said you guys were short on dancers tonight and that maybe you ladies could help me find something to wear."

Lyla thumbed through the rack of clothes and picked out a sequined pink number that made me question my decision to stay. As politely as I could, I scrunched my nose and shook my head.

"Something a bit darker, maybe?" I suggested.

I caught sight of a studded black outfit as she pushed

through and pulled it out. It was basically a one-piece leotard with several revealing slits along the sides, but I liked the silver studs. It was more my style than most of the other things I'd seen pass by.

"What about this one?" I asked, holding it up to myself in the mirror.

"Love it," Shay the redhead said. "What size shoes do you wear? There's a pair of kick ass black leather boots that would look amazing with that."

She got up from her seat in front of the mirror to go dig them out of a box for me.

"Seven, I think," I said.

"Perfect," she said with a smile. "These are eights, but just stuff some tissue down in the toe and they should fit fine."

I looked around for a private place to change, but quickly realized that this room was as private as it got.

"We've seen it all before," Cherish said with a laugh.

I wondered if that was her real name or not, because it wasn't doing much for my confidence that this wasn't a group of strippers.

"Have you ever danced before? Like, in public?" Lyla asked.

"No. I've worked at a lot of clubs and bars, but nothing like this," I said.

"I could kind of tell by the fact that your face is pale as a sheet," she said with a laugh. "It's not as bad as it seems. The club is dark, and no one is going to mess with you. We're more like decoration, really."

"Great," I said, trying to act happy about being a decorative accent in a room full of blood-thirsty vampires.

"It's really one of the best jobs in the place," Peri said. She was short with really long brown hair braided into one long braid down her back. She looked like she was about fifteen years old, but I knew she had to be older to be working here. Or at least I hoped. "The pay is great and all you have to do is have a good time."

"You better start getting dressed," Lyla said. "We have a staff meeting in half an hour before we open."

I slipped my shoes off and put them under one of the tables. I felt a bit nauseated looking down at the skimpy black outfit but remembered that I was supposed to be owning this like it was my choice. Not Azure's.

I can do this.

I undressed as fast as I could, relieved when I realized the others were too busy finishing up their makeup to pay attention to me.

I slid the black leotard on over my underwear, but quickly realized there was no way I could wear my bra with this thing. I unhooked it and slipped it off, feeling incredibly naked in this stupid outfit. I had never been more grateful to have freshly shaved legs.

Lyla whistled as I laced up the boots. "Wow, you look amazing," she said. She walked over and lowered her voice. "Are you using?"

I gave her a sideways look. "What do you mean? Like drugs?"

She looked at me like I was crazy. "No, silly. Magic. Glamours?"

"What's a glamour?"

All five of them turned to look at me.

"You're kidding, right?" the girl with the green shirt said.

Misty, I think, was her name. Her skin was dark and smooth and flawless, and her eyes were a deep lavender.

"No, I'm uh, totally new to this whole thing."

"A glamour is just a spell a lot of witches use to alter their appearance," Misty said. "Like plastic surgery or something, without the surgery."

My eyes widened. "You can do that?"

"Wow, Rend wasn't kidding when he said you would have a lot to learn," she said. "You never played around with stuff like that when you were a kid? Your mom never taught you about glamours?"

I shook my head, making an effort not to flinch at the mention of Mom.

"Watch," Misty said. She closed her eyes, took a deep breath, then opened them again. The deep lavender color of her eyes had been replaced by a bright green that matched her shirt.

"Holy shit," I whispered.

"We don't really have time to show you how to do it now, but if you get a chance later, we'll have some fun with it," Cherish said. "Shay here doesn't even really have red hair. She's really a brunette, but she keeps it red now all the time. I think it suits her."

"Thank you," Shay said with a little curtsy. "Me too."

"We'll help you with your makeup real quick and then we need to head out front," Lyla said. "Rend hates it if we're late for staff meetings, and I'm sure everyone will be dying to meet you."

My stomach flipped at the thought of the whole staff meeting me when I looked like this, but I had to find a way to embrace it. Fast.

"I just want to do some dark eyeliner, nothing too dramatic," I said. "I'm not really much of a heavy makeup person."

A few of the girls laughed, but I stood my ground when they tried to smear my cheeks with pink. I managed to get out of there with a light foundation, very dark eyeliner, mascara and a little bit of pink lip gloss.

"You really have some of the most gorgeous blue eyes I've ever seen," Shay said.

"Before you know it, she'll be copying them," Lyla said with a laugh.

"You're welcome to them," I said. "They kind of run in my family."

Not that I knew much about my family. My mother had refused to ever talk about them and she never, and I mean never, talked about my father. But I knew I'd gotten my eye color from her. She'd once slipped up in a moment of melancholy and told me that most of her sisters had the same bright blue eyes. It was the only time she'd even told me she had sisters and when I'd asked her about it, she got angry and told me to mind my own business.

"You ready?" Lyla asked. "It's time to go."

"Ready as I'll ever be, I guess."

I was grateful not to be walking out there alone. I positioned myself right in the middle of the group, trying to blend in and match their level of confidence. I had no idea how long they'd all been doing this, but they seemed to have no problem with what they were wearing. And to be honest, they all looked incredible. I hoped I looked like I belonged with them.

We walked together through the black curtain and out into the main part of the club. I sighed with relief when I saw that the harsh lights had been turned off and the place was back to the black and neon glow of the first night I'd been in here. The darkness made me feel a little bit more comfortable.

Azure was leaning against the bar, no doubt just waiting to see if I'd come out with the others like a good little girl. Every fiber of my being wanted to avoid her eyes, but instead, I met her gaze head-on, challenging her with a confident smile.

The anger that flashed through her eyes was all the reassurance I needed that I was doing the right thing by owning this instead of curling up in the corner like an abused kitten.

Her mouth dropped open a little as I passed, and my smile grew larger.

One of the guys standing in a group near the dance-floor whistled. "Looking gorgeous, as always, ladies."

Lyla walked up to him and held out her hand for him to kiss. They shared a look that made me wonder if there was a little something going on between the two of them.

I scanned the gathered crowd. It was about eighty percent women and every single person here was unreasonably good looking. A requirement of working here? Or were they all capable of using these glamours Misty was talking about? Did I measure up?

I had a feeling this job was going to be a constant test of my confidence.

"Let's get started," a familiar bass called out.

My heart jumped into my throat at the sound of Rend's voice. I hadn't been willing to admit to myself just how much I was looking forward to seeing him again. So much it was scary.

He didn't seem to notice me at first. The staff gathered in a half-circle around the edge of the dance-floor as Rend went through some basic instructions about how the night would go.

"I want everyone on their very best behavior tonight," he

said, glancing down at a clipboard in his hand. "And I want security at every exit and every single post around the club at all times. I don't want you ladies to much as think about going to the bathroom or getting a drink of water without making sure someone's got your post, understand."

A group of women off to his right nodded and I stared in awe. This was his security team? I had originally thought it was kind of odd to see a pretty woman working as the bouncer out front taking ID's, but for his entire security team to be women? That was unexpected. Especially in a place this dangerous.

At least they get to wear club staff t-shirts.

I adjusted my weight from one foot to the other and just that slight movement seemed to draw Rend's attention. He glanced up from his papers while he was talking about assignments, then looked back down.

But then, he stopped mid-sentence, and slowly looked back up, his eyes traveling very deliberately up my body from boot to boobs.

I expected him to say something. Introduce me. Cuss me out. Something. But he just stood there staring, his eyes finally reaching my own. I couldn't read his expression. Was he angry?

I lifted my chin, not letting myself so much as blink. I wanted him to see that I was still here, doing what needed to be done.

Tension gathered in the room as people looked from Rend to me, whispering. Behind me, Azure cleared her throat a little too loud to sound natural.

I wondered if they could all hear my heart beating. I

wondered if they could all see just how much I wanted Rend to cross over to me and take me in his arms.

I forced my eyes down, but that only made it worse. Instead of the jeans and black t-shirt he had on the other night, he wore a pair of perfectly tailored dark grey pants, a pristine white button-up shirt with the top button undone and a matching grey blazer. No tie. My body reacted in ways I hoped to God none of the others could sense.

Finally, Rend shook his head and tore his eyes away from me, looking back down at his clipboard. He flipped through his papers a few times, then found his voice again.

"I want someone stationed by that back door tonight, too. No one goes in or out that way tonight," he said. "No one in Paris tonight, either. If you need a smoke break or something, just go out to Hubbard and try to keep it to a minimum until we close."

A few people exchanged looks, as if this was definitely not normal. Was he saying this for my sake? I could have told him I wouldn't be stupid enough to go out that back door again for the rest of my life if I could help it. And what did he mean by Paris? Was that a special section of the club?

There was a part of me that was touched he seemed to care about keeping me safe. I had no idea what I'd done to deserve that. He could have easily just let me get eaten instead of offering me a job and personal protection.

"I'd also like to introduce everyone to our newest employee." Before he even said my name, everyone turned to look at me. "This is Franki. I'd like you guys to really welcome her to the club and take some time to introduce yourselves when you get a chance. Look out for her, too. She's new to all this."

A few people mumbled casual hello's, but Rend didn't give them time to come over and talk.

He went through the last of the instructions for the night and about ten minutes later called an end to the meeting.

Several people made a beeline straight to me to say hi and welcome me to the group. I knew I'd never remember everyone's names, but it was nice to meet some people who were nicer than Azure.

"Franki," Rend called out. When I turned to him, he cleared his throat. "Can I see you for a moment?"

"Sure," I said with a smile, doing my best to hide my nerves. I apologized and left the group that had surrounded me, then followed him into the same dark corner he'd brought me to that first night.

Standing this close to him again made my palms sweat.

His eyes drifted down to my cleavage and he ran a hand through his hair. "What are you wearing?"

Okay. Not what I expected him to say.

"I'm wearing what I was told to wear."

"Unless I'm going insane, I very clearly remember giving you a staff t-shirt to wear," he said. His voice was gruff. "That is most definitely not a staff t-shirt."

The girly, highly aroused part of me was loving the fact that he seemed so affected by my new clothing.

The confused, did-not-fucking-want-to-wear-this-outfit-in-the-first-place part of me was angry as hell.

"How observant of you," I said, standing as tall as I could next to him.

He reached out like he was going to grab my arm, but then spread his fingers wide and pulled back instead.

"Why are you wearing that, then?"

"I don't know why you're getting upset with me," I said. "I wake up Thursday night in my own bed with no memory of how I got there and no idea how you or anyone else here might have known where I lived. I show up to work not knowing if I'm expected to even be here, just because I don't want to upset you in case you were wanting me to work tonight. Then I get here and am told that Azure is in charge. Well, this is what she told me to wear, so I'm here, doing exactly everything I've been asked to do. If you don't think I look good enough to be one of the dancers on a night when you have friends coming—"

His eyes snapped up to mine. "Is that why you think I'm upset?"

"How am I supposed to know why you're upset?"

He took a deep breath in through his nose, his chest rising and falling. "Azure told you to wear this."

I wanted to tell him she threatened my life if I didn't, but I held my tongue. I didn't want to make her more of an enemy than she already was at this point.

"She said you were short a dancer tonight."

He glanced over toward the bar, his eyes narrowed.

When he turned his attention back to me, he softened just a little. "I brought you home Thursday," he said. "I thought you would be able to rest better at your own house. As to how I knew where you lived, well, let's just say I'm very good at finding people whether they want to be found or not."

I could hardly breathe as he spoke. He had this way of being hard edges and soft tones all at the same time. I had never met anyone sexier in my entire life.

"As for what you're wearing? Believe me, it has nothing to do with you not looking good enough." He cleared his throat again, and I could swear his bottom lip trembled ever so slightly. "I just would have rather had you working behind the scenes tonight instead of on display for everyone to see."

I moved one step closer to him and his eyes searched my face. "Why are you protecting me? You don't even know me. Why not just let those guys tear me apart the other night?"

He lifted a hand to my cheek and brushed a strand of hair out of my eyes. His fingers lingered for a moment on my skin and my insides went up in flames.

"There's something about you," he said, his walls down for the briefest of moments. "I can't explain it more than that. I just knew you were worth saving."

My breath was shallow, and my body yearned to move closer. I wanted to feel his hands on me again. My eyes were drawn to his lips, overcome by the desire to know what it would be like to kiss a man like Rend.

"You don't have to dance if you don't want to," he said. "I can find another job for you if you want to go back and get changed."

It was a tempting thought, but I refused to let Azure think I had complained to the boss and gotten my way like some child. I wanted her to know I was stronger than that.

"I'm good," I said, letting a smile tease my lips. "It might even be fun."

He groaned and clenched his jaw. "I'm going to keep my eye on you tonight," he said. "If you need anything or anyone so much as offers to buy you a drink, you come find me. I'll be in the bar or back in the private room behind the curtain most of the night."

I hoped he couldn't see me blush in the half-darkness. "I can take care of myself," I said. "Most of the time."

He paused, then put a finger under my chin, lifting my face to his. My lips parted, and I forced myself to keep breathing. Our eyes locked for a few intense seconds, then he dropped his hand and turned away.

"Azure. My office. Now."

I looked over just in time to see a look of terror cross her eyes.

WHAT OTHER TRUTHS

I rejoined the other dancers in a cluster near the black curtain.

Lyla grabbed my hand and pulled me to her side. "Oh, my God, what is going on with you and Rend?"

"You have to tell us everything," Shay said.

"I have never seen him look so—"

"So shaken." Lyla's eyes were huge and glimmering.

At this point, my face was probably beet red, and I was sure they could all see it, even in the sparse lighting.

"There's nothing going on," I said.

"Liar," Cherish said.

"Big, fat liar," Lyla said. "Listen, Rend is untouchable. Unshakable. He never lets himself get rattled. Not even when he's about to tear someone to pieces."

"Literally," Shay mumbled.

I snapped to look at her. "What do you mean, literally?"

"Why do you think everyone calls him Rend?" Cherish asked.

"Let's just say he's known around our kind of people as someone you don't cross," Lyla said.

My hand went to my forehead. The spot where his fingers had brushed my skin was still tingling. Surely, they didn't mean that he had killed people before? Is that what they were saying?

It seemed unbelievable, but I had seen the fear in the eyes of those vampires the other night. They had been terrified of him and he hadn't even lifted a finger toward them.

"I think you definitely picked the right outfit," Lyla said, giggling. "He could hardly take his eyes off you."

"I'm so jealous I could kill you," Peri said. "Seriously, I've never seen Rend with a woman and I've been working here for almost fifteen years."

I laughed out loud. "Yeah, right."

She eyed me. "What?"

"You can't be much older than I am. How have you been working here fifteen years? You would have been, what? Ten years old when you started?"

"Oh," she said, lifting the back of her hand up to her mouth to cover her laughter. "Girl, that's just the glamour. If you saw the real me underneath all this magic, you wouldn't question it. I'm thirty-nine."

My jaw dropped , and I shook my head. "There's no way."

"I would show you, but no one sees the real, unmagicked me. No one."

"I think we're all going to have to take a night off coming up and have a girl's night in where we teach Franki here some of our tricks," Shay said.

I couldn't take my eyes off Peri. Almost forty years old? It was incredible how young she looked. And I couldn't help but wonder what other truths were being hidden behind some curtain of magic in this place.

Nothing was as it seemed, and if I could no longer even trust my eyes, what could I trust?

"If you say nothing is happening between the two of you, I'll believe you," Lyla said. "But I saw the way you were looking at him, too."

"All I'm going to say is be careful," Misty said. "Prettier, more powerful women than you have fallen for him and ended up with nothing more than a broken heart. He's completely immune to love."

It occurred to me that I should probably be offended by the fact that she'd offhandedly insulted my looks, but the truth was that I didn't doubt it. Rend was gorgeous beyond words and it wouldn't surprise me if the hottest model in the world was in love with him.

"Don't worry about me," I said. "I have no delusions about his feelings for me. Besides, I'm just here because I happened to be in the wrong place at the wrong time. Rend saved me. End of story."

I didn't have a chance to say more, because the lights dimmed further, and the music turned up to near-deafening levels.

"Ooh, party time," Lyla said, raising her voice above the music. "Come with me, Franki. I'll show you to your spot."

I followed Lyla through the dark club, my knees weak at the thought of dancing in front of a crowd full of strangers.

She led me to an actual cage with strong black bars. "This is usually my spot, but I thought you might want to be back here where you had a good view of the bar," she said with a wink.

"Thank you," I said. I leaned in close to her ear. "What exactly do I do?"

She smiled and squeezed my arm. "Just dance," she said. Then she reached into a black bag she'd been carrying and pulled out two tubes of clear liquid. She uncapped them, handed one to me and downed the other. "And drink that. Trust me."

"What is it?" I stared at it, thinking about the shot from the other night. "Is this Red Dragon?"

"Mixed with a few other things," she said. Her eyes were glimmering again. "This is Rend's special brew for the dancers."

"Rend made this?"

She cocked her head to the side. "Rend makes everything we sell in here. He's the alchemist."

"Alchemist?" I stared at the tube. Just how much did I still have to learn about this world? It seemed like there was some new surprise around every corner.

"Just drink it and enjoy it," she said. "You won't regret it."

I took a deep breath and lifted the tube up in a kind of salute. "Here's to no regrets."

For some reason, an image from a dream appeared in my head. A hallway with a thousand doors, each one opening my eyes to some new secret. Some new mystery.

As I brought the shot up to my lips, I wondered just how far I could go before I lost myself to this new world. And to a man who was immune to love.

EPISODE THREE

THE DARKNESS

SO MUCH DARKNESS

The shot burned going down.

The heat started on my lips and flowed across my tongue, down my throat, spreading through my body like wildfire. I closed my eyes, drinking in the sensation of being lit up from the inside out. An intense energy filled me from head to toe, its power putting me on the edge of control, as if one more drop would have been too much.

"Good, right?" Lyla asked, smiling.

I opened my eyes and the entire room looked different. The light that flowed through the glass tubes running across the ceiling seemed brighter. The music seemed louder. Every wisp of air across my skin made me shiver. I felt it travel into my body and become a part of me.

"I never felt anything like it," I said, my voice unsteady. It was different from the plain Red Dragon shot I'd had the other night on my birthday. This was intensified. I was less fuzzy and more awake. On fire.

I felt sexy.

Lyla flipped a switch near the base of the iron cage and the door swung open. "Climb up," she said.

I gripped the bars and pulled myself into the cage with almost no effort. I had more raw energy flowing through me than I could ever remember in my whole life.

Lyla closed me inside. "Now all you have to do is dance," she said with a giggle. "I'll come get you when it's time for a break. Do you smoke?"

I shook my head, having a hard time concentrating on what she was saying. It was like sensory overload.

"Okay, well, you can come outside with us when it's time or you can go back to the break room or whatever," she said. "See you in a few hours. Have fun."

She winked, then made her way to a similar cage on the other side of the room.

The doors to the club must have opened, because there were suddenly all these people moving onto the dance floor and standing in line at the bar. A few minutes ago, the place was nearly empty and just like that, it was packed.

If they were selling these homemade potions instead of liquor, it was no wonder there were so many people here. Damn.

I briefly wondered if anything going on in this place was even legal and how in the hell they had managed to stay open this long without getting into trouble. But my mind couldn't focus on the question long enough to worry about it.

My body wanted to move.

At first, I was hyper-aware of my body. I judged every movement. Was I doing this right? Did I look okay? But then the music consumed me. It swallowed me whole, the beat controlling the beat of my own heart. I couldn't fight it anymore. I let go, not thinking about how I looked or who was watching me. I just let my body move the way it wanted. I had never felt so free in my life.

Hours must have gone by like that and not once did the energy from the shot let up. Sweat coated the back of my neck and the skin on my arms. My hair caressed my face and shoulders. I could have danced forever.

But then, the dark feeling from the other night was back. It was like being sucked into a black hole. Or maybe more like having a thick, heavy black cloak thrown over my body, covering me in a veil of fear.

I reached out and grabbed hold of the iron bars, for the first time really looking through the crowd. He was here. Whoever had been watching me that first night was back, and his eyes were locked on me.

I turned around in the cage, searching for a pair of eyes staring back at me, but no matter how hard I looked, I couldn't find him.

As long as I was having fun, the potion that flowed through my system felt good. It gave me energy and made me feel sexy and beautiful. But adding in that taste of fear was like an amplified version of the worst panic I'd ever felt. I suddenly couldn't breathe.

I turned my attention to the bar, searching for Rend. He had somehow sensed this darkness before. Did he sense it now?

He wasn't behind the bar, though, and I couldn't find him anywhere in the crowd. Was he behind the black curtain with his friends?

I knew I would look stupid rushing into their private room

with fear written all over my face. And I didn't want to give Azure the satisfaction of seeing me freaking out.

I glanced over and was relieved to see that she wasn't paying any attention to me. If I totally lost it, though, she'd see it. Everyone would. They would think I was crazy.

I had to pull myself together.

I took a deep breath and forced myself to focus on the music. Whoever was out there in the darkness was just watching me. They couldn't touch me here in this cage in front of everyone. As long as I worked for Rend, they couldn't hurt me.

After a few minutes, I was able to push the dark feeling to the edge of my consciousness and focus on the music again. Still, all sense of freedom was gone now. I was in survival mode, which was much more like my normal state of being. Instead of giving myself up to the potion running through my veins, I was fighting against it.

When Lyla finally came to tell me it was time for us to go on a break, I nearly jumped out of the cage and kissed her on the mouth. I wanted to get out of there and off display for a while.

"You doing okay?" she asked as we pushed through the crowd and made our way through the front doors and out on the street. "You don't look like you're having fun."

I bit my lower lip. Should I tell her about the strange feeling? She seemed cool, but Azure had seemed fine at first too. I didn't want her telling everyone the new girl had some panic attack over nothing.

"Do you ever get the feeling someone is watching you?" I asked.

She laughed. "Everyone is watching you," she said. "It's part of the job."

"No, that's not exactly what I meant," I said, trying to figure out how to put words to the feeling. "I'm talking about someone... specific. Someone dark."

Evil. The word was on the tip of my tongue, but I didn't dare speak it.

She lit a cigarette and took a long drag. "Did someone talk to you? Try to get inside your head? You have to just ignore those guys. They're harmless, really. No one would dare lay a hand on one of Rend's girls," she said. A smile crept across her features. "Not without permission, anyway."

"No, no one came up to me or anything," I said.

"What then?"

I wrapped my arms around my body. Despite the late summer air and the heat of the shot running through my veins, I was shivering.

"Nothing, I guess," I said. "Just a feeling I got when I was up there."

"You want another shot of Dragon's Breath?"

I laughed. "Is that seriously what it's called?"

She rolled her eyes and smiled. "Yeah. All the drinks here have crazy color-themed names," she said. "You'll eventually learn what they all are and what they do. The base drink is Red Dragon, but Rend's special mix for the dancers is called Dragon's Breath."

"Can I ask you something else?"

"Sure," she said, finishing her cigarette and immediately lighting another one.

"How long has this place been here? I tried looking it up online and it's like it doesn't even exist at all."

"Oh, gosh, Venom has been open for about sixty years, I guess?" She looked up, as if the answer were written on the sky. "Maybe sixty-five?"

"Oh," I said, surprised. "I got the impression this was Rend's place. You know, that he started it. How long has he owned it, then?"

She shook her head and tossed her cigarette onto the ground, stomping it out with her heel. "Girl, you have so much to learn, I can't even begin to know where to start."

I tried to ask her what she meant by that, but before I could, she was leading us back into the club.

Selena gave us a wave as we walked past the crowd waiting to get in. I smiled at her, but that smile was wiped right off my face the second we walked back inside. I hadn't realized it, but the darkness was gone when we were outside. Walking back in was like walking into a cave of fear.

I shivered.

"Maybe you should go rest in the back for a little bit," Lyla said, her face creased with worry. "Something's really got you shaken up."

"You really don't feel that?" I asked. "That darkness?"

She shook her head, the smile fading from her face. "I've been surrounded by so much darkness my whole life, it's the only thing I know how to feel."

Lyla patted my shoulder and made her way toward her spot on the dance floor, leaving me with an overwhelming feeling of sadness.

MORE THAN YOU

I wasn't sure I could face another three hours in that cage.

Not with someone evil watching me. What did he want with me, whoever he was? Was he the one who had sent the black roses? I wished he would just show himself. Tell me what he wanted. I couldn't take the not-knowing of it.

I should find Rend. He'd told me to find him if anything happened. I looked toward the bar again, but there was no sign of him.

I glanced toward the black curtain. I could just walk back there with a confident smile on my face and tell him I needed to see him for a second. No one would know I was a mess on the inside. He would be able to tell me if I was in danger or if this was all in my head. And if I was in danger, he would be able to help me.

I hoped.

I made it more than halfway to the curtain when a tall, thin man stepped in front of me out of nowhere. I knew him by the look in his eyes and the shadows that seemed to ooze from him like dark smoke.

I stopped cold, my chest constricting.

"I've been watching you," he said. His voice was oily.

"I know."

He tilted his chin and smiled a thin, papery smile. "Beautiful and intuitive."

"Are you the one who sent the roses?" I asked.

"Roses?" He lifted a long finger to his lips. "Perhaps."

I narrowed my eyes at him. What kind of an answer was that?

"I was not aware of any roses, but perhaps my associate sent them," he said. "You see, my associate is very interested in you, Franki."

His voice sent a shudder of disgust through me. "Your associate?"

"He sent me here to get a look at you," the dark man said.

"Who is he?" My voice hitched on my fear. If this guy was just some lackey, how dark was the man he worked for? And what the hell did he want with me?

"You'll find out in due time," he said. "For now, it's good your eyes have finally been opened to this world." He moved a step closer to me and I fought to stand my ground, no matter how badly I wanted to turn and run. "You belong in this world. You always have. Too bad you will soon have to leave it."

"I don't know what you or your boss want with me, but I'm not interested," I said. I sounded a lot more confident than I felt.

He laughed, and the sound grated on my insides. Even his laughter sounded ominous and devoid of joy. "How cute," he said. "You think your opinion matters."

I swallowed down my terror. I didn't like the fact that he talked about me as if I was already part of someone's plan. I didn't like for anyone to talk about me as if my life was out of my own control.

"You look so much like your mother," he said, lifting his bony finger to my cheek.

I pulled away, barely restraining myself from slapping his hand away. "What do you know about my mother?"

"More than you, my dear. So much more than you," he said.

Anger flared within me, amplified by the potion still working its way through my veins. A sudden breeze blew across my skin and the man's eyes widened.

"So much power inside that heart of yours. So much passion," he said. "It's a shame you'll never really have the chance to explore all that talent."

My heart thundered in my chest. I clenched my teeth and tried to force deep breaths. The last thing I needed to do was start a tornado with all these people in here. I squashed my anger as best I could, but it took everything I had just to keep my power from ripping this place apart.

"Your mother worked so hard to keep you from ever discovering this side of yourself," he said. "It's a shame she had to die before she saw your powers at work."

Tears sprang to my eyes and I cried out, forcing them back. I would not cry. Even if he was telling the truth, I would not break this promise to myself. Especially not for a woman who had long since abandoned me.

"Such control," he said. "Astounding. Truly."

"Just tell me what you want." I said. "Stop playing games."

"Sweet child," he said with a smile. "The games have only just begun."

THE DEVIL'S IN THE DETAILS

I couldn't move.

Anger, fear, and intense sadness pulsed through my veins as the dark man turned and disappeared into the crowd of club goers.

It took all my willpower to hold back the tears and rage I wanted to unleash.

Just who did he think he was, coming here and threatening me? Telling me my mother was dead and then walking away?

I wanted to kill him. I wanted to shove my hands inside his wide mouth and rip him in two, straight down the middle.

I turned to look for him in the crowd. This couldn't be it. If I let him get away now, he'd just keep finding me. Watching me. Toying with me until I'd lost my damned mind.

I sprinted after him, pushing people out of my way and not even bothering to stop and apologize.

I finally caught sight of him going through one of the doors Azure had told me was off limits. His movements were slow and deliberate. He slipped through the door as though covered in oil.

I pushed my way through the last group of dancers and followed him through the door, only taking a second to look around and make sure none of the other staff were paying attention to me. When I didn't see any eyes looking my way, I moved inside.

The room was nearly pitch-black, and I stopped as the door closed behind me with a thud, blocking off the only light.

Laughter rang out, echoing in the space.

"You really are something," the dark man said. "Ninety-nine out of a hundred girls wouldn't dare follow me. They'd still be out there shaking in their boots, but not you, Franki. You are special in every way."

I could hear him several feet away, in front of me, but I couldn't see so much as an outline of him in the blackness.

"I don't like games," I said. "If you want something from me, I'd rather know what it is now than go back and forth wondering when you're coming back for me."

"In this case, it's not up to you, I'm afraid," he said. Had he moved closer? I tried to mentally estimate the space between me and the door back into the club. Could I reach it in one or two steps?

It was stupid to have followed him. Impulsive.

In my fear, I reached for the only card in my hand. "I work for Rend now," I said. "I'm under his protection."

More laughter that cut me to my core. I had been hoping for some sign of fear, like those guys in the alley.

"Yes, that is a minor bump in the road for us, but Rend's protection only extends so far," the dark man said. "Rend would be a fool to deny my associate anything he asked. If he wants you, he will have you."

"So why tell me and then walk away?" I asked. "Why not just take me now if he wants me, whoever he is?"

"Because you're not ready," he said. This time he was definitely closer. I hadn't heard any footsteps, but his voice was inches from my face. Could he see me in the darkness? "When the time is right, he'll come for you and there will be nothing you can do about it. You are a very special girl, Franki. Your sacrifice will change the world."

"Sacrifice?" The word tasted sour on my lips.

He moved so close I could feel his clothing brushing against the bare skin on my arms and shoulders. His leg pressed against mine and one very cold hand snaked around my middle.

"Your death is inevitable."

My body shivered violently as he pulled me against his thin frame. I grew colder, warmth leaving me as if his very touch was draining my body of its will to live. My knees went weak and my head felt fuzzy.

"Don't touch me," I said, my voice trembling.

"Or you'll what?" he asked, amused.

Behind me, Rend's voice came out as a low growl. "Or I'll rip your goddamned arms off," he said. "Let her go."

The dark man's body slid off me like a shadow, more cloud than solid form.

I backed toward Rend's voice. The door to this room hadn't even opened. How had he gotten inside?

Rend extended his hand and an orb of light formed against the darkness, illuminating a long hallway instead of a room like

I'd expected. He moved in front of me, putting himself between me and the dark man.

"You aren't welcome here, Fallon." Rend said. "You know that."

"You cannot deny me entrance to this place," the dark man said. He didn't seem afraid despite the conviction in Rend's voice. "You and my master have an agreement, remember? I'm sure he would be happy to refresh your memory, if need be."

It wasn't lost on me that suddenly this man's associate had been upgraded to his master.

Rend dropped his hand, but the orb continued to float in the air in front of him. "Maybe your master is the one who needs reminding," Rend said. "The witches who work here are under my protection. He has no right to them, and he can't step foot into my club."

"The devil's in the details, my friend," the dark man said. "This girl is special. For him, she's worth breaking a few rules. Even your rules. I'll go for now, but you can't stop this, Rend. You would do well to politely step out of my master's way. You wouldn't want to risk everything you've built here, would you?"

"Get the hell out of my club," Rend said, raising his voice.

The dark man lowered his head in a bow, then disintegrated into black smoke and shadows.

HIS WORDS

Rend turned to me, and I threw my arms around him, my entire body trembling against him. He held me close until I'd calmed down enough to untangle myself from him.

"Who was that?" I asked.

"His name is Fallon," he said.

His face was all hard angles in the dim light of his glowing orb.

"Franki, I'm trying to be very patient and understanding here, because I know you've been through some shit over the past few days, but my patience is running thin," he said. His voice was calm and even, but his muscles were tense.

I pulled away, startled. Was he seriously reprimanding me after what I'd just been through?

"Why would you follow him back here?" he asked, some of his anger leaking into his tone. "After everything that happened the other night, why would you follow another stranger into a dark hallway, out of view from me and the rest of the staff?"

I closed my eyes and swallowed hard. It was a fair question. How did you explain to someone like him that sometimes I was too stubborn to be smart?

"I looked for you," I said. "I felt him watching me again, just like the other night. But you weren't at the bar, so I figured you were behind the curtain."

"Why didn't you come back there to talk to me, then?"

"I was going to," I said. "I was on my way back there when this guy appeared out of nowhere. He blocked my way, and I knew the second I looked at him that he was the one. He said things to me. He threatened me."

"So, you thought it would be a good idea to go with him into a dark, secluded place?"

"Hey, I didn't know this was a dark, secluded place," I said, gripping my arms, still shivering a little.

Rend shrugged out of his black jacket and put it around my shoulders. I mumbled a thank you and slipped my arms inside, inhaling the scent of him and wishing it didn't send a wave of desire through me.

"Azure told you this door was off limits, right? Staff isn't allowed back here in the first place, and you knew that. You better start explaining yourself, Franki."

"He said things," I repeated. I hadn't wanted to mention my mother, but it was becoming impossible to hide from him. "He told me my mother was dead."

Rend's eyes snapped to my face, questioning. "What?" He shook his head. "Your mother? How would a guy like that know your mom?"

"I have no idea," I said. "I haven't seen her in three years.

She took off on my eighteenth birthday without so much as a note to say goodbye. Now this creepy guy tells me I look like her and that she's dead. He threatened me, Rend. He told me his associate had his eye on me and that they were going to play games with me. He told me I'd make a good sacrifice. I couldn't just let him walk away after that. I wanted answers."

Rend grabbed his hair into his fist and paced the floor in front of me. "This doesn't make any sense," he said. "What kind of sacrifice?"

"I don't know. He said I would have to die." My voice came out like a scared third grader's, high-pitched and terrified. "I couldn't just let him threaten me and then walk away. I had to follow him."

"Dammit, Franki, he wanted you to follow him. He was playing with you," he said. "And you just walked right into it. He could have killed you. What if he had taken you out of here? I might not have been able to find you."

"I didn't say it was the smartest thing I ever did, but he really got to me."

"You should have come to find me before you went after him," he said.

"Look, I know you said you want to protect me, but you can't possibly keep an eye on me at all times," I said. "And just because I agreed to work here does not mean you own me. I am still free to make my own decisions, even if they're stupid ones. Even if I end up dead, it's my life to lose."

I was yelling at him. Here he was sticking his neck out for me, and I was yelling at him. The guy got under my skin in more ways than one.

Anger flashed in his eyes and he moved so close, my back

pushed against the wall. He placed his palm flat against the wall beside my head, leaning in.

"Why are you so determined to drive me insane?"

"Why do you care what happens to me?" I asked, breathless.

"I don't know," he said, his eyes locked on mine. "I haven't been able to get you out of my mind since the moment I first saw you standing there at the bar."

My heart pounded in my throat, and I couldn't help myself. I looked down at his lips again, just inches from my own. There was no denying how much I wanted him.

"I don't let women get to me like this," he said, his voice low and rough. "You've got me all mixed up."

His hand traveled slowly down the wall, grazing the edge of my shoulder and arm. I could feel the heat of him even through the jacket.

I never wanted a piece of clothing gone so badly in my life.

"I want to protect you, Franki," he said, softening. His hand moved to my hip. "You're making that incredibly difficult."

"I'm sorry," I whispered.

His eyes were as black as night, the silver running through them like stars, flashing in the near-darkness.

"I'm in a very dangerous position here," he said. "I run this place with a strict code. When a woman comes to work for me, I vow to protect her from the dangers she may encounter here. In order to do that for the entire staff, I have to keep my head on straight. I have to watch out for them at all times, the best I can. I can't get involved on a more... intimate level."

I shivered at his words.

"Then why are you standing so close to me?" I said.

The air in the space between us was electric. I wanted so badly to touch him. I wanted to wrap my arms around him and close that small space that kept us apart.

"Because I can't seem to help myself around you," he said, his eyes darting across my face, studying every inch of my expression.

My body ached for him. How could such little space feel like a cavern between us?

My mouth went dry while other parts of me grew wet with need.

Just touch me, I begged with my eyes. I thought I might die of anticipation.

"Tell me I'm wrong to feel this way," he said. "Tell me you're only here because I forced you to be here and that if you could, you would walk right out that door and go back to your normal life before you ever found this place."

"I can't," I said. Whatever I thought I wanted before now, I knew I couldn't walk away. Not just because of the danger or because I wanted the truth about my mother. I was here because of him.

"You have no idea how much I wish you would," he said.

His words burned me. How could someone want me to stay and want me to go at the same time? How could he stand here teasing me like this? Telling me he wanted me, too, but that I could never have him?

"Then tell me to go," I said. "Or tell me you'll never let anything happen between us and that I'm stupid for wanting you. But don't stand here like this and tell me you won't kiss me because of your own pride or some arbitrary rule you set for yourself long before I walked through your door."

I don't know where I'd found the courage to tell him what I was feeling, but the words poured out of me.

"I don't like to play games," I said. "So, if you're going to kiss me, you'd better do it before I go insane from being this close to something I can never have."

He didn't move at first. His breaths were fast and shallow, and his eyes darkened.

Then, with a swiftness that made me gasp, he moved the edge of the jacket aside and grabbed my hip with his hand, pulling my body toward his.

His other hand moved up behind my neck, both gentle and strong at the same time. A low moan rumbled in his chest as he dipped his head toward me, his kiss finally landing on my lips with a fire that ignited an even deeper need inside me.

My hands circled his neck, and I lifted onto my toes, wanting to be closer, always closer. My fingers slid up the back of his neck, gripping his hair as his fingers dug into my hip.

Our lips and tongues met and parted, joining then drawing back, opening and closing in rhythm as we explored our first taste of each other.

His thumb moved back and forth against the bare skin at my waist as his hips pushed against mine.

Passion erupted beneath the surface of my skin, his every touch, every kiss, setting off a wave of fireworks deep inside me. God, I never knew a man could make me feel this way. I never wanted it to end.

All I wanted was more.

A deep moan escaped Rend's lips, and he pulled himself away from my kiss, pressing his forehead against mine, his hands still holding me with passionate force.

"I shouldn't be doing this," he said between breaths. "I'm

supposed to be protecting you, not putting you in greater danger."

"How does kissing me put me in danger?" I asked, moving one hand slowly down his neck and around to his face.

I wanted to touch every part of him until he was mine by memory.

"You have no idea what kind of man I really am," he said. "If you knew, you wouldn't open yourself up to me like this."

I thought about what the other girls in the dressing room had said. How he was known for tearing men in two with his bare hands. Maybe I should have been afraid of him, but fear was the last thing on my mind.

He moved his hands from my body, and I nearly whimpered at the loss of his touch. He shook his head, then slipped out of my grasp, turning from me.

That's when we both noticed the orb of light. It's dim amber glow had been amplified to a bright sunlight.

"How did you do that?" he asked.

I laughed. "Me? I didn't do anything."

"I could never create a light this bright," he said. He moved his hand under the orb and moved it toward us.

I giggled, watching the light. Had I made it brighter?

But then my eyes opened to the space around us. My heart nearly stopped as I looked down the long hallway, now lit up from the bright glow. I fell back against the wall in shock, covering my mouth with my hand.

"What is it?" he asked.

I shook my head in disbelief. This wasn't possible.

"Franki? What's wrong?"

"I dreamed of this place," I said. "A hall of doorways."

I walked forward, studying the door closest to us. It was

made of a sturdy wood, just like in my dream. On the surface of the wood, there was a carving of a serpent, its fangs outstretched as if it were about to strike. I ran my hand across the carving to make sure I wasn't imagining this place.

Rend touched my hand, but I pulled away. I needed to see if it was here.

I started down the hallway, my eyes searching each image for the one that had haunted me.

Rend followed as I practically tore down the hallway.

"Franki wait, there's a reason this place is off-limits to staff," he said. "Don't open any of these doors."

"I just need to see," I said, not slowing down.

When I saw it, I nearly fell to the floor in front of it. I stopped, unable to breathe.

A black crow, its wings stretched wide.

I reached forward and ran my hand along the carving, feeling each groove in the wood. It was really here.

Rend grabbed my hand and cupped my chin with his other, turning my head toward him. He looked almost pale in the bright light. "Franki, I need to know why you were searching for this particular door," he said. "This is important."

I shook my head, feeling like I was still stuck inside that dream. "I don't know," I said. "In my dream, I was running down this hallway, chasing the sound of wings fluttering in the distance. When I reached this door, the one with the crow on it, I tried to go inside. That's when I woke up."

He swallowed and gripped my hand tighter.

"What's your name?" he asked, for the first time a hint of fear in his voice. It scared me to hear it there. "Your full name?"

I studied his face, not understanding his question. Why

did my name matter? Franki was a nickname my mother had given me when I was very young. I hated for anyone to call me by my full name, so I never gave it out unless I had to.

I was scared to know why he suddenly felt that it was important.

"Mary Francis," I said, finally.

Rend paled and dropped my hand. He looked from me to the door, then brought a fist to his mouth and closed his eyes.

"How did I not see this before?"

He seemed to be talking to himself more than he was to me.

"See what?"

"Your power. Your blue eyes and black hair," he said. "No wonder Fallon said I was risking everything by protecting you."

The tension in his face and jaw frightened me. Was he mad at me? "I still don't understand," I said. "What does my real name have to do with this?"

He turned to look at me, anger and frustration shining in his eyes. "Your first name is Mary, like all the women in your family."

I took a step back, suddenly cold with fear.

"How do you know that?"

I knew my mother's name was Mary Beth, but she had never told me about the other women in her family.

"Because I know your family," he said. "Everyone knows about your family."

I shook my head, my breath shallow. What was he saying?

"You're a crow witch," he said. He'd been avoiding my eyes, but now he looked up and stared right through to my very soul. "Fallon was right. I can't protect you."

NO LOGICAL WAY

My knees weakened, and I nearly fell.

Rend caught me, his arms encircling my waist as he pulled me against his body. The orb of light hovering near us dimmed to its original amber glow, and I realized he'd been right.

It was me who had been making the light brighter. I had no idea how, but as soon as the joy of kissing him dimmed, so did the light.

"I need to get you out of here," he said.

"I need to know what's behind that door," I said, trying to push against him. All my strength was gone, though, siphoned out of me with his words.

I hadn't taken the dark man's threats seriously because I believed Rend would protect me. Everyone had said so. I'd seen the fear in the eyes of those young vampires when he'd told them I belonged to him.

But the dark man—Fallon—had not been scared of him.

"You can't go through there," he said. "It would be the

worst, most dangerous thing you could do right now. I need to get you to a place where no one can touch you or find you for a while."

I gathered what little strength I could find inside and pushed against him. I leaned against the door for support. "I'm not going anywhere with you until you tell me what you know about my family."

His eyes widened, and he looked both ways down the hall. "There's way too much to try to explain it here."

"Give me the short version," I said, my jaw tensed. My breath came fast. He had to know he couldn't just drop a bomb like that and expect me to let it go until another time.

He let out a frustrated sigh. "Many witches have spirit animals or spirit objects, often tied to their family line. Some witches are so strongly tied to their spirit animals that they can actually shape-shift into them," he explained. "You come from a very long line of witches who are able to shift into crows."

I swallowed, my throat thick with anticipation. How long had I wanted to know about my family?

"You are the descendant of a particularly powerful witch called the Mother Crow," he said. "She is well over one hundred years old and she is one of the most truly evil creatures I have ever had the misfortune to come across, which is really saying something after what I've been through."

"Evil?" I shook my head. Not exactly what every girl wants to hear about her grandmother. Or great-grandmother. At over a hundred years old, what was she to me, exactly?

"Truly wicked, like the man Fallon works for," he said.

My hands began to tremble. I gathered them into fists and pressed them against my legs, willing them to stop. "And who is that?"

"We call him the Devil," Rend said. "And he lives up to that name. Getting his hands on one of Mother Crow's girls would mean..."

His voice trailed off and he looked away, his eyebrows pinched together with worry.

"What could he possibly want with me?" I asked.

"Your blood is valuable, Franki," he said. "Demons who come to this world cannot cast magic without being detected. When a demon casts, their magic pulls energy from every living thing around them. Trees, grass, even humans. It makes demons vulnerable and very easy to track. That's why vampires exist. I know it's difficult to understand, but when a demon consumes the blood of a powerful witch, that power lives inside them. The demon can draw from that power like a battery, allowing them to cast without damaging the world around them."

I shook my head. This was too much. My brain couldn't make sense of it all. The hallway spun, and I closed my eyes and pressed my back against the door.

"I promise I'll tell you everything after you're safe, but for now, you have to trust me," he said. "There is a war going on around us all the time and the most valuable weapon is the power that lives inside of you."

"My blood," I said with a whisper.

"Your blood. Your heritage. Your abilities. All of it," he said. "Different factions desire it for different reasons, but all you need to understand right now is that you're in danger. Until I figure this out, I need to make sure you're safe."

I wanted to protest and run away. I wanted to go home and try to forget any of this existed. But I knew I was in too deep now to walk away.

I opened my eyes and found Rend staring at me, concern written in every line on his gorgeous face. "Let me help you," he said.

"I thought you said you couldn't protect me," I said.

"I can't promise you anything right now," he said, lifting his hand to my face and tracing a path down my cheek. "But I swear to you I'll do everything I can. At least let me try."

I took a step forward, but my knees buckled.

Rend caught me and lifted me off the ground, cradling me in his arms as he walked with hurried steps back toward the door to at the other end of the hall. The door that would take us back into the club.

Instead, though, he stopped in front of the one with the carving of the serpent.

He turned the handle and pushed the door open wide, then carried me inside.

Lights flickered on as he nudged the door shut with his foot.

"Where are you taking me?" I asked.

"This is my house," he said. "It's the only place I can think of that will be totally safe right now."

"I don't understand," I said. "Is your house in the basement of the club?"

"Not exactly," he said. He carried me through a dark room and down a narrow set of stairs.

I don't know what I expected to see down there. A basement apartment of some kind maybe. Some kind of man cave with a big screen TV and a twin bed where he slept on nights when he worked too late to go all the way home.

I definitely didn't expect to see a real, full-size house down there. A mansion, really, with pristine dark wooden floors and paintings hanging in golden frames.

He carried me down another hallway and into a large bedroom with a gorgeous canopied bed carved from mahogany.

Very gently, he laid me down on top of a billowy white comforter. I sank into it as if he'd set me on top of a cloud.

I couldn't make sense of it. There was no logical way the club was so big it could hold a hundred rooms like this behind all those doors. And how had he built a huge mansion like this underneath the streets of Chicago?

My mind was spinning with questions, but Rend didn't give me a chance to ask them.

He sat on the edge of the bed, his eyes dark with worry.

"I can't stay here with you right now," he said. "I have some very important people in the club who will start asking questions if I'm gone too long. Besides, I need to make sure Fallon is gone and none of the Devil's other minions are hanging around the club."

"I can't stay here by myself," I said, sitting up.

He placed his hand on my leg. "Franki, this isn't a request," he said sternly. "You'll be safe here for now, I swear my life on it. Stay here. Rest if you can. I'll be back as soon as I can get away."

"You can't leave me with all these unanswered questions," I said, the panic growing inside my chest. "I'll go mad."

He ran his hand across my cheek. "I can't even imagine how difficult this is right now for you, to be thrust into this world you never even knew existed," he said. "But I cannot stay right now, and I can't bring you back to the club with me.

Until we know what their intentions are for you, it's just too dangerous."

"If you can't protect me from the Devil," I said, "then why are you still trying?"

He avoided my eyes. "I have to get back to the club before someone comes looking for me."

He took my hand in his and brushed his lips against it like a whisper.

"I should have made you leave the second I saw you walk into my club," he said. "I should have picked you up and taken you out myself."

My shoulders slumped against the mountain of pillows behind me. If it wasn't for the way I felt when he was near me, I would have wished the same thing.

But everything had changed with that kiss. I couldn't wish him out of my life now if I tried.

"Get some rest," he said.

Before I could protest any further, he was gone.

RIP ME APART

I woke to the sound of rain falling against the window.

But then, how could that be?

I sat up in bed, making sure I was still in Rend's house and that he hadn't brought me back to my own campus apartment sometime in the night.

The elegant white bedding was a dead giveaway. My comforter at home was five years old and well used. There was no accidentally mistaking the two.

So how were there windows in the basement?

I stood and made my way to the window, a bright light coming from outside. How long had I slept? It only felt like a few hours, but the light pouring through the glass was as bright as day.

I must have taken my boots off at some point in the night and the wood floor was cool against my bare feet. I trembled as I watched snowflakes, not rain, pelt the window.

I closed my eyes, thinking I must be stuck inside a dream.

I opened them again, wider this time, unable to believe my own eyes. A winter wonderland stretched out before me for miles. A cliff dropped off just a few feet from the edge of the house and mountain peaks rose from the fog that stretched out across the distance. Snow swirled everywhere.

I brought my hand to my mouth. I could hardly breathe.

Toto, we are so not in Chicago anymore.

I stepped back from the window. Where the hell was I? How was it possible that we had stepped through a doorway in the club in Chicago, come down a flight of stairs, and ended up on the edge of a mountain in the middle of nowhere?

It was summer in Chicago. This just wasn't possible.

For a brief moment, I wondered if maybe I was looking into some kind of TV screen. An illusion to make me believe we weren't underground.

But it looked too real. What kind of trick was my mind playing on me?

I looked around the room for a coat. I needed to see for myself. If it really was snowing outside, I couldn't go out in nothing but some dance leotard. I'd freeze to death.

My eyes landed on a white dress shirt thrown casually over the back of a large chair near the bed. I picked it up and breathed in the scent of him, my insides warming just from the thought of his kiss the night before.

Okay, so the guy was strange and obviously not like any man I'd ever met before in my life. But there was no denying that the smallest thought of him turned me upside down.

I slipped my arms inside the shirt. It was huge on me, but I loved the way it felt against my skin. I pulled it around me and headed for the bedroom door.

I made my way down the hallway with just a fleeting look back toward the small hidden staircase he'd originally brought me down. I knew he had said to stay put, but I needed to see what was really going on outside.

The main hallway opened up into a large landing with a wide wooden staircase. The banisters on either side were hand-carved, with ornate patterns. Everything looked antique and expensive and more beautiful than any house I'd ever stepped foot inside.

I raced down the stairs to the heavy front door, taking in the marble-tiled entryway and the large chandelier that hung above it.

I pulled the door open and stepped into another world.

Freezing cold wind whipped around my face and bare legs.

My feet sank into the newly fallen snow. I don't know if it was shock or the leftovers of last night's shot running through my veins, but I hardly felt affected by the cold at first.

I stood with my arms stretched out, lifting my face to the sky. Soft snowflakes landed on my cheeks and melted in an instant, icy water sliding across my warm skin.

I barely registered the sound of footsteps behind me before strong arms circled around my waist.

I jumped and struggled for an instant, afraid Fallon had found me again. But it was Rend's voice that rose above the growing wind.

"I told you not to leave the bedroom," he said.

I couldn't tell if he was angry or amused. Or both.

I flipped around to face him, glad when he didn't take his hands from my waist. "Did you really expect me to see a winter wonderland outside your window and not investigate?"

"That's not the point," he said, his voice stern, but his dark eyes somehow lighter here in the snow.

"How is this possible?" I asked, looking up at the white sky. "Where are we?"

He pulled me closer and suddenly the snow felt freezing on my skin compared to the inviting warmth of his body against mine.

"Italy," he said with a slight twitch of his eyebrow.

I shook my head, not able to make sense of this. Even with my feet buried in the snow, it didn't feel like reality.

"That's impossible," I said. "How is Italy in the basement of your club?"

"It's complicated." He ran a warm finger across my cheek, brushing away the melted snowflakes.

I shivered at the thought of all the things I had never known. All the things I still didn't know.

"You're freezing," he said. "Let's get you inside before you turn into an icicle."

He didn't ask my permission. He simply lifted me into his strong arms, carried me up the granite steps, and into the massive mansion on the cliff.

Rend brought me into a living room off to the right of the grand staircase. He laid me gently across a large leather couch facing a magnificent stone fireplace that looked big enough to hold a family of four.

He pulled a blanket from the back of the couch and wrapped it around my body, his eyes lingering on the unbuttoned shirt.

"I see you made yourself right at home," he said with a small hint of a smile.

The blanket was soft like fur, and I snuggled into it, my body shivering.

"Oh," I said, embarrassed. "I'll have it dry cleaned."

He shook his head and turned toward the fireplace. "Keep it," he said. "Seeing you in my shirt isn't exactly an unpleasant sight."

The hint of admission of his attraction to me sent a wave of warmth between my legs, and I squeezed them together under the blanket. I bit my lip as I watched him open a large wooden box beside the fireplace.

He was still dressed in the same suit he'd been wearing last night, but he'd taken off his tie and loosened the collar. I let my eyes travel over his body, devouring every inch of him, my mind imagining what he'd look like outside of those clothes.

A contented moan escaped from my lips and he glanced back at me, his eyes narrowed. "What are you thinking about?"

I hid my face behind the blanket. "Nothing," I said. "This blanket is gorgeous. It's so soft."

My attempt at distraction didn't seem to work because he smiled and shook his head.

I sank deeper into the couch, wishing I could disappear for a moment. I needed to get a handle on my own desires. I barely knew this guy. He was obviously part of a world I couldn't even begin to understand.

I forced my eyes away from his perfect silhouette and concentrated on the work he was doing in that wooden box. I assumed he was getting ready to build a fire, which meant the box was likely full of wood.

I was learning that it was stupid to assume anything about this new world. Instead of wood, he pulled out a well-worn leather bag that cinched with a long cord at the top. In his other hand, he held a vial of golden liquid.

Intrigued, I watched as he opened the bag just enough to put two fingers inside and grab a pinch of golden dust from it. He uttered words under his breath that I couldn't understand, and then threw the dust into the fireplace. He quickly followed this by tossing the vial of liquid against the stone. The glass shattered, and golden flames erupted from the fireplace, a wave of heat rushing toward me and blowing my hair around my face.

The slight smell of sulfur lingered in the air for a moment, and then disappeared. The flames roared bright and strong, despite the absence of logs or any actual material to burn.

My mouth fell open as I stared into the fire.

"How did you do that? Is that magic?"

"It's a special kind of magic," he said, placing the small leather bag back inside the wooden box. "My magic is a type of alchemy. Instead of using the force of magic within me to cast the spells like you did with the wind in my office the other day, I combine natural elements of the earth in ways that create magical effects. That way it doesn't drain me the way you were drained the other day."

"Does that mean I could go into your little box and take those same two items and create the fire on my own without using magic?"

He left the fire and came to sit next to me on the couch. I pulled my legs under my body and sat up, giving him room. Wanting him closer.

"Yes, anyone could use them now and create the same effect," he said. "The magical part is in the enchantments and the breaking down of the elements and materials in a way that brings out their natural magic. There's pure magic inside every living thing and every element of nature. Most humans just can't see it to appreciate its power."

Our eyes locked and my heart stopped beating for a long moment.

What was going on with me? I had never felt so intensely attracted to someone in my life. It was terrifying, but no matter how hard I tried, I couldn't force my gaze away from his.

I forced a breath instead, kick-starting my heart.

"Are you going to tell me how we got from a club in Chicago to a mountaintop in Italy by walking through a doorway?" I asked. My voice was softer than I'd intended, but he simply took my breath away.

He rested his arm across the length of the back of the couch, turning his body fully toward me. It took every ounce of self-control for me not to move closer to him. Instead, I clutched the blanket tighter in my fists.

"That's another type of magic," he said. "Each doorway is a portal that leads to another place inside this world."

The way he said this world sent a shiver up my spine. He said it as if he meant there were other worlds besides this one, and I wasn't sure I was ready to recognize that as a possibility.

"So, if we walked back upstairs and went through the door again, we'd be back inside the club in Chicago?"

He nodded, his eyes dipping for a moment to my lips. I felt self-conscious and vulnerable under his gaze.

I wasn't used to vulnerability. Being vulnerable meant being weak around someone. It meant trusting someone. And trust wasn't something I gave easily, especially to strange men who could do things like create fire out of dust.

I looked toward the flames as they danced and flickered. I could get lost inside a fire like that.

"Are you doing okay?" he asked. "I know this has to be a lot to take in."

A laugh escaped from my mouth, and it came out as a half-sob, nearly choking me. I clamped my hand over my mouth, surprised by the emotion that seemed to pour out of me when I was around him.

I turned my face away, not wanting him to even look at me. I had spent my whole life trying to hide who I was—what I was —and suddenly, I felt exposed. Raw.

He moved closer and placed his hand on my shoulder. As much as I yearned for his touch, part of me also wanted to run away and forget the past week had ever happened. I had fought to control my emotions for so long, and keep everyone at arm's length, that I couldn't handle the thought of opening myself up to someone like this.

But the warmth of his hand through the fabric of the shirt felt right. No matter how much my heart and mind rebelled against the desire of it, my body betrayed me.

I closed my eyes, unable to pull myself away from him even though I knew I should.

"Franki?"

The sound of my name on his lips made my breath catch in my throat, and I turned to him.

His black eyes searched mine, and I was certain the desire there mirrored my own. And not just the desire. The fear, too. Was he afraid of this attraction, just as much as I was? Was that possible?

It was hard to imagine a strong man like him being scared of anything, but I was sure I saw it there.

I swallowed, my mouth dry from need and want. My mind pushed against the growing ache, begging me not to move one inch toward him. Not to give him permission to act on that desire.

But I couldn't listen to my mind right now. Reason faded to the background like a loud stereo being turned down suddenly, leaving nothing but the intense silence of need.

With slow motion, almost unwillingly, I turned my shoulders slightly toward him, as if opening myself to him. And that was all it took, that one micro-movement.

He leaned toward me, fear replaced by hunger.

His hand slid behind my head, his fingers tangling in my hair as he pulled me toward him. I met him halfway, lifting up onto my knees. The soft blanket fell between us as our bodies collided, all hesitation defeated by the heat of the moment.

His lips descended on mine, opening to take my mouth entirely, his teeth grazing against the soft skin of my lips. My palms pressed hard against his chest, sliding around to his back and exploring every ripple of muscle. Without thinking, my hands gathered his shirt into fists, pulling until it was free of his pants, giving me access to the warm skin underneath.

He trembled as my fingers slipped up and under his shirt, touching the flushed heat of his skin. His mouth opened, and his breath fell hot against my cheek as I ran my hands up and down his back, my mouth on his cheek and chin, the rough stubble abrasive against the soft skin of my face.

His hand tensed against the back of my neck, and he tugged on my hair, pulling my head back from him so he could claim my mouth for himself.

Effortlessly, he lifted me from my knees, then pushed me

fully back onto the cushions of the couch, his body heavy against mine.

Finally, his hands left my face and neck and explored lower, my blood pulsing with need as his fingers dug into my thighs. I opened beneath him. My legs wrapped tight around him, drawing him closer.

His mouth moved from my lips and he traveled lower. My head dipped back against the couch, giving him access to my neck. My nails dug into his shoulder, desperately wanting more.

My breath came faster as I moved against him, cursing the clothing that kept us from fully knowing each other's bodies.

His teeth grazed against the sensitive spot just above my shoulder, and he tensed, his entire form growing rigid against me. His hands gripped me so tightly, the pain of it was almost ecstasy. Almost torture.

Then, suddenly, he released me, moving up and off of me so fast, the absence of him was disorienting.

I sat up, laboring for each breath as my heart pounded violently against my ribcage.

"What?" I asked. Had I done something wrong? He was turned completely away from me, one fist resting against the stone mantle of the large fireplace.

I stood to go to him, but he turned and the darkness in his eyes stunned me. Scared me. I stopped without taking another step, waiting for some kind of explanation.

"We need to get changed and get back to the club," he said. His entire demeanor and tone had changed, as if he had become another person in the space of ten seconds.

I adjusted the borrowed shirt on my body, covering myself back up as best I could. "That's all you have to say?"

His face was hard edges, his expression closed off. "What more do you want from me?"

I swallowed the hurt that threatened to rip me apart. I pushed back the desire that I had actually dared to let consume me. Instead, I invited in anger. I embraced it and let it flow up through me, burning me like those golden flames.

I knew how to be angry instead of hurt. I knew how to hide disappointment and pain. If he didn't care to even acknowledge what had just happened between us, and if he could honestly turn his desire on and off like that, then I wouldn't give him the satisfaction of seeing me protest.

I covered myself in I-don't-care. It was a mask I had created for myself after years of living with a mother who had never loved me.

"You're right, it's probably getting late," I said, grateful when my voice sounded relaxed and indifferent. I was good at hiding my bitterness. "I need to get home and change before my shift tonight anyway. My roommate is probably worried sick. In fact, maybe it's better if I take a few days off."

"No," he said, the volume of his protest making me jump.

I took a deep breath.

Stay calm. Don't let him see you upset. Don't be vulnerable.

"Why not?" I asked, meeting his gaze straight on as a challenge. "You said yourself you can't keep me safe from the Devil. And if you can't keep me safe, then why should I even bother working at Venom, anymore?"

His jaw tensed. "You'll be safer with me than out there alone."

I shook my head, sadness flushing through me. "I'm not so sure about that."

I turned on my heels and walked back toward the grand

staircase, feeling his eyes on me the entire time. It was a miracle my knees didn't give out on the way up. On the outside, I managed to hold myself together, but on the inside, my heart was aching. I cursed myself for caring about him this intensely. How had this happened so fast? I was usually more guarded than this. I should know better.

I found my way down the hallway and through the hidden entrance to the narrow staircase. The stairs opened up to a small room at the top with five doorways. Crap. Which one? It ruined my cool and confident exit if I opened up some stupid closet door and tried to walk inside. I didn't remember seeing four other doors in here last night, but the whole thing was kind of a blur.

I bit my lip, my heart racing as I heard his footsteps on the stairs behind me.

I reached for the handle of the first door to the right, but as my hand touched the antique bronze knob, Rend placed his hand on my arm.

"Not that one," he said.

I yanked my arm away as if his touch were poisonous to my soul.

"Franki, I know I owe you an apology," he said. "I should have never kissed you like that. I let a weak moment get the best of me."

It wasn't the kiss I wanted an apology for.

I held my feelings inside, unsure how to respond, but not wanting him to know how he'd hurt me.

"And you're right," he said. "I don't own you. Working at Venom is one hundred percent your choice, but if you come back, I promise I'll do my best to keep you safe for as long as I can."

I swallowed and turned toward the next door. "I can take care of myself."

The words came out of my mouth, but I knew I didn't really believe them. Who was I kidding? I didn't know the first thing about protecting myself from vampires and demons and witches. I had no idea how to control whatever power I happened to possess.

"Franki—"

"Don't," I said, raising my voice and lifting my chin. "I never should have come here."

I looked into his eyes and hoped he couldn't see the struggle deep inside.

And I don't ever plan to come back.

Those were the words I wanted to say, but I knew I would be lying. I couldn't walk away from him forever any more than I could deny that I belonged here in this world of magic.

"Come back tonight," he said softly. "At least to let me explain what it is you're up against."

I took a deep breath. How could I say no?

It would be torture to be around him. The memory of his kiss still burned on my lips, but something had made him pull away from me. My heart couldn't handle that kind of push and pull for long. I needed to get as far away from him as I could before I disintegrated into a pile of ashes in his hands.

But I needed to know about my family. I needed to understand who the Devil was and why he found my blood so valuable.

I sighed and looked at the door leading back into Venom. "I'll come back when and if I'm ready," I said. "Don't ask me for more than that."

Rend stepped toward me, but I pulled away, not wanting

to feel his touch on my skin. I was terrified that if he touched me again, he would own me, and I would never be able to get away from him. His eyes searched mine.

There was still so much unsaid between us, but for now, it would have to wait.

Instead, I opened the door and walked through, crossing back into Chicago and the hall of doorways.

NOT EXACTLY NOTHING

I closed the door behind me and took a deep breath. I threw a wishful glance back toward the door with the crow embedded on its front.

I hadn't even gotten the chance to really talk to Rend about the crows. How many of them were there? Why had they never come to find me? What did he know about my mother?

If the answers were behind that door, I wanted to go through and face them, no matter how dangerous.

But now was not the time to be going through strange doors. For all I knew, the crow door could lead me straight to hell. Or Kansas. Who knew?

Someday, though, I would go through that door and learn the truth.

I reached for the handle of the door that would lead me back to Venom and without another glance back at Rend's door, I stepped through to the main part of the club.

I ran straight into Azure.

Literally.

A tray full of glasses flew out of her hand. She cried out as they all went tumbling toward the floor. I jumped back, waiting for glass to shatter and spray across my legs and bare feet, but before the glasses hit the floor, they froze in midair.

I gasped, taking two steps back in surprise. My eyes traveled up to Azure's face. She stared down at the glasses with great concentration, one palm lifted and curled, as if she held them in her hand. She raised her palm up and all ten glasses followed her movement, rising through the air and back onto her outstretched tray.

"Whoa," I said. "That was amazing."

She glared at me, then slowly let her eyes travel down my body. Shit, I was still wearing Rend's shirt, and my hair was probably tousled, like I'd just had a good ride in the sack.

I straightened the shirt and squared my shoulders, daring her to say one damned word to me about it.

She cleared her throat, the muscles around her mouth tightening. "Well, I guess now we know where you disappeared to last night."

I was all ready to tell her to fuck off, except that there was a twinge of sadness mixed into her hateful tone. Even though she turned away to try to hide it, I saw her eyes fill with shiny tears.

Crap, did she have a thing for Rend? Had he treated her like this, too? Kissing her and leading her to believe there was something between them, only to back off just when things were getting intense? I felt cheap and used, suddenly sure that what I had thought was special between Rend and me was just some kind of game he liked to play.

"Look," I said, reaching out to put my hand on her arm. "It's not what you think, trust me."

She snapped away from my touch, her glare back. And this time it had daggers in it. "I'm sure it's completely innocent."

Sarcasm dripped from her tone like acid.

I crossed my arms in front of my chest, feeling slightly naked even though I still had my dance outfit underneath. "Fine, you don't have to believe me if you don't want to, but Rend was just trying to help me out," I said. "Nothing happened."

Okay, so not exactly nothing, but she didn't need to know that.

"You don't have to explain yourself to me," she said, sniffing and turning back toward the bar. "It's none of my business."

No, it isn't.

She obviously wasn't going to respond well to my attempts to be nice, so screw it. I had enough problems without worrying about her.

"Okay, well, see you around, then," I said. She didn't even bother to look back at me or say goodbye. She just continued to clear the used glasses from the tables.

I glanced back before I disappeared behind the black curtain and watched for a long moment as she used her magic to clean the place. Glasses flew through the air in perfect lines, lifting from the tables to the bar where they dipped gently into a large sink full of soapy bubbles.

I briefly wondered why, if she could do that with nothing more than a flick of her wrist, she'd been using the tray at all. I wondered what kind of things I might be capable of if I stayed in this world a little longer.

I shook my head and went back to the dressing room, changed back into my own clothes, and left for home.

SOMETHING IN THE SHADOWS

I got on the 'L' but didn't get off near campus. Instead, I kept going, taking the familiar route back to my mother's old house.

I hadn't been there in a full year.

Time had been hard on the place.

Greyish-white paint chipped off the exterior, leaving the boards shabby and dirty. The bushes that lined the front of the house were overgrown and misshapen. Paper cups and other trash disintegrated in the weeds that owned the small front yard. The bay window to the left of the porch that my mother had prized was now covered in dirt and grime, the lace curtains inside yellowed and torn in two places.

The bottom step had all but fallen in completely now, and I stepped over it to walk up to the small porch.

Guilt still twisted in my stomach. I should have taken better care of this place, but money was tight, and I needed every dime to pay for school.

The deed was still in my mother's name. Without a death

certificate or any idea where she was or if she was okay, there was nothing else to do with the house than just leave it to rot away. Looking at it now, I realized I should have made it more of a priority to pay someone to take care of the place.

Mom had loved this house. She'd fought so hard to pay for it and keep it, saying how proud she was when she'd finally been able to pay it off. And it had been a very rare thing to see my mother excited about anything.

She was such a loser, always numbed by drugs and alcohol.

But the day she closed on this house, she'd been completely sober. I still remembered her blue eyes being so bright, they almost sparkled.

She'd been happy.

At the time, I'd resented this stupid house. Yes, it was nice to get out of cramped apartments and not have to move around every few months. But at the same time, she had never once looked at me with the same pride and happiness. She'd rarely ever smiled at me, much less been happy about having me in her life. I was nothing but a nuisance to her my whole life, and she never let me forget it.

The leaves had just recently begun to change and fall, and they covered the small front porch entirely in orange and red and brown. They crackled under my feet.

The porch itself seemed to be holding up all right except for one area in the front corner that had collapsed, the boards sunken.

I sat down in the old swing hanging from the ceiling of the porch. I must have come out here a thousand times when I was younger and needed to get out of the house, so I didn't have to stare at her zombie eyes. Sometimes, the house had felt like a tomb. It often felt as if my mother was already dead. She was just waiting for her body to follow her to the grave, so she'd entombed herself inside this house.

I still wasn't sure how she had gotten the money to buy the place outright. It hadn't seemed that strange when I was little, but back then I didn't understand how money and loans worked. I just knew that one day we were worried about getting evicted from yet another apartment and the next, we were moving into this place, and Mom never mentioned needing to leave. She'd promised me we'd never have to move again.

And yet she had left. Three years ago, I had come home to find the entire place empty, as if she had packed up and moved again. Only, this time, she had forgotten to take me with her.

I stood and stilled the swing. The old memories here were already pulling me into their sadness. What was I even doing here?

I shook my head and looked around. Was I hoping to find some kind of answers here? Some kind of proof that Rend had been right about who I am and where I came from?

The front door was locked.

I stretched up and searched for the spare key above the door frame. It was still there after all this time. Probably, no one had even touched it since the last time I had come here to sulk.

I opened the door and put the key back where I'd found it.

"Hello?" I called into the house. I didn't even know why I said it. It was obvious no one had been in here in a long time, but I guess I just wanted to be sure.

Some stupid part of me imagined the furniture she'd sold off in the months before her disappearance would be back, set up just like it used to be. She'd be sitting there on the old flower-patterned couch smoking a joint, and in one of her better moods. I could picture it now as if it were real.

"About time you brought your lazy ass home," she'd have said. "Get into the kitchen and make us some dinner. I'm starving."

The very idea that I thought of this as a fond memory was so incredibly fucked up that I wanted to punch the wall. She had been a terrible mother, and if she was dead, the world was better for it.

But even as the thought came into my head, I knew it wasn't true. There were times when I had seen the light in my mother's eyes. Times when I had so desperately wanted to believe she loved me.

I realized then why I had come all this way. Why I had come back to this house of horrors.

I wanted to feel close to my mother. I had somehow believed that being back here, in her house, would allow me to see the truth. Was she really dead? Or had Fallon been lying just to upset me?

My eyes filled with tears, and for the first time in three years, I let them fall.

There was no one here to see me or judge me. I was alone with my memories and my pain.

I wiped the wetness off my cheek and walked into the empty living room.

Something in the shadows caught my eye, and I sniffed, then walked over to it, crouching to get a better look.

With a trembling hand, I reached for it, taking it between my fingers and twirling it around with wonder.

A single black feather.

Rend had been telling me the truth.

WHY HADN'T HE?

I stayed at my mother's house for a few hours, wandering around the empty rooms and looking for any clues that she had been here recently.

I kept the black feather in my pocket, convinced it was one of hers.

I thought of the dream I'd had and the flutter of wings in the alley the other night after I'd followed someone who looked like her out into the darkness. My mind raced ahead, trying to make sense of all the questions running through it.

Was my mother dead? Or had she been at Venom the other night?

But if that was her, why would she have turned herself into a crow and left me there with those other demons? It didn't make sense. Just because she didn't want to be around me anymore didn't mean she would willingly lead me to my death. I refused to believe that.

If it wasn't her, though, who could it have been?

Lyla and the other dancers used glamours to make themselves look younger and more beautiful. Did that mean they could make themselves look like another person?

Anything might be possible in this new world, which made it even more difficult to figure out what was really going on around me.

Then there was Rend.

There was no denying the way my body reacted to him, but I would be lying to say there wasn't more to it than that. I thought he had felt it, too, but just when we'd started to give in to our desires, he had pulled away as if I disgusted him.

I would be smart to stay away from him, but even the thought of him now made my whole body flush with warmth. It was dangerous to be around him, but dangerous to stay away. I was trapped.

I needed him in a hundred different ways.

Which was exactly why I needed to stay away from him until I could get this need under control. I would stay home and go about my normal life as best I could until I'd somehow managed to put some emotional distance between us.

I just had to hope Fallon and the Devil wouldn't come after me before that happened.

With a plan in place, I closed up my mother's house and headed back home on the train. I was looking forward to seeing Katy, even if I couldn't tell her everything that had been going on.

But Katy wasn't home.

Disappointment flooded through me. I could really use a friend right now, and the last thing I needed was to be alone.

She'd left a note on the whiteboard we'd mounted on the back of the door.

Sorry we keep missing each other. Derek's home this

weekend so going to stay with my parents for a few days. Hugs, Katy.

I sat down at the kitchen table where my open books were still waiting for me. Derek was Katy's older brother. He was two years older than she and was working on his law degree at Columbia. She didn't get to see him much, so whenever he came home, she usually went to stay with her parents in Highland Park for a few days, only coming back to campus for class.

Suddenly the thought of Rend's safe house in the mountains didn't sound so bad. I told myself I wasn't scared to be alone here all night, but I was lying to myself. I was terrified.

The Devil, whoever he was, had known about me before I even knew demons existed. I was fairly certain he was the one who had sent me those flowers, which meant he knew where I lived. What was stopping him from coming in here right now and killing me?

I rested my head in my hands.

So why hadn't he?

My brain worked through the problem, putting a question to his actions for the first time.

If he wanted to kill me so badly, why invite me to a club where I would be introduced to an entire world of people just like me? People who despised him. And most of all, why introduce me to someone like Rend when he was offering the only protection a girl like me could find?

It didn't make sense.

What kind of game was the Devil playing?

If he'd wanted me so badly, he could have come in and taken me without a powerful guy like Rend ever knowing about it. Or about me.

I stared at my homework and sighed. There was no way I

was getting this done tonight. Even if I wasn't completely exhausted, I couldn't get my mind off the events of the past few days. What I needed was sleep. I would have to ask my professor for an extension on the homework. I'd tell him I had a family emergency or something, which was actually somewhat close to the truth.

I closed the book with a thud, then headed back to my bedroom.

I stripped off my work clothes and went to grab my discarded PJ's from this morning when my eyes landed on the white dress shirt I'd laid across my chair.

Rend's shirt.

I knew I should have it cleaned and taken back to him, but right now, I wanted to curl up in it and fall asleep. I wanted a reminder that even if I was alone here tonight, no matter what his motivation for doing it, Rend was watching out for me. He wanted to keep me safe.

I pulled the shirt on, breathing in the lingering scent of his cologne and wishing he were here with me now.

I left the bedside-lamp on—something I hadn't done since I was a little girl—and crawled into bed.

INVITE ME IN

I am back in the hall of doorways. The sound of flapping wings ahead draws my attention, but I can't see anything in the darkness. I lift my palm and concentrate on creating light. It takes a few tries, but after a few minutes, a small spark of light forms, allowing me to see a few feet in front of me.

"Come to me, little bird," a voice says in a whisper.

"Mom?"

I move forward, glancing at each doorway until I'm standing in front of the one with a crow carved into its surface. I raise my free hand to the carving, letting my fingers slide over the bumps and ridges of it.

Slowly, I reach for the doorknob with a trembling hand.

RAIN PELTED the window and a tree branch squeaked across the glass, ripping me from sleep.

Sweat soaked the back of my neck and my breath came in short gasps.

I brought my knees to my chest and rubbed my eyes with weary hands. I glanced at the clock. Four in the morning.

I'd been dreaming of the door again, following my mother. She'd been leading me to that door. I needed to know what was behind it.

I knew Rend didn't want me going through the crow's door until we had some idea of what was behind it, but what if my mother was there? What if she could give me some of the answers I'd been looking for? What if she could keep me safe?

In my sleep I had tossed the covers off my body, and I stood to straighten them. I thought about getting back into bed and trying to get more sleep, but I'd been locked in the dream of that door for the past several hours.

I needed a break.

I carried a blanket out to the couch and walked to the fridge to get a glass of water, but a feeling seized me as I passed by the large window facing the street.

Someone is out there.

My heart skipped a beat, and I forced a deep breath. Weak-kneed, I went to the window and stared out into the storm.

Rain poured hard, and wind whipped the trees from side to side.

Cars zoomed by, their lights illuminating the sidewalk as they passed.

That's when I saw him.

Rend stood in the shadow of a large oak tree near the street, his black hooded sweatshirt soaked through from the rain. I couldn't see his face, but I knew it was him.

How long had he been down there?

I stepped away from the window and leaned against the arm of the couch for support. I wasn't sure my legs could hold me.

This was his solution? If I wouldn't come to the club, he would stand guard all night outside my apartment? In the pouring rain?

I knew my life was in danger, but what I still couldn't wrap my head around was why my life was so important to anyone.

Especially Rend.

If my blood was so valuable to the Devil, why not let him have me? Wouldn't that be easier on everyone?

I paced the floor in front of the window, anger giving me the strength to walk again.

Was he really going to just stand out there all night?

I contemplated just going back into my room and going to bed as if I hadn't seen him. Let him stay out there, miserable and uncomfortable all night. Why should I care? It's not like I asked him to protect me.

But I already knew I couldn't let this go.

I couldn't live my life under his constant supervision.

I'd told him I needed space and that I'd come back when I felt like it. How dare he show up here like this?

I had to put a stop to this now. I had to let him know I had my boundaries and that I needed him to respect that.

I threw open my door and stomped down the three flights of stairs to the front entrance of my building. I stepped out into the night, rain soaking my hair and clothes in seconds. I shivered as the wind picked up. It was still late summer, but the cold rain made it feel like fall.

My eyes struggled to find him out here in the dark. Oak

trees lined this entire street, and I couldn't figure out which one he'd been hiding behind.

As if he knew I was searching for him, Rend stepped around the tree and leaned against it, one leg propped up behind him.

I marched over to him, ready to battle to the death about this if that was what it took. He needed to understand that just because he was bigger and more powerful than I was, he couldn't just take over my life without asking me. Danger or not, I still needed to be in control of my own choices.

"What the hell are you doing out here?" I asked. I could hardly see through the rain. It pelted my face with thick drops that landed, then slid down my cheeks.

Even in the dim light of the street lamp, I couldn't see his eyes underneath that hood. His body position was so casual, so utterly unconcerned, that it just pissed me off more.

"I wake up in the middle of the night to find you lurking outside my apartment like some stalker." I placed a hand on my hip. "You'd better start explaining yourself. And take that stupid hood off."

I had to shout to be heard over the storm.

He slowly pulled the hood back from his face, and I sucked in a breath. God, he was gorgeous. Every time I saw him, he took my breath away.

I hated him for it.

"It's the only way I could be sure you would be safe."

I tensed and drew my hands into fists. "So, what? You're just going to stand out here every night for the rest of my life?"

"I'll do whatever it takes," he said.

"Right." I nodded. "And you do this for all your employees?"

"Of course not."

"Then what makes me so special that I get the privilege of your company twenty-four-seven?"

"First of all, you have no idea how to take care of yourself."

Anger pulsed through me.

"Don't even go there," I shouted. "I have been taking care of myself since I was five years old."

"Not against people like him."

"No, but from what I can tell, Azure and most of the staff there at Venom wouldn't be able to protect themselves against him. Even you had fear in your eyes when you were talking about him."

Rend pushed against the tree and moved a step closer. I took one step back.

"Just because I'm afraid of him doesn't mean I couldn't destroy him if I wanted to," he said.

"You're saying that's what you would do? If he showed up here tonight, right now? That's what you would do? You would risk your own life for me?"

He stepped toward me, and I backed away. My foot caught on the edge of the sidewalk, and I fell. Rend's form blurred, and his arms wrapped around me, pulling me to him.

Breathless, I stared up at him, rain falling from him onto me as he held me. "How did you do that?" I asked. "How did you move that fast?"

"I told you, there are so many things about this world you cannot even begin to comprehend." He stared down into my eyes and I was glad he was holding me because my entire body turned to liquid. "You shouldn't be out here in the rain like this."

I cursed my body for shivering against him, but the wind

had picked up and I was soaked through.

"I needed to talk to you," I said.

"We could talk inside," he said, glancing up at the apartment building.

He lifted me and set me back on my feet, but he didn't remove his arms from around me.

"I'm not inviting you up," I said.

He lifted his chin, his lips pressed tight. "You're infuriating, you know that?"

"Only because you make me that way," I said. "And you didn't answer my question."

"We can talk about it tomorrow. You're going to get sick if you stay out here."

"No, we need to talk about this right now," I said. I knew I should push away from him. My brain didn't work when he was this close. But the warmth of his body felt so incredible, I couldn't force myself away.

"Yes," he said. His eyes moving over my face. "I would risk my life for you."

My heart stopped for a moment and time stood still. Logically, I knew he didn't mean that he cared about me. I knew he had sworn to protect everyone who worked for him.

But there was something in his eyes that defied logic.

"Why?" I asked, my breath barely a whisper in the wind.

Against my hands, his chest rose and fell in short breaths.

"Why am I worth so much to you?" I felt the door inside my heart opening to him again, and even though a part of me wanted to slam it closed, there was a part of me that still hoped we could be something more. I realized I wasn't ready to give up on that hope just yet. "You barely know me. Why take this risk for me?"

I swallowed. I was scared to go any further into this conversation.

He didn't say anything, but I could feel his heart beating fast against the palm of my hand.

"I've tried to make sense of this in my mind ever since you kissed me earlier," I said, unable to stop myself. "It feels like there could be something between us. Something real that goes beyond you agreeing to protect me because I work for you. But every time you get close to me, you pull away, and I don't know what to believe anymore. Have I imagined this? Do you want me? Or are you just playing some kind of game with my heart?"

He was quiet for a long moment as my heart thundered against my chest. His jaw tensed, and his fingers curled into the skin on my back, drawing the shirt into his fist. His lips parted, but then he shook his head, as if there was a war going on inside of him.

He let out a breath and gripped my arm tighter. "Dammit, Franki," he said. "I don't want to feel this way about you. I wish I could stand here and tell you that was all you meant to me. I wish I could say you are nothing more than an employee."

Thunder boomed in the distance and a car passed beside us, the lights landing on the tortured expression of his face.

"I want you, but I can't afford to take sides. I'm supposed to be the neutral party, providing a place for those on both sides to come and talk things out and make deals. I don't take sides," he said. "I can't take sides."

He released me, both hands coming completely off my body as he stepped away and turned his back to me.

I wrapped my arms around myself, feeling that this was

the end. This is where the awful truth would come out. I would not let it break me.

"I can protect my employees against most of the evil that's out there, but with the Devil, things are different," he said. "I can't explain it to you now, but choosing you over him would mean choosing sides. It would mean getting involved in a war I've worked hard to stay out of."

He ran a shaking hand through his hair and leaned forward against the tree. He stood there for a long moment, his body as still and rigid as a statue.

Then, he turned back to me, his eyes finding mine even in the darkness of the night.

He shook his head again, then walked with sure steps to me.

My hands dropped to my side, and I looked up as he took my face in his hands.

"Fuck it," he said. "You're worth it."

He claimed my mouth with his, tasting of rain and licorice. His kisses were rough and unrelenting, and as my lips opened to him, he moved his hands down my neck and arms and around to my back. He gripped my shirt in his hands and pulled me to him with such force, it took my breath away.

I yielded to him, my heart split wide open by the passion in his touch.

"Invite me in," he said, finally pulling away. His words were tortured, as if he couldn't bear taking the moments from my lips to speak them. "Unless you want me to do this in front of all your neighbors."

I nodded, my arms circling around his neck and my body heating at the thought of what he meant by *this*.

"Say it," he said, his forehead pressed against mine. "I need you to say it. I need to know you want this as much as I do."

"Take me inside," I said, barely able to recognize my own voice.

He lifted me into his arms and carried me up the stairs into my building. He took the steps two at a time, all the way to the third floor, finding my door without ever taking his eyes from my face.

I had left the door unlocked. He threw it open and carried me across the threshold, then kicked it closed.

He kissed me again as soon as we were inside, the sound of his moans making me yearn for his hands on my body. The room was quiet after being out in the storm. The only sounds were our heavy breaths and the pounding of our hearts.

He set my feet on the floor but didn't take his hands from my body. They moved to my hips, pulling me tighter against him. He pushed me backward until my back hit the edge of the kitchen table.

"You are so beautiful," he said. His voice was rough and filled with longing. "I have wanted you from the moment I saw you beating up those vampires in the alley."

My skin was freezing from the rain and every time his hand brushed against the skin underneath the shirt, I trembled with fear and desire. The thought of his hands exploring every inch of my bare skin sent waves of longing through me, warmth growing between my thighs.

Impatient, I reached for the zipper on his sweatshirt, pulling it down and pushing it from his shoulders. Underneath, he was wearing a black t-shirt that clung to his body, every ridge of his muscles defined and hard beneath the thin fabric. Drops of water fell to the floor all around , and his skin glistened with rain. He lifted the shirt from his body in one

swift motion, then reached for the bottom of my shirt—his shirt
—and ripped it open, buttons flying.

His strong hands burned against the cold skin of my waist
as he pulled my black leggings down. I stepped out of them,
completely naked and vulnerable before him. In the back of
my mind, warning bells went off, telling me my heart couldn't
come back from this. My soul tried to warn me that all those
walls I'd spent years carefully constructing around myself
were being ripped down with every touch of his lips against
mine.

But I refused to listen.

I didn't care about tomorrow. All I cared about was right
now. This moment. And all I wanted was to feel him against
me. Inside me.

My hands reached for the belt at his waist and his stomach
rippled at the touch of my skin against his. He moaned and
kissed me harder as I pulled his belt from his jeans.

His hands explored my naked skin, leaving a trail of heat in
their wake. I shuddered against him as he leaned over me, our
bare chests pressed tightly against each other.

Rend kissed me, then moved his mouth across my cheek
and down toward my shoulder. He pushed the white shirt
down, exposing the skin at the base of my neck. Just as I had
earlier at his house, I lifted my chin, giving him complete
access. Wanting him more than ever.

His lips brushed against my sensitive skin, and I shivered,
digging my fingers into his biceps.

His body went rigid, and he let out a low growl. The sound
sent a wave of fear through me. His mouth opened against my
skin and two sharp points dug into me, breaking the skin as I
cried out in pain.

I jerked away from him, but he held me down against the top of the table, his strength too much for me. He seemed to be frozen in place as desire and fear waged war inside my core. What was happening to him?

Finally, he wrenched himself away from me, a loud groan escaping as he moved quickly across the room, his form nothing more than a blur of shadows.

I sat up and pulled what was left of the white dress shirt tight around my trembling form.

"Rend?" My voice wavered. I stood and backed as far as I could against the wall, my arms wrapped around myself like a bandage. Warm blood trickled from the small wounds at my neck, and I knew what he was. I knew it, but I didn't want to believe it.

I shook my head, unable to stop the tears from falling down my cheeks.

Rend stood beside the window, his hand gripping the wooden frame with such power it had partially crumbled in his hand. His back rose and fell with each deep, rapid breath.

"I thought I could control it," he finally said, his voice tense and filled with darkness. "This is why I'm dangerous for you, Franki."

I yearned for him and feared him in that moment, body and soul surrendered to a man I could never have. The pain of it split me in two as my body shivered against the wall of my small apartment.

"This is why we can never be together," he said.

He turned to me then, his face cloaked in shadow, but enough light coming through the window for me to see two white fangs protruding from his mouth, my red blood smeared across his lips.

EPISODE FOUR

THE DYING

HEARTSICK

Rend wiped the blood from his lips.

My blood.

But he couldn't wipe the hunger from his eyes. Hunger I had stupidly mistaken for something entirely different. His chest rose and fell with each labored breath, and I wondered what kind of self-control he still had at this point. Was I in danger?

I clutched the torn shirt that covered my body, pulling it tighter across my cold skin. I pressed my back against the wall of my small campus apartment, desperately trying to make sense of what had just happened.

I was torn between an intense desire for him and an even more intense desire to get the fuck out of dodge.

At my neck, blood pulsed and dripped from two small wounds. My skin throbbed. His teeth had barely punctured the surface, but it was enough to rip us apart.

"Why didn't you tell me you were one of them?" I asked. I could hear the judgment in my own tone, but I knew what I was feeling was less about hating what he was, and more about hating that he'd lied about it.

"I'm not one of them," he said. His voice was grating and rough, low, like an animal's growl.

A piece of the wooden frame of the window crumbled and fell to the floor at his feet. He released his hold on the wood and moved away.

I flinched and pushed back against the wall, realizing, with sudden terror, there was nowhere else to go. If he wanted to kill me there would be nothing I could do to stop him.

Rend took a couple of steps toward me, but when I flinched, he stopped cold. His forehead wrinkled with tension, and he swallowed hard. "You're afraid of me," he said, disgust dripping from his tone.

"You just grew fangs and bit me," I said. "Is there some other reaction I should be having right now?"

"Dammit, Franki, don't make jokes right now," he growled. "You don't understand."

"I understand perfectly," I said, lifting my eyes to his. "You lied to me about everything. About keeping me safe. About wanting to protect me. You lied about who you are."

Even as I said those words, I knew I was holding back the one thing that hurt most.

He had lied about wanting me.

I thought he wanted me the same way I wanted him. I believed there was something real between us. Something special. I thought there was true passion in the way he kissed me.

But the whole time, he wanted the same thing those three vampires in the alley behind his club had wanted. He wasn't attracted to me.

He was attracted to my blood.

I was disgusted and heartsick. I very rarely let myself be vulnerable around men—or anyone, really—and I felt stupid for letting down my guard around him.

He hadn't killed me, but he may as well have. I wanted him so badly, and to bring me so close and then take it all away was cruel.

"You should go," I said. It came out timid and weak. Just seconds ago, the last thing in the world I wanted was to be apart from him.

Now, I couldn't send him away fast enough.

"We need to talk about this," he said, taking two steps toward me. "You have to listen to me."

"I don't have to do anything," I said. My eyes flashed with anger, and he stopped moving. I welcomed the anger. Embraced it. The more I embraced the anger, the faster the heartache part of it descended into the darkness. "I want you to get the hell out of here."

Rend's eyes darkened to a deep pool of blackness.

My legs grew weak, and I had to lean against the wall for support. My heart thundered in my chest.

"Go," I said again, this time with less conviction and more fear.

Rend's hand closed into a tight fist. His jaw tensed as he slammed his fist into the wall, leaving a huge hole. He lifted the side table into the air, and threw it to the ground with such force the floor beneath my feet vibrated.

Then, in an instant, he crossed the room to me. His body pressed against mine, crushing me against the wall.

He brought a hand to my throat and used one finger to turn my head to the side. My bleeding neck was completely exposed to him, and in that moment, I was certain this was the end.

He leaned in close, his breath hot against my cheek.

"I didn't ask for any of this," he said. "I am not one of them, Franki. Not anymore."

I closed my eyes and waited, trembling. My body betrayed me by responding with desire instead of terror. Part of me understood, even then, that desire was a million times more dangerous.

"Please," I said in the tiniest whisper. A single tear slid down my cheek and onto his hand. "Please go."

Rend released his hold on my throat and ran his index finger softly along my skin, tracing the path of my tear. I opened my eyes and met his black stare.

"I'm sorry," he said. He shook his head and backed away. "I'm so sorry, Franki."

For a long moment, our eyes locked together in mutual regret and sorrow.

Rend looked away first, his gaze dropping to the floor. He opened his mouth as if to say something more, but then he shook his head and backed away. His body disintegrated into shadow. One minute he was whole and human, and the next, he was nothing more than a cloud of black smoke that hovered for only a moment before slipping through the crack under my door.

I slid down the wall until I hit the floor. I rested my head on bent knees, hugging them so tightly I could hardly breathe. I wanted nothing more than to rewind the night. I should have been more careful. I should have protected myself better.

Not from vampires or demons or even the Devil himself.

I should have protected myself from love.

STOP TRYING TO GUESS

"Franki?"

Katy shook my arm. I opened my eyes and found her standing above me, concern etched on her face.

"Are you all right?" she asked, an edge of panic in her voice. "What the hell happened?"

Oh, shit.

My eyes opened wider and I looked around, seeing the apartment and my torn clothes the way Katy must be seeing it. Our side table was smashed, my books were all over the floor, and there was dried blood all over my shirt and neck.

How the hell was I going to explain this? I sucked at lying, and I couldn't even begin to think of a good enough explanation for this. One that didn't sound insane.

Even the truth sounded insane.

I reached for her hand and she pulled me to my feet. I put my arms around her and hugged her as tightly as I could. "I need to tell you something, but you have to promise me you won't have me committed to an asylum."

Katy pulled away and narrowed her eyes at me. "You're seriously scaring me here," she said. "First, you don't come home from work. You don't call or text me to say what's up. Now, I come home to find you curled up asleep on the floor, wearing a ripped blood-stained shirt? This isn't like you at all, Franki."

"I know," I said. "I've had some serious shit going on the past few days. I promise I'll explain everything, but can you make a pot of coffee first, while I get cleaned up?"

"Are you on drugs or something?" she asked. Her entire body was tense.

"I wish," I muttered.

Her eyes flashed wide, and I shook my head.

"No, okay? I'm not on drugs. I don't want to be on drugs. I don't plan to do drugs," I said. "Just do me a favor and stop trying to guess or figure out what's going on, because trust me, you'll never in a million years guess this."

"Franki—"

"Coffee," I said, stepping around her and making my way to the bathroom. If I was really going to attempt to make enough sense of all this to explain it to her, I was going to need that coffee. And I had to get out of this stupid shirt.

I grabbed a clean washcloth from under the sink and ran the water until it got steaming hot. I carefully wiped the dried blood from my neck, then stared at the two small puncture-wounds. They looked exactly like what you'd expect a vampire bite to look like.

I must have seen more than a dozen vampire movies in my life, but not once had I ever believed they could really exist.

Even being attacked by those three in the alley hadn't made it feel as real as seeing the actual marks on my skin.

Rend is a vampire.

The thought brought on a wave of nausea. I gripped the edge of the sink and took several deep breaths. How could I have missed the fact that he was different?

I hadn't, though. Not completely. I'd caught the references to Rend being older than your average human. I'd seen the strange drawings in his office and known he was capable of great magic.

The truth was I hadn't allowed myself to put two-and-two together. I let my desire for him cloud my ability to care about anything else.

The hot water running in the sink had steamed up the mirror. I wiped a section clear and looked at myself in the mirror again. I brought my fingers up to the small teeth marks.

No matter how much I wanted him, there was no denying this. He had hurt me. Yes, it could have been much worse, but wasn't this bad enough? The one person I'd been trusting to keep me safe was the most dangerous person on the planet. I'd let my guard down around him, and that was just about worse than anything else. I'd let him into my heart in ways I'd never let a man in before.

I couldn't let it happen again.

"Franki?" Katy knocked on the door to the bathroom. "You can't seriously be making me wait to hear this. Are you sure you're okay?"

I cleared my throat and turned off the water.

"I'll be okay," I said. I rummaged in my makeup bag for a Band-Aid and placed it over the marks on my neck. She was going to think I was crazy, but I knew I had to tell her the truth. Lying to someone I cared about right now would make me the worst kind of hypocrite.

"The coffee's almost ready," Katy said.

"I'll be out in a second," I said.

I waited until I heard her walk back toward the kitchen before I slipped out of the bathroom and into my bedroom. I undressed quickly, shedding my bloodied clothes and pulling on a pair of sweat pants and a tank top.

I picked Rend's white shirt off the floor, thinking how I'd worn it last night to find comfort and feel close to him. And how, less than twelve hours later, I wasn't sure if I ever wanted to see him again.

I wadded the shirt up and tossed it into the trashcan under my desk.

I took another deep breath, then made my way out to have coffee with my best friend and tell her about how I'd almost been killed by vampires.

NOT EVER

Katy sat across from me, her mouth open.

She hadn't said a word in the past half hour and she hadn't taken so much as a sip of her coffee. Mostly, she just stared at me, listening in awe.

Or horror.

I wasn't sure which.

"When he left, I must have sat on the floor until I finally fell asleep," I said, coming to the end of my story. I'd told her almost everything, from the vampires in the alley to Fallon's threat and Rend's visit last night.

I bit my lip and waited for her to react. Tell me I was crazy. Something.

Instead, she sat still, her hands gripping her favorite Eiffel Tower coffee mug.

"Katy, say something. Please."

She took a deep breath in and raised her eyebrows. "Are you going to see him again?"

I pressed my hand against my forehead. "Wait, you heard all that and this is the burning question on your mind?"

Maybe she was the crazy one here.

"Franki, do you seriously think I haven't always known there was something different about you?" she asked in a soft voice. She placed her hand on mine and squeezed. "We've been friends for as long as I can remember. I notice things like unexplained gusts of wind when you get angry or the way you flinch every time someone uses the word witch."

I shook my head. "Why didn't you ever say anything?"

She shrugged and released my hand, finally taking a sip of her coffee. She stuck her tongue out and made a face. "Yuck, this is cold."

She stood up, dumped her cup out in the sink, and poured a fresh one.

"I'm serious," I said. "You're telling me you've known all this time I was a witch and you never once asked me about it or confronted me about it?"

"It was obvious you were sensitive about it," she said. "The same way I almost never ask you about your mom. It's just not important if it's going to hurt you to talk about it."

I ran a hand through my knotted hair. "Great. So, I'm the last one to find out who I really am," I mumbled. "Next, you'll be telling me you knew vampires were real."

She shrugged again. "It's not like I've ever met one before, but I guess I'm not really that surprised. There're all kinds of weird shit going on in the world that we never even hear about," she said. "And I'm definitely not surprised there's crazy shit going on at Venom. That place is definitely the kind of place where vampires would hang out."

I laughed and threw my arms around her neck. "Thank you," I said.

"For what?"

"For making me feel a little bit less crazy," I said. "I thought you were going to have me committed."

She smiled and went back to sit down on the barstool. "Oh, I still think you're crazy," she said. "I just don't think that's any different from any other day."

I rolled my eyes and opened the fridge. "I'm going to make eggs and bacon," I said. "Are you hungry?"

"Starving," she said. "But you still haven't answered my question."

My stomach flipped over. I grabbed the eggs and butter and set them down on the counter next to the stove.

I hadn't answered her partly because I had no idea what to say. Was I ever going to see Rend again? Should I go back to the club? Or just go back to my life before Venom?

As if I could.

"You really care about this guy, don't you?"

I groaned and put my hands over my face. "Is it that obvious?"

"As long as I've known you, I've never seen you this twisted up over someone," she said. "It just sucks he's a vampire."

I laughed, but kind of wanted to cry at the same time. "Yes. Yes it does." I cracked the eggs into a bowl and poured a little bit of milk inside. "The thing is, I honestly wasn't as hurt by the fact that he'd tried to kill me as I was by the fact that he lied to me."

"Did he ever tell you he wasn't a vampire?"

"Well, no, but leaving it out is just as bad, right?"

Katy leaned over the counter. "It's not exactly a lie," she said. "It's just not telling the whole truth. You can't expect a guy to confess his deepest, darkest secrets to you the second you meet."

"I can if it's a secret that could put me in danger."

She nodded. "Maybe."

My eyes widened, and I put a hand on my hip. "Are you taking his side, here?"

Katy held her hands up in defense. "Hey, you know I'm always on your side," she said. "I'm just saying that it sounds to me as if he's been risking a lot to keep you safe. I don't think he would intentionally turn around and put you in danger."

"What does that even mean? If he's a vampire, he should have known he was putting me in danger by even coming up here."

"Not necessarily," she said. "Hear me out. The girls at the club were quick to tell you Rend was off-limits, right? They probably all already know what he is and what he's capable of when he loses control. Only, the thing is, he doesn't normally lose control. He's usually the poster-child for control, am I right?"

I shrugged and turned back to the scrambled eggs.

"He's probably off-limits to most of the women there because he refuses to allow himself to lose control," she said. "Only, he couldn't resist you, and he went too far."

Her words sparked the most annoying little feeling of hope deep inside of me.

Part of me desperately wanted to believe that I was nothing special to him. Everything would be so much easier—for both of us—if he saw me as just another witch with delicious blood running through her veins. It was better if I could make myself believe he didn't care for me. If I could just stay angry with him, my heart was safe.

But hope had sparked, and I knew there was nothing I could do to kill it now.

"Couldn't resist me?" I asked. "Or just couldn't resist my blood?"

She rolled her eyes and made a clicking sound with her tongue. "How many witches does he work with on a daily basis? How many witches come in and out of that bar every single night? Hundreds? He's surrounded by the scent of powerful blood every day of his life and somehow, he manages to maintain control. If there wasn't something different about you, he wouldn't have had any trouble resisting you."

I shook my head and sighed. "Maybe I'm different some other way, you know? Maybe my blood is just more potent or something? Why else would this other guy—the Devil—be after me?"

Katy bit her lip. "I don't know for sure, but he scares me a lot more than Rend does," she said. "And you've never seen him?"

"No, just his lackey or whatever you would call him," I said. "Rend said the Devil isn't allowed in his club at all."

I scooped the finished eggs into a large bowl and doused them in salt. My mind was spinning. I definitely wasn't expecting Katy to believe me so easily, much less start applying her typical logic to the situation.

"You have to go back there," she said, sneaking a piece of bacon from the plate I'd set on the counter.

"What? Why?"

"Because, regardless of what happened between you and Rend last night, he's still your best chance of surviving whatever this other guy has planned for you," she said. "Plus, you have way too many questions to turn your back on that world so fast."

I leaned against the counter and nodded. She was right. Life as I knew it was over forever. There was no more denying who—or what—I was. Turning my back on Venom was the same as turning my back on myself. I knew Venom was my best chance at really figuring out who I was and where I came from. I had way too many questions to walk away now.

"What would I do without you?" I asked her, taking a piece of bacon for myself.

Katy smiled and looked up toward the ceiling. "I don't know. Probably make all the wrong decisions and end up an old maid who never got it on with a hot vampire."

I threw the rest of my bacon at her, hitting her squarely on the nose. "I did not get it on with a vampire," I protested.

She laughed and picked up the thrown bacon. She tossed it into her mouth. "Not yet," she said.

"Not ever," I mumbled, turning back to grab two plates from the cupboard.

Still, despite my protests, my stomach fluttered.

"I'll go back," I said. "But only because I need answers."

My fingertips traced the outline of the Band-Aid on my neck, and I shivered at the thought of someday finishing what Rend and I had started last night.

Would I be so lucky next time? Would I even survive a next time?

I closed my eyes and started the grueling work of cleaning up the mess we'd made of the apartment. Deep inside, I started the more taxing work of rebuilding the wall around my heart. The one Rend had managed to destroy with a single kiss.

EXTREME RESTRAINT

I stood in the drizzling rain outside Venom for a few minutes before going inside.

I felt like the second everyone saw me, they would know. My feelings for Rend would show on my face, and they would all feel sorry for me.

Poor girl. We told her he was off-limits. She really believed she was special.

How humiliating.

And worse than the humiliation of it all, was to be so close to Rend and know I could never be with him. It was going to be torture.

I almost turned around and ran back to the 'L', but I was determined to be strong. Let them laugh. I deserved it for believing there was something real between us when everyone had warned me against it.

I didn't care what Katy said. To Rend, I was just another tasty witch. He'd gotten too close and had shown his true nature. End of story. I had to believe that, if I was going to make it through my shift tonight.

A tap on my shoulder made me nearly jump out of my skin. I looked over to see Lyla waving and smiling. My hand flew to my heart.

"You scared me to death," I said.

"I'm sorry," she said. "I was walking by and saw you standing here like a zombie. Are you coming in? How are you feeling?"

"Yeah. I was totally zoned out there for a second," I said, laughing it off. "I didn't get much sleep last night."

"I wasn't even expecting to see you here tonight at all," she said as we made our way across the street to the club's entrance. "Rend told us you got sick last night and might not be in for a while."

"He did?" I shouldn't have been surprised. Of course, he would have some kind of explanation ready for when I disappeared and never came back.

But until now, I hadn't really considered his reaction when he saw me tonight. I'd been thinking so much about what I wanted to do that I hadn't even thought about what Rend might want. What if he kicked me out and told me he never wanted to see me again?

"Maybe I should go home," I said, turning back toward the train. "If Rend isn't expecting me in tonight—"

Lyla grabbed my arm and pulled me back toward the club's entrance. "Oh, hush. He'll be so glad you're here," she said. "I know I am. We could really use the extra help now that Amber's been flaking out on us."

"I thought she's only been gone a couple nights?"

Lyla shrugged. "Yeah, but even two nights is too many," she said. "I haven't had a night off in at least five years."

"You're here every night?" I asked. "Like, always?"

"Of course," she said. "Everyone's here every night. Once you start working here, it becomes home, in a way."

I had never heard anyone say they didn't get a night off from their job every once in a while. The club was fun, but it wasn't easy being on your feet every night, having to always be on for the crowd.

Selena, the bouncer, said hey to us as we walked in, but her eyes lingered on me. I thought I detected a hint of anger there, but before I could stop to ask her about it, Lyla pulled me inside.

"Did Rend tell you guys why he hired me?" I asked Lyla as we headed back to the dressing rooms.

"Why do you ask that?" Lyla turned to me and put her hand on my wrist.

"I was just curious to know if he explained why someone who obviously knows almost nothing about your world was given a job here."

She smiled and squeezed my wrist. "Honey, everyone who works here was hired for the same reason."

"What reason is that?"

She twisted her mouth into a frown and shrugged. "We had nowhere else to turn and he was the only one who could save us."

She turned and walked through the black curtain, leaving me to wonder what kind of trouble always led people to him. And why Rend—a vampire—felt it was his job to save them.

To save us.

Back in my apartment, he'd said he was dangerous. But

why would someone so dangerous go to such great lengths to save so many?

"You made it," Azure said from behind me. "I wasn't expecting you in again tonight."

Her disappointment was obvious.

"Well, I'm here," I said.

"Lovely."

I wanted to ask her what her problem was with me, but I already knew. It was obvious she had a thing for Rend. I had no idea if she had ever acted on those feelings or not, but she definitely had feelings for him.

After she'd seen me coming out of his doorway yesterday morning wearing his shirt, she had every right to assume something had happened between us. That was enough to make me the enemy. I couldn't really blame her, because truth be told, if I walked in here tomorrow and saw her wearing his shirt, I'd want to claw her eyes out. Azure was acting with extreme restraint, considering the circumstances.

I wanted to tell her she had nothing to worry about. Rend wasn't interested in me the way I thought, after all, but there was no use explaining it to her or anyone. They would see for themselves soon enough.

I followed Lyla through the black curtain and into the dressing rooms.

"You okay?" Shay asked as she came in the room and nearly ran straight into me.

"She's fine," Lyla called out with a laugh. "Just give her some space. I think she's a little overwhelmed. I found her outside just now, staring at the entrance like she wasn't sure she wanted to come inside."

"Hey, you girls remember how tough the first few nights

were for us, right?" Cherish said. She walked over and put her arms around me with a tight squeeze. "And we had all known about magic and demons and witches for most of our lives. I can't imagine what it must be like for you to find out this world exists, and then get thrown into it all at once."

"You're doing great, hon," Shay said.

"If you need anything, you just let us know," Peri said.

I sat down at the makeup station I'd used yesterday and tugged at the scarf I'd wrapped around my neck before I left the apartment.

"There is one thing you can do," I said.

"Anything," Lyla said.

I swiveled around in my chair and took a deep breath. "Teach me how to do a glamour."

TAPPING INTO IT

The five dancers rushed over and gathered around me.

"I have been dying for you to ask us about this," Shay said. She ran her hand down my straight black hair. "What do you want to look like? Have you given it some thought?"

I squirmed in my chair. I didn't expect them to all come running over like we were at some girly sleepover or something.

"Oh, gosh, I don't know," I said. I studied myself in the mirror. There was really only one thing I wanted to get rid of—two bite marks on my neck. But, I knew I'd better come up with something more creative. "I was thinking about making my eyes green instead of blue for a change. Maybe wearing something to match?"

"Yes," Lyla said. She actually giggled with excitement. "I know the perfect outfit."

She went over to the rack of clothes and pulled out a little green... I honestly don't even know what to call it. It was like a silky one-piece leotard with a slit running all the way up the front.

I swallowed, my palms growing sweaty.

"I might need an entirely new body to pull that off."

Lyla rolled her eyes. "Pshh. You're perfect," she said. "Besides, you wear it with this."

She held up a small black sequined bandeau top that didn't make me feel one bit better.

"Your eyes will be so pretty that color of green," Misty said. She had chosen a bright pink halter top and the world's shortest skirt for herself tonight.

"All you have to do is find a way to connect to the power deep inside yourself," Shay said. She sat down in the chair next to mine and crossed both palms over her heart. She closed her eyes and took several deep breaths. On the third breath, her hair changed from a deep red color to a black as dark as mine. When she opened her eyes, they were exactly the same color of green as the outfit Lyla was holding.

I blew out, releasing the air from my lungs in a moment of pure awe. "Wow, that completely changes the way you look," I said. "But I have no idea how to connect to my power. What does that feel like?"

"It feels like finding your true self," Peri said, coming around to lean against the counter beside me. "Like dipping your fingers into some secret well of magical energy that lives inside you."

I raised an eyebrow. That sounded wonderfully vague. A secret well inside me? How the hell was I supposed to recognize that? Or connect to it?

"I still can't believe your mama didn't teach you all this growing up," Shay said, shaking her head.

"My mom wasn't exactly the nurturing type," I said. I left it at that and hoped they wouldn't bring her up again. I didn't want to get started on just how not-nurturing my mother really was. "Okay, so I close my eyes and breathe in. Then I put my hands on my heart."

"It doesn't have to be your heart," Lyla said. "I usually just place my hands on my legs, palm-up. Just do whatever feels natural and relaxing for you."

I closed my eyes and placed my hands over my heart, but it was hard to concentrate knowing five other girls were staring at me, expecting something magical to happen. I tried to take a few deep breaths but started laughing instead.

"I can't," I said. "Not with you goons watching me like that."

Shay laughed and grabbed my hand. "Here," she said. "Come sit here in the middle of the room. Peri, turn off the lights. Misty, can you give us some mood lighting?"

Shay grabbed a big blanket from a couch in the back of the dressing room and spread it out across the floor. She pointed for me to sit down, so I did, cross-legged with my back straight. Lyla sat across from me and took my hands in hers. She placed them palm-up against my knee, then took a deep breath.

"Breathe with me," she said. "Just like this."

I felt stupid at first, but I was touched at how hard they were all trying to help me understand this type of magic. Peri switched the lights off, throwing the room into complete darkness. A moment later, Misty conjured a very light pink orb of light that she sent up into the air above our heads like a solitary star.

"Close your eyes," Shay whispered. "Try to search for a spark of something deep inside, like a warmth in the distance. An energy. Trust me, you'll recognize it when you feel it."

I sighed, wondering if I'd ever get the hang of this. Lyla nudged me with her knee, and I closed my eyes, determined to give it one more try.

I inhaled, concentrating on the flow of air as it passed into my body and made its way deep down into my lungs and beyond. I focused only on the breath at first, as I had learned to do as such a young girl. Back then, my mother had taught me this technique as a way to control my power and to hold it at bay, not as a way to connect with it and use it.

But as I breathed, I did start to feel a warm energy pulsing in my core. It was like a separate heartbeat alive inside me. I imagined dipping my fingers into that power, tapping into it.

I gasped as the energy blossomed, expanding from that single point until chill bumps formed on my skin and my eyelids fluttered. Around me, the other girls stirred, but someone shushed them.

"Now, picture the color of green you want," Shay said. "Imagine your own eyes are that exact color. Concentrate on it as hard as you can, filling your eyes with that color until they're saturated with it."

I did exactly as she said, imagining it so clearly in my mind's eye. A pulse of energy warmed my eyelids and I opened my eyes in surprise. "I think I messed it up," I said in a whisper. "Shit."

Lyla bit her lip and smiled. "No, you didn't," she said, clapping. "Go look."

I stood and walked over to the mirror. I pressed my face

close and opened my eyes wide, hardly able to believe what I was seeing.

My eyes were the perfect shade of green.

BACK TO BUSINESS

Before I removed the scarf around my neck, I performed a second, more secret, glamour.

I imagined the skin on my neck to be smooth and perfect, hiding all evidence of a vampire's bite. When I unraveled the scarf a few moments later, I sucked in a grateful breath. I had done it.

"How long do these glamours last?" I asked Lyla as I changed into the green outfit she'd laid out for me.

"It depends on your skill and level of magic ability," she said. "One of my glamours typically lasts about twelve hours if I want it to, but for someone new like you, I'd guess about four hours tops unless you redo it."

Four hours. That should be enough to get me through enough of my shift. I could take a break if I needed to and freshen the glamour later.

"You did great, by the way," she said, giving me a little hug. "I know you don't really like to talk about your mom, but it's going to be okay. Not all witches grow up with moms who will teach them how to use their magic. You can still learn how to control it now. I can help, if you want."

I smiled and squeezed her hand. "Thanks, I'd really appreciate that."

I wasn't even sure what other kinds of magic were available to me, but I knew that if I hoped to have a chance at surviving whatever the Devil had planned for me, I'd be better off learning how to fight instead of how to change my eye color. I'd have to figure out a way to ask her what she knew about fighting, later. Now didn't seem like the right time.

"You want another shot of Dragon's Breath?" she asked, holding out a tube of liquid.

"No, thanks," I said. "I need all my wits about me tonight."

She studied me. "What really happened last night?" she asked. "One minute we were outside, and you seemed fine, and the next you were gone and Rend said you had gone home sick. Was it the shot that made you sick?"

I knew from the way she asked the question that she already knew the answer. "No," I said. She may have figured out that I wasn't really sick, but that didn't mean I wanted her to know the truth, either. Lyla had been super nice to me so far, but I didn't know who I could really trust with the whole story. How much had Rend told them, anyway? How much did he want them to know?

Luckily, I didn't have to worry about it, because Shay interrupted us and told us the staff meeting was about to start.

"We can talk about it later," Lyla said, looping her arm in mine as we made our way out to the main room of the club. "If you want."

I gave her a half smile and concentrated on walking in the ridiculously high heels she'd given me to wear. I mean, I usually loved high heels, but these things were sky-scraper-high. How the heck was I going to dance in them all night?

I nearly tripped my way into the bar area where Rend was already addressing the small staff of the club. When I stumbled, he looked up from his clipboard for a moment, and his eyes froze on mine. The smile was ripped from my face as his expression smoldered with anger.

"Franki, I wasn't expecting you to come in tonight." His words were tense and harsh.

Everyone in the room turned to look at me. I cleared my throat and did my best to act completely unaffected by his obvious rage. "I was feeling better," I said, challenging him with a single raised eyebrow.

Only, challenging him turned out to be exactly the wrong thing to do in that moment.

Rend slammed his clipboard down on the top of the bar. "Excuse us a moment," he said. "Azure, can you take over for me, please?"

Lyla slipped her arm from mine and took a few steps in the other direction as Rend came straight at me. He locked his hand around my arm and pulled me into the room behind the black curtain. I stumbled in the high shoes, but he didn't pause to let me take them off. He just kept pulling me along.

And he didn't stop there. He continued past the velvet couch and into a smaller room behind another private door. This room held a small table with two chairs. Rend shut the door and pushed me back against it.

"Let me go," I said through clenched teeth. "You're hurting me."

His eyes flashed silver and he released me, then cursed. He

didn't back away, though, and his body was still pressed close to mine. "What the hell are you doing here?"

I flinched. Yes, the possibility that he might not be happy to see me had crossed my mind, but hearing the anger in his voice startled me.

"This is my job, isn't it?"

He ran a hand through his hair. "I thought you understood," he said. "You can't just—"

"I can do whatever I damned well please," I said. "Unless you're firing me, in which case I'll take my pay for last night and get out of here."

My heart was beating so fast against my chest, I was sure he could feel it through the jacket of his black suit. Why did he have to stand so close to me? Couldn't he see that he was driving me insane? No matter how hard I had tried to rebuild the walls between us I knew, in that moment, that it was no use. He would just keep tearing them down every time he got close to me.

I couldn't resist him even if I tried.

"Of course I'm not firing you, but I don't want you here looking like that," he said. Mercifully, he backed away, running a hand through his dark hair. "You can't possibly understand how difficult this is for me."

"I have an idea," I said, my voice a whisper.

What I didn't understand was exactly why he was having such a hard time being around me. Was this just about the smell of the blood running through my veins? Or was Katy right? Was it more than that? Was I special?

I wanted to ask him, but the words caught in my throat.

"Do you want me to leave?"

He closed his eyes, his profile half in shadow here in the

dimly lit room. "No," he said. "I just wasn't expecting you to show up after what happened before. I was afraid you weren't ever coming back."

"Would you have come looking for me?" I asked, my breath hitching on the last word. "Or would you have let me go?"

He turned to me, dark eyes flashing with intensity. The muscles in his jaw rippled as he clenched his teeth, his lips tight and his shoulders rigid.

"I don't think I could let you go even if I tried," he said.

He took two long steps toward me and slid one hand behind my back, pulling me into his arms. I pushed against his chest, my heart in panic-mode. I wanted him and hated him at the same time. How did he always have this power over me? How could I possibly protect myself against this?

"Rend." His name was a prayer against my lips. Only, I wasn't sure what I was praying for most. I knew what I really wanted from him, but I was overcome by fear of never being able to have him that way. And if I couldn't have him all, I didn't want any of him. It would destroy me, piece by piece.

His eyes locked on mine and our bodies pressed tightly against one another. My struggle stopped, and I grabbed his jacket into my fists instead, urging him closer.

His lips descended on mine, and I gave in to him, releasing my grip so that I could wrap my arms around his neck. I knew first-hand how dangerous kissing him could be, but I didn't care. Let him take my blood if he wanted it. I couldn't deny him anything.

Rend pulled me close, his hands roaming over my back as his lips explored mine. We broke apart and came together in fits of passion, my leg hooking around his as he pressed my back hard against the closed door. He groaned, then pulled away, but he didn't release me. Instead, his eyes met mine and he placed his thumb along my jawline as his hand cradled my head. "Franki, I don't ever want to hurt you again," he said. "But I don't know how to resist you."

"I can't keep playing this game," I said. "I need to know how you feel. I need to understand what it is you want from me."

His eyes searched my face, but before he could answer, someone knocked on the door.

"Rend?"

It was Azure. Rend's body tensed and he released his hold on me. "I'll be out in a minute," he said.

"Sorry to interrupt, but we've only got about ten minutes before the doors open," she said.

"I said I'll be there in a minute," he said.

I ducked under his arm and moved away, feeling exposed in the skimpy outfit, my body pulsing with desire for a man I swore I would protect myself from. I immediately regretted our kiss now that it was over. Was I really this girl? The kind who let a man constantly get away with this push and pull, never committing or fully giving in? I didn't want to be her. I swore I'd never be her.

"I have to go," he said. "I want you to get changed and come back out as soon as you can."

He was back to business now.

"Rend, I—"

"I know," he said, cutting me off with a gruff tone. "We'll talk later, I promise. After your shift. For now, get out of those clothes before I rip them off of you."

I shivered at the thought, remembering last night and the way he'd practically torn the white shirt from my body.

"I'll see you out there," he said. He straightened his suit jacket and opened the door, but then he turned back to me before he walked out. "And by the way. I like your natural blue better."

My hand fluttered toward my eyes as he walked away. There was no doubt the desire was still there between us, but I was no closer to understanding whether he wanted me for the right reasons or the most horribly wrong ones.

LADY LUCK

When I had changed back into jeans and a Venom Staff t-shirt, I walked into the main room to catch the tail end of the staff meeting. As I'd feared, most people turned to stare when I walked in. Probably, they all thought I had done something horrible to incur Rend's wrath the way I had, which was actually better than if they suspected the truth.

I was so confused, I didn't even know what the truth was at this point.

"Why did you change?" Lyla whispered. "Are you not dancing again tonight?"

"No, she's going to be behind the bar with Azure tonight."

Rend had this terrible habit of stepping into conversations when I least expected it. I hadn't realized he was even listening to Lyla's question.

At the sound of his voice, my heart raced. My cheeks flushed, and I prayed no one could tell in the half-darkness of the room. I took a deep breath before I dared to look up at him.

All it would take was one very competent observer and everyone in this room would know we'd kissed. And more.

I needed to get myself under control. If I was going to be working here, I'd have to keep my feelings for him under tight lock and key.

Thankfully, when I finally did turn toward him, he had already moved away. If I'd had to stare into those dark black eyes right now, I might have cracked. Instead, I was able to collect myself with no one watching.

And did he just say I'd be working with Azure tonight? Awesome. And here I'd thought this night couldn't get any worse.

As Rend finished going through the instructions for the evening, I picked a random spot behind him to focus on. The glowing exit sign on the back door. That way I didn't have to stare directly at him in those black pants that clung to his body in all the right ways. I didn't have to think about how the white dress shirt he wore reminded me of the fact that hours earlier he'd practically torn a shirt just like that off my body.

"Franki?"

I snapped to attention, embarrassed I'd been caught not listening.

"Yes?"

He raised an eyebrow and tensed his jaw. "Is that good with you?"

I had no idea what he'd been talking about, and I looked to Lyla as if she could somehow telepathically fill me in on the last ten minutes.

Rend sighed. "These meetings aren't just for my own amusement, Franki. I need you to pay attention."

I wanted to crawl under one of the tables and disappear into shadow.

"Sorry," I mumbled.

Lyla reached over and squeezed my hand. I gave her a half-smile and she looked at me with pity. Poor Franki. What a complete idiot.

"I was asking if you would mind spending a few minutes behind the bar with me before your shift, so I can show you the basics of what we offer."

"Oh. Sure," I said. Did it matter if I was okay with it or not? It wasn't like I had other options. I damned well wasn't going to say I'd rather be dancing. Or cleaning toilets. Being behind the bar was probably one of the best jobs in this place. I especially liked the idea of the actual bar standing between me and most of the people coming in here. There was a feeling of safety in that barrier.

Still, the thought of spending time that close to Rend right now made me all tingly and nervous.

Was it too much to hope that he would stay twenty feet away from me at all times for the next few hours? At least until his kiss wasn't still raw on my lips?

When the meeting was over, Lyla squeezed my hand one more time. She leaned close to me, her back turned so Rend couldn't see or hear her. "If you need anything, just let me know, okay? He can be a real ball-buster sometimes. Don't let him get to you."

Too late.

"Thanks," I said, genuinely touched that she cared. And relieved that she had obviously mistaken my awkward nervousness for fear that I was in trouble.

Azure however, was staring daggers at me again from behind the bar as I approached.

"Looks like we'll be working together tonight," I said, trying to infuse my voice with some level of enthusiasm.

"Oh, joy," she said. She gave me a sickly-sweet smile.

This promised to be an interesting night. Maybe I should channel all my nervous energy into annoying the shit out of Azure. That would help to keep my mind off Rend, at least.

I waited for him behind the bar, busying myself with cleaning glasses and getting acclimated to the arrangement of everything back there, but my eyes kept drifting over to where he stood talking to Selena.

God, he really was the most gorgeous man I'd ever seen in my life. Just catching him out of the corner of my eye made my body yearn for him. How was I going to survive working so close to him and not being able to touch him?

I was crazy if I thought I could convince myself I didn't have real feelings for him. The moment his lips had touched mine, I knew it was hopeless to deny it.

But, at the same time, it was dangerous to give in to those feelings.

Normally, I would have just walked away and cut him from my life. A clean break was the only way to get over feelings like this. But, that wasn't even a possibility for me right now.

I sighed and glanced up at him again, unable to keep my eyes off him. He'd been talking to Selena for quite a while and now their discussion had escalated into more of an argument. I couldn't hear what they were saying, but from the tension in their shoulders and faces, I could tell they were both angry.

I looked to Azure, and she raised her shoulders in a shrug.

"Then do it yourself, dammit," Selena shouted, throwing her hands up in the air. "I'm not about to put my life at risk for some—"

Rend grabbed her arm and leaned in to say something in her ear.

Selena's body grew softer as she listened. Rend loosened his grip on her, and she looked over her shoulder, her eyes meeting mine for a brief moment. She nodded at him, then opened her palm. Rend took something out of his pocket and handed it to her. Selena closed her fist around it before I could see what it was. She dropped the object into the back pocket of her jeans and stormed out to take her place in front of the club.

"What was that all about?" I asked when Rend came over to stand beside me behind the bar.

"What makes you think that's any of your business?" Anger rolled off him like a dark cloud.

"Oh, I don't know. Maybe the fact that she said she wasn't going to risk her life for someone and then looked directly at me?"

He shook his head. "You never let up, do you? Have you always been so blunt?"

I shrugged. I couldn't tell if he meant it as a compliment or an insult.

"I just don't like it when people keep things from me," I said.

He gave me a sideways glance, and I met his eyes, letting him know that yes, I meant that exactly the way it sounded.

"I asked her not to let Fallon or any of the Devil's other minions into the club tonight," he said.

I swallowed. "Do you think he'd actually try to come back?"

"I have no idea," he said, keeping his voice low and looking around to make sure no one was listening.

Azure stood at the end of the bar polishing glasses, but I'm sure she was listening to every word. He didn't seem to mind, though. Maybe he trusted Azure more than most of his other workers. I wondered again exactly what their story was. And whether there had ever been more between them than a simple boss-employee relationship.

"Thanks," I said. "You know, for trying to keep me safe in here."

"It's my job," he said. He reached for a shot glass and set it up on the top of the bar. "Okay, so here's all you need to know for tonight. We serve five basic drinks to ninety percent of the people who come in here."

He leaned over the top of the bar and pointed to the first of five bottles lined up in a row just beneath the bar top. "We call this one Blue Frost. It goes down with a cooling effect, drawing the heat from your body and heightening the senses, particularly touch and sight. Drinking this makes people remember details more clearly. They think better. A lot of the people who ask for this drink are here to have some kind of meeting where they need to be sharp and clear and calm."

He nodded to the bottle. "Pour me a shot," he said.

I had worked behind bars before, so I was comfortable with pouring a normal shot. But when I picked the bottle up, it was much lighter than I expected. I used way too much force to lift it, banging the top hard against the underside of the counter.

"Oh, shit." I jumped back as the spout on the top shot off and disappeared under a mini-fridge behind me.

At the end of the bar, Azure snorted. I shot her a look.

"Potions aren't like normal liquids," Rend said. "They

aren't like water or scotch or whatever. They actually have different weights, so something you'll have to get used to is how each bottle feels. You don't want to break any of these bottles because you weren't prepared for the weight of the correct color."

I nodded, my heart racing. Okay, so now I was a little bit nervous. Not that I wasn't smart enough to figure out five basic shots. It was more that I knew he and Azure would be watching my every move tonight. Azure in particular would be waiting for me to mess up, snickering each time, I'm sure.

"How can I tell them apart? You said they're each a color, but they all look clear to me."

Rend's eyes questioned me, then he seemed to remember something and softened. "I can't believe I forgot," he said. "You never got your mark."

"Mark?"

"When someone becomes an employee here, I give them the mark of the serpent," he said. "The mark holds power and allows the staff to see things normal patrons can't see."

"Like the colors of the drinks?"

"Among other things," he said. He came around to my side of the bar and reached inside a cabinet to pull out a long needle filled with silver liquid.

I shook my head and backed away. "No way am I letting you near me with that thing," I said.

He lifted the needle and smiled, his eyes dancing. "This little thing?"

The needle was huge. Just looking at it made me want to pass out.

"Are you serious? What are you going to do with it?"

He kept coming toward me, and I kept backing up, but eventually, my ass hit the wall and I had nowhere else to go.

Rend reached toward me with his free hand and swept my hair back on the right side, exposing the skin just behind my ear. I shivered at his touch.

"This won't hurt, I promise."

I closed my eyes and turned my head to the side as Rend inserted the needle into that strip of flesh. I braced myself for pain, but he was right, it didn't hurt at all. Instead, my skin flushed with warmth as the liquid gushed under the surface of my skin, writhing around like a snake.

Rend backed away, and I lifted my hand to the spot.

"What did you do to me?"

He looked from side to side, then grabbed a silver mixing tumbler and lifted it up in front of me like a mirror. "I just gave you my mark," he said. "A silver serpent. Like a tattoo. And don't worry, it's only temporary. When you want it removed, just say the word, and I'll take it out."

I pulled my hair back and stared at the snake tattoo just behind my ear. Everyone had one of these? How had I not noticed that before?

The spot still felt tender and warm, but at least the thing had stopped wiggling around.

"Now look at the bottles of liquid," he said. "What do you see?"

I looked down, and my eyes grew wide. "Holy crap, they're all different colors."

"Exactly," he said with a laugh. "It's a little trick I came up with to give patrons of the club a little bit of extra privacy. That way no one else really knows what type of shot they're drinking tonight."

"Except us."

"Right."

He moved back down to where we had started our lesson and placed a new spout on top of the blue bottle. "Try again."

I picked it up much more carefully this time, ready for how light it would be, then poured. The liquid flowed much slower than I expected, confusing me. It should have flowed faster if it was lighter than normal liquid, right?

I lifted the bottom of the bottle higher and the liquid poured out faster. I stopped when I'd poured the standard three-ounce shot.

"Great," he said. "You're getting a feel for the weight of it and how it works. These potions don't always act the way you're expecting them to because they don't follow the basic rules of physics. Everything in this world acts a little differently than you might expect."

"So I'm learning," I said.

His eyes met mine for a long beat before he looked away and grabbed another empty glass. He set it on top of the bar. "Red."

I reached for the bottle of red liquid. I lifted it carefully, ready for anything. This time, it felt totally normal, just like any bottle of liquor. I relaxed.

But then the bottle grew warm beneath my hand. In seconds it began to burn my skin and on instinct, I opened my palm and watched in horror as it dropped toward the ground.

Rend leaned across the bar top and caught it without a second thought, his movements so fast my eyes barely registered them. I drew in a surprised breath.

"The red liquid gets extremely hot," he said. "We call this Red Dragon."

"This is what Azure gave me the first night I came in here," I said.

"And then Lyla gave you a version of it last night, too, right?"

"She said it was something you made especially for the dancers."

"Right," he said. "Dragon's Breath. It's the same as Red Dragon, but with a little something extra added in. We'll cover specialty drinks later, but for now, at least you understand the basics of how Red Dragon makes you feel. Instead of heightening the senses like Blue Frost, it does the opposite. Red Dragon relaxes you and takes away some of your inhibitions. It's almost like getting drunk, but without the hangover."

He handed the bottle to me again, and this time I made sure to grab it from the top instead of the bottom. I poured a shot into the second glass, relieved when it poured easily.

He pointed to the yellow bottle in the center next. "Yellow Sunshine. This one is our happy drink," he said with a laugh. "Anyone who is feeling depressed or down or just generally drained of energy can have a shot of this to lift them up and make them feel better."

"The ultimate anti-depressant," I said.

Rend smiled and for an instant, his eyes dipped to my lips. He cleared his throat and forced his eyes away. "Pour a shot," he said.

I lifted the bottle and found this one to be so heavy it nearly slipped out of my hands from the sheer weight of it. "So, this one lifts people's moods, but weighs a freaking ton. That makes sense."

"Like I said, not everything is going to make sense in a logical way," he said. "Someday, if we get the chance, I'll take you to my lab and show you how all this works when I mix the potions, but for now, just learn the basics."

A shiver went through me at the thought of being alone with him in his lab. Getting to know him and really being a part of his life. Was that too much to hope for, considering the circumstances? I was getting way ahead of myself here.

Focus, Franki.

"Purple?" I asked, staring down at the next one in line.

I wanted to get through these as fast as possible so Rend would leave and go about his business. I couldn't hope to focus with him standing so close to me and looking at my lips or brushing his hand against mine. It was pure torture.

The doors to the club had opened for the night, and the lights had all been dimmed. Azure served anyone who came up to the bar, leaving Rend and me alone at the other end.

"Purple," he said. "Lady Luck. It gives people a sense of confidence, as if luck is on their side. It doesn't actually make them lucky, so they couldn't leave here and go win the lottery or anything. It just gives them the illusion of luck. A lot of people come in and request this one when they have a big business meeting or a performance coming up."

I poured the purple shot and found that it felt relatively normal compared to the others. No big tricks there.

I nodded to the last of the five basic shots. Green.

"Green Monster," he said. "You won't be asked for this one nearly as often, but we keep it on the menu for certain guests who crave it."

"What does it do?" I asked. I picked up the bottle and the liquid inside began to bubble up as if it were agitated with my touch. I set it back down, scared it was about to burn me like the red one did.

"Green Monster gives you courage," he said.

"How is that different from Lady Luck?"

"Luck is about confidence and feeling good about your decisions. It's about presenting yourself in a way that makes others believe you are a confident, sure person," Rend explained. "Courage, on the other hand, is about believing in yourself. It's about gathering that inner strength you need to get the job done."

"Why did it act so agitated when I picked it up?" I asked.

"Because Green Monster is all about fearlessness and daring," he said. "It's a very energy-focused drink. To keep it from bubbling up like that, just hold it closer to the top. In fact, you'll do better to just grab them all at the neck and pour from there. That way people can't read the drinks by the way you're holding them."

I nodded, pouring the final shot to complete the set in front of me. I was in awe of the glamours and the other magic I'd seen so far, but alchemy was something different. It was like bottling magic and gifting it to other people. I wondered if I could learn how to make potions like this someday.

"How do you feel? Do you want to go over it again?" he asked.

I stared at the line of glowing shots. I briefly went over the basics of them in my mind. "No, I think I've got it," I said, amazed I could even concentrate when the sleeve of his jacket was touching the bare skin on my arm.

"It's Sunday night, so it should be much slower tonight than what you've seen in here so far," he said. "When it really gets going back here, it can be intense and some of the people who come in can be less than patient when they really need a drink."

"I've worked behind a bar before," I said. "I know how fast-paced it can be. I'll be fine."

"This isn't like any bar you've worked in before." He picked up each glass and dumped the contents into the sink.

"Really? I hadn't noticed," I said, then regretted my sarcasm. I didn't want him to think I wasn't taking this seriously, but did that really have to be said? I may have been naive, but I wasn't stupid.

"This isn't a joke, Franki. This isn't some game I'm playing with you," he said. His voice grew rough, and a few of the staff serving at nearby tables turned to look at us. Rend turned away from them, leaning so close to me, a warm rush of desire spread through my veins. "If anyone so much as says a single word that makes you feel uncomfortable or frightened in any way, I want you to come to me."

"Okay," I said, wanting to tell him that he was making me uncomfortable.

He let out a breath and ran a hand through his dark hair. He moved over toward the register and opened a mirrored cabinet filled with dozens of smaller, rounded bottles. He selected three of them and set them down beside a fresh glass on the bar.

Two of these smaller ones glowed much brighter than any of the basic bottles. The other was pitch black, like ink. He poured an ounce of Blue Frost, then carefully poured a tiny bit from each of the smaller bottles. The colors mixed together, then the entire glass-full turned to black, a dark mist rising from it.

He threw it back, downing the shot in one smooth motion, and then set the glass down hard against the bar.

He placed both hands on the edge of the bar and leaned into it, his head dipped low.

I waited, watching to see if I could tell what kind of effect the drink would have on him. The only physical response I could see was that his tense shoulders relaxed, and his breathing steadied.

What it was doing to his insides, I had no idea.

"What do these do?" I reached for the bottle of black liquid but the moment I touched it, his hand closed over mine.

The touch of his skin against mine made me ache for something I knew I couldn't have. At least, not in front of all these people.

"These are special," he said. "Not for the average customer and definitely not for you to touch until you've studied them, and you understand how the different potions mix and combine. The wrong combination could be fatal."

He released my hand, and I pulled it back, my stomach twisting and turning.

"What did these three do mixed with the blue, then?" I asked. My voice came out unsteady and breathless. I cleared my throat and forced myself to relax. He couldn't know how much he was getting to me.

"I don't have a name for this mix," he said. "Azure, what would you call this?"

"Rend's Addiction," She called out, laughing.

Rend smiled and nodded. "It's just something that takes the edge off for me when I need it," he said.

He didn't give me any more details than that. He just put the three smaller bottles back in their case and closed it up again.

"Azure will take care of any orders that require mixing," he said. "All you have to do is serve the basic five. Like I said, most of the people who come up will ask for one of those."

I had been staring down at the five bottles, running through what he'd taught me so far, but when he paused, I looked up to find him watching me. The look in his eyes took my breath away. There was something unsaid behind them, and I suddenly couldn't wait for my shift to be over. What was he waiting to tell me? Would he break it off? Or would he kiss me again?

I bit my lower lip, and his eyes dipped to my mouth. His lips parted slightly, and he sucked in a ragged breath. When his eyes returned to mine, they were full of undeniable desire.

But desire for what?

"I'm going to make sure everything is set up and ready for us to open," he said. He left me standing there behind the bar without another word.

Pure torture.

CURRENCY

Once the customers started pouring in, the night flew by.

I got used to the weight and flow of each of the five basic drinks and before too long, I was able to choose the right bottle without even looking down.

Most of the people who came in seemed happy to see a new face behind the bar. I began to relax into the rhythm of the work, having fun meeting new people and listening to the kinds of conversations taking place.

Since the music was loud, most people practically yelled at each other, laying their business out in front of everyone close enough to hear.

I paid attention without making eye contact or showing any indication that I was listening, but I was getting a kick out of things like complaints about girlfriends who had cast spells on them when they refused to help with the dishes.

I was sure the more serious conversations were happening back in the shadowy booths and in the darkness of the second-floor tables, but I liked the energy up here away from the darker places. I liked the neon glow of the bar, and the energy of the place.

I also liked the fact that no one could come up and threaten me in front of everyone. I felt safer up here.

The people who crowded around the bar were like most customers at bars I'd worked in the past, here to have a good time and be around friends and people who were like them.

People like me.

"Where's Rend?" A man wearing a black baseball cap leaned across the bar near me. From what I could see of his face under the cap, he was handsome.

I moved toward him, the mention of Rend's name sending an involuntary flare of heat though my middle. "I'm not sure," I said. I glanced around the crowded room, but I didn't spot him anywhere. "I don't see him. Wait here just a second."

Azure had barely spoken two words to me all night. She'd mostly kept to her side of the bar all night, only coming over when someone requested one of the more complicated drinks and she had to get into the cabinet behind me. She would know what to do, though, and possibly where to find Rend.

"Hey, the guy in the black hat down there is looking for Rend," I said, walking over to where she was openly flirting with a group of guys at the end of the bar. "Do you know where he is?"

She sighed audibly. "Do you?"

I bit back a sarcastic reply and played nice. "What should I tell this guy, then?"

"I'll go see if I can find him. Tell him to hang on to his britches."

"Thanks."

I asked the man to wait here while Azure went to see if she could find Rend. I served a few customers who all wanted Red Dragon. A few minutes later, Rend appeared on the other side of the bar and shook the man's hand. They half-embraced, clapping each other on the back.

The pure smile that spread across Rend's face mesmerized me. I'd never seen him so joyful. He always seemed angry or amused or passionate, but this was a new side to him. The smile animated him, and I was struck by the intense desire to someday see him smile at me that way.

Watch yourself, kiddo.

Forcing myself not to care was an exercise in futility. He was magnetic. I was drawn to him despite myself. No amount of logic could keep me from wanting him, and I might as well accept that.

As I looked up from pouring another shot for a new customer, I knew honestly and completely that I was falling for him.

I was falling for a freaking vampire. What the hell was wrong with me?

"He's beautiful when he's happy, isn't he?"

Azure stood next to me, mixing some new concoction that glowed bright pink in the glass.

"I don't know what you mean," I said. I don't even know why I denied it. She'd obviously seen me staring at him like a love-struck schoolgirl.

She laughed. "Okay," she said. "But just so you know, whatever it is you think the two of you have, it isn't going to end well for you."

I bristled. Who was she to tell me what Rend and I had?

"I know you don't believe me, but nothing happened the

other morning," I said. I had no idea why I wanted her to believe nothing had happened between us, when something obviously had. She just brought out the worst in me. "He's just trying to protect me. So whatever bug you have up your ass about it can just die a slow, painful death. There's nothing to be jealous about."

Her eyes widened and both of her eyebrows rose. "You think I'm jealous of you?" She threw her head back and laughed. "Girly, you've been here what? Three or four days? I've been with Rend for decades, working right here beside him every minute of every day. Trust me, I'm not jealous of you."

Decades? I swallowed and glanced back at Rend. If he was a vampire, that also meant he was old. Possibly centuries old. If she'd been with him that long, maybe she did know a lot more about him than I did.

The thought unnerved me.

"Then why are you so intent on making me feel like I don't belong here?" I asked. "I've been nothing but nice to you, and you keep coming back at me with anger and sarcasm, like I don't matter."

"Oh, you matter," she said, finishing the mixture and using a clear glass rod to stir it around. "Just not the way you think you matter."

She replaced the bottles she'd taken from the cabinet and returned to her side of the bar to deliver the drink to a beautiful blond woman wearing a hot pink dress that matched the color of the drink exactly. I couldn't help wondering what the special drink would make her feel. The woman leaned over the bar and planted a kiss on Azure's cheek, then slid her a one-hundred-dollar bill.

I glanced back at Rend. He was still standing with the handsome man in the black hat, smiling and laughing. I couldn't hear what they were saying, but they were obviously old friends.

Azure's words kept playing in my head like a broken record. What did she even mean by that? What way did I matter, then?

A woman leaned over the bar and asked for a shot of Red Dragon, and I held up a finger and told her I'd be right back. I wiped my hands off on a towel and threw it back down on the shelf beneath the bar, then marched over to where Azure had resumed her flirting with the group of guys who'd been lingering around her all night.

"What exactly did you mean by that?" I asked. I knew I sounded like a petulant child demanding an explanation, but I didn't care.

"Excuse me, guys," she said, throwing them a smile. "I'll be right back."

She turned to me, her head leaning to one side and her hand on her hip.

"What did you mean by I matter, but not the way I think?" I was almost more scared than angry.

"Look, I know Rend better than someone like you ever will," she said. "He's been through things your tiny brain can't even imagine, and he escaped all that when he created Venom. This club is his life, and he cares more about what he's built here than anything else in this world or the next."

As she spoke, I bit down on the inside of my lip, the pain anchoring me so that I didn't get emotional or let her words tear me apart.

"He doesn't do anything to risk this club," she said. "Sure, he may stick his neck out sometimes to help one of us out or to get someone like you out of trouble, especially when he sees great potential in someone or he senses their brokenness. But he never, and I mean never, risks his heart."

My heart thumped in my chest, and I breathed in slowly as she spoke.

"Whatever happened—or didn't happen—between you two has nothing to do with Rend falling in love with you."

"I never said anything about love."

"I see the way you look at him like a little lost puppy dog looking for someone to save her. I see that heady mix of panic and desire flash through your eyes when you look at him. You're not fooling anyone," she said, shaking her head. "But don't you even think for a second he's going to return that affection. Rend doesn't fall in love. Period. He's incapable of love. At least, the kind you're looking for."

I regretted coming over here to talk to her. I never should have even let her know I gave a shit about what she had to say. I wished I had the nerve to just turn around and walk away and not listen to another word of this, but I couldn't. I needed to know. I needed to hear this so I would stop hoping for something that would never happen.

"What I meant when I said you don't matter in the way you think is that you've somehow convinced yourself there's a chance with him and that if you could just break through that hard, outer shell of his, you'll find a soft, loving boyfriend on the inside," she said. "I'm telling you this for your own good before you end up with your heart broken into a million pieces. If he's done anything to make you think he cares for you, or if he's giving you a taste of what it would be like to be with him, he's doing it for one reason and one reason only. To get you wrapped so tightly around his little finger you wouldn't dream of taking a single step without his permission or acceptance.

"Because if there's one thing I know for sure, it's that Rend will do anything to make sure his club stays exactly the way it is. He'll do whatever it takes and hurt whoever he has to in order to protect what he's built here."

"I don't understand what protecting the club has to do with me," I said. My mouth was dry.

"I thought you said you were smart?" she said, taking a few steps into my personal space. "Do I really have to spell this out for you? You show up here because were invited by some anonymous stranger. You're threatened by a guy who works for one of the most dangerous vampires in existence—a vampire who wouldn't think twice about just taking any witch he wanted from the safety of her own bed in the middle of the night while she was sleeping. You're the descendant of one of the most evil witches who ever walked this earth. All these things lead to one conclusion. Have you figured out what that is yet?"

My hands trembled, and I pressed them hard against my legs to make them stop. I hadn't realized he'd been keeping Azure in the loop about me and everything he'd learned about me. It was unsettling.

"My blood is valuable," I said.

"Ah, so you're not entirely stupid," she said. "Yes, your blood is extremely valuable, which means you matter to a lot of people right now. Some evil and some just looking to profit from you in some way. Which do you think Rend is?"

I swallowed, the realization of what she was saying to me finally soaking in. I bit down harder on the inside of my lip tasting the sting of blood as my teeth pierced the sensitive skin.

"The truth isn't always easy to hear, but I'm telling you this for your own good, Franki." She moved in closer, her face uncomfortably close to mine. "Because I don't want you to ever think for one second that you're anything more than currency to him."

The room around me began to spin, throwing me off-balance internally. Anger and regret and disappointment swirled around me and the slightest wisp of wind blew across my skin.

Breathe, little bird.

I breathed in through my nose, filling my lungs with air, but my heart continued to pump faster.

Currency.

My blood was valuable, which meant Rend only cared what he could get for me in trade or negotiation, anything to keep the Devil, one of the only vampires he feared, from destroying everything he'd built.

He'd all but told me this himself, but I had failed to connect the dots.

Was this really all just a game to him? Were we back to this?

Azure didn't even bother to wait for a response from me. She casually grabbed a clean glass from the stack and poured a shot of Blue Frost, filling the glass to the rim so that some of it spilled out onto the floor at her feet.

She shoved it toward me, the neon liquid sloshing onto my shirt. "Do yourself a favor," she said. "Drink some of this. Get some clarity before you end up making some huge mistakes that put us all in danger."

I wanted to throw it in her face, but instead I took it from her. My hand trembled slightly as I held it, but I didn't drink it. Not yet.

Azure rolled her eyes and turned around, going right back to her friends without missing a beat, as if she hadn't just turned my entire world upside-down, all over again.

I wanted to leave. To walk away from this place and never look back, but in the space of a few short days, my life had become so entangled in this new world it felt like there was no way out.

Or at least no way out alive.

I couldn't leave. Even if Rend had only kissed me to try to convince me to stay or to drag me deeper under his spell, he was still the only one who could offer me any kind of protection from the evil that wanted to destroy my life.

I needed to stay strong.

I thought I had faced dangers in my life before this, but my life since receiving those black roses had brought new meaning to the word danger. There was so much darkness surrounding me now, maybe the only way out was to start looking for the light.

And right now, the light meant taking the veil from my eyes and seeing things for what they really were.

I downed the shot of Blue Frost, a cold chill spreading through my body like ice through my veins.

I closed my eyes and held onto the edge of the bar as the magic worked its way through my system. I felt my head begin to clear and my skin cool. My heartbeat slowed back down to normal, control restored.

And when I felt my head clear, I opened my eyes, ready to find my way out of the darkness.

A NATURAL

"**R**ed Dragon."

A guy at the far end of the bar snapped his fingers at me, and when I glanced his way, he held up three fingers and tapped them on the top of the bar.

Normally, snapping your fingers at me will get you damn slapped in your face. Tonight, though, with the shot of Blue Frost cooling me down, I offered him a smile instead.

Out of the corner of my eye, I saw three other previous customers step to the bar and look my way expectantly. The clarity of mind the potion provided gave me access to memories I never would have been able to recall without it. I remembered each customer and exactly what they'd ordered. Even without looking directly at them, I could tell from the angle of their bodies and the tension in their bodies that they weren't coming to order something different.

I lined six glasses up on the bar and poured from two bottles at the same time, my brain working on extra channels, processing the weight and pour of each liquid with no effort.

All six shots were poured and delivered in less than thirty seconds.

The customers nodded in appreciation.

"Thanks," the guy with three Red Dragons said when I pushed the shots toward him. He looked to be about my age, maybe a few years older. He had long brown hair that dusted the top of his shoulders and light green eyes that were locked on my face.

He flashed a smile and tucked his hair behind one ear on the left side. "I don't think I've seen you here before," he said. "Are you new?"

"Yes," I said, smiling back and leaning against the bar. "This is my first night behind the bar slinging drinks."

"Well, you'd never know it," he said. "You're a natural. I'm Ashton, by the way."

He extended his hand to me, and I wiped mine on my jeans and placed it in his. He held onto it a beat too long, but I easily kept my cool.

"Nice to meet you," I said. "I'm Franki."

"Very nice to meet you, too." He finally released my hand. "So, did you just move into town or—"

"Oh, no," I said. "I've actually lived here my whole life. What about you?"

His eyes narrowed slightly. His head twitched and his smile changed. "I was brought through when I was pretty young," he said. "I've been on this side for the past twenty years, but of course, only free for the past six months or so."

"Brought through?" I asked. I had no idea what he was talking about.

He gave a shake of his head and twisted one of the shot glasses around in a circle. "You know, by the Order. They—"

Rend's hand landed on the guy's shoulder. "Ashton, it's really nice to see you here, again," he said. The sound came out nicely enough, but there was an edge of annoyance there. "I see you've met my Franki."

My Franki? Was he jealous?

"Yeah, she's doing a great job for it being her first night," Ashton said. "We were just talking about how she grew up here in Chicago."

Rend waved his index finger over the three full shot glasses. "Did you have some friends waiting for these?"

"Oh." Ashton glanced over toward one of the booths closest to the bar where a few other guys sat. "Yeah, I guess I should probably get these out to them. It was nice to meet you, Franki. I hope we'll be seeing more of you in here from now on."

"You, too," I said, flashing a smile that was perhaps a bit brighter than it would have been had Rend not been watching me, the tension in his shoulders growing with every second that went by.

"What was that about?" he asked when Ashton had rejoined his friends.

"We were just talking." I grabbed a towel from the rack behind me and started wiping the counter with it, forcing Rend to lift his elbow so I could clean under it.

"Just talking about your personal life and where you live?" He raised his voice. "Franki, you don't know most of these people. Until you get a feel for what kind of temperament they may have, I think you should be careful not to share anything about your personal and home life with any of these people."

"It wasn't like I gave him my home address," I said. "Besides, he seemed sweet."

Rend shook his head and tightened his jaw. "I don't want you talking to anyone in here about your personal life, sweet or not," he said. "There are things about the people who come in here that you don't understand and you never know who might be working for the Devil."

"The Devil already knows where I live, remember? He sent me flowers before I even knew he existed." I poured a few more drinks for waiting customers. "Besides, I understand a lot more than you think I do. I may not know all the dangers of this world, but I am still the one in control of my own life. Just because I agreed to work here doesn't mean you own me."

His eyes darkened and his shoulders tensed. "I want you to be careful."

You want to protect your investment.

"I am being careful," I said. "And one thing you need to learn about me is that if you ever hope to earn my trust, you had better start trusting me too."

He swallowed and pushed off from the edge of the bar. He looked around at the rest of the people in the bar, taking his time to respond.

"We've only got about an hour left before last call," he said finally. "You've done a great job tonight, but let's try to get through the rest of this evening without anyone making threats or learning more about you than they need to know."

"Yes, sir," I said, saluting him.

He narrowed his eyes at me, then shook his head. "I'll see you after your shift," he said. His eyes softened. "I have something important I want to show you."

He walked away, and I let my head fall back slightly. Why did I always have to open my smart mouth and talk back to him? Why couldn't I make him smile like he had earlier?

The only thing that made me feel better was that it was obvious, from the way he was acting, that I was getting under his skin just as much as he was getting under mine.

THE DEVIL

Though rush of orders from before slowed to a crawl. I
was dying for this last hour to go by faster, so of
course, it was the slowest hour of the entire night.

I busied myself by cleaning up the glassware and wiping
down the bar, sweeping the floors and straightening up in
general.

Lyla leaned across the top of the bar and yanked on my
hair. "Hey, girl, how was your night?"

I had never been so happy to see someone. "Great until
about half an hour ago when everything slowed down," I said.
"I'm turning into a zombie back here."

"Want to sneak out and grab a cigarette with me?"
she asked.

I looked around, mainly checking to see what Azure was
up to and whether Rend was paying attention. "Won't we get
in trouble for ducking out early?"

She shrugged. "Nah. It's Sunday night and it's slow," she

said. "Come on, we'll just pop out for a few minutes and be back before anyone even notices."

"Okay," I said. I tossed the towel I'd been cleaning with into the sink and came around the bar to meet Lyla near the door.

Azure didn't even flinch when I walked by.

Selena nodded as we walked out into the humid night air. "Hi," she said. "Fun night?"

Lyly made a face. "Slow," she said. "But I guess you already know that."

Selena laughed.

The two of us walked down the alley to get away from the main entrance, moving up onto the main street a little more. Lyla leaned against the brick exterior of a nearby restaurant and lit her cigarette. She offered one to me, but I declined.

The city was alive for me in a way it had never been before. I could hear every sound with complete clarity. Footsteps on the pavement. Laughter from the outdoor patio of the restaurant across the street.

I could see and register so much of what was going on around me. It was a very cool feeling without being too overwhelming.

Lyla laughed, and I turned to question her.

"Blue Frost for the first time?" she asked.

"How did you know?"

"I've seen that look a dozen times before," she said. "It's like you're seeing the world for the first time, right? Noticing every crack in the pavement and hearing every blade of grass as it blows in the wind."

I laughed. "Maybe not quite that many details, but yeah.

It's amazing. Rend's amazing. Do you know where he learned to make all those?"

"He taught himself, mostly," she said. "Back in the Shadow World, he had a teacher, but I can't remember his name. Still, I think he learned most of his alchemy through experimenting in his own lab and shit."

"Incredible," I said.

"What's going on there?" she asked.

"What do you mean?"

"Come on," she said, laughing. "You and Rend. What's up?"

I blushed. What was I supposed to say to that? I guess I knew this was coming. There was no way I was going to be able to hide my feelings from everyone, but at the same time, I knew he wouldn't want me telling anyone what had really happened between us. Not that I really understood it, anyway.

This sucked.

She took another drag from her cigarette. "Damn, you've got it bad."

"No, I don't," I said, turning my face away from her and watching a group of girls make their way into the club. I wondered if they realized they had less than half an hour left to drink and dance before closing?

"Oh, yes, you do," Lyla said. "You are one hundred percent fucked."

I snapped my head toward her. "What do you mean? No, I'm not."

She shook her head. "Rend is complicated, to say the least," she said. "But I know there's no talking you out of it now. You're already in love with him."

I pressed my lips together and raised my chin. My insides

twisted. "No, I'm not in love with him," I said. "I just like him. A lot."

"Uh huh," she said, obviously not buying it. "Just be careful, okay? Rend can be amazing. He can be the first person to pull a girl off the streets, and he'd do anything to keep us all safe from the Order or the Others. But at the same time, I've seen him do things that have haunted my dreams for months."

Her face went pale, and the expression was like a dagger in my gut.

"What kinds of things?" I asked, my mouth dry.

"Do you know what it means? His name?" she asked.

"Rend?"

She raised an eyebrow. "Yeah. Rend. To tear something into two or more pieces. It's not his real name, you know. Just a nickname he got a very long time ago for doing exactly that to vampires and witches who crossed him in any way."

My heart stopped beating for a moment and my mouth opened, but I couldn't even think of what to say. I felt suddenly very cold. "He tore them apart?"

"Literally. He's not going to do that to you," she said. "You're one of his girls. He wouldn't hurt you. I just think you should be careful. He's worked hard to get himself under control, but with guys like him, you just never know when something's gonna set them off? You know?"

She patted my shoulder and threw her cigarette to the ground. She lit a second one, and I glanced back toward the club, thinking of Rend.

A strange man caught my eye, though, and I couldn't tear my gaze away. He was tall and thin, dressed in a perfectly tailored pinstripe suit with a red tie. There was something about him that unnerved me and made me instantly afraid. It was as if there was a darkness that surrounded him.

He strolled out of the shadows and opened the door to Venom, a thin-lipped smile teasing the corners of his mouth.

Lyla continued to talk about relationships, which turned into a rant about men in general, but I was barely paying attention to her.

I couldn't get the strange man out of my head.

Panic gathered in my core, eating away at me. Something was wrong. I could feel it in every fiber of my being, but I had no idea what to do about it.

"What's wrong?" Lyla asked, tossing her last cigarette to the ground and stomping it out with her high heeled boots. "Franki? You okay?"

I tried to swallow, but my throat was thick with worry.

The group of girls I'd watched walk in a few moments ago came running back out through the club's front door, their screams echoing off the building across from us.

"Shit, something's up." Lyla grabbed my arm and started to run toward the club, but I held my ground.

I pulled her back into the shadows with me, crouching low. "What?" she asked.

I put my finger over her mouth and shook my head. I couldn't find my voice, and I certainly didn't know how to explain what I was feeling, but I followed my instincts. Stay hidden. Wait for Rend.

Lyla nodded back and leaned against the bricks here in the half-shadows at the mouth of the alley. Her eyes were wide and filled with panic.

Another scream rang out into the night. Slowly, a shadow of a man walked out from the entrance to the club. It was the same man I'd seen walk through just a few seconds ago, but he was only half-formed. Part shadow, part man. His eyes burned red.

In his hand, he held a silver dagger coated in red blood. He took his time, pulling a pristine white cloth from his pocket and wiping each side of the blade on it. He tucked the dagger back into his coat and threw the discarded white cloth onto the ground.

I stared at the streaks of bright red blood that stained the cloth.

My hand rose to my mouth. Whose blood was that?

But I didn't have to wonder for long. The door to the club opened one last time and a woman stumbled through, falling to her knees as blood ran from a large wound in her side. She reached for him, barely grabbing the back of his pants before collapsing completely onto the graveled pavement in the alley.

Selena.

Hot tears filled my eyes. Lyla tried to stand, but I held onto her for dear life, suddenly sure of who the shadowed man must be. And who he had come here to find.

I stared at Selena, torn between staying hidden and going to try to help her. But the light was already dimming in her beautifully clear eyes. There was nothing anyone could do to help her now.

She groaned and let her head fall to the pavement.

I couldn't believe we were going to just hide here, watching her die. Where was Rend?

I shook my head as tears streamed down my face.

I'm so sorry, I wanted to tell her. *This is all my fault.*

I knew she couldn't hear me, but I could swear for an instant, her eyes locked with mine. She saw me, and her lips parted. She sucked in a surprised breath, then struggled to lift her head from the ground.

The Devil, in his half-shadowed form, looked down at her and laughed. "Die already," he said. "I need to get inside that club."

Selena's blood ran like a river against the ground, but she managed to move her hand toward the pocket of her jeans. With labored movements, she reached inside her pocket and pulled something out. Her palm opened and I caught a glimpse of a small clear bead with a red spark glowing inside.

I gasped.

Rend's gift to her earlier tonight.

I couldn't breath as I watched her hand close around the small bead. Then, with her eyes locked on mine, she gave me a sad smile and mouthed a singled word.

Run.

With her last breath, she gathered her strength and squeezed.

The world in front of me exploded in fire. The front of the building went up in flames, and the Devil flew backward, his body slamming against the brick wall behind him and disappearing into a cloud of ash and flame.

I shielded my face from the flames, coughing on the growing cloud of smoke. Lyla clawed at my arm, urging me to run, but I couldn't hear her. I couldn't force myself to move.

All I could do was stare dumbly at the destroyed building that used to be Venom.

EPISODE FIVE

THE DEVIL

VENOM IS GONE

Debris floated through the air. Ash coated the side of my face. I screamed, but my voice was lost amidst the wail of sirens. My ears rang from the noise of the explosion and blood trickled into my eyes from a cut on my forehead.

Venom is gone.

Lyla pulled furiously on my arm, but I was too numb to move.

Rend was still inside that building.

But in the flames and smoke, I couldn't tell how much of the building was still standing.

"Franki, we have to go now," Lyla said, her voice desperate.

"I can't," I yelled, yanking my arm away from her.

I ran toward the fire, but she blocked my way. She placed both hands on my face, forcing me to look at her.

"We have to go," she said.

"I can't just leave," I shouted. I shook my head, not wanting to believe this could be happening. This was all my fault.

Selena and the others, they were all dead because of me. "We have to find them. What if someone's still alive in there? We have to go back."

Lyla shook her head, panic in her wide eyes. "Dammit, Franki, you have to listen to me. It's not what you think, but we have to go now. If we don't go, you're going to be dead, too. Do you hear me?"

I nodded, still in shock. I couldn't focus with the weight of panic and sorrow on my heart.

We couldn't just leave them here like this. We couldn't just walk away and leave them. I couldn't leave Rend like this. Not if there was a chance. Didn't she understand? But a part of my mind registered what she was saying. The Devil had come here for me. He'd been knocked back by the blast, but how long would that keep him down? If he woke up, he'd be coming for me.

"Come on," she said. "I'll explain as we go, but we have to move."

I let her grab my hand and pull me back toward the main street. She led us through the crowd gathered on the sidewalk. A fire truck pulled up on the curb and rescue workers were yelling, running, and directing people to stay away from the alley.

We ducked our heads and ran through the crowd, past the rows of bars and restaurants, and toward the nearest 'L' station.

Cars were stopped all along Hubbard street, and people were getting out of their cars to see what was going on. A cab driver motioned to us.

"What's going on up there?" he asked. "Someone get hurt?"

I just shook my head, unable to put words to what I'd seen.

It didn't seem real. The entire club was gone. Just like that, the building destroyed.

I pictured the Devil flying back against the brick wall, shock registering on his pale face. I pictured Selena's sad smile and the way she had told me to run. Chills broke out along my skin.

Had she died for me? Because of me?

I would never be able to forgive myself.

Lyla got us on the first train that pulled up and led me toward a pair of seats in the back.

We sat down, and I stared straight ahead. It took all my willpower just to force breath into my lungs.

I couldn't lose him now. Not when we hadn't even had a chance to decide what we meant to each other. I might never know if I meant anything to Rend or not, but with the possibility of him being gone forever, I gained a new clarity about my own feelings.

And now it was too late.

My hands were ice cold and shaking uncontrollably. I held them in my lap, unable to stop them.

Lyla leaned over and placed both her hands on top of mine. She put her mouth close to my ear. "You have to get control of that," she said. "People are going to stare. Franki?"

I shook my head, as if waking from a dream.

I blinked several times. What did she mean? Why would people stare?

Then I saw it. A series of small whirlwinds kicking up dust from the floor of the train. It looked like four miniature tornadoes traveling along down the center of the aisle.

My mouth fell open, and I forced a deeper breath. Had I done that?

"I don't know how to stop it," I said.

"Yes, you do," she said. "Just breathe. Focus. All you have to do is calm down and find where that energy is coming from and tell it to stop."

I closed my eyes and took several deep breaths. I focused on my body, connecting in a new way to what was going on inside of me. And she was right. Somewhere in the core of my being, a fire burned. Rage. Sorrow. Fear. Regret. My magic was so closely tied to my emotions that I had created small tornadoes of dust and wind right here on the train in downtown Chicago.

I pictured it slowing down and dissipating into nothingness, and the whirlwinds obeyed, collapsing into piles of dust and dirt on the floor at my feet.

Lyla squeezed my hands and looked around at the other passengers on the train.

"We're okay for now," she said. "But I have to get you someplace safe."

"I don't even understand what's going on," I said. I felt more helpless than ever before in my life. "How could this happen?"

"You saw him, didn't you? Before I even saw what was going on, you noticed him."

I nodded. "I saw him going in. The second I laid eyes on him, I got this weird feeling. I knew he was a bad man, but it wasn't until he came out with blood on his hands that I realized who he really was. That was the Devil, wasn't it?"

She swallowed. "Yes. He's the worst of the vampires," she said. "The evillest demon I've ever seen. Well, I'd never actually seen him in person, before tonight, but I'm sure that's who he was."

"He killed Selena," I said.

"She's the gatekeeper here in Chicago," Lyla said. "She understood that danger when she took the job. The gatekeeper decides who is allowed inside that particular gate. If she told him he couldn't go in, there was no way he could cross that barrier. The only way in would be to kill her. Once a gatekeeper dies, the gate opens to everyone. At least until another gatekeeper arrives. Selena knew that going in. She volunteered for the job."

I closed my eyes. "She died because of me," I said. "The Devil was there for me."

"The Devil was there for you? How do you know that?"

I slumped down in my seat. I wasn't sure I had the energy to explain all of this to her right now, but I knew she had a right to know the truth.

"He's the whole reason I ever found Venom in the first place," I said. "He sent me black roses on my twenty-first birthday, inviting me to the club."

"That doesn't even make sense," she said. "He's been banned from Venom for more than a decade. Why would he invite you there?"

"I don't know," I said. "I think he wanted to make me discover my own magic. He wanted to make sure I really was who he thought I was."

"And who is that?" she asked, her voice soft and full of fear.

I swallowed and looked out the window at the city lights. It was just after one in the morning, and I had no idea where we were going. Or what the hell I was going to do once morning came. I couldn't just go home and go back to my life before Venom. Before Rend.

He had opened my eyes to a whole new world. A whole new life. Finding the club had changed me forever. There was no way to turn my back on that now, even if I wanted to.

Of course, without Rend and the club, I wasn't sure how much life I'd have left to live. If the Devil had come to Venom for me, he was going to find me no matter where I tried to hide. Without Rend, there would be no one who could protect me.

"What are we going to do?" I asked. "I can't go home."

"No," she said. "We're going to a safe-house just outside the city. Rend will come looking for you there."

I snapped my head toward her. My heart skipped a beat. "Rend? But—"

"I know what it looked like, Franki, but that's what I was trying to explain to you on the street. The club itself wasn't destroyed. It was only the Chicago entrance that was destroyed."

My head pounded. She wasn't making sense. "What do you mean? How is that possible?"

"There are six entrances to Venom around the world," she said. "Chicago, Paris, New York City, Berlin, Moscow, and Havana. Only that one entrance to the club was destroyed."

Hope fluttered in my heart and tears sprang to my eyes. "You mean he's okay? Don't fuck with me."

She smiled and shook her head. "I'm not fucking with you. Anyone who was inside Venom is fine," she said. "But they won't be able to get here to Chicago without going through another gateway."

I felt the first true breath of hope enter my body, and my hands stopped trembling. I needed to talk to Rend and tell him what I saw.

My heart was still sick for Selena, but I was relieved everyone else was okay.

"How does this work?" I asked. "We're just supposed to wait for word from him? Or do you have some other way of contacting him to let him know we're okay?"

I groaned, realizing Rend wouldn't know where I was. Not for sure. He hadn't seen me leave the club with Lyla. I wasn't sure Azure had been paying attention, either. The only person I could be sure who knew we had walked out into the streets of Chicago was Selena. And she wouldn't be telling anyone.

"Did you tell anyone else you were going out to smoke?" I asked. "Any of the other dancers?"

She shook her head. "No, I just came to see if you wanted to go out," she said. "But when they realize I'm not there, they'll guess where I went, I'm sure."

"But they won't know I was with you," I said, thinking out loud. "Rend won't even know the Devil was there."

"I'm sure he has a good idea of what happened," she said. "It's not like the doorways get destroyed very often. Selena wouldn't have blown the door unless it was absolutely necessary. An explosion like that is rare. It's a fail-safe to make sure no one dangerous gets inside the club."

I closed my eyes, my stomach rolling at the thought of Selena's death. "I saw Rend arguing with her before we opened tonight," I said. "She said she didn't want to risk her life for me."

Lyla pressed her lips together and shook her head. "You can't blame yourself."

"Who else can I blame?" I asked. "This is all my fault."

"Look, we're family at Venom. We look out for each other. Remember what I told you earlier? Every single one of us came to be there because we were in some kind of trouble," she said. "Rend gave us jobs to protect us from people like The Order and The Others."

I shook my head. "I don't even know who those people are," I said. "It feels like the more I learn about this world, the more I don't know."

"All you need to know is that there is a constant war going on in this world for the souls and power that witches hold," she said. "There are those who think we're evil just for existing and there are others who want to control us. Once these people realize a witch has great power, they will do whatever it takes to get control of that power. Rend has been around for a very long time, Franki. He's seen the worst of it first hand, and he wants to do everything he can to save as many people from falling into the hands of evil as he can."

I sat back against the cold plastic seat on the train and tried to process what she was telling me. How could I have been so clueless to the war between good and evil happening all around me? How could I have missed it?

"If the Devil is after you, you must be extremely valuable to him for some reason," Lyla said. She chewed on the fingernail on her thumb for a moment. "Something beyond the average witch. Do you have any idea what it could be?"

I bit the inside of my lip. How much could I really trust Lyla? Rend obviously trusted her or he wouldn't have her working at Venom. On the other hand, I barely knew anything about her. I was still getting used to the idea that I was a descendant of the Mother Crow. Did I want to confide in her about it?

I looked around at the other people on the train. This late at night, there weren't many people on board, but I didn't want to take any chances that someone could be listening in on our conversation.

"Rend and I figured out something about my family that makes me unique." I knew I was being vague, but vague was my only option right now. "I'll tell you more about it when we get to a safe place, but for now, can we just leave it at that?"

Lyla nodded and sat back in her seat. "Good idea," she said. "We're going to have to get off the train at the next stop anyway. Then we'll get a cab and go the rest of the way. We'll get to the safe-house in half an hour or so, and we should be able to relax until Rend can get word to us."

"He'll be expecting us to go there?" I asked.

"Yeah, he'll know that's where I'll go if I'm still alive," she said. "He'll definitely come looking for us, but I have no idea how long it will take him to find a way here. New York is the closest doorway, and then he'll have to catch a flight from there. We probably won't hear from him until tomorrow at the earliest."

I nodded, knowing I had no choice but to trust her and follow her to this safe-house.

I wished I had time to call Katy and let her know I was okay and that I would be gone for a while, but my cell phone and purse were both still inside the club. God, I hope she wasn't in any danger. When I talked to Rend, I'd have to see if he could get someone to watch over her for me. Just in case.

"So, if there are all these doorways into the club from all these different cities, what city is the club itself actually in?" I asked.

Lyla twisted her mouth to the side. "Huh," she said. "I have no idea."

I didn't have time to ask more questions because the train

pulled up to the next station. We both got off and descended the stairs to the street below. Lyla hailed a cab and gave directions to one of the nearby suburbs.

Neither of us said a word the rest of the way to the safe-house, but we clasped tightly to each other's hands in the darkness.

THE LORE OF VAMPIRES

The cab pulled up to a very normal-looking house in the middle of suburbia. The lights were all off and the lawn looked like it could use a good mowing, but there was nothing strange or unusual looking about the place. It wasn't at all what I was expecting for a vampire's chosen safe-house, but maybe that was exactly the point.

Lyla pulled a fifty out of her bra and told the driver to keep the change.

As we got out, she turned back to him and touched his hand. His expression went slack, and he stared at her with empty eyes.

"You never saw us," she said in an even tone. "You will drive back into the city and forget about this fare."

The driver nodded, then blinked and smiled at her with a dazed expression on his face.

He drove away, and I raised an eyebrow at Lyla.

"What just happened there?" I asked.

She winked at me but didn't elaborate. Once again, I was

amazed at the possibilities that opened up when magic was involved.

Lyla took a good look around the neighborhood. It looked like the typical middle-class suburban street. Brick houses built close together. Basketball goals in the driveway. Shrubbery. Most of the lights in the nearby houses were off. A red tricycle sat in the driveway of the house next door. A dog barked in the distance.

"Notice anything out of the ordinary?" she asked. "Or did the effects of the Blue Frost wear off after the explosion?"

I looked around, trying to notice the kinds of tiny details I had noticed earlier. But the shot seemed to be out of my system. Maybe the shock of the explosion had sobered me up.

Nothing seemed strange or out of place about the area. There were no strange cars parked on the street. No one looking out of windows. No dark feeling. But without the shot, I knew I could be missing a hundred important details.

"I have no idea," I said. "The shot is gone, but I don't see anything weird."

"Okay, follow me."

Lyla walked around to the back door of the house. I expected her to look around for a spare key, the way I'd done at my mom's abandoned house. Instead, she placed her palm on a small clear stone embedded in the door frame.

The door popped open, and she took one last look around before stepping inside.

The inside of the house smelled like dust and mildew. It was dark, and when she flipped the switch near the back door, nothing happened.

"Shit, the power's off," she said.

"I'm guessing from the smell no one's used this place in

quite some time."

She laughed. "Years, probably. At least four, I think."

"So, you've been here before?" I closed the back door and carefully followed her into what seemed to be a living room. The light coming in from the street through the front windows illuminated the outline of a couch and recliner.

"It's been a while, but yeah. I came here maybe seven years ago when I had a scare with an ex-boyfriend of mine who came after me. Rend put me up here for a little while to keep me safe until he could... deal with it."

I shivered at the thought of what Rend's version of dealing with a dangerous ex might be. Had he torn him apart?

"The power was on back then," she said. She tripped over something on the floor and cursed.

"You okay?"

"I'm fine," she said. "Do you know how to make an orb?"

"Definitely not," I said. "You can just assume my answer is no when you ask if I can do anything magic-related."

She giggled. "You seemed to create a small tornado just fine earlier."

I groaned. "That was an accident."

"Powerful accident," she murmured.

Was it? I had no idea what power really meant anymore.

"Can you do it?" I asked. "Make an orb, I mean."

"I'm not great at it," she said. "It's not one of my gifts. Plus, I don't want to waste any of my power in case we have to leave again. I think I know where some candles are, though. Wait here."

She tripped over a few more things as she made her way into another room off the main hall. A few minutes later, she came back carrying a long white pillar candle. She held her hand over the small flame to keep it from going out as she walked.

"Success," she said. "I'm much better with fire."

I raised an eyebrow. "So it seems."

"Come on, let's go upstairs. I need to get out of these ridiculous clothes and into something more comfortable," she said. "Tomorrow's going to be hell with no air conditioning."

I followed her up the stairs, noticing along the way that there were no pictures or decorations of any kind here. It felt very empty and hollow.

We made our way into a bedroom in the back of the house. It was sparsely furnished with nothing more than a basic queen bed and a side table. Lyla set the candle on the table and pulled open the sliding doors of the closet.

"Rend keeps a bunch of spare clothes here for anyone who might have to hide out for a while without more than a moment's notice to gather our things," she explained. "There should be some toothbrushes and shampoo and stuff in the bathroom, too. Oh god, what if there's no water, either?"

"You said Rend might be here tomorrow," I said. "We shouldn't have to rough it for too long before someone shows up."

"We could both use a shower, though," she said. "We smell like smoke from the fire. Besides, we need to get that cut on your forehead cleaned up and see what kind of damage there is."

I raised my hand to the sore spot above my eye and traced my fingers along a two-inch cut caked with blood. "Shit, no wonder people were staring at us. I probably look like I've been in a fight."

"We're both caked in ash, too," she said.

She rummaged through the closet and came out with a pair of yoga pants and a tank top. "Here, these look about your size if you want to change."

I took the clothes and waited for her to find something for herself before we both made our way into the master bathroom. She crossed her fingers, then turned the faucet. Water sputtered out, then flowed freely.

"Yay, thank you Jesus."

I smiled. "That's something at least," I said. "You'd think if he was going to keep this as a permanent safe-house, he would have kept the power on, though. It's not like he's hurting for money. I mean, have you seen his house?"

I said it as an off-handed comment, not really thinking, but Lyla nearly dropped the candle.

"Um, excuse me? Are you saying you have?"

I cleared my throat. Shit. I really needed to watch my stupid mouth.

"You have," she said, her eyes wide. "I'm going to clean that cut and get changed, and then you're going to dish the good stuff. We might be here for days, but now at least I know we'll have something fun to talk about."

She seemed giddy at the thought of me knowing secrets about Rend, but it made my stomach hurt. I'm sure Rend didn't want me telling the rest of the staff what had been going on between us the past few days. Hell, I wasn't even sure what was going on with us. I'd been hoping to get more clarity about our relationship after the club closed tonight, but now everything had changed.

"It's not as juicy as you think," I said.

I winced as she rubbed a cold washcloth on my forehead. Blood trickled down my cheek and she wiped it off.

"Hold still," she said.

"I'm trying, but that stings."

"Sorry, I'm just trying to get a better look at the damage. I don't think the cut went too deep, so it should heal fine," she said. "Let me see if I can find some bandages."

She found a first-aid kit under the sink, rubbed ointment on the cut, and fixed a bandage over the top.

"Let's get changed and see if there's anything here to eat."

"Are you serious? You said no one's been here in four years. What could there possibly be to eat?" I asked.

She made a face. "Good point," she said. "I would say let's order pizza, but it's too risky at this point to let anyone know we're here. I'm starving, though."

My stomach rumbled at the thought of food. "Me, too," I said. "We'll figure something out."

We went back into the bedroom and changed out of our dirty clothes. I took my time, hoping by the time we got downstairs, Lyla would have forgotten what I'd said about Rend's house.

"Does this place have a phone? Or do you happen to have your cell on you?" I asked as we made our way back down to the kitchen.

"No," she said. "But don't worry, Rend will come for us. Everything's going to be okay."

I nodded and followed her into the kitchen. I wished I could be so confident, but I didn't like the feeling of being so far away from him right now. And I really didn't like not knowing for sure that he was okay.

Lyla and I searched the cabinets, but there was nothing here other than a few packs of stale saltines and a very old can of baked beans.

"What if we ordered pizza and you did your little magical memory thing on the delivery guy?"

She shook her head. "I don't know any place that's going to deliver after two in the morning on a Sunday," she said. "We'll have to just wait until morning. We can walk down to the gas station around the corner when they open and grab something for breakfast. They should be open in about four hours or so."

I groaned. I wished she had never mentioned food, because now I was starving, too.

"Do you want to try to get some rest?"

"I don't think I could sleep right now even if I tried," I said. I probably wouldn't be able to sleep until I saw Rend walk through that door.

Lyla set the candle down on the coffee table in front of the couch and walked over to the large window in the living room. She reached over and pulled a thick, dusty curtain across the window, closing off nearly all the outside light.

"I don't want someone out there to notice the candle and call the police or anything," she said, sitting down on the couch. She pulled her feet up and placed them under her, turning to me with a sparkle in her eyes. "I'm dying to know what's been going on, Franki. When did you see Rend's house? What's it like? And what did the two of you do there, exactly?"

I sighed. So much for hoping she'd forget. I had a feeling she wasn't going to let it go until I gave her something.

"I don't really know how much there is to tell," I said, sitting across from her. "To be honest, I'm still confused about what's going on between Rend and me. He's confusing."

"Give me the basics, and I'll see if I can interpret," she said with a giggle.

I sighed. Other than Katy, I'd never had true girlfriends to chat with and spill my secrets. Somehow, this terrible night had turned into a gossip session, and I was mega-uncomfortable.

"Let's start with this," she said. "Has he kissed you?"

I closed my eyes and tensed my lips.

"Oh, my God, he has," she said. She grabbed my hand. "Franki, this is huge. I have known Rend for years, and he has never, and I mean ne-ver, gotten romantically involved with anyone in all the time I've known him."

"Until right now, you didn't know he was romantically involved with me, either," I said, raising one eyebrow.

"True," she said. "But I had my suspicions. I've never even almost suspected he was dating someone before this."

"We're not dating." I bit the inside of my lip and gave her a sideways look, my heart beating a little faster. "Not even Azure?"

I said it so quietly, it was almost a non-question. I was terrified the moment the words left my lips. I definitely had my suspicions about Azure's feelings for Rend. What I didn't know was how Rend felt about her.

"What? Are you serious? Never," she said. She narrowed her eyes at me. "Why? Did she tell you there was something between them?"

I shrugged, wondering if I'd already said too much. "Not exactly," I said. "She's just been really hard on me from the moment I walked into Venom, and the closer I get to Rend, the more she treats me like shit. Then tonight..."

My voice trailed off. I had almost let myself forget the horrible things she'd said to me tonight, behind the bar. She'd called me currency. I hoped he thought of me as more than that, but what if this was all some game he was playing with me?

"What?" Lyla put her hand on my leg and leaned closer. "What did she do?"

"She said something awful to me tonight when we were working together behind the bar," I said. "It made me wonder if there had ever been something more between them. Something romantic."

"Not that I've ever known about," she said. "Azure has been with him from the beginning, so she's known him a lot longer than I have. Still, I think everyone would know if there had ever been something between them."

"He trusts her," I said. "He's apparently filled her in on all the things he found out about me, when he obviously didn't tell everyone else."

"Like what?"

"Like who my real family is," I said. "When she was talking to me tonight, she mentioned it, so he had to have told her. How else would she have known?"

Lyla went back to chewing on her fingernail. "What if he didn't tell her? What if she had some other way of finding out information about you?"

I shook my head. "Like what?"

"I don't know," she said, shaking her head. "Forget it. I'm just thinking out loud. What was it she said to you tonight that was so awful?"

I shrugged. I hated even to utter the words, because they had been so hurtful. Mainly because I was worried they were true. I wasn't sure I wanted to lay my heart on the line in front of Lyla.

"You can tell me," she said. "I'm not going to go blabbing

back to the rest of the girls, if that's what you're afraid of."

"I don't know," I said. I felt terrible talking about the people in the club when we didn't even know how they were doing or where they were right now. Were they really okay? "Don't get me wrong, I think you're awesome and you've made me feel welcome from the second I started working at Venom."

"But?"

"I haven't had a lot of people in my life that I've gotten close to," I said. "When I was growing up my mother kept me very sheltered. We moved around a lot and I didn't have many friends. She never really let me have girlfriends over or get too close to anyone. It's hard for me to really open up sometimes."

Lyla leaned over and put her arms around me. "I'm sorry," she said. "You've been going through a lot the past week and here I am, forcing you to spill all your personal shit. I didn't mean to make you feel uncomfortable."

I hugged her back, grateful she was at least willing to listen and empathize.

But the truth was, now that she'd basically given me a pass, I realized I wanted to tell her. I desperately wanted someone I could talk to about all this.

Talking to Katy was one thing. She was my dearest friend, and I knew I could talk to her about anything. At the same time, she had no clue about how this new world worked. She didn't know any of the players involved so she couldn't completely understand what I was going through.

It would be nice to have someone, apart from Rend, to confide in and ask for advice.

I took a deep breath. "Do you know who Rend is?" I asked. "I mean, do you know what he is?"

Lyla leaned back against the arm of the couch. She opened

her mouth in a moment of realization. "Ah, you mean the vampire thing? I wasn't sure if you knew. He doesn't keep it a secret, but he also doesn't exactly advertise the fact."

So, she knew. That was a relief, because even if I decided to spill my own secrets, I wouldn't feel right spilling his.

"I just found out last night," I said, leaving out the details of how I'd found out. She didn't need to know everything. "I almost didn't come back to the club tonight, which is why you found me outside before we opened. I was trying to make up my mind about whether to even go inside."

"He's not like the rest of them," she said. "Not all of them are like the Devil, you know. I mean, some of them are, but a lot of the vampires are really great."

"They drink the blood of witches," I said. "That's hard to redeem."

She shrugged. "Did Rend explain why they do it?"

I shook my head.

"Do you know where demons come from? Has anyone explained that to you, at least?"

I shook my head again, feeling for the millionth time like a clueless child.

"Okay, so I'll give you the short version. Demons are not native to this world. Neither are witches. Demons come from another world called The Shadow World. They came here hundreds of years ago through a portal. The first demon was named Mythic, and he fell in love with a human woman. They had a child together. The very first human with magical powers. The first witch. See, a witch is just a human woman with the blood of a demon running through her veins."

"What about men? Are there male witches?"

"No, only women," she said. "I don't really know why, but

only daughters get magical powers through demons. The strength of a witch's line begins to diminish the farther the line gets from the original demon union, but any girl who has magical abilities is a descendent of a demon somewhere along the way."

I ran a hand through my hair, allowing her story to sink in.

"When a witch casts spells here in the human world, she connects to the power within herself to cast. But when a demon from the Shadow World casts magic, they pull energy from the life around them," she said.

"What does that mean, exactly?"

"It means that if a demon was standing here and he or she wanted to cast, they would need to pull energy from you or me or the grass outside or a bug sitting on the windowsill. Something living. Does that make sense?"

"Yeah."

The candle on the coffee table flickered, throwing eerie shadows across the wall.

"The problem early demons had with this, is that every time they cast, they left a mark on this world. Grass or animals around them died when they used their magic. It made them easy to track. They had reasons they needed to keep their presence secret from the rest of the human world, so one of the demons in charge came up with a very creative solution."

I nodded, my skin tingling. "They drank the blood of witches."

"Exactly," she said. "You catch on fast."

"It makes sense," I said. "If they can drink the blood of a witch, they can pull from the power inside without anyone ever knowing."

"Yes," she said. "Of course, they still left dead bodies of the witches they drained completely, but they could drain a witch of her blood in Chicago and then go to New York and cast in secret without anyone being able to detect their presence," she said. "That's where the lore of vampires began and, of course, humans took that to the cinema and glorified it."

"Fascinating," I said. "And very creative, when you think about it."

"The tough part is that when a demon took the oath to become a part of the Brotherhood of Darkness, which is the order of the vampires, they had to undergo a very painful transformation that allowed them to use the blood in the most efficient way possible. Over time, the demons who transformed into vampires became unable to cast without the blood."

"So, they lost their ability to cast in the normal way demons cast?"

"Yes," she said. "Some of them, like Rend, got tired of all the senseless killing of the Brotherhood. They rebelled, refusing to drink the blood of witches. That's when Rend came up with the idea of opening Venom. For him, it became a refuge from the evils of this world."

I leaned against the cushions on the couch and thought about how hard it must have been for Rend to make that decision. To turn away from what he had become and start a new life.

But I had seen him cast an orb. How did he do that without blood?

Or was he still drinking blood in secret?

I reached up and touched the spot on my neck where he had bitten me. With horror, I realized that after the excitement of the explosion, I had forgotten all about re-casting the glamour that hid the wounds.

Lyla grabbed my hand and pulled it away from my neck. "Holy fuck," she said. "Who did that to you?"

I pulled away from her, wishing I'd never touched the spot. In the dim light of the candle she might not have noticed it without me drawing attention to it.

"Did Rend do that?" she asked. Her hands were shaking.

I swallowed and stood up, avoiding her eyes.

"Franki, I'm serious. Did he hurt you?"

"I think it surprised him as much as it surprised me, to be honest. He barely broke the skin before he stopped himself."

Lyla brought a trembling hand to her mouth. "I have never seen him lose control like that," she said. "What happened between the two of you?"

I blushed as butterflies stirred in my stomach. Thankfully, there was no way she could see the flush of my cheeks in the darkness, but every time I thought about how close we had come to making love, my body grew warm.

"Oh," she said. "OH."

"Please, don't tell anyone else," I said, turning to her. The candlelight flickered across her shocked face.

"I don't even know what to say," she said. "I've just never seen him lose control, especially not over a woman. You must really get to him."

"He gets to me, too," I said. "I—"

My words caught in my throat as the back door clicked open and footsteps rushed across the tile in the kitchen.

Lyla sucked in a scared breath and grabbed me, pulling me back toward the stairs as a tall black man with thick dreadlocks stepped into the dim light of the candle still burning on the table.

YOU BELONG TO THE DEVIL

"It's me," a voice whispered in the darkness. Someone walked around the black man and reached for us. "Lyla?"

"Marco?" Lyla's grip on me softened and she reached for his hand. "Oh, thank God. Who's with you?"

"This is Mordecai," he said, turning to the other man. "You don't know him, but he's an old friend of Rend's."

"Is Rend okay?" I asked, my heart pumping.

"Franki?" Marco moved into the small ring of light coming from the candle. He had a big smile on his face. "You have no idea how happy Rend is going to be when he finds out you're okay."

"We got to get moving, man," Mordecai said, glancing toward the back door. "They're close."

Chills ran down my spine. "Who's close?"

"Fallon and some of his friends," Marco said. "I don't know how they found you, but they've been tracking the two of you since you left the club. Did you guys use magic? We barely made it here ahead of them."

I touched the cut on my forehead, wondering if the vampires had been able to track my blood. Before we could answer him, though, the front window shattered. I jumped back as two shadowy forms flew through the gaping hole in the living room.

Instantly, the room filled with a dark energy that shot fear through my veins.

Mordecai reacted first. He lifted his two large hands in the air and every piece of furniture in the room rose and flew toward the two intruders.

"Run," Lyla yelled, grabbing me for the second time that night. She pushed past Marco and Mordecai and made a break for the back door, but before we could find our way out, two more dark smoky forms broke through the door.

"Shit," she said, turning back toward the others. "We're trapped."

Marco moved around behind us, heading off the two new demons. A bright white light shot out from his fingertips, forming a rope that he whipped around the neck of the first demon. He yanked on the magical rope and pulled. The demon screamed. It was a high-pitched, painful sound that nearly brought me to my knees. With another whip of his rope, Marco brought the demon to the ground, but before he could get close to him, the demon turned to smoke and flew backward.

I stood in the middle of the attack, helpless to defend myself. My mind could barely register what was happening, much less how to join the attack.

The candle blew out, leaving us in darkness. Somehow,

they must have broken the street light outside. Now, the only light came from the flash of the spells cast back and forth around me.

Lyla stood completely still, her eyes closed and her hand outstretched. One of the first attackers stood equally still just inches from her hand, his eyes wide open in terror. I had no idea what she was doing to him, but whatever it was, it looked like he couldn't move or control his own body.

Mordecai fought one of the others, a silver dagger flashing in his hand.

Marco battled with the two at the back door, but without me helping, we were outnumbered. I had to do something.

I tried to calm the panic in my heart and instead, I remembered what the girls had taught me earlier that night in the dressing room.

Connect to your power, Franki. You can do this.

It took a few tries to calm down enough. I felt the pressure of time, knowing that if I didn't figure this out fast, we might all die right here and now.

Or worse.

They might kill the others and take me to the Devil. I did not want to find out what he wanted to do with me.

I forced a deeper breath, searching for that spark of power deep within myself. I imagined dipping my fingers into that well of power, then opened my eyes and knew I had found it.

I had no idea how to fuel it, but before I could even think about it, I knew I had all the fuel I needed right here. My power had always been closely tied to my darkest emotions. Anger. Rage. Sorrow. My whole life, these emotions had been dangerous for me. Now, they were my best hope at surviving the night.

I embraced the anger inside me, picturing Selena's eyes as the light drained from them.

I fueled my power with rage, letting it blossom deep inside, radiating from my center until it consumed me. I could feel the buzz of it travel along my nerves until my hands shook with tension.

My hair blew back from my shoulders as a great wave of wind washed through the room.

I focused my gaze on the second demon fighting Marco. He was half-human, half-smoke. I imagined harnessing the power of that wind-force, gathering it into my hands. I pulled it back toward my body, and then pushed outward, sending a strong wind straight at him.

The demon's eyes flashed with surprise as he flew up and back, his body slamming into the back wall of the house so hard the drywall split into pieces. He fell to the floor, his eyes closed and his head limp against his shoulder.

I turned to the one who had come in the back door with him, but before I could repeat the spell, a coil of black smoke wrapped around my neck and yanked me backward.

I clawed at the smoke but couldn't get hold of it. It was as if a ghost held me, there, but completely unformed. I could feel it against my skin, but when I tried to grab it with my hands, it was like it wasn't really there.

How did you fight an enemy like this?

I struggled for breath but couldn't draw a single wisp of air into my lungs.

My bare feet dragged along the floor until my back hit the muscled chest of the demon who held me captive.

Mordecai lay unconscious on the floor at my feet.

Lyla's eyes flew open, and she seemed to lose her concentration when she saw me. The demon she'd been holding under her spell broke free and descended on her so fast she didn't have time to react.

I tried to scream, but had no air left to make a sound. My pulse throbbed in my neck where the demon's coil of smoke held me.

He leaned close to my ear and in a deep, ominous voice, he whispered, "Forget her. You belong to the Devil now."

ASH AND CHALK

My vision blurred, and my knees weakened.

I couldn't breathe.

I used every ounce of strength in my body to struggle against him, desperate to break free long enough to draw a breath. If I passed out now, I might never wake up.

I refused to let this be the end of me.

The rage I'd felt before he grabbed me intensified. A strong wind blew through the room.

I pushed my hand forward, then drew my elbow back into the demon's stomach. It wasn't enough to make him drop me, but it was enough to make him loosen his grip long enough for me to take one glorious breath of air.

I inhaled, filling my lungs. Inside me, the breath connected with the fear and rage rising inside me. The air descended into the very core of my power.

Darkness consumed me, and I felt a shift in my power. Instead of rage, I moved toward hatred. It expanded like a tumor in my heart, black and malignant, poisoning my power.

All I could think about was how much I wanted to hurt this demon who held me. I wanted him dead.

Acting on that instinct, I turned my head to the side and opened my mouth wide, exhaling that dark breath. A black, oily smoke oozed from my mouth. It tasted of ash and chalk. The shadow took on a life of its own, shifting into a thousand tiny mosquitoes. The winged bugs swarmed around the head of the demon holding me. He screamed and dropped the smoky rope coiled around my neck. I pulled away, gasping for breath.

In horror, I watched as the swarm of bugs flew into his mouth, nose, ears and eyes. The demon clawed at his face. He screamed and fell to the floor, scratching at his chest and arms furiously as his now-human skin bubbled with large black welts.

The mosquitoes were inside him, eating him from the inside. His body began to shrivel and decay right before my eyes, as if the bugs were eating him alive.

My screams joined with his. How could this darkness have come from me?

What had I done?

I watched in terror as his body jerked and shook and turned to bone and ash before me. Dark smoke rose from the decayed form of the dead demon. I backed away, but the energy of whatever was left of him found me, entering me through my mouth, the bugs returning to wherever they'd come from.

His life-power filled me up, fueling me with a dark energy that oozed through my veins, thick and slow. Wind whipped around us, sweeping the remaining ash against the wall near the stairs.

I gasped and fell to my knees, unable to believe what I'd done. Yes, I had wanted him to stop hurting me, but I hadn't meant to kill him. Not like that. I felt sick.

But at the same time, I felt alive. The darkness running through me made me feel invincible and powerful, as if I could kill them all with a flick of my wrist. I struggled against that darkness, but its power fought to seduce me.

"Franki?"

Lyla's voice was thin and shaky.

I looked up, remembering there were still more demons left to fight. But all of the fighting in the room had stopped. The night descended into a silence so complete I could hear nothing but the beating of my own heart and the call of the darkness within.

I turned to the other three vampires in the room. Their eyes filled with awe and complete terror.

Part of me wanted to collapse completely at their feet and beg for forgiveness. I wanted to tell them I hadn't meant it. Killing him was an accident. At the same time, another part of me wanted to rise up stronger than ever and kill them all. They attacked us. They brought this on themselves.

It was fight or die right now, for all of us. And I wasn't ready to die.

I turned to the demon who still had Lyla pinned to the floor. I pointed my index finger at him.

"Let her go," I said. My voice did not even sound like my own. It was deeper. Richer. And most definitely darker.

The demon obeyed, releasing his hold on Lyla's arms. She stood and rushed over to Marco's side, grabbing his arm. When she looked at me, it was impossible to miss the fear in her eyes.

I turned my gaze to the other two demons, but my vision

tinted, making them hard to see in the darkness of the night. I shook my head, blinking.

The room spun, and I placed a hand on my forehead. I gasped for breath, unable to focus on anything or anyone. I couldn't seem to get my bearings. My stomach lurched, and I doubled over, leaning against the toppled couch for support.

Lyla ran to my side. She took my hand in hers and helped me stand up straight. Before I could decide what should be done about the three demons still facing us, she raised her free hand toward them. The three of them froze. Lyla's hand wobbled, every muscle in her body tense as she stared them down.

Marco nodded toward Mordecai and the tall black demon stepped forward. He lifted his silver dagger to the throat of each demon, slicing them from ear-to-ear. Black blood ran down their bodies like obsidian waterfalls.

When their eyes were closed and their bodies drained, Lyla lowered her hand. All three bodies fell to the floor like ragdolls.

I stared at the carnage, my mouth open. A final gust of wind whipped my hair across my face.

Lyla leaned against me, resting her hip against the overturned couch. "Franki, sweetheart, it's okay," she said. Her voice was strained and she struggled to catch her breath. "You're safe."

I swallowed, barely able to hear her over the panic that rang in my ears. Panic and fear.

I had become someone else, completely overcome by a darkness that scared the shit out of me. How could any of them still be standing here by my side after what had come out of me? If I were them, I would have run as far away as I could.

"I'm so sorry," I said. The deep tone had left my voice, replaced by a trembling terror. "I swear I didn't mean to do that. I didn't mean to hurt him like that. I just wanted him to leave me alone."

Mordecai smiled and laughed, a deep rumbling sound that seemed out of place among the bodies of the dead. "Are you kidding me?" he asked. "That was the singularly most bad-ass thing I've seen a human witch do in a very long time."

He seemed happy and impressed, but I felt sick.

It hadn't felt impressive to me at all. It felt wrong and evil.

An image of the Mother Crow flashed through my mind. She was known to be one of the most evil witches who ever lived, and tonight, I had shown my connection to her in the most raw, horrific way imaginable.

"I hate to bring it up, but we're still in danger," Marco said. "Knowing the Devil, this is just the first wave. And we just barely managed to defeat them. I don't know about you guys, but I don't want to find out what happens when more of them show up."

"Or the Devil himself," Lyla said in a whisper.

"Where will we go?" I asked. All I wanted was to find Rend. I wanted him to explain what had just happened to me.

And how to make sure it never happened again.

"We have a plan, but it's going to take considerable power to pull it off," Mordecai said. He looked to me and lifted his chin. "You up for it?"

I swallowed back the bile that coated my throat. Was I? Did I have a choice?

If it was death or my best attempt, I was willing to give it every ounce of whatever power lay inside my body.

"I can try," I said. "What does it involve?"

"Are you familiar with glamours?" Marco asked.

Lyla took my hand in hers again, and I was grateful for the reassuring motion. It was good to know she wasn't horrified by me.

"We actually just showed her how to do one earlier tonight," Lyla said. She glanced at the marks on my neck. "Think you can do it again?"

I nodded. As long as it didn't involve vomiting mosquitoes, I was good to go.

"What do you want me to do?"

Marco locked eyes with Lyla. "This involves you, too," he said. "And it's asking a lot, so if you want to say no, there's no shame in that."

Lyla's mouth opened in surprise. "What is it?"

"We need the two of you to change places," Mordecai said. He walked over to the broken window in the living room and looked out. "I'm guessing we don't have much time to pull this off. I can feel their energy moving closer. We'll have to time it just right to make it work."

"What do you mean switch places?" I asked.

"I need for you to glamour yourself to look like Lyla, and for her to do the same with you," he said. "That way anyone following Franki gets confused and follows the wrong trail."

"You want me to be a decoy Franki?" Lyla asked. Her hand slipped from mine. I couldn't tell from her voice if she was upset or resigned. "They'll all follow me instead."

"Lyla, I can't ask you to do this," I said. "I'll run. If we go now, we could leave before the others arrive."

She turned to me. "Franki, there's no way I'm letting you leave without at least trying this," she said. "I'll do whatever I can to save you."

"Why?" I asked, shaking my head. "Why are so many people risking their lives to save me?"

She gave me a small smile. "You're a part of our family now. Our Venom family. And if you mean this much to Rend, you mean this much to all of us."

"If something happens to you, I'll never forgive myself."

"It's going to put you in serious danger," Marco said. He stood in front of Lyla and put his hands on her shoulders. "Like I said, I know this is way too much to ask of you. If you don't want to do it, we can just take our chances and hope Franki gets away without our help."

"But you need to decide now," Mordecai said. His dark eyes searched the yard in front of the house, his shoulders tensing.

"She's really important, isn't she?" Lyla asked, almost as if I wasn't standing here beside her. "What does the Devil want with her?"

"We don't know exactly, but Rend suspects the Devil wants to perform a permanent spell of some sort. One that requires a powerful blood sacrifice."

Lyla turned to me. "Who are you?"

I shook my head. Now was not the time for secrets, but I had never been more ashamed of my family line than I was at that moment. "I'm a descendant of the Mother Crow," I said, giving voice to the truth for the first time.

"Oh my God," Lyla said in a whisper. She backed away from Marco and lifted a hand to her mouth. "So, it's not just powerful blood that runs through your veins. It's blood that's tainted with the darkest kinds of magic."

I flinched, knowing she was right. But also knowing I had never asked for this darkness.

There was no way Lyla would risk her life for me, not after finding out who I really was. I couldn't blame her.

"If the Devil is able to use you for a blood sacrifice, he'll be unstoppable," she said. "He could gain enough power to rule this world if we don't stop him."

"We have to stop him," Mordecai said. "No matter what it takes."

Lyla faced Mordecai and took a deep breath in through her nose.

"Let's do it," she said.

"No, Lyla, please." I grabbed her hand and shook my head, but no one seemed to care what I had to say about the matter. Lyla had said yes. That was all that mattered.

"I'll watch the back door," Marco said. "Mordecai, you keep an eye on the front. Ladies? Hurry."

"Let's go upstairs where it's quiet and, um, less bloody." Lyla pulled me toward the stairs. When we got to the landing, she sat down and motioned for me to sit across from her.

We sat in exactly the same position we had earlier tonight, knee-to-knee, our legs crossed beneath us and our hands clasped.

"Just breathe," she said. "Focus on that energy deep inside, like we talked about earlier."

Tears sprang to my eyes. "I'm not sure I can do this," I said. "Not after what happened earlier."

"You can and you will," she said. "All our lives depend on this. Don't be scared, Franki. Your power manifested the way it did because you were angry and full of fear. Concentrate on something else. Control the power. Don't let it control you. You can do this."

My breath hitched in my throat.

Could I? How could I be sure my power wouldn't consume me again? How could I be sure I wasn't going to kill anyone else?

"You ready?" she asked.

"No. But let's try this anyway."

She squeezed my hands. "Take a moment to study my face. Take in every detail you can, from my hair to my eyes, everything that would make me immediately recognizable at a glance. It doesn't have to be perfect, but it has to at least be enough to fool someone in the dark."

I nodded. I studied her, taking in her chin-length brown hair and her dark brown eyes. I knew she was several inches shorter than I was. I studied the curve of her lips and the shape of her nose.

Mordecai peered around the bottom of the stairs. "Hurry up, ladies, we have to move. They're coming."

"Shh," Lyla said to him without taking her eyes off my face. "Don't let panic cloud your energy. It's going to be okay. Now, close your eyes."

I took one last look at her face, then closed my eyes. I felt us both breathe in together. We clasped hands, knowing our lives depended on this moment right here, right now.

We had to get this right the first try or there might never be a second chance.

I focused on the energy inside my core, pulling away at first, then pushing forward. I had to trust that I could embrace the power inside me without allowing it to turn to darkness.

I focused on the spark of power buzzing through me, then tapped into it slowly, allowing the warm strength of it to flow through me. When I felt connected and ready, I pictured every detail of Lyla's face and skin and hair. I saw her clearly in my mind's eye, picturing myself becoming her.

I felt the change of my hair immediately. Instead of my long, heavy hair, it was suddenly light and slightly curled around my face. Curls tickled my cheek and I opened my eyes.

I gasped, the sight of her a shock to my system.

I was looking at a perfect replica of myself.

NOT A CHANCE

M arco stared at us, narrowing his eyes, as if trying to catch any missing details.

"Either it didn't work at all or you guys are fucking good at this," he said.

I exhaled. If we could fool Marco—someone who had known Lyla for many years—we could fool anyone.

I hoped.

"You'll never know," Lyla said, winking.

Marco leaned toward her. "You may look like Franki, but you're still acting like Lyla."

"Shit," she said, wrinkling her nose. My nose. Sort of. "I didn't think of that."

"Just don't speak and do your best to act and walk like the other girl," Mordecai said. "You'll be fine. Hopefully no one will ever get close enough to see the details, anyway."

"Where will we go?" I asked.

"Separate ways," Marco said. "That's all you need to know for now."

Shadows moved across the lawn and all of us tensed. Fear rippled across my skin.

"Here we go," Lyla said, squeezing my hand one last time. "Be safe."

"You too," I said. I pulled her into a hug. I still couldn't believe she was willing to do this for me. To save me. "Thank you."

"You owe me one," she said, smiling.

Marco grabbed her hand and nodded to Mordecai. "See you in this world or the next, my friend."

Mordecai clasped his large hand around my bicep and raised his eyebrows at me. "Let's go," he said. "Hold on as long as you can."

I nodded, understanding what he'd meant earlier about this glamour taking more power to complete. Hiding the marks on my neck had only taken a small amount of my energy, but becoming Lyla had taken more out of me than I expected. A headache was forming behind my eyes and my knees felt weak.

I knew if we were forced to fight again, I would be of no use to any of them.

The shadowy figures on the lawn burst through the front door and the window just as Marco and the fake Franki took off through the back.

Mordecai and I followed, the vampires close behind us. Just as we passed through the back door, Mordecai pulled a vial from his pocket and smashed it onto the floor. A thick silver fog rose around us, hiding us all as we made our escape.

Two cars waited for us out back—a large black Escalade and a sporty white Mercedes. I followed Mordecai's lead toward the Escalade as Marco and Lyla ran to the Mercedes.

Just before I ducked my head inside the car, Lyla and I

locked eyes. I hoped this would not be the last time we saw each other.

"Go," Marco yelled. "I've got Franki."

He said it loud enough for the shadowy figures to hear as they emerged from the rubble and fog inside the house.

Mordecai started up the car and took off before I could even get my door closed. I slid across the seat and quickly buckled up. I had a feeling this was going to be one hell of a bumpy ride.

I turned to look behind us as we raced down the driveway. Marco and Lyla got into the Mercedes and tore off in the other direction.

I waited, watching with nerves tingling. I bit down hard on my lip. The vampires didn't have cars, but they could fly. The leader of their group of six turned to watch the two cars.

In the distance, sirens sounded. Someone in the neighborhood must have called the cops.

The vampire leader pointed a shadowy finger toward the Mercedes. The leader and three of his followers shifted to smoke and flew off after Marco's car. The remaining two followed us.

Mordecai took a corner so hard I slammed against the seat and had to grab the handle to keep from crashing into the side of him.

"Hold on," he said.

He pushed his foot down hard on the gas pedal, blasting through a four-way stop without any hesitation. The vampires followed, their bodies nothing but blurred shadows hovering in the air behind us.

"Can we outrun them?" I asked.

"Not a chance," Mordecai said. He flashed a smile. "But I have other plans."

He let up on the gas just a little as we approached a red light up ahead. Thankfully, it was so late at night no one else was out on the road. If he kept driving like this, though, the cops we heard would find us and we'd be forced to stop.

The shadows of the two vampires hovered near my window. I looked at them, hoping they couldn't tell the difference between me and the real Lyla. I concentrated on the power holding the glamour, begging it to hold up just a little bit longer.

Mordecai punched the gas again, then turned the wheel hard to the left and slammed on the brakes. The two vampires crashed into the side of the Escalade, their bodies shifting back into human form and falling onto the pavement.

Mordecai laughed, then hit the gas as hard as he could. "That should hold them a few minutes."

He turned down several side streets before coming out near a major intersection and pulling onto the highway. When we'd made it several miles away, he checked the rear-view mirror again, then slowed to a normal speed. Our car blended in with the rest of the late-night traffic on the Interstate.

I let out a deep sigh of relief. At least for now, we were safe.

Over the miles that followed, I didn't say a word. I had a million questions about where we were heading and if Rend would be waiting for me there. But the question that kept me silent was one Mordecai couldn't answer any better than I could.

Would Marco and Lyla be okay? What would happen to them if the other vampires caught up to them?

And what if even more came after them?

I slumped down in the soft leather seat, staring straight ahead as Mordecai drove south, away from the city.

I still couldn't believe Lyla had been willing to put herself in so much danger to save my life. What had I ever done to deserve that kind of loyalty?

I didn't understand it. I didn't deserve it.

And Lyla wasn't the only one willing to risk her life. Selena had died to save me. She had argued with Rend about the explosive device. She didn't want to take it from him. I'd heard her clearly say she wasn't going to risk her life for me.

And yet she had.

What had Rend whispered in her ear last night to make her change her mind? What could he have possibly said to make her take the small bead and put it in her pocket?

And as she lay dying, when her eyes locked with mine, what thought had gone through her head? Why did she choose to make that sacrifice to save me?

I closed my eyes, letting the sound of the tires on the highway calm me.

I might never know why these people I'd just met were so willing to lay down their lives for me, or why Rend had taken a chance to protect me. But I vowed that night to make sure their sacrifices had not been in vain.

I vowed to make sure I did not become the sacrifice the Devil wanted to turn me into.

I would not let him win.

I would do whatever it took to take him down and make sure my new family at Venom never had to risk their lives for me again.

I drifted off to sleep with that thought heavy on my heart.

Several hours later, as Mordecai slowed and pulled off the interstate, the change in rhythm pulled me from my sleep. The sun colored the sky in pinks and purples on the horizon.

I rubbed my eyes and sat up in my seat. "Where are we?"

"About an hour north of Nashville," Mordecai said.

Nashville? How long had I been asleep? The clock on the dashboard read seven thirty-three.

"I didn't mean to fall asleep," I said.

Mordecai glanced over at me and smiled. For such a big man, he had a soft smile that warmed me and made me trust him.

"You needed your rest," he said. He reached behind the seat and pulled out an Atlanta Braves baseball cap. "Here, put this on. We're in the clear for now, but you lost your glamour in your sleep, and I don't want to risk anyone recognizing you."

I leaned over and glanced at myself in the rear-view mirror. My eyes were ringed with dark circles and my skin looked awful with no makeup, but I had my own face back for now. I pulled my hair up and slipped the ball cap over it.

"Have you heard anything from Marco?" I asked. "Did they get away?"

"I don't know," he said. "We can't have any contact with anyone from Venom for now. It's too risky."

My face crumpled. What if something terrible happened to them? I would never forgive myself.

Mordecai glanced over at me. "I think they'll be all right," he said. "Marco's a lot stronger than he looks, and there were a few other friends waiting to help them out on their journey. As long as they were able to make it to the airport, they're okay. Probably halfway to Las Vegas by now."

"Vegas?"

"Rend had a private jet waiting for them at the airport. He filed a false flight plan to New York, but that's not really going to fool anyone for long. They're really headed to Vegas, and once they get there, Marco knows where to hide out. He's got people there."

I nodded. "And what about us?" I asked. "Where are we heading?"

A smile played across his lips. When he turned his head, the beads in his dreadlocks clicked together. "A place called Peachville, Georgia," he said. "I'm taking you to meet your cousin."

MORE TO YOUR POWER

The rest of the trip flew by. All I could think about was meeting a member of my extended family for the first time in my life.

I had a cousin! And somehow, despite what Rend told me about the crows never breaking free of the control of the Mother Crow, this girl had managed to break free all on her own.

Mary Anne.

I couldn't wait to meet her.

But at the same time, I wondered if going to her house would put her in danger.

"You said she's there with a group of other witches?"

"Witches and demons," Mordecai said. "Some real bad asses." He smiled again and cut his eyes toward me. "You'll fit right in."

I couldn't help but smile back at him. He looked intimidating with his broad shoulders and muscular build, but he had an easy way about him that put me at ease.

"The group there has been through a lot, but they know how to handle their shit," he said. "You'll be safe there. And Rend thinks it'll be the last place the Devil will think to look right now. Truthfully, even if he finds out you're there, I don't think he'd want to draw this crowd into the fight."

"I hope," I said. "But I don't want to put anyone else in danger. It's not right that everyone is taking so many chances to keep me alive."

"It's like Lyla said. If you're important to Rend, you're important to all of us," Mordecai said. "He doesn't take his relationships lightly, and he doesn't ask us to back him up unless he has a reason. I've known Rend for many years, and I've never seen him so concerned for a woman. You're very special, Franki."

"So I'm told," I mumbled. "I just wish I understood why."

"Did Rend ever explain to you about blood sacrifice?"

"Not really," I said. "Lyla mentioned it earlier, but I didn't really know what it meant."

"A blood sacrifice is one of the darkest magics there is," he said. "When you cast a spell like a glamour, or a rope of smoke or whatever, it's temporary. It takes power and energy to maintain, which is why, when you fell asleep, your glamour dropped."

I nodded. It made sense so far.

"With blood sacrifice, a witch or demon can cast a spell that is permanent and can never be broken. The more powerful or difficult the spell, the more powerful the blood needed to sustain it for eternity," he said. "You following me?"

"So, if the Devil were to get his hands on a powerful witch, he could kill her in a blood sacrifice in order to maintain a permanent spell?"

"Exactly. Some spells are much too powerful to sustain forever," he said. "They might require several sacrifices over the course of time. But, it's very difficult to fight against a blood sacrifice. Whatever the Devil has planned, it can't be good. Not for any of us."

"Is my blood really that powerful?" I asked. "Just because I'm a descendent of the Mother Crow? If that's true, why isn't he after my cousin, Mary Anne?"

"It's also possible you were just an easier target," he said. "But I have a feeling there's more to your power than just your mother's heritage, if you know what I mean."

I sucked in a breath and turned my face to the window, letting the sun warm my skin. I suddenly felt very cold inside.

"So, the real question," I said after a few moments to let his words sink in, "is who is my father?"

He raised his eyebrows. "Yes, I believe that is a very good question."

I shivered, wishing I had a blanket or something. I felt exposed and vulnerable. A feeling I hated with everything I had.

My mother had refused to discuss my father. I must have asked her a thousand times, but as I grew older, I learned to avoid the subject at all costs. I had always assumed he was some loser who had beat her or something. Someone she obviously wanted to forget.

But what if there was more to it than that?

I curled my feet under me on the seat and rested my head against the window.

I didn't say another word until we had crossed over the Georgia state line and were well on our way to Peachville.

MIRRORS OF MY OWN

Mordecai turned on a gravel road in the middle of nowhere. It was almost four in the afternoon, and we had been traveling on back roads in Georgia for more than half an hour. The main feature of the scenery was pine trees that lined both sides of the road for miles. I had never seen so many trees in my life.

It started to give me some confidence that Rend had chosen a good place for me to hide. We had definitely found the middle of nowhere.

Mordecai took a winding driveway down a bumpy road and, in a clearing at the end, stood a huge white house.

Flowers bloomed in a gorgeous garden to the left. A fountain flowed with crystal-clear water, surrounded by bright blue and pink hydrangeas. Crepe myrtles with pink and white flowers lined the final drive up to the house. It was like a fairyland back here, and not at all what I was expecting.

The house itself had been newly painted a brilliant white. Tall stately columns rose from the wide porch, and there on the top step sat two teenagers. They straightened when they saw the SUV approach.

The boy was tall and lanky with sandy brown hair. He looked over at the girl and clasped her hand tightly as they stood.

It was the girl who took my breath away. I knew the instant I saw her that she was Mary Anne. There was no mistaking the family resemblance. Her hair was shorter than mine but had the same dark blue-black shine.

Mordecai parked out front. I reached for the door handle with trembling hands. Was this real? After every horrible thing that had happened in the past few hours, was fate truly tossing me this beautiful gift?

My heart sped up as I stepped from the Escalade.

I pulled the baseball cap from my hair and smoothed it out with my fingers. This was not exactly how I would have wanted to look when meeting the first member of my family outside my mother, but it would have to do. Mordecai came around the car and nodded to me.

I took a deep breath and walked toward the girl on the steps. I made it about four steps before she released the boy's hand and ran toward me, throwing her arms around me.

I laughed, the breath nearly knocked from my body. It felt so amazing to wrap my arms around her small frame, knowing she was a part of me. A part of my real, true family. This was a moment I had dreamed of my whole life and never dared hope could ever come true.

We held tight to each other for a long moment until someone near the house laughed, and Mary Anne pulled away, her porcelain skin flushing with a light pink blush.

When she lifted her eyes to mine, they were mirrors of my own—a clear blue as true as the sky above.

"I'm Franki," I said awkwardly. "Mary Francis, really, but everyone calls me Franki."

Her face broke out into a smile. "I'm Mary Anne," she said.

"I can't believe you're real," I said. Emotion released from me in a sudden gulp of air, and I lifted my hand to my mouth as tears welled up in my eyes. "I'm sorry."

"Don't apologize," a girl said. "We're so glad you guys made it here safely."

I looked up to see a beautiful girl with wavy blonde hair and deep, brown eyes, smiling at me.

"I'm Harper," she said. She held her hand out to me, and I shook it. The instant our skin touched, a tiny static shock went through me, and I pulled away. Harper laughed and rolled her eyes. "That happens to me all the time, sorry."

I smiled, feeling the warmth coming from her, as if I were meeting with old friends instead of complete strangers.

"Come on in and meet everyone," she said. She put one arm around Mordecai and gave him a brief hug.

Mary Anne held her hand out to the boy who had been sitting beside her. "This is Essex."

When she said his name, her face blushed again.

"Hi Essex," I said, unable to hide my smile. "Nice to meet you."

Essex bowed his head. "I am very honored to be meeting you as well," he said. His voice had a slight foreign accent to it that I couldn't quite place, and I wondered briefly where he'd come from.

He took Mary Anne's hand and together we all walked up the steps to the house.

Harper led us to a room just off the main entryway where a group of teens were gathered, playing video games. They were shouting and laughing as zombies came after their characters on the screen.

"Shoot it," one guy shouted. He lifted his hands up as if moving the controller up would save his character.

A gorgeous girl with tanned skin and a long black braid laughed and punched buttons on her controller faster. "I'm trying," she shouted. "Get out of my way."

A couple of other guys sat around watching them, cheering them on.

Another guy stood in the corner, alone, his expression sad even in the midst of all this laughter.

Harper cleared her throat and everyone turned and looked at us all at once.

"Hey guys, this is the girl I told you about," she said. "Her name is Franki, and she's Mary Anne's cousin. We're going to help keep her safe for a little while, so no one outside this group needs to know she's here."

The two playing the game abandoned their controllers and stood to introduce themselves.

"I'm Lea," the brunette said. She pointed to the other two guys on the couch. "The guy with the glasses there is Joost and this is Cristo."

I waved, feeling self-conscious, but amazed at how welcoming everyone was.

"I'm Jackson." The guy who'd been playing video games lifted his chin in a nod. "And over there, that's my twin brother Aerden."

I glanced over at the quiet guy in the corner and noticed that the two of them were nearly identical except for the color of their eyes—one had green and the other blue.

"Nice to meet you guys."

"You've been through a lot, so I'm sure you're anxious to take a shower and get settled," Harper said. She came over and put a hand on my wrist. "You can meet the rest of the group later. If you want, Mary Anne can show you to her room and you can shower and change or whatever. You can take anything you want out of my closet. We should be about the same size, I think."

I looked around the room at the group and wondered what their story was. Why were they all so willing to just accept me in and protect me when I could be putting them all in danger? And how were a bunch of teens all living in this big house together with no parents or guardians? It was a strange situation. They seemed to act like a family, but I knew Mordecai had said some were human and some were demons.

Mary Anne slipped her small hand into mine. "I'll show you upstairs."

Essex winked at her as we passed and Mary Anne smiled and ducked her head. They were so cute, I wanted to just grab them up and hug them. I wondered how long they'd been together.

"So, do you guys all live here?" I asked as we made our way up the stairs.

"Not everyone and not full-time, but yeah, sometimes," she said. "This is kind of our headquarters, if you want to call it that."

I had so many questions I wanted to ask her, but no idea where to even begin. I didn't want to step over any boundaries, either, and I didn't know if there were any topics that were off-limits.

"Thank you for taking me in like this," I said. "I don't want to put any of you guys in danger, though."

Mary Anne gave me a stoic look. "Trust me, there's nothing you can bring to the table that we haven't faced, and then some," she said. "We've been through a lot the past couple of years."

I wanted to ask their story. I'd heard the name Harper from one of the dancers before, and I wondered if this could be the same girl. An orphan who grew up never knowing about her powers, but then quickly becoming extremely powerful. It had to be her, right?

Mary Anne showed me into a room decorated in rich black fabrics with blue accents that was off the main hallway. Black silk curtains hung from high windows, blocking out most of the outside light. A black bedspread with dark blue piping was on the bed. Even the rug covering part of the wood floors was a rich black wool.

"Big fan of black," I said.

"I'm comforted by the darkness," she said. "Which I guess is kind of ironic considering where we come from."

I bit the inside of my lip. "Did you grow up with them? The other crows?" I asked. I wasn't even sure if that's what I was supposed to call them.

Mary Anne sat down on the edge of her bed. "For a little while," she said. "It's kind of a long story, but when I was about ten, the Mother Crow sent me here. This place used to be called Shadowford Home for Girls. It was set up to look like a kind of orphanage, but it was really a way for the Order of

Shadows to look for someone who was very important to them."

"Harper?" I asked, piecing together small parts of the story from the bits and pieces I'd gotten along the way.

"How did you know that? Has someone already told you the story?" she asked.

"No, but I've heard people talking about her."

"Yeah, she's kind of well-known all over these days," Mary Anne said. "The Mother Crow originally sent me here knowing that if the Order ever found Harper, I could report back to her about it."

I nodded, wondering what it would have been like to grow up with the rest of them, following orders and having no control over my own life.

"That must have been really hard. To leave your family like that."

Mary Anne shrugged. "It was, in a way, but life in the village wasn't exactly paradise either."

"The village?"

She nodded. "It's a small city above the trees that the Mother Crow built for all of us," she said. "It's where she kept us hidden all these years. She cast a spell on the village that made it impossible for anyone to see it or enter into it without having the blood of a crow."

"Wow," I whispered, taking a spot next to her on the bed. I never would have dreamed of a secret village above the trees. "And no one was allowed to leave?"

"Not unless they had a specific job to do," she said. "And none of us who left were ever allowed to tell anyone who we were."

"So, how did you get away from all that?" I asked.

"When the Mother Crow found out about Harper, she tried to kill her. I was supposed to be a part of it, but I'd already made friends with Harper," she said. "I couldn't let them do that to her."

I shivered, remembering what Mordecai had told me earlier about blood sacrifice. Was that what they were doing to Harper?

"You saved her?"

Mary Anne shrugged and gave a small smile. "I helped," she said. "But Harper's amazingly good at saving herself in situations like that."

"Situations? As in plural?"

"Like I said, we've been through a lot."

"You guys seem really happy here," I said. "Are you guys alone? What happened to the people running the orphanage?"

Mary Anne laughed and scrunched her nose. "We killed them," she said. "Or Harper killed the main woman in charge, Mrs. Shadowford. And the ones who set up the orphanage to begin with. It's been just us ever since."

An awkward silence stretched out between us. I had so many questions I wanted to ask, but I didn't want to pry. I was relieved when Mary Anne asked me a question instead.

"How did you get away?" she asked. "I never knew of anyone who wasn't part of the village. No one ever talked about a family that got out."

"My mother's name was Mary Beth. Growing up, she refused to tell me about her family or my father or anything. I didn't even know I had a family or that we were witches," I said. "To be honest, I just found out about everything a few days ago. It feels like I've lived a lifetime since then. And there's still so much I don't know."

"Where's your mother now?"

Sadness flooded my heart, but I pushed it back, refusing to let myself be upset about a woman who had kept everything from me. Who had abandoned me when I needed her most.

"She left three years ago. Just disappeared without a trace," I said. "Someone told me recently that she died."

"I'm sorry. I don't know where my mother is, either." Mary Anne reached out for my hand again. "I hope someday soon we'll be able to sit down and really talk about all of it," she said. "We'll do everything we can to keep you safe."

I shook my head. "It seems like no matter where I go, the Devil finds me. What if no place is safe anymore?"

She stood and looked me in the eyes, her face serious. "There's one place I know is safe," she said. "As soon as Rend gets here, we'll take you there."

I brought in a quick breath, a lump forming in my throat. "Rend's coming here?"

Her face broke out in a smile. "Yes." She glanced at her watch. "In fact, he should be here soon. If you want to clean up, I'll go find you something in Harper's closet to wear."

I touched my hair and the cut along my forehead. I looked awful. I most definitely wanted to clean up and wash last night's blood off my hands. I didn't want Rend to see me like this, but I also didn't want to miss it when he got here.

"Thanks," I said. "I won't take long."

Mary Anne showed me where I could find everything I needed in her bathroom, then left to give me some privacy.

As I climbed into the hot shower, I smiled and repeated the same words over and over to myself.

Rend is coming.

THERE IS EVIL ALL AROUND US

I changed into some of Harper's clothes and made my way toward the stairs, planning to go down and see what everyone else was up to. And to see if anyone had an idea when Rend would be here.

It was probably close to dinner time, and I hadn't had anything to eat since before my shift last night at Venom. I was starving.

I found the group in the kitchen sitting around a scarred wooden table that looked like it had seen many similar gatherings in the past. It looked to be the same people as before, only the sad guy—the twin with the blue eyes—was missing. A girl with very straight white-blonde hair and pale skin had taken his place.

"Is this her?" the blonde girl asked. Her voice was like tinkling bells, high-pitched and musical. She stood and rushed over to hug me. "I'm so happy to meet you, Franki. Welcome to our home."

I smiled and hugged her back. There was nothing but

joyful energy coming from her, as if she were some kind of fairy. And from what I'd learned the past few days, I wouldn't be surprised to learn she actually was a fairy.

"Don't worry," she whispered loudly. "I won't hold it against you that you're related to Mary Anne."

Mary Anne sighed and walked over. She pushed the girl to the side with a playful nudge. "This is Zara," she said. "Our resident gardener."

My eyes widened. "Did you plant all those flowers in the garden by the fountain?" I asked. "They're gorgeous."

Zara smiled and her entire face shone with joy. "Plant?" She giggled.

"She would never dare get her pristine little hands dirty," Mary Anne said. "She grew them with magic."

"Oh," I said. "I didn't realize you could—"

"Where is she? Is she okay?"

Rend's voice stopped me mid-sentence. I spun around and saw him coming around the corner near the staircase. My eyes filled with tears, and I swallowed a thick lump in my throat. I wanted to run to him and feel his strong arms around me, but I had no idea how he felt about me right now. Was he angry at me for what happened? Did he blame me?

His lips parted as our eyes met, and I was relieved to see passion, not anger. Relief instead of rage.

He tightened his jaw, the muscles in his face rippling with tension. "Franki."

His voice was strained, and I was dying to know what was going on in his head. Was he feeling the same longing I was?

If I had doubted how I was feeling before this moment, seeing him again made everything clear. I wanted him. There was no denying it. I didn't even care if he did want my blood. I wanted him anyway.

And I couldn't tell him.

Not here in front of all these strangers.

I waited for him to walk to me, each step agonizingly slow. When he made it over to where I stood, he lifted his hands as if to hug me, then lowered them.

"Are you okay?" he said, his voice shaking.

"I'm a little shaken up, but I'm okay," I said. "I thought you were dead."

"I know," he said. "I should have explained to you how the club's entrance worked when you first started there, but it never seemed like the right time. After work last night, I was going to..."

His voice trailed off and he looked up to find half the room staring at us. They all quickly turned around and went back to what they were doing, but we knew they were listening in. They were probably wondering what was going on just as much as I was.

The corner of Rend's mouth lifted into a smirk. "We can talk about it later," he said softly.

I pressed my lips together hard to keep from smiling like a complete dork. "Okay," I said. A shiver of anticipation rippled up my spine at the thought of what else might come later. Would we have a chance to be alone?

God, I hope so.

"What about Lyla and Marco?" I asked, trying to shake the thought of him possibly kissing me again out of my mind. "Have you heard from them?"

"They made it to Las Vegas, but I haven't heard from them

since they landed," he said. "Marco's family is there, so I think they'll be okay. At least for a while."

"Thank God. I don't know if I can handle anyone else getting hurt." I licked my lips and looked down at the floor. "Selena's dead."

"I know," Rend said. He put a hand on my shoulder. "She did what she had to do to keep all of us safe."

"None of you would have been in any danger if it wasn't for me."

"You can't blame yourself," he said. "There is evil all around us. You can't hold yourself responsible for that."

"What's your plan?" Harper asked. She leaned against an island in the kitchen. "What else can we do to help?"

"You've already done so much," Rend said. "Just giving Franki a place to stay until I could get to her was help enough."

"Where will you go?" Jackson asked. He stood behind Harper, his hand resting on hers, their pinkies entwined. "You guys are welcome to stay here as long as you need to."

"We wouldn't want to put you in any more danger than you're already in," Rend said. "I was planning to take her back to my place. Through the hall of doorways."

"No," Mary Anne said, standing up from her spot at the dinner table and walking over to us. "It's not safe."

I hid a smile and glanced toward Rend. I knew he wasn't used to someone telling him no or questioning his judgment. I was liking my cousin more and more, just for having the guts to speak up.

"It's probably the safest place there is," Rend said. He shook his head, his shoulders tense. "There's a spell on my door keeping everyone out."

"What about your Brotherhood?" Mary Anne asked. "All of them are barred from your home?"

Rend's eyebrows came together in a pinched expression. "No, not all of them. But I trust them."

"Do you?" she challenged. "Isn't the Devil himself one of the Brotherhood?"

Rend cleared his throat. "Yes, but he is banned from my home, as is anyone working for him."

"Anyone you know is working for him," she corrected. "But from what I understand, a lot of the Brotherhood of Darkness is upset with you for your decision to stop drinking blood. Any chance someone you once considered a friend would be willing to betray you? Someone who was maybe looking to teach you a lesson?"

"Shit," Rend said. He ran a hand through his thick black hair. "You have a good point."

He paced the floor in front of the island.

"We could place another spell on the door," he said. "Something that would keep everyone else out even if they originally had passage through the door to my house."

"Can you cast something strong enough so quickly?" Harper asked.

"I don't know," Rend said. "The barrier spell that's on there now is very strong, but it took me weeks to gather the power and items I needed in order to create the binding."

"Besides, the Devil will expect you to take her there," Mary Anne said. "He's already seen how far you're willing to go to keep her safe. Bringing her back to your place is the most logical response."

Rend nodded. "We'll have to run," he said.

"He'll follow you," Harper said.

"Yes," Rend said. "But we can't very well hide out here forever. This isn't your fight. You have important work of your own to do right now."

"You can stay as long as you need to," Harper said. "Any fight against evil is our fight."

"I know where you can go," Mary Anne said. She put her hand in mine again and squeezed. "We'll take you to the crow village."

SWEET

Excitement and fear buzzed across my skin.

The crow village. The place where my mother grew up. I was dying to see it, but I was also afraid of what seeing it would make me feel.

"Is it safe there? What about the crows?" Rend asked.

"No one would go back there," Harper said. "We used it as a staging ground for our army when we were fighting the Order of Shadows. It's safe."

"If no one can get in besides crows, how did you bring all those people up there?" Rend asked.

I could tell he wasn't completely sold on the idea. I stayed silent, not knowing whether I wanted to see it or get as far away from that place as I could.

"We had Essex make ribbons that were infused with a drop of Mary Anne's blood," Harper said. "Anyone wearing the ribbon was able to pass through the barrier."

"Do those people all still have their ribbons?"

I was touched Rend was grilling them so hard. The fact

that he wanted so badly to keep me safe was a great comfort. I just wished I knew the real motivation behind his desire. Our late-night meeting to talk it through had been canceled when Venom's entrance exploded, but I hoped we would still be able to find time to talk about it.

Was it weird for me to care about things like that at a time like this? His kiss should be the last thing on my mind, but it wasn't. It was all I could think about.

"We collected the ribbons from everyone after the battle, and burned them," Mary Anne said. "It's been abandoned since the fall of the blue gates. You'll be safe there, I promise."

Rend nodded, then met my eyes. "How do you feel about this?"

I raised an eyebrow, surprised he was even asking for my opinion. "I'll go wherever you think is best."

I just want to be with you.

Rend's eyes flashed with hunger, as if he'd heard that last part. I hadn't said it out loud, but maybe I'd said it with my eyes.

He cleared his throat. "Show us where to go."

Mary Anne nodded and started toward the back door.

"Wait," I said. Everyone turned to look, and I laughed nervously. "Do you guys have anything to eat first? I'm starving."

Rend relaxed and nodded. "Of course, I didn't think about that." He punched Mordecai in the shoulder. "You didn't think to stop and get her something to eat?"

Mordecai held his hands up in surrender. "All I could think about was getting her here as fast as possible, man."

"Thanks for that," Rend said, his voice growing more serious. "I owe you big time."

Mordecai patted Rend's hand. "No worries. Seriously, anything you need, you just let me know."

Harper and Zara rummaged through cabinets and the fridge and within fifteen minutes, an entire buffet of food was spread out on the island, along with a stack of paper plates.

"Help yourself," Harper said.

"Thank you so much."

I piled a plate with fried chicken, baked beans, biscuits, and cole slaw. Real southern food. Mary Anne even poured me a glass of sweet tea. I nearly choked on it, not expecting something so sweet.

"Wow, that's sweet," I said with a laugh.

"That's how we do it down here in Georgia," Mary Anne joked. "Besides, Zara made it. She always puts in too much sugar."

"I do not," Zara said, sticking her bottom lip out in a pout. "It's delicious."

"It's great," I said. "I've just never had sweet tea before."

Mary Anne shook her head. "You have so much to learn."

I laughed, knowing just how right she was.

I took a seat at the big table in the kitchen and soon everyone joined me. I almost forgot to eat, watching them interact with each other. It nearly brought tears to my eyes. My whole life, I'd never had what these people have. True friendship. Family. They loved each other in this house. I wanted to be a part of something like that someday.

Then Rend caught my eye from across the table. He hadn't even made a plate of food. He just sat there, watching me with that same hunger blazing in his dark eyes.

That's when I realized I was a part of something. I was part of the Venom family, and now I had ties to this new group in

Peachville. I had a real cousin who could tell me stories about the family I'd never known. And it was all because of Rend. If he hadn't chosen to save my life that night in the alley, I never would have had any of this.

Yes, this new life was terrifying, and dangerous, and confusing, but it was also real and beautiful. It held the promise of finally belonging to something—or someone—for the first time.

Staring into Rend's eyes, my stomach fluttered, and my heart beat faster. My body warmed at the thought of those lips on mine again.

I forced my gaze away and concentrated on finishing my food so we could get out of here and get to the village where we might finally be alone.

Footsteps pounded on the stairs, and I turned to face the door to the kitchen. Aerden rushed in.

"Rend, Franki, you guys have to go now," he said. He was out of breath from running.

"What's going on?" Rend asked, standing.

"Azure just checked in and sent a message," Aerden said. "She said the group tracking her in Paris destroyed her glamour. They know you tricked them, and now they're tracking Mordecai's vehicle. It won't be long before they figure out where he was."

"Is Azure okay?"

"Why was she in Paris?" I asked.

"She was a second decoy," Rend said. "We sent Lyla to Vegas and Azure to Paris."

"She's fine," Aerden said. "She managed to dodge them and get back through the Venom door before they could get to her."

"Someone just reported four dead witches from a coven near Nashville," Lea said, coming around the corner. "The vampires could be here in less than an hour."

"And if they've just fed, they'll be nearly impossible to track from there," Rend said. I was still trying to wrap my head around the fact that Azure had agreed to glamour herself as a fake me and put her own life in danger. I knew she would do anything Rend asked of her, but I'm sure it killed her to have to wear my face for a while.

As hard as she'd been on me so far, though, I was still thankful she was safe. I didn't want her blood on my hands, too.

"We should just stay here and fight them," Lea said. "We can take them. I've been wanting a good fight, anyway. Things have been way too calm lately for my taste."

"He'll just send more," Rend said. "I'd rather not get you guys involved."

"We're already involved," Lea said.

She had a definite attitude on her, but I liked the fact that she didn't seem scared of anything.

"You haven't fought them directly," Rend said.

"Mordecai killed a few of them," I said, remembering the way his silver dagger had sliced through the skin of the vampires back at the safe-house.

Everyone grew quiet, and I realized after a few beats that they were all looking to Harper for an answer.

Harper finally looked up and met Rend's eyes. "I think you should go," she said finally. "If it comes down to a fight, we're behind you. But if we can avoid bringing a fight to Brighton Manor, I'd at least like to try."

Lea grumbled and turned away, shaking her head. But

Rend nodded. He took my hand in his, and my entire body lit up at his touch.

"I understand," he said. "Mary Anne, can you show us where to go?"

Mary Anne nodded. "Do you know how to shift?" she asked me.

I bit my lip and shook my head.

She scrunched her nose in disappointment. "Okay, what's the best way to get them both up there without leaving a trail?" she asked. "They'll track Rend if he casts, unless you've had something to drink lately."

His hand tensed against mine and I swallowed nervously, realizing the bites on my neck were still visible to anyone paying enough attention.

"No," he said.

My face warmed. I knew I should keep my mouth shut, but we were in danger and running out of time. "You can drink from me," I said.

Mary Anne's eyes grew wide, and she looked from me to Rend, questioning our relationship.

Rend tensed and dropped my hand. "Absolutely not," he said. "Who here has the ability to fly us up there without being tracked?"

I backed away, hurt that he had been so quick to dismiss my offer. It wasn't like I was telling him to drain me and leave me for dead. One little drink and we would be up in the safety of the crow village in minutes. Instead, he had to be difficult. As usual.

Zara stepped forward. "I can float you up there," she said. "Come on."

She and Mary Anne led us out the back door. Mary Anne

nodded to Zara and shifted, her body shrinking and transforming in the blink of an eye. A black crow with bright blue eyes cawed at us, then flew into the air.

Zara nodded to us. "Ready?"

Rend took my hand. "Let's go." He turned back toward the door and nodded to Harper and the others. "Thank you."

"Let us know if you need us," Harper said, waving as Zara lifted her hands into the air.

Our feet rose off the ground. I clung tightly to Rend's hand, feeling unbalanced as my body flew forward and up, above the trees. He pulled me close to him and over the sound of the wind in my ears, I was sure I heard him laugh.

"A crow afraid to fly," he said.

If we had been on solid ground, I would have smacked him. Instead, I held on tighter.

"I'm not afraid to fly," I said. "I'm just new at it."

We flew over the tops of the trees. I couldn't believe how many trees. Miles in every direction. Growing up in the city all my life, I'd never seen anything like it.

In the distance, the sun had started to set. I breathed in the beauty of it as Zara and Mary Anne led us toward the village where my mother was born.

The place where we landed was nothing more than a platform of air and nothingness. I couldn't see a village here, or a landing zone for that matter, but Mary Anne shifted back to her human form and landed in mid-air.

Zara joined her, setting Rend and me down next to them.

I knew as a natural crow, I shouldn't be scared, but I was seriously about to pee my pants. We were literally standing on nothing, at least twenty feet above the tallest pine tree.

"I'll wait here," Zara said.

"Thanks for your help," I said, wondering how exactly we were going to get back down without her. I really didn't want to fall from way up here.

Mary Anne motioned for us to join her. I stepped carefully, unsure what we were even standing on, much less where it started and ended.

"Follow me," she said. "Hold his hand as you come in."

She stepped forward, and her body disappeared

completely. I gasped. I knew I had to trust this, but I was learning more and more that I could no longer trust my eyes. It was a weird feeling.

I squeezed Rend's hand and raised an eyebrow. He smiled and nodded. With a deep breath, I followed Mary Anne, trying my best to place my foot exactly where she had stepped.

My body buzzed with a peculiar energy, similar to the static shock I'd felt when I touched Harper's hand, but more intense and all throughout my body. I shook my head, shivering from the strangeness of it as it pulsed through me.

Then I looked up and truly opened my eyes.

I dropped Rend's hand, and brought both my hands to my mouth. Holy crap. The forest of tree-tops was gone, replaced by a small village filled with colorful houses. A real sidewalk—just like in a normal neighborhood—wound around the whole village. Houses lined the walkway on one side and in the middle of the entire village was a large covered pavilion with a stone altar in the middle. I shivered, thinking of what that altar must have been used for. Had the Mother Crow performed dark rituals here? Blood sacrifice?

How was she tied to the Devil?

I looked around, trying to picture what it must have been like when the entire family of crow witches lived here. Some of them were evil like the Mother Crow, but many of them had to be more like Mary Anne and me. There might be darkness inside us, but we were always fighting for more light. We couldn't be the only ones.

Mary Anne gave me a brief hug. "I'm sorry to bring you up here and leave, but I have to go," she said. "If we're going to face the vampires and prove to them that you were never here, we all need to be there. Especially me. If I'm gone, they might suspect where we've hidden you."

"Thanks for everything," I said. "You have no idea how much meeting you means to me."

"I feel the same way," she said. "I'll be back, if I can, when things blow over. We still have so much to talk about."

She gave us a small wave, then shifted back into the form of a crow and flew down into the cover of the trees.

"Do you think they'll be okay?" I asked. "Or did we just put them all in danger?"

"They're tough," Rend said. "The Devil wouldn't dare attack them right now. It would start a war he'd be too scared to lose."

"They're really that powerful?" I asked. It was a solid group of people, but they were mostly teenagers from the looks of it.

"More than you can imagine," he said. "They conquered a group of evil witches when all the odds were stacked against them. That's a war they're still fighting, though, which is why Harper was reluctant to get involved beyond what she did."

I walked with Rend through the streets of the small village. Being here felt like an out-of-body experience. The houses and the altar in the center. It was like walking through a ghost town, but the energy of my people called to me here.

This is where my mother grew up.

Knowing this about her and picturing her as a child here in this place changed her for me. Made her more real than she'd ever been, even when she was alive.

"Think of the secrets this village holds," I said. "What was my mother's childhood like, I wonder?"

"Sheltered, I imagine," Rend said. He walked beside me as we passed in front of the empty houses. "Extremely strict."

"But also filled with family," I said. "Traditions. Can you imagine the closeness you would feel if you grew up in this small village your entire life and never once got to leave?"

Rend shook his head. "Don't romanticize it," he said. "These women and children were prisoners, but they were also expendable if it suited the Mother Crow's purposes. She had no problem sacrificing one of her daughters to give herself a longer life. Her pursuit of power knew no limits."

"Knew?" I asked. "I thought she was still alive."

"Technically, she is," Rend said. "Or we all assume she is, but after she tried to kill Harper, she was severely wounded and only just managed to escape. The coven scattered for a while, but no one knows if the Mother Crow created a new village for her family and gathered them all back by her side or if many of the ones who escaped are still in hiding, praying the Mother Crow never finds them."

I shook my head, overcome with emotion. "Why do you think my mother took me away from here?"

"I have no idea," he said. "There are many possible explanations, but the one that makes the most sense is that she wanted to keep you safe. She didn't want you to grow up a part of this."

"I just keep thinking there has to be more to it than that," I said. I walked up the steps of a two-story house painted the color of rust and looked out on the village. "My mother was never affectionate with me. Growing up, I never felt like I was valued, you know? I never once felt as if she loved me so much she would do anything to protect me."

"What was it like, then?"

"It was like she resented me," I said. "As if she'd been faced with an impossible choice and took the lesser of two evils—a life raising a child she never wanted."

Rend grabbed my hand and the connection started a fire in my heart. We were alone now, with so much left unsaid between us. I had no idea how to say all those things. I was terrified of being vulnerable around him again. What if he turned me away again? What if he admitted that Azure was right?

What if I really was nothing more than currency to him and he was here to protect his investment?

"That sounds like a difficult way to grow up," he said.

I shrugged. Talking about my mother wasn't pleasant, but it was easier than admitting how I felt about him.

"It was all I ever knew, but I'd be lying if I said I didn't long for her to tell me she loved me," I said, my tongue stumbling over the word love. "Instead, she spent a lot of time drunk or on drugs, as if she hated her life so much she would do anything to escape it."

I looked out at the peaceful, quiet village that used to be filled with laughter, solidarity, and commitment, even if it was in loyalty to an evil witch. Yes, the ghost of fear still haunted these halls, but it had also been a place of happiness and love.

"I have longed for love my entire life," I told him, my heart open so wide it was terrifying. "So much so that my greatest fear became the idea of falling for someone—trusting someone—who didn't love me back. At a young age, I decided the best way to protect myself was to never allow myself to let anyone close enough to have that power over me."

"Franki—"

"Let me get this out," I said. "I need for you to understand how important this is for me."

I took a deep breath and chose my words carefully.

"The problem with that plan was that while I was so busy protecting myself from pain, I was also denying myself the one thing I wanted most in the world," I said. "Falling in love is not something I could ever take lightly. It's risky and dangerous and terrifying.

"Up until I met you, I was successful at protecting my heart. But there's been nothing I could do to push you away. Every time I decided never to see you again or let you into my heart, all you had to do was look at me with those silver-black eyes of yours and I was falling all over again."

"I know exactly how you feel," he said.

"Do you?" I asked in a whisper. I was too afraid to look into his eyes. Scared of what I might see there.

Instead, I leaned my cheek against his chest, concentrating on the beat of his heart. He was here. He was really alive. Every fear I'd held inside, from the moment that club exploded before my eyes, was tied to my separation from Rend.

In the span of less than a week, I had fallen for him so hard, I couldn't imagine my life without him.

And in some ways, that was the scariest part of this whole thing.

"When Selena set off that bomb and the club exploded, I thought Venom had been destroyed," I said. "I thought I had lost you forever."

"I'm sorry, I should have told you—"

I looked up and placed my fingertips across his lips. "Rend, I never want to feel that way again," I said. "I know we haven't known each other for long, and every step of the way I've questioned what I was feeling, not believing I could feel something so intense for someone I barely knew."

I took a shallow breath, unable to control the racing of my pulse and the words coming directly from my heart. As afraid as I was, I knew I couldn't hold this inside any longer.

"Ever since the other night when you bit me, I've been completely clueless about your feelings for me," I said. "I've agonized over whether you ever were attracted to me, or if it was just the power of the blood running through my veins that drew you to me."

He opened his mouth again, but I shook my head. I wanted to say what I had to say before I realized how vulnerable I was allowing myself to be in front of him. I wanted to lay it out there before fear took hold of my voice and silenced me.

"Just when I thought I felt something between us again last night at the club when we kissed, Azure turned it all upside down by telling me that you would never risk your heart. She told me that if you pretended to care for me, it was only so that you could manipulate and control me." I was talking so fast, I could barely catch my breath, but I had to know the truth. I couldn't wait another moment, and I couldn't keep questioning this. "She said I was nothing more than currency to you. An asset you could trade to keep yourself and everyone else safe."

His eyes flashed with specks of silver and his arms tensed around me.

"After everything that's happened since the explosion, I keep coming back to that," I said. "I have to know if you're doing all this to save me just because you think you can use me, or if you care about me in a deeper way. Because if you're playing games to control my heart, you might as well walk away right now and never look back. I'll never be yours because of some game of make believe. The only way I'll be yours is if you're mine, too. You need to understand that about me right now. Right now, you need to tell me the truth, no matter how much it may hurt me to hear it."

Rend placed his hands on my face and forced my eyes to his. A smile curled the corners of his luscious lips and his eyes darkened.

"You are the most insufferable woman I've ever met in my life," he said. "You never let me get a word in edgewise, and you never let me get away with anything."

My heart beat fast, pounding against my ribs. I had never put myself out there with anyone the way I'd just opened up to him, and if he looked me in the eyes and said he didn't feel the same way, I wasn't sure how I'd survive it.

"Azure's right. I'm no good at love, Franki. I care about a great deal of people and would do anything—even risk my own life—to save the lives of those who are closest to me. But I have never in all my hundreds of years been the kind of man who could fall in love," he said.

I couldn't control the tears that spilled down my cheeks. I didn't want to believe what he was saying.

"But maybe in all that time, it wasn't me at all," he said. "Maybe it was never about my inability to love a woman. Maybe it was about never having found the one woman I was always destined to love."

He lifted my face to his and kissed me with a fury that took my breath away. His mouth closed over mine, his tongue brushing the soft skin on my lips, coaxing them open.

I wanted him with a fierceness that set my body aflame, but I was terrified of what might happen if he lost control again. Would he be able to stop this time?

"I want you so badly, but I'd be lying if I said I wasn't scared," I said, breathless. "How do we do this without ending up right back where we were the other night in my apartment?"

He licked his lips and breathed in through his nose. "Believe me when I say I've thought of this a million times since that night," he said. "I haven't taken the blood of a witch without her consent in decades. I have practiced the art of control for so long, I never imagined I could still lose myself to the passion of the moment. But if there's one thing I've learned since we met, it's that you can surprise me in ways no one ever has."

I smiled, but my insides quivered. I wasn't sure I could take knowing he felt the same way, but that we could never be together the way I longed to be with him.

"I'll take you however I can get you," I said. "Even if that means we can't ever—"

"Oh, hell no," Rend said. "Being with you and not being able to make love to you is not an option for me. We're going to figure this out."

"How?"

"One step at a time," he said. "We'll take it slowly, and if I feel close to losing control, we'll slow down."

"Can you do that?" I asked. "I mean, the very nature of sex is about losing control. It's about surrender."

"I don't know if I can or not," he said. "But I'm willing to try if you are."

"Oh, I'm willing," I said, biting back a smile.

Rend lifted me into his arms and carried me over the threshold of the little red house. He kissed me as he made his way through the house, searching for a bedroom. We found one at the end of the hall, equipped with nothing more than a small bed covered with a tattered blanket.

"I'm sorry this isn't more glamorous," he said.

"Trust me. I don't care about anything fancy," I said. "I just want you."

He set my feet on the floor. The fiery passion on the porch had been replaced by the heated realization that we were really doing this. Time slowed between us and every inch of my body trembled in anticipation.

I reached down and grabbed the bottom of my tank top, crossing my arms as I pulled it up and over my head. I tossed it onto the floor, my heart beating wildly as his eyes devoured me.

"You are so beautiful," he said. His voice was rough and filled with longing. "I have wanted to touch you since the moment I saw you beating up those vampires behind my club."

My skin quivered as his fingers brushed the skin beneath my breasts, following the curves of my body. The thought of his hands exploring every inch of my bare skin sent waves of longing through me.

This wasn't the first time I'd been with a man, but it was the first time I'd ever been with someone I wanted on this level. Someone I could really be with.

Impatient, I reached for the edge of his black t-shirt, running my fingertips along the waistband of his jeans. His stomach trembled at my touch, and I looked up to meet his eyes. They were the darkest black now, filled with passion and hunger.

The only light around us was the amber glow of the setting sun pouring through a small window in the room. He pulled his shirt from his body, and I bit my lip as I ran my palm across his taut muscles. His body was lean and solid, every muscle clearly defined and hard as a rock.

And even then, I knew his muscles were only the beginning of his strength.

He could rip me apart at any moment if he wanted, and here I was surrendering my body to him. It was either the dumbest, or the bravest, thing I'd ever done in my life.

He moved his hands along the curve of my hips, his hands gathering the cotton into tight fists as he leaned down to kiss me again. His bare chest pressed against me, our bodies skin-to-skin for the first time. He slid his hands around to my back and pulled me harder against him.

I gasped for air as his hands explored me and his mouth claimed mine. I circled my arms around his neck, pressing my hips against him, yearning for more.

He grew hard against me, and I moaned. Just the thought of seeing him naked and touching him—pleasing him—was enough to send my mind spiraling out of control.

His body tensed and he pulled away, breathing hard. He turned away and in the dim light, I could see the flash of white fangs.

I couldn't speak. I knew he was struggling to control himself and that there was nothing I could do to help him, but god, I wanted him so badly. I wasn't sure I would survive the push and pull of it. I wasn't sure I could take it slowly.

But I also didn't want him to lose control and really hurt me.

I couldn't trust him completely, but I also couldn't resist him.

"Are you okay?" I asked, finally finding my voice. "Is there anything I can do?"

He shook his head and leaned one hand against the frame of the door.

I waited, my stomach in knots and my body flushed with warmth. Need circled in my veins, but I couldn't rush him.

After a few agonizing minutes, he finally turned, his eyes black as night, but his fangs retracted. He walked over without a word and pushed me down on the bed.

With his eyes locked on mine, he hooked his fingers inside the waistband of my pants and pulled them down. I writhed against the bed. Each piece of clothing we removed brought us one step closer to abandonment.

He ran his fingers gently up the inside of my legs. My thighs trembled as his fingertips brushed past, almost reaching the hot core between my legs, but torturously bypassing it to explore farther up my body.

Rend crawled onto the bed beside me, taking his time as his fingers moved up my stomach to my breasts. He circled them with the lightest of touches, his breath deep and controlled, but his eyes hungry.

My chest rose against his hand with each breath, fear mingling with pleasure and need. I wasn't sure I could take much more teasing, but I didn't want to push him past his breaking point either.

I decided maybe it was time to test the boundaries a little, though.

I rose, pushing him back against the pillows with both hands on his bare chest.

He kissed me again, the heat growing between us. He moaned and moved around me, as if we were in a constant battle for who was in control.

I had a feeling neither of us were in control, anymore.

He stood and met my eyes, as if making sure this is really what I wanted. I sat up on my knees and crawled across the bed toward him, placing my hands on the waist of his jeans. His heart was racing so hard, I could see it pulsing against his skin as if it were trying to escape.

There was no doubt I wanted this. No doubt we both wanted this. I had no idea how joining our bodies together would change things between us, but I knew it was inevitable. I knew we could no longer keep ourselves from it.

I unbuttoned the top of his jeans and slid the metal zipper down, my hand brushing him. He closed his eyes and breathed in through his nose.

I watched his face, every pained expression, every flash of desire, as I pushed his jeans to the floor.

Rend grabbed my wrist as I moved to touch him, his grip hard and unrelenting. He moved his other hand to my face, brushing my hair off my cheek. "I don't want to hurt you, Franki," he said, his voice deep and low. "But one step further, and I'm not sure I'll be able to stop myself."

There were only two pieces of clothing separating us now. Two moments of hesitation.

I had to make a decision. Should I trust this man I'd only known for a few days? Or was I playing with fire here? How many times did I need to learn that the danger in this new world was far greater than I could ever imagine?

My hands trembled as I slipped my wrist from his grasp. I moved my palms across his taut stomach, his muscles jumping with each touch. I slid them down the length of his stomach, never taking my eyes off his as I removed one of the final barriers between us.

No more hesitation or indecision.

Now, there was only passion.

Rend moaned and joined me on the bed. He stripped me down until we were both naked and vulnerable, finally giving in to something we'd both wanted from the moment we laid eyes on each other. He pulled me into his arms, passionately at first, then softening.

His eyes met mine in one final moment of question.

I swallowed and nodded. I was ready to surrender to him, come what may.

He positioned himself above me, his dark eyes closing as he took several deep breaths. The struggle for control was evident in his tense jaw and furrowed brow. I ran my hands in soft circles against his back, my body lying still beneath him. It was torture not to move toward him, press against him. I pushed my hips down into the bed, my legs slightly parted, waiting, but my thighs trembling.

Finally, Rend opened his eyes and lowered himself, pushing into me with one glorious stroke. I gasped and cried out from the fullness of him. My hands tensed and scratched at his back, pulling him down as my hips rose.

We found a rhythm as we danced along the edge of abandon, taking our time exploring and learning each other's limits. It was a game of push and pull, reaching one limit, then backing away until control could be found again.

Wind whipped around us, cooling our heated bodies as my magic took over. When it got too strong, Rend slowed and waited until the wind died down. If he moved his lips toward my neck, I pulled him back, forcing his eyes to mine until he calmed.

But eventually, desire took hold. We brought each other to the edge, then pushed past. Debris moved around as passion exploded within my core. I cried his name as the window broke and glass fell to the floor.

Rend groaned as he moved inside me. He pushed a hand into my black hair and pulled my head back hard against the bed, exposing my neck. I screamed in both pleasure and pain as his fangs grew long and he lowered his head to my bare skin.

His teeth drew blood just as he reached his climax. I dug my nails into his side, trying to push him off me, even while a part of me still wanted to draw him closer.

"Rend," I cried as I pushed against him. My mouth grew dry and fear pounded through my veins.

He let out a low, unearthly growl, then pushed me away. In an instant, his body shifted to smoke and flew from the room, leaving me panting there on the bed alone and exposed.

I reached up to touch the sticky wet blood on my neck, then fell back against the bed and smiled, exhausted and satisfied.

And still very much alive.

THE FLUTTER OF BLACK WINGS

I crawled out of bed and pulled the tattered blanket around my body. I tiptoed across the creaky old floor and made my way out the front door of the house.

I wasn't sure how long I'd slept or where Rend had disappeared to, but I wanted to make sure he knew I was okay.

I moved to the edge of the front porch railing and looked out across the crow village. Rend sat near the stone altar in the center of town, wearing nothing but his jeans. He was bent over, his head in his hands.

But as my eyes landed on him, he looked up and straightened. I smiled and lifted a hand in a wave and his shoulders relaxed. His eyes tensed, but I noticed a smile playing at the corners of his mouth.

I knew we still had a long way to go and so much we still needed to discuss and figure out, but for now, I was happy just to be here with him. Just to have had this one night with him.

I sat down on the railing and imagined what my life would have been if my mother had never left this place behind.

Where would I be now? What kind of woman would I be?

I had spent so much of my life being angry with my mom for her choices and her regrets. I would have given almost anything for the chance to talk to her about why she'd left in the first place. And why she didn't love me the way I deserved to be loved as a small child.

I wiped a tear from my cheek. Now was not the time for sadness and regret, but somehow opening myself to Rend had also opened a chamber in my heart that held memories and sorrow. I was overcome by more emotion than I'd allowed myself to feel in a very long time.

Part of me wished Rend and I could stay here forever, never having to face the dangers of the outside world. I was sure we could learn to find a balance between surrender and control. But I knew our time here was limited. When the sun came up in the morning, I knew we would have to get serious about making a long-term plan.

We couldn't run forever, which meant only one thing.

We would have to stand and fight.

Movement near the entrance caught my eye, and I pulled the blanket tighter around my body.

Mary Anne must have come back already. Did that mean there was trouble back at the house? Had they been attacked?

Rend saw my concern and moved to my side in seconds.

"Who is it?" he said.

"Mary Anne, I think," I said. "We're safe here, right? No one else can get in."

"Stay here," he said.

I heard him but didn't want him to go out there without me, so I followed right behind him.

Near the entrance, I saw the flutter of black wings.

I sped up and moved ahead of Rend to the entrance to greet her, not even caring that I was dressed in nothing more than an old rag.

Only, the figure shifting into human form at the entrance to the crow village was not Mary Anne at all.

The sight of the woman standing there froze my feet to the ground. The breath was knocked from my lungs with the sheer force of surprise.

I opened my mouth to speak, my lower lip trembling. Could this be real?

She stepped forward, a sad smile etched on her familiar face. "Franki," she said.

I shook my head and took two steps back, a tear falling down my cheek at the sight of her.

"Mom?"

EPISODE SIX

THE DOORWAY

MISUNDERSTOOD

"**M**om?"

My mother stood at the entrance to the crow village, her eyes bulging. Her entire body shook with fear.

"Franki, thank God you're here," she said. Her voice sounded foreign. Almost child-like in her terror. She ran toward me and grabbed my arm. "You're in serious danger. We have to get out of here. He's on his way."

"Who?" I asked. My breath came in short bursts. "The Devil?"

Mom looked behind her at the entrance to the village. Her head twitched. "Yes. He's been holding me prisoner for a very long time. I finally managed to escape, but we don't have much time."

"How did you know where to find us?" Rend asked.

She looked at him as if realizing, for the first time, that he was here. "Rend. Thank goodness you're here with my little bird," she said. "I don't know what I would have done if you hadn't been able to keep her safe."

"Answer my question," he said.

She blinked several times, tears filling her eyes. "The Devil knows you're here. I heard him talking about it to one of his servants. He can't be far behind me."

"It's okay, Mom. We're safe here. He can't get in. This village is enchanted, remember? You have to know that."

She shook her head violently and pulled hard on my arm. "You don't understand." She pushed her hair back from her neck to reveal two swollen puncture wounds. "He's been drinking from me for months, taking me down to almost death before letting go. He let me heal, and then he drained me again. Over and over."

I gasped and reached up toward the wounds, pulling back before touching them. Her neck looked infected. What horror had she been through? My stomach turned at the thought of her as his prisoner all this time.

"That means he can get inside the village," Rend said. "When was the last time he drank from you?"

"Hours ago," she said. "He'll still have some of my power inside him. The spell won't keep him out as long as he has some of my blood running through him."

"Shit," Rend said. He grabbed my hand. "We'll go to my house. Or to Venom."

"No," my mother said. Her hand was cold and clammy against my arm. "There's another way, but we have to go now. We can't risk him finding us here."

I looked at Rend and could tell he wasn't happy about being told no. The line of his jaw was straight and tense, and his eyes flashed with veins of silver in the blackness.

"What other way?"

"There's a doorway here inside the village," she said. "The Devil doesn't know about it. No one outside of the crow witches even knows it exists."

"Where does it lead?" I asked. She was digging into my arm so hard, I was afraid she was going to draw blood. I had to wrench my arm from her grasp. Rend was already tense enough. I didn't want to aggravate him.

"To a secret network of doors belonging only to the crows," she said.

"Like the hall of doorways at Venom?" I asked. I wasn't sure she knew about the hall there, but apparently hallways like that existed all over the world and most witches and demons knew they existed.

"Similar," she said. "But these doors only lead to secret hiding places of the crows. It's the Mother Crow's personal hallway. If we can get inside before he arrives, he'll never know what happened to you."

"Franki, I don't know about this," Rend said, turning me toward him. "I don't know that turning to the other crows at a time like this is the best plan. The Mother Crow may be just as dangerous as the Devil right now."

"I won't take her to the Mother Crow," Mom said. "I swear it."

I squeezed my eyes shut. I couldn't think straight. Rend and I had just gotten here. We hadn't even had a chance to talk about what had happened between us, much less what we were going to do about the Devil. This was all moving way too fast. I didn't know who to trust or what to do. One wrong move could mean all our lives.

"I have to get dressed," I said. "I need a minute to wrap my head around this and figure out what we should do."

My mother stepped back and studied me, her eyes traveling from my face all the way down to my toes. Her gaze snapped toward Rend. "You were supposed to be protecting her, not taking advantage of her."

She lashed out at him, but Rend stepped back. I moved between them and held up a hand. "Stop," I said. "I've been taking care of myself for the past three years. I'm not a child anymore. I know you're scared and you're trying to help, but I'm not going to let you just barrel back into my life and start criticizing my choices."

Tears fell from my mother's eyes, and she swiped at them. "You're right. I'm sorry, but you have to understand how this looks to me," she said. "I didn't want to leave you, Franki, but at the time, I thought it was for the best. You have no idea all the things I've sacrificed to keep you safe."

My heart tightened in my chest. Was that the truth? Had I completely misunderstood her all this time?

"Let me get dressed," I said. "I'll be right back."

Mom nodded but jerked her head back toward the entrance. "Hurry, please," she said. "I couldn't bear it if anything happened to you."

I studied her face for a long beat. She seemed to be genuinely worried about me. I had never seen her act this way my entire life. Had I been wrong about everything?

I squeezed her hand once and hurried toward the small rust-colored house Rend and I had claimed as our own.

THE LAST KISS

Rend followed me into the room. I searched for my clothes on the floor and began dressing as fast as I could.

"Franki, something doesn't feel right about this," he said.

I shook my head. "Nothing has felt right for the past week or two," I said. "My entire life has been completely turned upside down."

"No, I mean your mother showing up here like this," he said. He sat down next to me on the bed as I pulled the tank top over my head. "If the Devil had her prisoner for the past several months, how did she suddenly get free on her own? He wouldn't have just let her go. Not after what she'd heard."

"I don't know," I said. I pulled my pants up and started searching for my shoes under the bed. "She's obviously terrified. You saw the marks on her neck. I think she's telling the truth."

"I'm not saying she's lying to you," he said. "I just think we need to be careful."

I stretched to reach one of the shoes that had somehow gotten pushed way under the bed. My hands were shaking. "What do you think we should do, then? Where can we possibly go that is going to be safe from him?" I asked. I finally grabbed the edge of the shoe and dragged it out. "How did he even figure out that we were here in the first place? It's like he has eyes everywhere. I don't even know where to begin to fight back against that."

"I don't know," he said. He stood and punched a fist against the wall. "I hate this. I want to keep you safe, but I feel powerless. If we can get you to Venom, we can regroup there. I can call in any favors and friends who might be willing to stand and fight."

I finished dressing and stood. My head throbbed with a sudden headache. "If we can even get there at all," I said. "The Chicago entrance is ruined. He's already got eyes on Paris. Probably all the others, too. What about the entrance from your house? Could we go through the hall in Harper's house to get there?"

He shook his head. "It's not that easy," he said. "The only entrance to Venom from my house is through a specific hallway outside of Venom. It's a trick I put in place with my own magic. If we go through the hallway in Harper's house, we can get to my house, but not back to Venom. Not directly, anyway. It's complicated."

I ran a hand through my knotted hair, still tousled from sleeping. I glanced over at the bed. I would have given anything for just one more peaceful night here alone with Rend. I wanted nothing more than to be lost in his arms again.

"We have no choice," I said. "Anything else is too risky. If we leave the safety of this village, we're vulnerable until we can get back to Venom. For all we know, the Devil is already out there waiting for us to leave."

Rend turned to me, his chest rising with each labored breath. "Okay. We'll follow her through this secret doorway of the crows, but at the first sign of trouble, we bail," he said. He moved toward me and put a hand on my cheek. "I won't let anything happen to you, Franki."

I wasn't sure it was entirely up to him, but I wanted to believe he could keep me safe. I wanted to believe there was a future for us, outside of this constant danger.

"I won't let anything happen to you either," I said with a smile.

Rend smiled and lowered his lips to mine. I wrapped my arms around him, pressing my body tightly against his. Our kiss deepened as we opened to each other. I dug my fingers into his back, wanting him closer.

His hand slipped behind my head, tangling in my hair. His other hand gripped my shirt into a fist, desire overcoming us as our bodies went up in flames. Now that I'd had a taste of what it was like to be with him, I wanted more.

But there was no time.

I groaned and pulled away, pressing my forehead against his as we both panted and caught our breath.

"We have to go," I said.

"I know," he said. He pulled back and locked his eyes on mine. "When all this is over, we're going to finish this. I'll figure out a way for us to be together, Franki."

I blushed. "We were pretty together last night," I reminded him.

He bit his lower lip, and his eyes sparkled. "Yeah, but I was holding back," he said.

His words made my stomach flip in a rush of desire and anticipation. If that had been him holding back, dear God I wanted to know what it felt like when he gave all of himself.

Someone began knocking furiously on the door of the house, and Rend groaned.

"Franki, we have to hurry," Mom said. "I think I saw movement outside."

"I'll be right out," I called.

I lifted onto my tiptoes and kissed Rend one more time. As our lips met, I sent up a silent prayer that this would not be the last kiss.

THE DOOR

Mom sat on the top step of the porch, waiting. She stood as we came out, her eyes full of fear.

"I think he's close," she said. "We need to get to that door as soon as we can."

She took my hand and pulled me down the stairs. Rend followed closely behind.

"Where is this door?" he asked.

"It's below the stone altar in the center of the village," she said. "The Mother Crow created it decades ago. None of us were ever allowed inside without permission, but I've been through the doorway once before, when I was younger."

"Where will we go once we get inside?" I held tightly to her hand, trying to remember the last time I had actually held my mother's hand.

"There's another village similar to this one that was set up about thirty years ago," she said. "Some of the other crows lived there for a while, but it's been abandoned for the past ten years or so."

"Wait," I said, slowing. "How do you know the rest of the crows aren't all living there now? Mary Anne said they all disappeared after the Mother Crow's fight against Harper here in Peachville."

She shook her head and yanked on my arm, putting all of her weight into it. "I just know," she said. "The Mother Crow wouldn't have gone anywhere Mary Anne and her friends could go after her. She would have hidden somewhere new. I imagine she's set up a new village somewhere, by now."

My stomach knotted. Were we doing the right thing trusting my mom?

I wasn't sure, but we couldn't stay here. Rend was right, though, something didn't feel right about all of this. I needed to know she could be trusted. I needed to know that, after all this time, she was willing to tell me the truth.

I paused when we reached the stone altar. I took my hand from hers and watched as she lifted the stone, revealing a staircase that led down into the darkness.

"Come on," she said, motioning for me to follow her.

"Hold on." My heart raced.

She had already started down the stairs, but she stopped to look up at me. "Franki, there's no time for this."

"There's something I need to know before I can follow you down there," I said. I crossed my arms over my chest, holding myself tightly, afraid even to ask for the truth after all this time. I wasn't sure I was prepared to hear the answer. "I need to know why the Devil is after me specifically," I said. "Out of all the witches in the world, why me?"

She shook her head, and her eyes searched my face. "We can discuss this later," she said.

"No. We need to talk about it now," I said. I remembered my conversation with Mordecai on the ride down to Peachville. He had said the secret to my unusual strength was not my crow heritage. It was my father's. "I need to know who my father is."

Mom narrowed her eyes at me, her entire forehead wrinkling. She leaned against the edge of the stone stairway. "I don't understand—"

"My whole life you kept my powers a secret," I said. "You made me feel ashamed of myself for having these abilities, always warning me not to use my power or to let anyone know what I was capable of. Why? It was because of him, wasn't it? Because of his darkness?"

She lifted a hand to her mouth and sat down on the steps. "Franki, I just need you to come with me now," she said softly, her voice barely more than a whisper.

"You have to see this from my point of view," I said. "You abandon me without a word three years ago, and now you show up out of nowhere, asking me to trust you. If you really want me to trust you, you have to give me this one thing. This one truth."

She shook her head and avoided my eyes. Her shoulders shook with sobs. "Okay," she said. When she looked up, it was Rend's eyes she met, not mine. "You have to understand that I didn't know who he was when I met him. You have to know that I had no idea the things he was capable of."

Rend's eyes darkened. "Who?"

She turned to me. "Your father was a vampire," she said. "A very powerful one by the name of Solomon."

Rend gasped and backed away from the altar. "Solomon is Franki's father?"

My eyes widened. The name meant nothing to me, but Rend's face said it all. He actually looked frightened.

"Who is Solomon?" I asked.

"One of the original founders of the Brotherhood of Darkness," Rend said. He met my eyes, and I could see the disbelief inside. "Solomon is the Devil's brother, Franki."

My mouth fell open, and I brought a hand to my heart. "What? You're telling me I'm related to the Devil?"

"Technically, he's your uncle," Mom said. "You have to see why I could never tell you about him. You would have wanted to know more. You would have wanted to meet him or find him, and I couldn't explain to you what had happened to him or why you could never know him."

"What happened to him?"

"Franki, I know you want answers, but if the Devil comes through that door, none of us will leave here alive," she said. "I can explain everything to you once we get inside."

I nodded, my hands numb from holding them in such tight fists against my ribcage. My father was a demon. A vampire. The darkness I had struggled with my entire life was his darkness.

Mom stood and reached for my hand.

I stared at it a moment, feeling that I finally understood why she had kept all this from me. Maybe it was true that I had been too hard on her. Maybe I had been seeing her from the wrong eyes all this time.

I put my hand in hers and followed her down the stairs, trusting her for the first time since I was a child.

The room beneath the altar was so dark I couldn't see anything more than the outline of what looked to be furniture arranged in rows.

Mom released my hand. "Wait here a second," she said. She descended the final steps and a few seconds later, lit a match that sparked red in the darkness. She used the match to light a small candle at the base of the stairs that illuminated the entire room with a deep red glow.

"The Mother Crow put a series of traps in place down here," she said. "The candle disables them, so it's safe to come down now."

I looked around, seeing now that the furniture was actually rows and rows of bookcases. "What is this place? A library?"

"All the spells and history of the crows," she said. She moved toward the corner under the stairs. "The door is this way."

I glanced back at Rend and he nodded but looked worried. We were putting our lives in her hands, not even knowing where we might end up next.

She led us to a wall that looked like solid stone. No doorway in sight.

Silently, she placed both her palms on the smooth stone, her eyes closed. In an instant, the outline of a door appeared, the wing of a crow carved into its center.

I gasped, reaching forward to run my fingers along the wing. It looked nearly identical to the one carved on the doorway in the hall at Venom. The door there had been made of wood, but the symbol was the same. I wondered if they led to the same place, but before I could ask, Mom pushed on the stone and it gave way, revealing a small dark hallway.

She took my hand and pulled me through.

I stepped around her and peered into the darkness. Rather than a long hall of nearly endless doorways, there was only a handful here, just as she had said.

I turned back just as Rend approached the doorway. He stepped forward but slammed against an invisible barrier. His forehead wrinkled and he pushed his hands against the spot where the door had been. Again, they hit a barrier like glass, completely see-through, but very real.

Horror flashed in his eyes, and he reared back, ramming the barrier with all his might. He shifted to smoke and tried again, but the door would not let him through.

I reached for him, thinking that maybe it was like the entrance to the crow village. Maybe I had to be holding his hand to pull him through.

But my mother pushed me backwards with such strength, it took my breath away. My body slammed against the wall behind me, stars exploding in my vision as my head hit stone. I screamed as the realization of betrayal finally dawned on me.

I ran toward the door, knowing in that moment, that I had made a very terrible mistake trusting my mother.

I watched as my mother's face drew up into a horrible smile.

She slammed the door closed before I could get there, closing me off from Rend. And locking me inside with her.

BETRAYAL

I pounded my fist against the stone.

"What have you done?" I shouted. "We have to go back."

My mother placed her hand on my chest and pushed me again. Where had she gotten such strength? She stepped in front of the door, that evil smile still plastered on her face. I wanted to rip it off her.

"Get out of my way," I said. A fierce wind blew her back against the door.

She raised her eyebrows. "You always had such a temper," she said. "I'm glad to see your power has been growing. It's going to come in handy when you die."

Fury consumed me, and I reached back, gathering my power in my hands. I threw it back at her in a rage, the power of it knocking her to her knees. I walked over and lifted my foot to her shoulder, kicking as hard as I could. She cried out and fell to the ground beside the door.

I searched for a handle, but the door was smooth except for

the cracks that outlined its shape. I placed my palms flat against the wall like I'd seen her do inside and to my relief, it opened toward me.

I stepped out of the way of the moving door, prepared to rush through to Rend on the other side.

Only, it wasn't Rend who stood there.

The crow library had been replaced by a room made of deep gray stones. There, just on the other side of the opening, stood the Devil, his eyes red and hungry.

I stepped back and reached for the edge of the door, but it was too late.

He grabbed my arm with one hand and placed the other on my forehead. I struggled against him, but he was too powerful. Too strong.

"Sleep," he said.

A bright light flashed across my vision. My knees gave out and my body went limp. The Devil's arms encircled me, and even though I fought it with everything I had inside, sleep beckoned—its call too strong to resist.

The last thing I saw before darkness consumed me was the image of my mother's satisfied smile of betrayal.

REND

BROTHERHOOD

The moment my body slammed against the invisible barrier, I knew I had lost her.

I had never felt so powerless. Or so consumed by rage.

I pushed, clawed, and drove every ounce of my power toward that doorway, but there was no breaking through. That witch had known exactly what she was doing, and we had played into it like blind children.

The stone door slammed closed, cutting Franki off from me entirely. The door's outline disappeared, leaving nothing more than a smooth stone wall. Without Crow blood in my veins, there was no way to make the door reopen. A roar escaped from me, shaking the books from their cases.

How could I have let this happen?

I had promised to protect her. I never should have let her go through the door first. What was I thinking?

My gut had told me not to trust her mother. Something had felt off about her behavior from the moment she stepped into the crow village. I should have trusted that, but I had let myself be ruled by fear and desperation.

Without my normal level of power, there was no way I could defeat the Devil in a direct fight. I had been so anxious to see Franki and make sure she really was safe that I hadn't brought any of my potions with me to Peachville. I had been completely unprepared and now Franki's life was in more danger than ever.

I had to find my way to her.

I shifted to my demon form and flew up the stairs and out into the village. I crossed the barrier and didn't stop until I had reached Brighton Manor. I had no idea how much time I had until the Devil carried out his plans, but I was now sure Franki's mother had been a part of his game all along.

He never had been on his way to the crow village. He wouldn't have risked getting tied up with Harper and her friends. He would want Franki brought to him. If there was going to be a fight, he would want it fought on his terms. His turf.

I banged on the back door. The moment it opened, I barreled into the kitchen where Harper, Jackson and a handful of others were just sitting down to breakfast.

Harper stood, pushing her chair back. "What is it?"

My jaw tensed. I hated even to admit what I had let happen, but there was no avoiding it now. I was going to need all the help I could get, and the group here in Peachville was made up of some of the strongest witches and demons I knew.

"Franki's been taken," I said, my mind filtering out the unnecessary details. "Her mother showed up this morning claiming the Devil had been holding her captive for months.

She said she'd escaped just in time to warn us that he was on his way to the village to attack."

Mary Anne rushed in from the other room, her bright blue eyes wide with fear. "What? How? There's no way he could even get into the village."

My gut twisted. "She showed us marks on her neck and said he had been feeding on her," I said. "Her blood was in his veins, and she said he'd be able to get in that way."

"Oh my God," Mary Anne said. "We have to go after her. Where did he take her?"

I ran a hand through my hair. I was so mad I just wanted to rip it out. "He didn't. Not directly. Franki's mom betrayed us," I explained. "She said the only way out of the village without risking the Devil capturing Franki was through a special doorway in the library."

"The one under the altar?" Jackson asked, standing to join me near the door.

"Yes," I said. I looked to Mary Anne, hopeful. "Do you know that door? Do you know where it leads to?"

Mary Anne's mouth hung open. "It's a shifting doorway," she said. "Her mom could have taken her anywhere from the other side of that door."

I leaned a hand against the table, trying to control my anger. If anything happened to Franki, I would never be able to forgive myself.

"She's taken her to the Devil's castle," I said. "I'm sure of it. That had to have been their plan all along. Dammit. I knew something was wrong, but she was so convincing. She kept rushing us toward that door, telling us it was our only chance to escape. I can't believe we trusted her."

"You can't blame yourself for the betrayal of others,"

Harper said. "All you can do is learn from it and move forward. What can we do to help?"

I rubbed my hands across my weary face. I needed to think. If I was going after the Devil, I needed an army. "The Devil's castle is in Germany," I said. "It's not too far from my own house in the mountains. I can use the doorway here to get us close. We'll have to fly the rest of the way. He'll have it heavily guarded, I imagine. Possibly a hundred or more of the lesser vampires. Worst case, some of the Brotherhood will be there, as well. I know it's a lot to ask for you to join me in this fight, but there's something I haven't told you."

"What?" Jackson said. He and Harper shared a look.

"Before she took her through the doorway, Franki's mother told her who her real father is," I said. "She lied about a lot of things, but I don't think she was lying about this."

Mordecai, who'd been sitting quietly at the table, listening, stood, his hands pressed against the top of the wooden table. "I knew her father was the key to this. Who is it?"

I closed my eyes and swallowed. My entire throat had gone dry. The implications of why the Devil would be after Franki took on a whole new meaning now.

"Solomon is Franki's father."

Every demon in the room went quiet.

Mary Anne shook her head. "I don't understand," she said. "Who is Solomon?"

"He's the Devil's brother," I said. "And one of the original founding members of the Brotherhood of Darkness."

"He's one of the most evil bastards ever to walk this world or the next," Mordecai said, sitting back down and resting his head in his hands. "What does this mean? What do you think the Devil wants with her?"

"I have an idea, but I need to talk to someone first to be sure," I said.

"Who?" Harper asked.

I looked at her, hoping she was up for this fight. After all I'd heard about her powers, I was going to need her.

"I have to find my friend Silas," I said. "And tell him he's Franki's brother."

HAUNTED

"Franki has a brother?" Mary Anne asked.

"A half-brother," I said. "Solomon's son. He's a member of the Brotherhood and one of my best friends. He came into the club the other night. He said he was in Chicago and thought he'd stop by to say hello, but I never thought to ask him what he was doing there. Ten to one he was looking into the Devil's activities. I need to talk to him and find out what he knows."

"What do you think the Devil is after?" Harper asked. She moved around the table and came to stand beside Jackson. "I haven't heard of Solomon before, but he sounds dangerous. Do you think he's behind all this?"

"Solomon is dead," Mordecai said.

"Not exactly," I said. "Twenty-one years ago, the Mother Crow banished Solomon's spirit to a black stone."

"A soul stone?" Harper asked.

I nodded. "A very large soul stone," I said. "He was too

powerful for her to kill, so she trapped him inside the stone and hid it somewhere no one would ever find it."

"And you're afraid the Devil has found it," Jackson said.

"Yes."

"What would that mean?" Harper asked. "Do you think he's trying to set him free?"

"I don't know if that's even possible," I said. "After he was locked inside the stone, the Devil led a group of brothers on a witch hunt. They searched for the stone and for the Mother Crow, but at the time, she had gone deep into hiding. No one knew the location of the crow's secret village and after a few years of searching, Solomon was mourned by the Brotherhood and considered dead. We all knew that even if the Devil had found the stone, the magic trapping Solomon inside would be too powerful for us to break without a significant blood sacrifice."

"Franki," Mary Anne whispered.

"If I had to guess, the Devil plans to use her to try to free Solomon's power," I said.

"From what I know about soul stones, I don't think Solomon would ever be able to regain his true form," Jackson said.

"Maybe he's planning to use someone as a vessel," Mordecai said. "There is a precedent."

"Alijah," Lea said from the hallway.

I hadn't seen or heard her come in, but she must have been listening. "Yes."

Harper and Mary Anne, the only two in the room who had not grown up in the Shadow World, looked confused.

Lea stepped inside the room. "Alijah was a powerful demon on my father's council. She was his friend once. They had grown up together as shadowlings," she explained. "But Alijah had aspirations to overthrow my father's rule and take over the Northern Kingdom. When he discovered her plan, he captured her. Out of respect for her family's service to the throne for centuries, he banished her spirit to a soul stone where her power might be used for good."

"That's not exactly how it worked out, though," Jackson said. "I remember this story. The stone was in a case inside the castle where it was used to power parts of the city for decades."

"But her brother stole the stone and brought it here to the human world," Lea continued. "He traded her stone to the Order of Shadows in exchange for the freedom of a demon girl he had fallen in love with who had been taken from his village."

"What did the Order do with the stone?" Harper asked.

"They did what they always do," Lea said. "They used it to gain power. They sacrificed an entire coven of witches to free Alijah's spirit. One of the priestesses consumed the power, becoming a vessel."

"Which priestess?" Harper asked.

"I can't remember her name, but I think it was the priestess who rules over the emerald portals," Lea said. "The power nearly drove her mad, it was so great. She went into hiding for a while, but resurfaced years later, more powerful than ever."

"If the Devil intends to release Solomon's power into a human vessel, we'd better all pray it's not one of the priestesses," Harper said. "That's a fight we don't need right now."

Harper and her friends had waged war against the Order of Shadows—a powerful group of witches who had made a habit of stealing innocent demons from my world and using them as batteries for their power. Thanks to Harper, the five priestesses who ruled the Order had been whittled down to only four after the death of Priestess Winter. I knew they had plans to go after the other four, as well as the mysterious High Priestess who ruled them all.

"We need to stop him before it's too late," I said. "We may not have much time."

"Just tell us what we need to do," Harper said. She placed a hand on Jackson's shoulder. "This is our fight now, too."

I nodded to her. "Thank you," I said. "Gather as many as you can. Anyone you trust who is willing to help. Meet me at my house at midnight tonight. I'll show you the door and alter the spell to allow anyone with you to enter. We'll fly from there and hit him at night."

Harper and Jackson followed me up to the hall of doorways, and I showed them where to find the door with the cobra etched into the surface. They wished me luck and said they'd be there.

I said my goodbyes and went in search of Silas' door.

His symbol was easy to recognize. It was an animal closely associated with the devil of human lore. I searched for the goat, finally finding it about a hundred doors down from my own. I didn't bother knocking. If Silas was home, he would be down in his study.

Which is where I found him, his back hunched over a large book spread open on his desk.

I knocked twice on the door to his study and he looked up, startled.

"Rend? What are you doing here?"

"I'm sorry to walk in like this, but I have something urgent I need to talk to you about," I said.

He closed the book and stood, stretching his arms above his

head. I wondered how long he'd been sitting in that same position and what he'd been studying this time.

"I wasn't expecting to see you again so soon," he said.

"When you were in Chicago, why didn't you tell me the truth about Solomon's stone?" I asked.

His eyes widened and he looked away. "I don't know what you mean."

"Yes, you do," I said. "He's found it, hasn't he?"

Silas closed his eyes and took a deep breath before turning back to me. "How did you know? Has something happened?"

"Dammit, Silas, you should have told me." My muscles tightened in anger. If he had been open with me from the beginning, I might have been able to put this all together faster. I might have been able to save Franki from whatever hell she was in right now.

"I didn't want anyone inside the Brotherhood to find out before I had a better idea what his intentions were." He tapped the top of the book. "He must want to use the stone somehow, but how? I've been studying these damned old manuscripts for weeks, trying to make sense of it, but there's no way he can free my father from that stone. It's impossible."

"Impossible unless he had the blood of your father's only daughter," I said.

Silas' head snapped up. "What?"

"The girl you met at the club the other night," I said. "The bartender with the black hair? Her name is Franki—Mary Francis—and she's the daughter of a crow witch. The Devil has been trying to get his hands on her, and until today, I couldn't figure out why he was so intent on her, in particular."

"Solomon is her father?" he asked, his tongue tripping over the words. "This can't be possible."

"It is," I said. "And I think she might be the reason the Mother Crow banished your father to that stone in the first place. Silas, she just turned twenty-one years old."

His mouth fell open and he leaned against his desk, his head down. "Oh my God," he said. "We have to make sure he doesn't get to her. With her blood, he could—"

"He already has her," I said. My fangs pressed against the inside of my mouth, begging to be let loose. "I know he's your father, but you know better than anyone what he's capable of. We can't let him go free. You should have told me about the stone.

"You should have told me the Devil was after this girl," he said. "Together we might have figured this out."

"We still would have been missing the most important piece of the puzzle," I said.

"I could have helped you keep her safe," he said. He slammed his hands down on the top of the desk. "How could you have let him get to her?"

My fangs extended fully this time, and I shifted, reappearing behind him, my arm wrapped around his throat. "You don't want to mess with me right now, Silas."

Silas shifted and slid from my grasp. He reformed on the other side of the desk. "I am not your enemy," he said. "Save your anger for the Devil."

I closed my eyes and turned away. He was right, but I had been on the edge of losing control ever since Franki's mother took her through that doorway. Anger and fear boiled just beneath the surface of my resolve. I wasn't used to caring this much for someone. I didn't know how to deal with it when they were in danger. All I wanted to do was tear apart the demon responsible.

Silas rubbed a hand across his jaw. "Where is she now?"

"I'm not certain," I said, a lump forming in my throat. "I think he's taken her to his castle. We don't have much time."

"A ritual like that would take several hours to prepare," he said. "Maybe days, if we're lucky. I hope your friend is strong, because the type of preparations he'll have to put her through will be painful, to say the least."

I swallowed, the feeling of loss and fear in my heart foreign to me. I had lost many friends in my lifetime, but Franki was so much more to me than a friend. After last night, I realized just how much I had begun to care for her. I couldn't lose her now. I wouldn't.

"I have to get her back," I said.

Silas studied me. "You care for this girl," he said.

I moved toward him again, lifting my lips in a snarl. "She's not just a girl, Silas. She's your half-sister. And up until about a week ago, she had no idea our world even existed. Now she's probably being tortured in the Devil's dungeons." I cleared my throat and took a deep breath, stepping away. "We can't let him go through with whatever he's got planned. He and Solomon tried to destroy this world once. What's to stop them from trying again?"

Silas shook his head. "We are," he said. "We're going to stop them."

I let out the breath I'd been holding since I first stepped through his door. He was going to help me, and I was going to need him. It would take great power to even get close enough to the Devil's ritual room, much less defeat him and stop him from killing Franki.

"There are others," Silas said. "Some of our Brotherhood have been meeting in secret for a while, discussing taking control away from the Devil. He's grown too power-hungry lately, going too far with his killing. His actions have put us all in danger of being discovered."

"Gather anyone you think is on our side, but be careful. We can't afford to have anyone betray us and warn the Devil that we're coming," I said. My jaw tensed as I thought of Franki all alone in his dungeons. "I want to catch him by surprise. And I want to rip him apart with my bare hands when I do."

"There are eight or nine I know we can trust, with no doubts," he said. "I'll call a meeting and fill them in on what's happened."

"Thank you," I said. "Meet at my house at midnight. There will be others there. Some human witches. Make sure everyone is well fed before they arrive."

He nodded. "And what about you? Will you feed?"

Hunger echoed in my empty stomach. The need for blood haunted my dreams, but I had fought long and hard for the ability to survive without it. I hated what being a vampire had come to mean. I hated what it had done to the demon I used to be.

But Silas had a point. I needed all my strength if I was going to fight the Devil.

I walked to the door of his study. "I'll figure something out," I said. "Don't be late."

I KNEW THE SADNESS IN HER EYES

I hurried through the hall of doorways. I needed to get back to my own home in the mountains. At best, I had twelve hours until everyone started to arrive. That was barely enough time to extract the ingredients I'd need from the stones, much less create the potions I wanted for tonight's battle.

For the past seventy years, I'd refused to feed from humans, developing stronger and stronger potions to enhance my powers here in the human world.

But Silas was right. Nothing would bring me the strength I needed tonight like a real meal.

I shook the thought from my mind. I couldn't hunt. Not after all this time. That would mean trading an innocent witch's life for a chance at saving Franki. It wasn't right or fair.

As much as I wanted to get Franki back, I wouldn't sacrifice an innocent to increase my power. There were other ways.

There were some who were not so innocent.

I did a quick check of the house to make sure none of the devil's guards had gotten inside or set traps. I cast a spell near the entrance that would give access to Harper when she arrived. Silas and the others of the Brotherhood were already allowed to enter. All that was left to do was focus on the potions.

I needed to get down to my lab in the basement of the large mansion. I'd built this home into the side of the mountain for two reasons. One was that there was no road leading to the house. It was literally carved into the rock by magic, inaccessible by cars or any other normal human transportation, except maybe a helicopter, or in extreme cases, snowboard.

My second reason for building the house here was that this particular section of the Alps had pockets of iron and copper, useful base metals for many of my potions. Deep inside the mountain, veins of gold and silver also ran through the stone. Very few even knew it existed because of how difficult and expensive it would be to mine. But as a demon, I had access to tools and resources most humans did not. I was able to extract gold from the tiniest of deposits without as much as a hammer.

I built my lab several floors down from the main house and deep into the rock, where it would be easier to access the minerals and stone I needed.

The elevator leading down into the basement was hidden behind the main staircase. I stepped inside and pressed the only button. When the doors opened, I sucked in a startled breath. Movement caught my eye, and I lifted my hands, ready to fight. But as she turned, my heart filled with sadness and worry.

"Azure, oh my god, are you okay?" I crossed to her, taking

her face in my hands. I moved her head from side-to-side, surveying the damage.

Her left eye was bruised and black. A gash ran along her cheekbone, a scab already formed across it. Her bottom lip was split and cracked. Bruises wrapped around her neck. The Devil's vamps had really done a number on her.

"I'm fine," she said. "It's nothing that won't heal in a couple of days. But Rend, I heard from Marco."

The quiver in her voice stopped me cold. "What's happened?"

"The Devil's got Lyla and Misty and Shay."

"What?" My heart tightened in my chest. "How?"

"Lyla left Marco's house to go meet the other girls and bring them back to where she was hiding, and Fallon cornered them," she said. "We have to go after them."

"That's what I'm preparing to do," I said.

She looked up, her eyes meeting mine in that familiar expression of hope mixed with terrible sorrow. I took my hand from her and backed away, guilt churning my stomach.

I cleared my throat. "Azure, the Devil has Franki, too," I said.

She looked away, her eyes closed as she took several deep breaths.

"I was hoping you'd come back to Venom after you heard about what happened in Paris," she said. "But when you didn't, I knew you were with her."

She turned and walked around a large table that held a maze of glass tubes and beakers and other equipment. She ran her hand along the glass.

"I used to love coming down here to watch you work in the early days."

I swallowed and held my breath. I knew this was coming eventually, but this was the worst possible time for it.

Or, maybe, it was exactly the right time. Maybe, after what happened last night between Franki and me, this was the way this conversation was always meant to go.

"My whole life, I grew up around magic," she said. "But I had never seen anyone do what you do down here, taking solid stone and gems and metal and turning them to liquid and powder. The way you combine these seemingly powerless elements into these incredibly powerful potions and elixirs. It's like poetry or art."

"Azure—"

"Just let me say what I need to say." She closed her eyes and took a deep breath. When she opened them, her tears shone like diamonds. She laughed and looked up toward the ceiling, blinking fast to keep them from falling. "I swore I was going to be strong and not cry, but I can't seem to help myself."

I took a step toward her, but she held up a hand.

"I have loved you for so long, I don't even remember what it's like not to want you," she said. "I wanted to tell you from that first day you brought me down here, almost seventy years ago. I watched you work and knew that you were the only one for me. I knew I could never love anyone else."

I looked down at the floor and shifted my weight from one foot to the other. I guess I always knew Azure felt more for me than what I felt for her, but she'd never put words to it. She'd never once pushed or demanded anything of me. But I knew the sadness in her eyes. I knew the longing.

"The thing is, though, I had convinced myself that the reason you didn't love me back was because you couldn't love anyone," she said. "I told myself that I was content to be working there by your side, making Venom what it was. Being a part of your life was all I needed. But then, this girl walks in and you..."

I swallowed and looked up as her voice trailed off. The tears flowed down her cheeks, but she just wiped them away and kept moving around the lab, as if she was remembering every night we'd ever spent in here working.

"I consider myself a strong person," she said. "It takes a lot to break me, but the way you look at her tears me apart. You love her, don't you?"

I breathed in, not knowing what she wanted me to say. I couldn't deny it, but I didn't want to break her heart. Azure was one of my best friends in the world.

She shook her head and rolled her eyes. "You don't have to say it, Rend. I can see it there between you," she said. "I've known you for seventy-five years and could never earn your love. She's known you for seven days and you're ready to give up everything you've ever known to save her. Your club. Your Brotherhood. Even your own life."

"What do you want me to say?" I asked. "I can't explain the way I feel about her any more than you can. It just happened. A couple of weeks ago, if you had asked me if I was capable of loving a woman, I would have laughed in your face and told you love was not part of my destiny."

"And now?"

"Now, I feel more alive than I have my whole life," I said, realizing the truth of my words for the first time.

"And you never felt anything like that for me? This whole time?"

I closed my eyes. Why was she forcing this on me now? "I never meant to hurt you," I said. "This had nothing to do with you."

She shrugged and gave me a sad half-smile. "That's the problem," she said. "Since the day my father introduced us, everything in my life has revolved around you."

"I never asked for that," I said.

Azure lifted an eyebrow and wiped the last of her tears from her face. "No, you didn't," she said. "That's the thing about love, though. You don't have to ask for the things you need."

She picked up a glass tube and twirled it around in her fingers. With a swift motion, she smashed part of the tube against the table. Confused, I watched as she lifted the broken glass to her wrist.

My mouth fell open. "No. Azure, don't," I said. I shifted and flew to her side, but it was too late.

The cut was deep and blood flowed freely. She raised the wound above a larger glass container and let the warm red of her blood run into it.

I tore my t-shirt off and ripped it in two. Quickly, I grabbed her wrist and wrapped the strip of fabric tightly around her wound several times. I applied pressure and lowered her to the floor.

Her eyes closed and she rested her head on my chest.

"What were you thinking?" I asked.

She laughed, her eyes closed. "I just wanted you to know that even though you're in love with her, nothing can ever change the way I feel about you. All I've ever wanted is for you to be happy, Rend. If she makes you happy, then I will do anything to help you get her back." Her voice grew sleepy and weak.

Just before she lost consciousness, her eyes fluttered open for a moment and she smiled.

"Don't let me die."

ALCHEMY

I checked Azure's bandage to make sure the worst of the bleeding had stopped. I wanted to keep an eye on her, so I pulled out an old cot I sometimes used when I was working in the lab for days at a time. I made her as comfortable as I could and turned back to my laboratory.

The glass full of her blood beckoned to me.

My hunger was decades old, gnawing at my insides. I yearned for the taste of it in my mouth and the way its power filled me up.

But now was not the time.

I moved the glass to the other side of the room where its smell would be less potent, and forced myself to concentrate on the potions. If I was lucky, Harper would bring at least ten people with her. Silas said he thought he could recruit eight or nine. Including me, that meant I could hope for twenty-one, a significant number these days.

I got to work, drawing metals and minerals from the earth. When I had several vials full of each ingredient, I began mixing, crushing, and breaking down the raw elements. The work of it kept my mind occupied, but Franki's face crept into my consciousness at even intervals.

What had the Devil done with her? Where was she right now? Was she still alive?

I sent up prayer after prayer.

Please hold on. Just give me time. I'm coming for you. Hold on.

Once I had the raw powders and liquids I needed, I moved on to transmuting. It was work I had done countless times before. For me, my lab was my sanctuary where I prayed to the gods of alchemy and earth. I both lost and found myself in this room. Here, I had real power. Real control. When the rest of the world made no sense, I could always come here to feel centered.

My life had purpose in this lab, tonight more than ever.

I molded and transformed the raw elements into potions of unique power, concocting a mix of the clarity of Blue Frost and the passion of Red Dragon. I tested the limits of my own skill and knowledge, creating one potion for the witches who would join the fight, one for the demons, and one for the vampires.

As the clock struck eleven-thirty, I stared down at twenty-one perfect vials, knowing we would need every single drop.

ONE DEVIL AT A TIME

I corked each of the vials and put them inside my large leather satchel. I disappeared into my storeroom for a moment and added more than a hundred other vials of various potions to a second bag.

And it still didn't seem like enough.

The Devil would have his castle well-fortified by now. He would expect me to come. I just hoped he didn't expect me to bring an army along with me.

In all the years the Brotherhood of Darkness had been in existence, no one had ever challenged its leadership. Its principles. The most radical act of rebellion had been my own refusal to partake of human blood. I knew my actions tonight would change the Brotherhood forever. Once the battle was over—regardless of the outcome—the brothers who stood with me tonight would face judgment for attacking one of our own.

But even if it meant a death sentence, I knew I would die with honor. I would die for love. As long as Franki survived, it would be worth it.

I slung the satchels over my shoulder. I needed to get upstairs to meet the others. Some were likely already gathered in the main room of the house, waiting.

But before I could join them, there was one last thing I needed to do.

Something I had sworn never to do again.

I found the glass of blood where I had left it in the back of the lab. I closed my eyes and lifted it to my lips, my hand trembling with need. I drank it slowly, savoring the taste and the raw power that flowed through me.

Azure's sacrifice was one of love and true friendship. I would have never asked for such devotion, but the fact that she offered it willingly made it less of a betrayal.

My muscles rippled with new strength. I gripped the exposed rock, the blood pulsing through me like a powerful drug. It spread like wildfire, igniting my senses. God, I had forgotten how good this felt.

I was drunk with power, remembering the demon I used to be. The demon who had earned the name Rend all those years ago when I first became a vampire.

I opened my eyes, seeing every detail of the lab with new eyes. New clarity.

I shifted to demon smoke, amazed at the ease of it. I had grown used to fighting for every use of magic, learning to utilize every drop of my potions in order to cast. But with the blood of a powerful half-witch, half-demon, I felt as if I had been reborn.

I was tempted to leave the elevator behind and fly to the first floor, but I reminded myself that this was only the beginning of the night's work. I couldn't afford to waste a single drop.

Riding up on the elevator was torture. Energy buzzed inside every cell of my body, begging to be set free. I focused my thoughts on the Devil's face, and how good it would feel to rip him in two from mouth to cock.

Upstairs, a small group had already gathered around the massive fireplace in the main room. Harper was there, Jackson, Aerden, Lea, Essex and Mary Anne at her side. Mordecai, Joost, Cristo and Erick—friends of Lea's from the Shadow World—stood by the door. A teenaged girl I hadn't seen before sat alone on the leather couch, her blond hair covering half of her face. She looked up as I entered and smiled nervously.

I joined Harper's group, nodding to her in thanks.

She smiled. "I hope you don't mind. We made ourselves at home," she said. "I think you've met everyone."

I glanced at the girl on the couch and she ducked her head. I frowned. I didn't want to bring anyone into this fight if they weren't ready. This girl seemed very shy.

"That's Courtney," Harper said.

"Are you sure she's up for this?" I asked.

Harper nodded. "Trust me. She's very shy, but she has a unique power that will really come in handy tonight."

When I raised an eyebrow, she continued.

"She can recharge powers," she said. "Like a human battery."

My mouth fell open. I had heard of similar powers before, but never actually met someone who could do it. "That's a rare talent," I said.

Courtney's face blushed a bright red and she lowered her head, her hair falling across her face.

"She'll be fine," Harper whispered, smiling. "And we have one more coming. Zara said she'd be here, but—"

"She's notoriously late for everything these days," Mary Anne said. "She gets wrapped up in something and loses track of time. It's annoying."

"I'm here," a sing-songy voice called from the stairs. "And for the record, I wasn't wrapped up in something frivolous. I remembered a trick my mother taught me about fighting vampires."

Zara, a fairy-like young girl I'd met once or twice before, descended the last of the steps and held up a small blue bag.

"What's that?" I took a quick step back from her, repelled by the power of whatever she held concealed in her tiny hands.

She smiled. "My secret weapon," she said. "Mother called them black pearls, but really they are just very small, very concentrated soul stones with a special enchantment on them."

Black pearls. Dear Lord, this girl was waving them around like they were marbles.

"Get them away from me." The order came out darker than I intended, but what she held in her hand was extremely dangerous for any vampire. Especially one who had just fed on a witch's blood.

Zara's innocent smile faded from her pale face. She pulled the blue bag tightly against her body. "I'm sorry, I wasn't thinking," she said. "I've never actually worked on the same side as a vampire. I was just thinking about how useful they might be for tonight."

I softened. "I didn't mean to scare you," I said. "They will definitely come in handy tonight. I just don't want them anywhere near me or the others who will soon join us."

She nodded, her blue eyes wide. "Where should I put them?"

I looked around the room. We needed a more protective box for the black pearls. I'd only had them used on me once, many years ago, but it was an experience I was not keen to repeat any time soon. Or ever.

The black pearls were, as she'd said, small, concentrated soul stones enchanted in such a way that when thrown at the feet of a vampire, they were able to pull the lifeblood's power from their body, leaving them weak and defenseless, completely unable to cast or use magic. The effects of the pearls could last years if powerful enough.

And since Zara was the daughter of one of the original five priestesses of the Order of Shadows, I felt certain the black pearls in her bag were the real deal.

"I think, perhaps, I can be helping with this," Essex said in his strange accent. "If you have any spare materials around that I might use in weaving, I can make for this, special bags, enchanted, so that the power of these pearls does not escape. I can make one for each of the witches who are needing one."

I nodded, relaxing. I hadn't realized he was a weaver. "Thank you," I said. I disappeared upstairs for a moment and returned with straps of extra leather I'd used to make my own potion bags.

Essex took them from me and bowed. "I will get to working on this."

I thanked him and turned to the rest of the group.

"It's important to anyone here who plans to use them, that you memorize the faces of the vampires on our side. Several members of the Brotherhood of Darkness will be joining us soon. They are taking a great risk fighting one of our own, and I don't want any harm to come to them because one of these pearls was used on them accidentally."

Zara nodded and wisely went to sit near Essex on the other side the room, far away from the group gathered near me.

A door opened upstairs and I raised my eyes to see Marco and most of the Venom staff descending toward us.

"What are you guys doing here?" I asked. "I don't want to put any more of my staff at risk. You guys have been through enough."

Marco lifted his hands. "Do you really expect us to miss out on the greatest battle this world has seen in a while?" His eyes dipped toward Harper. "Well, since Peachville, anyway."

Harper smiled. "I like this guy."

Marco reached out to clasp my hand. "We all want to help however we can," he said sincerely. "You've done so much for us. We're a family, remember? We're all in this together."

Minutes later, I felt the presence of power enter the room.

My brothers flew down the stairs, streaks of black and white smoke trailing behind them.

Silas was the first to regain his human form. He reached for my hand.

"Brother."

"Thank you for being here," I said. "All of you."

I looked at the group of vampires who had come to fight at my side. Ten demons I had known for more than a century. After tonight, I would forever be in their debt.

Everyone gathered around me, and I knew the time for action had finally come.

"Never before in the history of this world or the next has such a group come together to fight against evil," I said. "When Solomon was bound to a stone, we mourned his passing, but those of us who knew the great evils he had performed since coming to this world, also knew that his passing was for the best. He and his brother had become addicted to power, not caring who they killed in their quest to obtain it. If Solomon had not been stopped, who knows what might have become of the human world."

Many of the Brotherhood nodded in agreement. Most of Harper's crew knew nothing of the great evils Solomon and the Devil had done, but they were no strangers to evil and senseless killing.

"Tonight, the Devil has plans to sacrifice a young witch in order to free Solomon's power from the soul stone where he's been trapped for more than twenty years," I said. Franki's face passed before my eyes and I took a deep breath, praying we were not too late. "This young witch is Solomon's daughter. A woman named Mary Francis. Half crow. Half demon. The power that runs through her veins is dark and powerful, but she is nothing like her father. She does not deserve to die. And we must do everything in our power to make sure the Devil does not follow through with this ritual."

"What's our plan?" Silas asked.

I pulled a map from one of the leather satchels I'd carried up from the basement laboratory. "While I was working downstairs, I drew up a crude blueprint of the Devil's castle. I know many of the Brotherhood have been there, but this will be the first time for most of the rest of you."

I spread the map out on the large table in front of the couch and everyone gathered around it in a circle.

"The Devil will likely have guards stationed at every entrance." I pointed out the four entrances I was aware of—the front door, an old servant's entrance at the back, an underground tunnel through the hills and a hidden half-door on the side. "I think our best bet is to send a pair to each entrance and hit all four at the same time. We'll confuse them and split their defenses. Zara here brought black pearls that used to belong to Priestess Winter of the blue demon gates. If we use the element of surprise to hit the guards at each entrance with these pearls, we can take their power and defeat them very quickly."

I sensed the fear and discomfort of the other vampires at the mention of the black pearls. Several threw odd glances at Zara.

"An attack like this will mean the witches of the group will have to go in first," I said. "We'll split you into groups of two. Harper and Mary Anne at the main entrance. Zara and Courtney here at the servant's entrance. Peri, you and Cherish go to the underground tunnel here. Brandy and Kianna, you'll take this half-door."

The witches all studied the map as I spoke.

"As soon as the attack begins, we'll concentrate the rest of our force here at the back entrance," I said, pointing to the old servant's entrance. "It's the closest both to the dungeons where Franki is likely being held and to the ritual room where the Devil will be preparing."

"He'll probably have Solomon's stone there as well," Silas said.

"Yes," I said. I looked into his eyes, knowing how difficult this must be for him. "Your primary focus tonight needs to be retrieving that stone, Silas. Do whatever you have to do to get the stone and take it far away from the Devil's castle."

"If I do manage to get it, what do I do with it?" he asked.

"Destroy it," I said.

Silas swallowed and his eyes grew dark.

"I know it's difficult, but you're the only one who can do

it," I said. "Destroying the stone is the only way to make sure his spirit can never be used for harm."

Silas nodded slowly. I could see the struggle going on inside him. He'd loved his father. Worshipped him. But that was before he saw what his father was capable of doing. I knew destroying the stone would be difficult for him, but I also trusted him to do the right thing.

I went over the rest of the plan as quickly as I could. I had no idea how long Franki had left, but I knew we didn't have a minute to lose.

"There's one more thing," I said. I walked to the satchel of potions I'd set by the fireplace. I hadn't made enough for everyone, but what we had would have to do.

I handed the red ones to the demons, deep cobalt blue potions to the witches and the purple potions to the vampires, saving one for myself.

"I spent the better part of the day crafting these special potions to give us all heightened senses and clarity," I said. "Their magic is strong, but the effects won't last long. Two hours at most. Let's pray to the gods we don't need more time than that to put an end to the Devil's plans. Some of you will have to share yours, which will give you even less time. I wasn't expecting such an amazing turnout, but I am grateful to each of you for being here."

"Cheers," Mordecai said, lifting his red vial into the air.

"Here's to conquering evil," Mary Anne said. "One devil at a time."

Everyone raised their vials to their lips and drank of the potions I'd prepared.

I passed out the rest of the vials from the second satchel. These were mostly bombs and weapons, illusions and tricks.

I'd grabbed anything that might be useful in a fight, knowing that even with the thirty of us gathered here, we would still be massively outnumbered.

When everyone was ready, I opened the front door and stared out at the rocky cliffs.

Here's to first love, I thought as I downed my own potion and flew into the darkness.

Never in all my centuries of life had I ever thought of myself as a demon who deserved love. And never had I wanted so badly to have the chance to tell her how desperately I loved her back.

FRANKI

ANNABELLE

I struggled against sleep, my head pounding. I forced my eyes open. Every inch of my body ached, and darkness threatened to pull me under once more.

I pushed back, refusing to become its slave. I was lucky to have regained consciousness. If I let sleep claim me again, would I ever wake up?

I couldn't risk the answer being no.

I took several pained breaths, my ribs sore and my lips so dry they cracked when I opened them. I swallowed, but my mouth was a desert.

My head rested against my arm. My numb hands were bound above me, and my weight hung limply from the cold metal clamped around my wrists.

I lifted my head, fighting against the pain. My vision blurred for a moment and my stomach lurched.

The smell of blood and piss invaded my nostrils.

I adjusted my weight, forming my hands into fists to wake them up. My legs ached from being in the same position for a long time. I stretched them out across the stone floor, sucking in a breath as the feeling rushed back into them.

Whatever the Devil had cast on me had left me only half of myself. My awareness was fuzzy, as if I couldn't quite access all of my brain. How long had I been asleep?

I couldn't tell if it had been hours or days.

Even in my haze, I knew I needed to act quickly.

First, that meant trying to stand up and figure out how the hell I was going to escape. I closed my eyes and took three deep breaths in and out. I calmed the panic that lived just under the surface of my skin and focused instead on finding that spark of power deep inside.

If I had any chance of surviving this night, tapping into that well of energy was my greatest hope.

On the third breath in, I felt a twinge of it, there on the edge of my awareness. Power that sent chills up my arms.

I grabbed hold of it, pulling it up from the depths of darkness and forcing it into the light. I pushed that power through my veins, feeding off it until my skin buzzed with it.

My eyes snapped open, my vision no longer fuzzy and blurred.

For the first time, I got a good look at the room where I was confined. Cell would have been a better name for it. It looked like something out of an old Dracula film. The floor and walls were made of huge gray stones of various sizes. Decades worth of dirt lined the floors. Streaks of blood ran down the walls as if someone had literally tried to claw their way through the stones.

Iron bars locked me inside.

I almost smiled. Was I really so dangerous that one of the

most powerful vampires in existence felt the need to knock me out and chain me up inside a cell with iron bars?

Maybe I really was capable of so much more than I realized.

If that was true, I'd better wake up my inner bad-ass before the Devil came back.

Across from me, I could see an identical cell. At first, it looked empty, but when I looked away, movement caught the corner of my eye.

I turned back and squinted. There, in the shadows, stood a young girl. She couldn't have been more than eight or nine years old. My lips parted. What kind of monster would imprison a child?

I pulled my feet under me and pushed my back against the stone wall. My muscles were weakened and quivering, but with the support of the wall, I was finally on my feet.

I lowered my arms, my hands pulsing as the blood rushed back into them. My head spun, and I had to close my eyes again and take several deep breaths. I waited, letting my blood redistribute itself through my body, concentrating on that tiny spark of power still lit inside my core. That spark was all that mattered right now. Not the pain or the discomfort. Not the hunger that gnarled at my stomach. Nothing else mattered but the power.

When I felt better, I rolled my shoulders out, my joints cracking.

Okay, I was up. Now what?

I turned my attention to the chains and shackles that held me to the wall. There had to be a way out.

There was just enough give in the chains when I was standing to allow me to move a few steps forward and to each side. I moved carefully, testing my boundaries without making much sound.

The chains rattled slightly, and I slowed, making very deliberate movements.

I had enough space to turn around and study the way the chains were embedded into the wall. I reached up and pulled on them, knowing it would be way too easy if I could just pull them off.

The thick links of chain were hooked to a metal plate bolted into the stone. The metal looked old and rusted in some places, covered with dirt and blood in others, but it was sturdy and strong, showing no signs of give or damage.

I looked over and saw the child in the opposite cell staring at me. She had moved closer to the front now, her small hands grasping the iron as her head rested against the bars.

She didn't seem to have any chains around her arms or legs, like I did.

Of course, her wrists were so skinny, she could have just slipped out of any chains.

I twisted my wrists around inside the shackles to see if I could possibly wiggle my hands through, but it was no use. The metal shackles were way too freaking tight. Even if I dislocated my thumb, I'd never be able to pull free.

Maybe I could use magic to get them off.

I didn't know much about how to control my magical powers, but what I'd done so far had mostly come instinctively. So, what did I know about magic? I knew how to do glamours, but a glamour would only hide or cover things, it couldn't actually change the substance of them.

When I got angry or emotional, I could control or manipulate the wind, but even a tornado wouldn't get me out of these chains unless I managed to bring the whole damn building down. Which would kill me and everyone down here. That might be a good option if I was totally out of others, but I wasn't ready to choose suicide over impending ritual sacrifice just yet.

Wind wasn't the answer.

Women in my family were all supposed to be able to shift into the form of a crow. I'd seen both Mary Anne and my mother do it, but I had no idea how to make myself shift.

Still, it was worth a shot. If I became a crow, the chains would slide right off. I might even be able to fly through the iron bars of my cell and find a window.

Hope lifted my heart.

I could do this.

I closed my eyes and breathed deeply. I concentrated on the warm spark of energy inside me. Like when I'd used a glamour to change my eye color, I used the power of my imagination. I imagined myself turning into a crow. I pictured sleek, black wings spreading from my back as my body grew smaller. I pictured a beak and dark feathers. I imagined myself slipping from the chains and flying free.

But nothing happened.

Frustrated, I opened my eyes and balled my hands into fists. How hard could this be, really? If everyone—even a teenage girl like Mary Anne—could do this, surely I could do it, too. It was part of my heritage. I was a crow witch.

There had to be some trick to it that I wasn't getting.

I turned and leaned my back against the stone wall for support. I raised my arms to the side as if they were wings and closed my eyes. I calmed the panic and fear in my chest as best I could and tried again.

The spark of power in my core spread outward like fingers of energy, reaching toward my arms and legs. I imagined that energy blossoming, changing me from the inside out.

But something held me back.

I couldn't explain it or put my finger on it exactly, but I knew something was wrong. It was as if my magic had been muzzled.

"You can't cast magic in here, if that's what you're trying to do," a small voice said in a slight British accent.

I opened one eye and peered over at the child in the opposite cell. "Why not?"

She shrugged. "Don't know. You just can't," she said. "No one can but them."

"Them who?"

She looked to her left, as if making sure no one was listening. "The vampires," she said in a whisper.

I bit the inside of my lip. No magic. That was definitely not good news.

"Do you know where we are?" I stepped forward as far as my chains would let me go.

She shook her head.

"Do you know how long I've been here?"

She glanced up toward the ceiling. "About day, I think," she said. "You've been sleeping. I thought maybe you were dead there for a while."

I nodded. "Me, too," I said with a laugh. "I'm Franki, by the way."

"I'm Annabelle," she said.

"How old are you Annabelle? If you don't mind me asking."

"Eight," she said. "Or at least I think I turned eight already.

I tried to keep track of the days, but it's hard because there isn't any light."

My heart ached for this girl. Had she really been in here so long she wasn't even sure if she'd had a birthday? "You've been in here a while?" I asked.

She nodded, her eyes going shiny with tears.

"All alone?"

She nodded again. "My mum used to be in the cell next to me, but the guards took her away a few days ago," she said. She swiped at her face and sniffed. "I don't think she's coming back."

I swallowed back tears of my own.

The Devil truly is a monster.

I clenched my teeth and pulled hard against the chains. I was going to make him pay for this. I was going to find a way out of this cell, and I was going to make him suffer.

I threw all my weight against the chains, not caring that the shackles were cutting into my skin. I ignored the pain and fought as hard as I could. I pulled and clawed at the ancient handcuffs, begging my hands to slip through.

But it was no use.

My head fell against the stone as I struggled to catch my breath. I was trapped. Powerless. Dead on arrival.

In the distance, a door creaked open. I froze and listened.

Across from me, Annabelle slipped back into the shadows.

Shoes clicked against the stones as someone walked through the dungeon toward my cell. I pressed my back against the wall. My knees trembled and nearly buckled beneath me.

I told myself not to be afraid, but who was I kidding? Impending death by ritual was one of those occasions where I think you're allowed to be scared. I was lucky I hadn't peed my pants.

But as the footsteps drew closer, I straightened my shoulders, determined not to let them see how frightened I really was.

If this was the end of my life, I wanted to face it with strength.

And, if possible, I wanted to end as many of theirs as I could before I died.

Starting with the woman who'd just stepped in front of the iron bars of my cell.

REVENGE

I had never felt such hatred in my life.

The spark of power at my core roared to life, its flames licking at the surface of my skin. For a moment, I wondered if I might be burned alive by my own rage.

My mother smiled at me through the bars of my cell. "You have no idea how long I've waited to see you locked up inside this cage, little bird," she said. "Three long years I've been planning for this moment. I can hardly believe the time has finally come."

My veins strained against my skin, the magic inside of me begging to be let loose.

"Why?" I asked through gritted teeth.

"Revenge," she said. "For every day of my life I sacrificed for you."

I flinched. What kind of woman could want revenge from her own child? "I never did anything to you," I said.

"You were born," she said. "Isn't that enough?"

I clenched my fists tighter. "Isn't that partially your fault?" I asked. "Since you were the one who gave birth to me?"

She moved closer, placing a hand on the bars. "I keep forgetting you don't know the truth."

My heart went cold. "What are you talking about?"

"I was not the one who gave birth to you, Franki," she said, laughter in her voice. As if breaking my heart was a thing of joy. "You were born in the crow village to a young woman named Mary Kathryn. She held you. She nursed you. And then, like some cruel joke, the Mother Crow snatched you from her arms and handed you to me, a rebellious loser who had disobeyed the rules one too many times. You were my punishment for all the sins of my childhood."

My mouth fell open and a strangled cry escaped my throat.

"I honestly thought you'd be happy to hear the news," she said, raising an eyebrow.

"Where is she now?" I asked. "Is she still alive?"

She walked down the length of the cell, her hand trailing along each bar. "Yes. In fact, I think you've seen her," she said.

I stopped breathing for a moment. "What?"

"At Venom that first night," she said, narrowing her eyes. "The Devil had finally located Solomon's stone, and we were preparing to kidnap you and bring you here, but your real mother intervened at the last minute. I don't know how she even knew you were in danger, but I guess she'd been keeping an eye on us both. Her little stunt put a temporary halt to our plans, especially when Rend asked you to come work for him."

I stared ahead in a daze. "She's the one who sent me those flowers," I whispered.

"Yes, sending you right into the arms of the one vampire she thought could keep you safe," she said. "Little bird was actually her name for you. She called you that the moment you were born."

Tears welled up in my eyes. How long had she been watching me? How many times had I been in the same room with her and not even known it?

"God knows she would never be strong enough to protect you on her own. Poor Mary Kathryn. Her pregnancy with you was extremely difficult. It practically killed her, growing such an evil seed in her belly. She used to be the Mother Crow's golden child, destined for great things. She was showered with love and attention, groomed for an important role in the family. But she chose the wrong mate."

I closed my eyes, a single tear escaping down my cheek. "Solomon."

"Yes. She had no idea who he was, of course. It was her duty to get pregnant, and Mary Kathryn was merely doing as she was told," she said. "Back then, the Mother Crow sent all the girls out of the village when they turned eighteen. They were instructed to find a strong man, get pregnant, and return home. The Mother Crow didn't want men living in our village, so it was the easiest way to continue the family line."

I shook my head, disgusted. It sounded barbaric. Girls who had never once been allowed to leave the safety and confinement of their small village were sent out at eighteen to find a man and get pregnant? Never allowed to love or have a normal family life with a husband and children?

"Don't look so horrified. We all grew up knowing it was our duty," she said. "We also knew that if you gave birth to a boy, he was immediately offered up to the Mother Crow to be used as a blood sacrifice. If you gave birth to a baby girl, she would take her place in the family."

Her voice grew sad and she looked down at the floor of the dungeon.

"My first and only child was a boy," she said. "I still remember the moment he was taken from my arms. He was so chubby and pink and lovely."

There was more tenderness in her voice for that lost child than I had ever heard from her the entire time she'd raised me as her own. I couldn't imagine the horror of having your child taken like that, but my sympathy for what she'd been through was tainted by the fact that she'd been planning the details of my death for the past three years.

"I begged the Mother Crow for another chance to have a child of my own. A daughter to raise." She laughed and wiped away a tear. "Instead, she gave me you. A baby whose very existence was cursed from the moment of conception."

I swallowed back words of hatred.

"I resented you from the moment you were first placed in my arms," she said. "The Mother Crow cast a spell binding me to you until your eighteenth birthday when you would come of age. The spell ruined my womb, making sure I would never have another child that might distract me from my duty of taking care of you."

"Why did she send me away?" I asked. "I don't understand."

"Because your life put every crow in that village at risk," she said. "When she first found out Mary Kathryn was pregnant with Solomon's baby, she had to make sure he would never come after you. She hunted him down and bound his spirit in a stone. But she knew others would eventually come looking for you. She was willing to risk my life, but not her own."

"You were the one who told the Devil about me," I said.

"I was supposed to hide you and make sure you never used your magic and could never be tracked," she said. "I did such a good job, not even the Mother Crow could find you. She trusted me to return you to the crows when you turned eighteen, but I wasn't about to hand such a powerful asset over to the monster who had murdered my son and destroyed my youth."

"Instead, you found another monster." Bile rose in my throat.

My false mother turned to me, a triumphant smile spreading across her treacherous mouth.

"Instead, I became a monster," she said. "And through your death, I will finally gain enough power to take my revenge on the crows, once and for all."

NOTHING HERE BUT NIGHTMARES

New footsteps sounded on the stone. I counted each foot-fall until the edge of a boot came into view, followed by the rest of the weaselly servant I knew as Fallon.

He put one hand on my mother's shoulder and smiled. His white skin looked translucent in the dim lighting.

"Someone's awake," he said. "The Devil will be pleased. He's very close to finishing his preparations for the ritual and he needs for you to be wide awake when he pierces your heart and bleeds you dry."

I swallowed back any signs of fear and met his stare. "Fallon. It's so nice to see you again," I said. "You look so much more at home in a creepy dungeon. It matches your pasty coloring."

"I see the sleep spell hasn't slowed your tongue," he said. He raised a thin eyebrow at me. "I would have liked to be the one silencing it for you."

"You aren't worthy of my death," I said. "You know as well

as I do that if I'd had time to fully learn to use my powers, neither one of us would be standing here right now."

"Perhaps," he said. "But that's something we'll never know, will we?"

I raised an eyebrow right back at him. "Time will tell."

He laughed. The empty sound echoed through the dungeons, and for the first time, I heard the movement of others in nearby cells.

"Who else is down here with us?" I asked, wondering what the girl across from me, and the others locked down here, had done to deserve such torture.

Fallon shrugged and glanced down the corridor. "Other witches. Ones less powerful than yourself. Or rather, witches who have a less significant heritage."

"Are they a part of this ritual, too? Or is it just me who has that honor today?"

"We have prisoners of all kinds," Fallon said. "Some are witches we wish to punish. We drain them of their blood until they are almost dead. We make them cry for mercy and beg to die. Then we let them live. We let their blood replenish so that in a few months, we can drain them all over again," he said. A wicked smile lit his entire face as he spoke. "Others are here only as meals. None have the rare privilege of being held for ritual sacrifice such as yourself, but they may yet be of use to the Devil today. When he awakens Solomon's power from the stone, he might find Solomon's thirst after twenty years of solitude is quite strong. If his new host is to survive, she will need blood to sustain her."

My stomach twisted. His new host?

I closed my eyes, understanding how this all fit together.

My mother—I had no other name for her despite the lie of calling her that—had traded information for ultimate power.

"In fact, you may know some of the witches we've reserved as snacks for after the ritual," she said. "Now, if you'll excuse me, I have to go upstairs and get ready as well."

She turned and disappeared from view, her heels clicking on the stone.

I jerked my head toward Fallon, panic seizing my chest.

"Who was she talking about?" My voice hitched on the words even though I'd sworn not to show any signs of weakness or fear.

"Some of your friends from the club," he said, lifting a finger for each one he counted off. "Misty. Shay. And what was the other one's name? Something that reminds me of a flower. Lilac? Oh, I can't remember."

My heart stopped beating for a moment.

"Lyla?" I whispered her name.

"Ah, yes, that's the one," he said. "Tricky little bitch, really. She has this nasty ability to control minds. It took a few of our senior vampires to catch her, but she'll make a wonderful meal when the time comes."

He pulled a ring of keys from his pocket and held them up, but I could barely see through the angry tears that welled up in my eyes.

Not Lyla. Not after all she had done for me.

Rend had said she was safe. Marco had taken her to safety somewhere on the west coast. How had the Devil's lackeys gotten their hands on her?

Fallon went through the dozens of keys on the looped keyring, finally selecting a rusted bronze key from the mix. He inserted it into a slot on the outside of the cell, and the door popped open.

If I hadn't been chained to the wall, I would have murdered him. I would have clawed at his eyes until he screamed for mercy.

But I could only take a couple steps toward him before my chains pulled me back.

He laughed. "I can feel your anger in the air around us," he said. "It's lovely, really. To me, the best part of killing is watching the faces of their loved ones as the light slips from their eyes. The rage and helplessness. The pure sorrow. It's the most delicious thing in the world. I'm glad to see we chose a few people you'll be sad to miss. It makes today a lot more fun for me."

"You're vile," I said.

He cocked his head toward me. "A compliment? I wasn't expecting such kindness."

"That wasn't a compliment," I said, knowing he was just toying with me and that I was playing right into his hands. "You disgust me."

"I am who I am," he said. "Being true to your own nature is the only thing that matters in this world or the next. If you had learned that sooner, you might not be here in chains. You might have been standing at the Devil's side."

"Never," I said. "Don't even pretend to think that just because you knew my father it means you understand my true nature."

He shrugged and walked toward me. "You still have so much to learn about the darkness inside you," he said. "And so little time. Mere hours and your light will go out forever."

I drew in a breath. Hours. I still wanted years. Decades.

I wanted a lifetime.

Fallon moved toward me, stopping just outside of my reach.

"What happens now?" I asked.

"Now I take you to the preparation room," he said. He didn't explain further, but I didn't like the sound of it.

Getting out of these chains sounded nice, though.

I held them up for him and waited.

He shook his head. "Don't get any grand ideas about escaping," he said. "Your magic is completely useless in the dungeons. Only vampires can cast down here."

I pressed my lips together. Annabelle had already told me as much, but hearing it confirmed by Fallon made it feel more real.

It made sense. If they were using these dungeons to hold witches against their will, they would need some kind of assurance that those witches wouldn't be able to use their magic to go free or fight back.

Fallon looked at my outstretched hands. "When I remove these chains, I expect you to come without a fight," he said. "As much as I would enjoy finding ways to punish you, the Devil wouldn't appreciate it if I harmed you before the ritual. He needs you to be mostly intact."

He waved his hand over the shackles, and they fell from my wrists, clanging to the ground.

I smiled. "You shouldn't have told me that."

I lifted a knee to his crotch, putting all my strength behind it.

Fallon doubled over, and I quickly reached into his pocket for the keys to the cell. I scrambled through the open door and slammed it shut. With trembling hands, I searched for the rusted bronze key he'd used to open it. Before I could find it, Fallon shifted to smoke and moved through the bars like a ghost. His bony hands wrapped around my throat and squeezed.

Damn. I'd forgotten demons could do that little trick.

"I warned you not to struggle," he said, the musical quality of his voice replaced with a grating shrillness.

I couldn't breathe. I gripped the keys as tightly as I could and swung them back toward his face. The pointed end of one of the keys sank into his flesh, and he released me, screaming.

The sound echoed through the dungeon, and the witches nearby began to clang against their bars.

I turned around to face him, keys lifted between us. "Don't come near me again," I threatened.

Fallon held a hand over the gash in his face. No blood poured from the wound, but I was sure I had injured him at least a little. Maybe vampires didn't bleed.

I wish I knew more about how to kill him. I wanted to gouge his eyes out with my bare hands, but the way he'd shifted to smoke so quickly, I doubted I'd have the chance.

He lowered his hand. The skin beneath it was torn and black, but not bloodied. Within seconds, it healed itself completely, becoming the familiar flawless white skin he'd had before.

But his eyes had changed. Instead of black, they glowed a faint red. His fangs came out, protruding past his lips in a snarl.

"You won't get away with that again," he said.

"You can't hurt me, remember?" I said. "Not without making the Devil angry. And I'm sure you'd rather deal with me than with him."

He narrowed his red eyes at me, anger boiling inside them. "I am looking forward to watching you die."

He turned his head to the side and nodded. "Take her to the preparation chamber," he said.

I followed his gaze toward the entrance to the dungeons. Six rows of cells stood between me and the stairway out of this hell, and guarding those stairs were six vampires dressed in black cloaks, their faces hidden behind black masks. Only their red eyes showed through the masks.

I backed toward the bars of the closed cell, but there was no escape. Four of the guards marched in my direction.

Frantic, I looked around for any way to escape. In the cell diagonal to me, another young girl stood just a stone's throw from the bars. She was not locked in chains like mine, but from the looks of it, she had been here much longer.

Her eyes were ringed with bruises, as if she hadn't slept in weeks. Her body was nothing more than skin and bones, and I wondered if they'd even been feeding her.

"Move a muscle and I'll torture every young witch in here," Fallon said. "Starting with her and moving on to the younger one next door. I'll make you watch as they scream."

This girl looked to be no more than fourteen or fifteen years old, and she had sandy blonde hair that fell all the way down her back. It was matted in places and greasy, but I could tell that it had once been beautiful. She had been beautiful.

Marks on her neck and arms showed that she had been feasted on by vampires. More than one by the looks of it.

I thought about what Fallon had said. How they punished witches by draining them over and over.

I couldn't stand to watch them hurt her or Annabelle. Not for something I had done.

As the guards approached, I locked eyes with the girl, memorizing her face and her features and swearing that if I ever made it out of here, I was taking her with me.

Two of the guards grabbed my arms as Fallon wrenched the keys out of my hand.

"I'll take those," he said, straightening his clothes and lifting his chin. "Take her to the preparation chamber. The maidens have their work cut out for them today."

I didn't struggle. With so many of them, I knew it was a waste of energy. I needed to save whatever I had left in reserve for a time when I might have a real chance for escape. I would keep my wits about me and look for any opportunity to run or hide.

As the guards guided me past the cells, I looked inside each one, searching for my friends from Venom.

I saw other witches who looked abused and weak, but there was no sign of Lyla and the others. Had Fallon been lying just to rile me up? God, I hoped so. I could face my own death if I had to, but I wasn't sure my heart could handle watching them die.

I peered into the final cell and saw a young mother lying on the floor, a child no more than two clutched in her arms. Their eyes were closed, the mother's body curled around the infant.

Don't ever wake up, I whispered to them in my head. *There is nothing here but nightmares.*

EMPTY OF LIFE

The preparation room was through a large wooden door at the end of the hallway, opposite from the stairs.

As soon as the door opened, a rush of steam escaped from the room. My skin moistened with heat, and I turned my head away, finding it difficult to breathe.

It was like walking into a steam-bath.

The guards pulled me deeper into the room, and I saw the source of the heat and steam.

A huge tiled tub took up an entire corner of the large room. Three steps led up to it and a woman dressed in a pristine white gown with flowing white hair sat on the top step with her hand dipped into the water. She turned as we entered, and I gasped.

Where her eyes should be, she had black holes, completely empty of life.

I yanked my arms from the guards' grasp and backed away, but they had already closed the door behind us. One of the four guards looped a thick chain through the lock and secured it by melting the metal together with his bare hands.

My chest tightened. There was no getting out of this place.

A second woman in white appeared through the gathering steam. She took my hand and led me to the center of the room. Her skin was ice cold, and I shivered, wondering what kind of creature she was.

With a single nod from her, the four guards who had brought me here shifted to smoke and disappeared through a small crack at the bottom of the door. I was glad to see them go, but I had no doubt they were now stationed outside the door, waiting.

And I wasn't exactly happy about my present company.

When I looked up, two more women in white had joined the group. They began pulling on my clothes, tugging my pants down and lifting my shirt over my head.

"Get your hands off me," I said. I tried to step back, but that wasn't easy considering my pants were now down around my ankles.

I pushed at their hands and tried to pull my pants back on, but there was only one of me versus four of them.

They didn't say a word or show any expression. They stripped me naked in seconds. I lifted my hands to cover my breasts, but they grabbed my arms and pulled me toward the steaming water.

From the amount of heat coming off that bath, I did not want to go anywhere near it.

"Stop," I said, fear filling my heart. I pushed my heels against the stone floor and struggled against their hold on me, but they were abnormally strong.

I managed to yank my arm away from one of them, but when I did, she turned her hollow eyes on me, and I froze.

I couldn't move at all, and when I tried to speak, my lips would not part. I reached up to touch my mouth, screaming on the inside. I couldn't pry my lips open. Something she had done to me had completely sealed them shut.

I shook my head violently as they continued to lead me to the bath. They forced me up the steps. I bent over, pulling back with every bit of strength I had, but it was no use.

The maidens arranged my feet on two orange stones embedded into the tile and backed away. I struggled to lift my feet, but they were locked on the stones. I couldn't move.

The four women in white moved to spots at each of the four corners of the square-shaped pool.

They moved in perfect unison, lifting their hands into the air. My body straightened, as if I were a puppet on a string. I lost all ability to control my own movements.

I wanted to be strong, but my heart pounded against my ribs in terror. What were they going to do to me?

The maidens reached down and each one grabbed a small vial of clear liquid from the steps of the pool. One by one, they poured the contents of their vials into the water.

The first vial made the water begin to move and swirl violently, as if a current ran through it.

The second vial calmed the thrashing, turning the water to a crystal-clear blue.

The contents of the third vial spread through the water like a dark disease, making it thick and muddy.

As the fourth maiden poured her vial into the pool, the entire surface of the water burst into flames.

Air. Water. Earth. Fire.

They had called the four elements, drawing power from the world around us.

Moving in unison once again, the four women pushed their palms down, sending my body forward into the water.

I cried out as the flames licked my flesh. I passed through fire into mud, sinking deep down into the thick muck.

I couldn't draw a breath. I was completely submerged, my lungs burning with the need for air.

Just when I felt like I couldn't take it anymore, a hand grabbed the top of my hair and pulled my head from the mud.

The flames were gone, and I gasped for air. I clawed at the mud, desperate to find my way out.

But the hand that held me pushed me back under. The mud turned to clear, cool water that cleansed my skin and took the sting of pain from my burns.

Soon, the pain in my lungs returned, and I struggled to find my way above the surface of the water. My hand reached up and grabbed the maiden's wrist, but I was losing strength rapidly.

My body went limp as I blacked out. I regained consciousness when the woman lifted me back up, allowing only the top of my head to rest above the water.

I opened my eyes and gasped for breath, not knowing how long I had before she pushed me back under again. I held on to her wrist as my legs kicked wildly beneath me. From the edge of the pool, she stared with unseeing eyes.

As I kicked, the water swirled and moved, waves lapping the sides of the pool. The maiden released me and the undertow pulled me under.

I tumbled head over feet, losing all sense of direction. Black shadows oozed from my skin, turning the water around me black as night. I kicked and swam and begged for it all to end. I held my breath for as long as I could before the pain grew too great.

My lungs screamed for air, and I couldn't deny them any longer.

I finally gave in, sucking in with one final desperate wish for life.

FIGHTING THE DARKER SIDE

Air, not water, entered my lungs, and I sat up,
startled.

All four of the women in white stood around
me. They placed their cold hands on my bare shoulders and
pushed me back down. Black vines grew from the stone, wrapping around my arms and legs to bind me to this spot. One
final vine slithered around my neck.

I stared up at the ceiling, focusing on anything other than
the empty sockets of the maidens' eyes. I took in the circular
chandeliers that hung from the ceiling. Instead of modern
light-bulbs, they held dozens of lit red candles.

I closed my eyes against their light. I'd been burned
enough for one day, thank you very much.

A soft hand touched my leg, and my eyes flew open again.
I struggled to sit up, but I could barely lift my head to see what
she was doing to me. The vine choked me, and I fell back
against the stone, not wanting to deny myself air.

A woman in white hovered over me, studying my body.

She leaned over, and I heard a sloshing sound but couldn't tell for sure what she was doing. When she came back up, she had a cloth in her hand, covered in a white paste that dripped thick blobs back onto the floor.

She spread the white paste along my entire body, having no sensitivity to my privacy or shame. She covered me and when every inch was painted white, the four maidens lay their hands on me. Their mouths did not move, but I could hear a faint chanting in my head.

The spark of power that still burned deeply in my core flashed warm, my body somehow reacting to whatever they'd put on my skin. My body heated, growing feverish. I alternated between cold chills and flashes of intense heat as the fire of my power spread through me, rising from the core of my body to the surface of my skin. I screamed as the heat consumed me.

Rage tore through my heart and dark visions appeared before me. I saw the world's evil flash before my eyes. Children tortured. Women drained of their blood and discarded like trash.

Shadows swirled around the room, racing across my skin, turning the white paste a dark, oily black.

The darkness in my soul grew, but I stubbornly clung to the light.

I understood now what these preparations were meant to do. They were meant to bring Solomon's darkness to the surface of my soul. They were drawing the black heart of him out so that the part of me that had come from him would be fresh and strong for the ritual.

With each horrible image, I forced thoughts of love into my heart. I thought of Katy. The way the sun felt on my face on the first day of spring. I thought of Lyla's friendship and her willingness to risk her own life for mine.

I thought of Mary Anne. A crow witch who had defied her family to save a friend.

I thought of my real mother. Somehow, despite how hard they had tried to keep her from me, she had found me. She had risked everything to lead me to the one person whose strength might keep me safe from evil.

And finally, when the darkness threatened to eat me alive, I thought of Rend. Tears of love and loss flooded my eyes, keeping the horror at bay. Fallon had said we all must be true to our nature, but Rend had spent years fighting the darker side of his nature in order to bring hope to those who had none left. He had found a way to hold back the monster inside so that he could make love to me.

As I felt the darker side of my own nature struggle for control, I knew it would never win. Not as long as there was love in my heart. Love and hope.

And trust that somewhere, Rend was out there trying to find his way back to me.

SACRIFICE ME

I woke from the fever dream with passion burning in my heart.

I would not give up. They had tortured me for hours, but I knew they could never break my spirit. I had too much to live for.

All they had done was teach me that my strength knew no limits. My capacity for love could not be destroyed.

I would fight until there was no fight left.

My body ached all over, and my skin was raw and sensitive. The maidens had removed the black paste while I slept, but the vines still bound me to the slab of stone.

The ritual grew closer now. I could feel it.

I took deep, calming breaths, the darkness inside never far from the surface. Its dark fingers scratched at my heart, begging for entry. But I would not let it in.

After what seemed an eternity, the four women in white appeared again. With a wave of their hands, the vines drew back. The maidens lifted me from the stone, lowering my feet to the floor. They spread a sweet-smelling oil across my skin and dressed me in a simple black gown that flowed to the floor. They brushed my hair and took care with each aspect of my appearance, readying me for death.

In some cultures, human sacrifice was a religious ritual, offering up a human life to appease a god or spirit.

But the idea of being sacrificed in order to give new life to my own father felt so backwards. So against the natural order of things. What god would demand such a sacrifice?

But there was no god here. Only monsters and devils. This was a house of pure evil, and I would not allow myself to become their sacrifice.

As the maidens dressed me, I vowed to find a way to put a stop to the Devil's plans. Even if I died in the process, I could not let him complete the ritual.

When they were finished, the women in white led me toward the wooden door and knocked once.

Smoke seeped in from beneath the door, and a faceless guard appeared. He studied me, nodded to the women in white, and then lifted the chain binding the door, crushing its links in his fist until it turned to silvery dust in his hand. He opened the door and motioned for me to move.

I knew by instinct that he was not allowed to touch me. I was a holy vessel now, a sacrificial lamb led to the slaughter.

I contemplated running but wondered if that would mean having to go through all those horrible preparations again. It would buy me some time in case Rend was still trying to get to me, but I wasn't sure I could push against the darkness and pain much longer. Its presence was heavy inside me.

No, I needed to save my energy. I would wait and keep my eyes open for any chance to put an end to their plans.

The four guards from earlier positioned themselves around me in a square—two in front, two behind. We walked down the row of cells in the dungeon. I studied them one last time, looking for my friends.

The young girl I'd locked eyes with earlier had retreated to the back of her cell, lost in the shadows somewhere. There was no sign of Annabelle. Had they taken her? Killed her? How long had they been torturing me?

There was also no sign of my friends. Only strangers whose fate was similar to my own. These women were all nothing but blood and fuel to these demon vampires. Nothing but meaningless sacrifices.

I walked up the steps, leaving the dungeon area for the first time since they'd brought me into the Devil's castle. The guards led me down an even longer hallway to a circular staircase that seemed to go on forever. I counted the steps as we went, to occupy my mind. Anything not to think about the fate that awaited me once we got upstairs.

I lost count at one hundred when my knees buckled, and I collapsed onto the steps. The guards shared a nervous look. I pressed my hands against the dirty stone step, smiling up at them, sure that my gown and cleansed skin would be marred with dirt and blood.

But when I stood, every inch of me was still pristine, as if the preparations had put an invisible barrier around me to keep impurities out.

Or to keep the darkness in.

At the top of the long staircase, the room opened into a large chamber adorned with intricately woven tapestries and oversized wooden furniture that dated back centuries. The guards led me past suits of polished armor and weapons that seemed to be created for giants, not men.

What was this place?

The ceilings were high, and the guard's footsteps echoed as we crossed the chamber and entered another hallway. They took me through several rooms before we reached a narrow hallway lined with a deep red carpet.

The guards stopped, motioning for me to continue alone.

I held my ground. They couldn't seriously expect me to walk freely to my own death. But something propelled me forward against my will. My bare feet rose from the stone floor, hovering for a moment above the ground. I moved forward through the narrow hallway, the bottom of my gown trailing along the red carpet.

I kicked my legs and reached out for anything I might grab onto, but the room at the end of the hall beckoned me forward. Just before I reached the large wooden door, it opened, revealing a room lit with thousands of red candles that hovered in the air above.

My hands fell to my side, no longer under my own control.

As I entered the room, fear crashed over me like a mighty wave. The heavy door slammed closed behind me, leaving no escape.

The red carpet continued all the way up through the great ritual room. All along each side of the carpet, hundreds of vampires stood in rows, here to witness my death and the rebirth of one of their founders. They were dressed in black cloaks, their faces hidden under thick hoods, only their red eyes visible through the shadows.

I floated forward, my body trembling as their red eyes watched.

As I passed near the front of the crowd of vampires, a row of trembling witches caught my eye and I gasped, tears springing to my eyes.

Lyla, Misty, and Shay were bound together in chains, along with the child who'd been in the cell across from mine. They all wept as I passed by them, and I prayed that somehow, we would all make it through this horror alive.

I turned my eyes forward and there, at the end of the carpet, was a large black altar. Behind it stood the Devil. He was cloaked in dark robes of his own, adorned with red jewels. He wore no hood, but his eyes were the reddest of all, hungry for my death and the power it would bring to him.

A flash of fire spread through me, and my eyes were suddenly drawn to a stone. The woman I'd known my whole life as my mother wore it around her neck. She smiled when my eyes met hers, pure evil reflected in her gaze.

She wore a long black dress that looked like something from a century ago. Layers of fabric stretched out behind her, the gown covering her completely, except for her hands and her chest. The large black stone rested above her heart, and when my eyes landed on it, I felt Solomon's power locked within its murky depths.

My mother's smile faded, and her hand fluttered to the stone. She tried to pull it away from her skin, but it wouldn't move. Her face twisted into a grimace of pain.

I hoped it was burning the shit out of her.

She fell to her knees, and some of the vampires in the room shifted uncomfortably.

The Devil narrowed his red eyes at her, and she swallowed. She gripped the edge of the black altar and pulled herself up, but her eyes were now wide with panic and fear.

When I reached the front of the room, my body dropped to the floor near the steps leading up to the platform where the Devil and my mother waited. My head bowed to them, as if someone were physically holding me down. My hands pressed deep into the lush red carpet.

"Stand, girl." The Devil's voice echoed through the room.

I lifted my eyes to him, hatred burning inside me.

A thin smile spread across his pale lips. He wanted me to hate him. He wanted me to embrace every dark corner of my heart.

Part of me fought against it, wanting to go back to that place of love I had found earlier, but my anger was too strong now. I had never asked for any of this. A child should not be punished for the evil deeds of its parents. I should not be judged by my father's darkness.

The hatred that lived inside me was not born of evil or a thirst for power. It was born of strength and light and a desire for life.

I pushed myself up from the ground, placing my feet carefully beneath me. I stood straight and tall, wanting him to see that his torture had not broken me. Darkness had not claimed me yet.

The Devil raised his hands and the vampires moved in unison, their eyes and bodies facing forward like obedient soldiers.

Shadows danced across his face.

"Mary Francis, spawn of Solomon, come to me."

I fought against the puppetry that moved my feet forward, but it was no use. I was compelled to obey. My bare feet walked up the six steps leading to the altar, the black gown flowing softly against my legs.

When I reached the top step, my entire body rose into the air and twisted so that my eyes looked toward the ceiling and my back was now prostrate to the altar. The Devil pulled his hand toward him, and I floated just above the flat, black stone. He lowered his hand and my body obeyed, slowly lowering me to the cold surface.

He nodded to my mother, and she rushed forward, taking my left hand in hers. For all her talk of power and revenge, her fear was evident in the cold clammy hand that clasped mine.

The stone around her neck seemed to respond to me. It began to emit a dark glow. My mother's hand gripped me tighter, and a whimper escaped from her throat.

She closed her eyes and clenched her teeth, her chest rising rapidly with each fear-filled breath.

When her eyes snapped open again, they were darker, the whites of her eyes turning murky as shadows swirled inside them. She yanked on my arm, pulling it straight out to the side. She pressed my wrist down on the shiny black surface of the stone, and an onyx chain snapped around it, locking my left arm in place.

My mouth went dry. All my hopes of escape or sabotage were quickly disappearing. I had been a fool to think I would have any control over this situation. The Devil's magic was too strong. His plans too detailed.

My mother moved around to the other side and clasped my right hand.

Another wave of pain rushed through her and she jerked, her muscles tensing. Her lips parted, and she cried out, but did not lose hold of my hand.

As she had done on the other side, she pressed my right wrist against the stone and another onyx shackle locked my hand in place. She repeated the gesture with both of my ankles.

My breaths came in rapid succession, my heart beating so fast I thought it might burst right out of my chest. I couldn't let this happen. I would not let them sacrifice me. I couldn't allow Solomon's spirit to be reborn. I would not be the cause of so much pain and death in this world.

Rend, where the hell are you? I need you now.

I struggled against the glass-like shackles that held me to the altar, but I knew my strength was not in my arms and legs or my physical body. My true power was within. I had to find a way to connect to that power.

I closed my eyes and took a deep breath in. I focused on the light inside. The light I knew still burned for all that was good and beautiful in this world. I calmed my racing heart, knowing this was my one chance to save myself.

A breeze blew across my skin, ruffling the fabric of my gown.

I reached deeper, imagining an endless well of power at my core. I thrust my consciousness into that well, tapping into that unseen essence and letting it flow through me like the blood pulsing through my veins.

My hair blew around my face as the power ignited within me.

My eyes snapped open, and I saw the flash of fear in the Devil's eyes. His nostrils flared, and his fangs extended as his lips parted. He snarled and snapped his fingers.

"Bring me the sword." His voice was deep and commanding.

Footsteps sounded on the steps and Fallon appeared. He

handed the Devil a large sword made of pure silver, a diamond embedded in its hilt.

Solomon's sword.

I knew it without question. I could feel his power surrounding it. The memories of the evil deeds he had committed with this sword clung to it.

The Devil wrapped both his bony hands around it, lifting it up with its sharp blade pointed downward toward my heart.

The room around us hung thick with anticipation.

He pressed the tip of the blade against my chest, just above my heart. I cried out as a black shadow forced its way through my body and out of my mouth. The smoke swirled around my body rapidly and the darkness of my father's spirit threatened to consume me. It pushed against my skin, boiling to the surface.

All around us, a great wind roared as my power begged for release.

"Solomon, my brother, how I have waited for this day," the Devil said, his voice rising above the sound of the whirlwind I'd created.

I had held back for far too long, afraid that if I let the dark side of my heritage grow, I would be lost to it forever. But at the moment just before death, I knew that the only way to win was to embrace both sides of myself. To welcome the darkness and use it in my own way. For my own purpose.

Fallon was right. I could no longer deny who I was.

"Do it," my mother screamed. Long tendrils of hair blew across her face, and she clasped a hand around the stone at her neck. "Do it now."

I sucked in a breath, taking those dark shadows back into

my body. I stopped fighting the dark side of my power, drawing it into myself instead.

The spell that held my power at bay, shattered. My spirit broke free, power blazing through me like hot flames.

I lifted my arms, and the onyx shackles exploded. I gripped the blade of the sword with both hands and pulled it upward.

The Devil fell back, taking the sword with him. The sharp blade sliced through my skin and my hands began to bleed, but I ignored the pain. I rose, breaking the shackles that bound my legs and flying into the air. Great black wings spread out from my back.

The vampires near the front cowered, their robes whipping around them as the wind grew stronger.

"Seize her," the Devil cried.

Several of his servants shifted to smoke and flew toward me. I drew my hands inward, close to my body, then pushed out. The vampires sailed back into the crowd, slamming against the floor at their brothers' feet.

I waited for the next wave to attack, but the assault came from behind. The Devil sliced through one of my wings with his sword, and I cried out in pain. I fell, descending to the altar as a black rope of smoke curled around my neck, cutting off my breath.

My hands scratched at the rope but couldn't grasp its smoky form.

I remembered this feeling. I remembered the way the vampire had held me back at Rend's safe-house and how, no matter how hard I tried, I couldn't grasp the demon rope.

The Devil leapt onto the altar. He grabbed my hair and wrenched my head to the side. His fangs pressed against my neck, and he brought the blade of my father's sword to my throat.

Tears of rage spilled down my cheeks.

Was this the end? Had I lost this fight? What more did I have to give?

My wings disappeared, and I closed my eyes, pain throbbing in my chest.

But just when I thought all hope was lost, the door at the back of the room crashed open. I lifted my eyes just as Rend rushed through the doorway.

NO GREATER SACRIFICE

Our eyes met across the great expanse of the ritual room, and love washed through me.

Several witches moved in behind him, Mary Anne leading the way. They dipped their hands into small leather bags and drew out fistfuls of tiny black beads. They crouched low and rolled the beads onto the floor at the feet of the vampires gathered in rows.

Screams echoed through the room as the vampires shifted to smoke, the essence of their beings writhing in pain as their power was sucked down into the stones.

The Devil tightened his grip on my hair and pulled his other hand backward, the sword slicing into the skin at my neck.

I drew in a breath, connecting with the last drop of power inside me. In an instant, my body disappeared, shifting to shadow as I embraced the demon half of my heritage. The sword sliced through nothingness.

I twirled around, reforming as I gripped the hilt of the sword, pulling it from the Devil's trembling hand.

His eyes flashed deep red as I lifted my father's sword and sliced his arm from his body.

He screamed and fell backward, scrambling off the altar, black sludge oozing from his severed limb.

Chaos erupted around me.

Vampires shifted and fled in fear while those most loyal to the Devil stayed behind to fight.

I glanced back and saw the familiar faces of those I'd met in Peachville as they joined the battle.

I turned my attention back to the Devil. Fallon had crawled to his master's side, but when I lifted the powerful sword toward him, he backed away, disappearing into the shadows at the back of the room.

Black smoke swirled around the Devil's form as he struggled to shift, but the pain of his wound had dampened his power. He pushed back with his legs, scurrying across the floor.

I jumped down from the altar, vengeance gleaming in my eyes.

I walked toward him with deliberate steps. "I am my father's daughter," I said with a smile. "You of all people should have known better than to underestimate that power."

The sword was heavy in my hand, but I wielded it well. I lifted it high into the air, but before I could end the Devil's life, a dagger plunged into my back.

I gasped and fell to my knees, the sword clanging to the ground at my feet. Warm blood flowed down my back.

A trembling hand removed the dagger, and my mother stepped around my fallen form, her eyes mad with panic. The stone at her neck pulsed with light, as if a heart were beating deep inside. My mother clawed at the stone with her free hand, her movements jerky and frantic.

She kicked Solomon's sword from my reach and pointed the small dagger toward me.

"I am not going to let you ruin this for me," she spat. "I had a life before you came into this world, and you took it away from me. Eighteen long years I wasted taking care of you, and I hated you every second of it. I was meant for more than this. I should have been the one the Mother Crow loved most. I should have been the one she showered with love. But she couldn't see my potential. She couldn't see the great things I was capable of."

My vision blurred and sweat beaded on my forehead. Fever spread through my body, and I collapsed to the floor, barely able to lift my head.

Smoke swirled around the large black stone at her neck as Solomon's power pushed against its cage. My mother twitched, her face contorted and wrinkled.

I pressed my hands flat against the ground and pushed up with all my might, trying to stand. My knees buckled, and I fell again to the stone floor. "I refuse to be your sacrifice," I said.

I crawled toward her, clawing at her gown.

A wisp of black smoke rushed up from behind me and coiled itself around my mother's body. Rend emerged from the shadowy smoke, his fangs sinking into my mother's throat. She screamed and dropped her dagger. She convulsed against him as he drained every last drop of her blood. Her face went slack and pale, her body limp.

Rend tossed her to the ground and turned his blazing red eyes on the Devil, who was inching toward Solomon's sword.

Rend placed his boot on the sword's blade, and the Devil's head snapped up in terror.

"The Brotherhood will punish you for this," the Devil said. "Your life will be over and for what? A human witch? You're a disgrace to everything Solomon and I built in this world."

"I would give my life a thousand times for love," Rend said, his voice strong and deep. "There is no greater sacrifice than that."

He grabbed the Devil up by his robes, lifting him high into the air.

My heart swelled, and I found the strength to stand. Rend kicked the silver sword toward me and I bent down, wrapping my hand tightly around the hilt.

I nodded to Rend, and he opened his fist, letting the Devil fall to the ground like a ragdoll.

He stepped aside as I approached the evil vampire.

"This is for every innocent life taken by you and by my father," I said.

I plunged the blade deep into the vampire's chest. His eyes grew wide as he clutched the blade with both hands. The red fire in his eyes faded to a deep black as his life faded.

I pulled the blade back and Rend stepped forward. He placed his hands inside the Devil's mouth and with a terrible cry, he tore him apart, the Devil's body splitting down the middle and erupting into ashes that crumbled to dust in Rend's hands.

I fell to my knees, the wound in my back throbbing.

Rend dropped to my side and gathered me into his arms. My eyelids fluttered as I struggled against the darkness.

He pulled me tight against his chest, rocking back and forth as tears cascaded down his cheeks.

He shouted, but his voice was distant.

He kissed my cheeks and stroked my hair, his body shaking with sobs. I wanted to tell him that I loved him, but I couldn't find my voice.

Flashes of light and shadow moved around us as the battle continued, and someone knelt beside us. I recognized Jackson as he placed his hands on my back.

I closed my eyes, feeling death brush against my soul. Knowing there was no other place I'd rather die than in the arms of the man I loved.

A cold chill spread through me.

When you are about to die, they say your life flashes before your eyes. Life's last gift. A single moment of clarity so you can see all the things you did wrong.

Every bad decision.

Every mistake.

Every horrible word you said to someone when you really just wanted them to love you as much as you loved them.

It's easy to get lost in the regrets of our past, thinking that if we'd only chosen something different, we might have been able to save ourselves a hell of a lot of heartbreak. If we'd only been born to difference circumstances or been given a second chance, we might have become someone different. Someone better.

Only, the thing is, we should really be giving ourselves credit for just surviving the best way we know how.

At any given moment, we're all just doing the best we can to survive and make a place for ourselves in this shit-storm we call life.

Looking back, it's easy to forget just how broken we were when we made those bad decisions. And most importantly, it's easy to overlook the fact that if we really were able to go back in time and change things, sure, we might avoid some of the worst heartaches of our lives, but at the same time, we also might not be here, right now, with the one person we love most in all the world.

What if my mother had never met Solomon?

What if the Mother Crow had never sent me away?

What if the Devil had never known I existed?

These questions flash through my mind in these last moments, but then all I can think is that one small change—one *"better"* decision—and I might have missed him altogether.

So, you know what? If I had the chance to go back and do it all over again, I wouldn't change one painful, gut-wrenching, dangerous, terrifying moment of what I've been through the past two weeks.

Even knowing it meant the death of me, I'd go through it all over again, just for him.

SOMEDAY SOON

Warm sunshine fell across my cheek.

I opened my eyes, expecting heaven. Or hell.

But what I found was life. A second chance.

Rend slept in a chair at my bedside, his body twisted uncomfortably, and his face pressed against the back cushion.

Love and gratitude washed through me as tears sprang to my eyes. My body ached, and my head pounded, but I was alive. Somehow, I had survived.

I struggled to sit up, wincing as pain shot through the wound in my back.

Rend jerked awake. His eyes met mine and he slid from the chair, falling to his knees at the side of the bed. He grabbed my hand and brought it to his lips like a prayer.

I squeezed his hand.

"Please tell me I'm not dreaming," I whispered.

He shook his head and smiled. "I was about to say the same thing."

He moved to my side on the bed and ran the back of his hand across my cheek.

"I was so afraid you'd never wake up," he said.

"How long have I been sleeping?" I asked.

"Weeks," he said. "Sixteen days to be exact."

I forced myself to sit up, my head swimming. "Katy, she—"

"Katy's fine," he said. He moved to place a few extra pillows behind me to help prop me up. "I sent Marco to check on her and give her some excuse as to why you weren't home. Of course, she raised hell and demanded to know the truth. I distinctly remember telling you not to give Katy the details of what was going on at the club."

I raised an eyebrow. "I've never really been a rule follower."

He laughed. "Really? I didn't know that about you."

I smiled. "So, she's okay? She's not completely freaking out?"

"Oh, she freaked out big time. She demanded to see proof that I hadn't gone all vampire on you and sucked your blood," he said. "Her words, not mine."

I laughed, and my ribs protested. I sucked a breath through my teeth and raised my hand to my side.

Rend furrowed his brow. "I'm sorry. I shouldn't make you laugh right now. How are you feeling?"

"Like I almost got murdered in a sacrificial ritual performed by the Devil and the woman formerly known as my mother."

Rend bit his lower lip to suppress a smile. "It's good to know they didn't destroy your sense of humor in the process."

I sighed. "I'm just glad to know they didn't destroy me, period."

"Me, too," he said softly, trailing a fingertip down my arm.

"What happened that night?" I asked. "How did you guys even get inside the castle?"

"We brought a bad-ass army," he said. "Harper and most of the Peachville crew came, some of the staff from the club, and ten members of the Brotherhood."

"Is everyone okay?" I asked, my heart tightening in my chest. I wasn't sure I was ready to hear bad news if someone else had died trying to save my life.

"We all made it out alive," he said. "A few nicks and bruises here and there, but nothing that won't heal."

I let out a sigh of relief. "Even Lyla and the others?"

"Yes," he said. "A lot of them have been by to see you, but I told them you needed your rest. When you're ready for visitors, I'm sure you'll have all the company you could ever want while you're recovering."

A child's face flashed into my memory.

"There were others," I said. "Witches locked in the dungeons of the castle. Rend, some of them were only children. Babies."

He nodded and stroked my hair. "We got everyone out of there," he said. "One girl in particular has been asking about you nonstop. Annabelle, I think her name is."

I held back tears of relief. "She was in the cell across from mine," I said. "Her mother was killed while she was in there. I can't even imagine the horror some of those witches have been through."

"Most of them returned to their families, but Annabelle had no one left," he said. "She's been staying at Harper's."

"I really owe her one for helping us. I owe all of them, really," I said.

Someone knocked on the door, and I looked up to see Jackson standing in the doorway. "We were just glad we could help," he said. He stepped into the room. "I came to check on my patient, but I see you're doing better."

"Patient?" The memory of him kneeling at my side flashed into my mind. "You're a healer?"

"It's one of my gifts," he said. "I'm not as strong as some, like Harper's sister, but I can heal some basic wounds. You didn't get a chance to meet her, but she came here to Rend's as soon as he brought you back here. She's been busy with some things in the Shadow World, but it was really her power that healed the worst of the wounds from the dagger. How are you feeling?"

"I wonder how many times I'm going to be asked that over the next few weeks," I said with a laugh. "I'm sore and weak, but I'm glad to be alive. And please, if you speak to Harper's sister, tell her thank you."

"I will. You're one of the strongest witches I've ever seen," he said, his lips curling into a half-smile. "I think you and Harper will be good friends. You two seem to have a lot in common."

I could tell just from the way he said her name that he loved her very much. From all I knew of her, I felt honored to even be mentioned in the same sentence as her.

He did a quick check of my wounds, changing a bandage on my back and laying his hands on the spot where the dagger had cut deepest. A cold chill spread through the wound like ice, relieving some of the pain.

"Better?" he asked.

"Wow." I took a deep breath, feeling an immediate improvement. "Yes, thank you."

"Good," he said. "I'll come back every day to check on you for the next few days. I'm going to let the others know you're awake. I'm sure Mary Anne is dying to come visit."

Over the weeks that followed, Rend's once-quiet and secluded house became a social hub. We had visitors from Venom and Peachville nearly every day. Azure even came to sit with me from time to time. I could tell something had changed between her and Rend. She still ribbed me and joked, but some of the mean-spiritedness I'd felt from her when we first met was gone now. As if she'd come to accept our relationship, even if she didn't like it.

Some of Rend's friends from the Brotherhood stopped by to see how I was doing. Mostly, though, the vampires came to see Rend. They never spoke of their fear of the Brotherhood's punishment around me. I knew Rend didn't want me worrying about it, but it was always there between us.

The Brotherhood consisted of hundreds, if not thousands, of vampires across the world. Some had been there at the Devil's side that night, ready to watch me die. Eventually, the main council of the Brotherhood of Darkness would hold the eleven vampires who had fought against the Devil accountable for their actions.

They had killed many of their own kind, including one of the original founders.

When I asked Rend about Solomon's stone, he told me Silas had taken it from my mother's body and disappeared. No one had heard from him since, but he'd been given orders to destroy it. They were all still waiting for Silas to return and confirm that the stone had been either hidden or destroyed.

I was anxious for his return for an entirely different reason.

My whole life, I never dreamed I might have a sibling. The

idea of a half-brother—even a vampire one—excited me. I had so many questions I wanted to ask him about our father and about their life in the Shadow World before they came to live here in mine.

I hoped he would come back before the Brotherhood made their decision about how to punish those who had stood with Rend.

And I hoped the Brotherhood would see the truth of what happened. The justice in it. I couldn't bear it if they sentenced Rend to death for what he'd done to protect me. Strangely, Rend didn't seem worried about it. He said, after all we'd survived so far together, he didn't plan on going anywhere anytime soon.

While Rend met with his fellow vampires, Mary Anne and I sat together for hours every day talking about what her life was like before she was sent to Shadowford. She told me stories about my real mother, Mary Kathryn. Mary Anne remembered her as a very sad, but beautiful woman who mostly kept to herself. She said Mary Kathryn had no children of her own, but that her eyes always lit up when a new baby was born, and she'd offer to hold them for hours upon hours, rocking them in an old rocking chair in the Mother Crow's house.

I prayed she was still alive and that the invitation she'd sent to me had not gotten her in trouble. Was she still living with the other crows? Or had she broken free of them when the coven split up?

There were so many questions still left unanswered.

In the evenings, Rend never left my side. He held me close, my head resting against his strong chest. We kissed and talked late into the night, until I fell asleep in his arms, always waking up still wrapped in his warmth.

As my body healed, I yearned to make love to him again, but he refused, saying it was too dangerous. He'd tasted the power of blood again and until he'd learned to control the thirst again, he didn't want to put my life in danger.

Sometimes, when the nightmares got to be too much, and I couldn't get back to sleep, I would sneak away and climb up the stairs to the hall of doorways.

I'd make my way down the long, narrow hallway until I found the door with the crow's wing etched deep into the wood. I would run my finger along its outline and wonder what secrets were hidden behind that door.

What evils.

Someday, I promised myself, when my strength had returned, I would go through that door. I would find my mother. I would find out more about who I really was and where I had come from.

And someday, I would face the Mother Crow herself and make her pay for all she'd stolen from me.

Someday soon.

ABOUT THE AUTHOR

Sarra Cannon is the author of several series featuring young adult and college-aged characters, including the bestselling Shadow Demons Saga. Her novels often stem from her own experiences growing up in the small town of Hawkinsville, Georgia, where she learned that being popular always comes at a price and relationships are rarely as simple as they seem.

Sarra recently celebrated seven years in indie publishing and has sold over half a million copies of her books. She currently lives in Charleston, South Carolina with her programmer husband and adorable redheaded son.

Love Sarra's books? Join Sarra's Mailing List to be notified of new releases and giveaways!

Also, please come hang out with me in my Facebook Fan Group: Sarra Cannon's Coven. We have a lot of fun in there, and I often share exclusive short stories and teasers in the group. Join now.

Want more? Get insider information on my writing process, inspiration, and what it's like to be an author with weekly videos on my YouTube channel.

Connect With Sarra Online:
www.sarracannon.com

Made in the USA
Middletown, DE
21 September 2020